TERMINATION
JC RYAN

TERMINATION
JC RYAN

By JC Ryan

Rossler Foundation Mysteries

The Tenth Cycle

Ninth Cycle Antarctica

Genetic Bullets

The Sword of Cyrus

The Skywalkers

The Phoenix Agenda

The Rowen

Termination

Vinci Books

vinci-books.com

Published by Vinci Books Ltd in 2025

1

Copyright © JC Ryan 2019

The author has asserted their moral right to be identified as the author of this work in accordance with the Copyright, Designs and Patents Act 1988. This work is a work of fiction. Names, characters, places and incidents are the product of the author's imagination or are used fictitiously. Any resemblance to actual persons, living or dead, places and incidents is entirely coincidental.

All rights reserved. No part of this publication may be copied, reproduced, distributed, stored in any retrieval system, or transmitted in any form or by any means, including photocopying, recording, or other electronic or mechanical methods, nor used as a source for any form of machine learning including AI datasets, without the prior written permission of the publisher.

The publisher and the author have made every effort to obtain permissions for any third party material used in this book and to comply with copyright law. Any queries in this respect should be brought to the attention of the publisher and any omissions will be corrected in future editions.

A CIP catalogue record for this book is available from the British Library.

Paperback ISBN: 9781036700454

The EU GPSR authorised representative is Logos Europe, 9 rue Nicolas Poussion, 17000 La Rochelle, France
contact@logoseurope.eu

Chapter One

Onboard the *Itinerant* en route to the Chukchi Sea

Captain Timothy Marcus was in his cabin aboard the Itinerant—a small, one of a kind, but extremely efficient, rescue submarine, discussing possible scenarios with the Rescue Team Leader Karl Dunlap and his Second-In-Command, Michael Sommers.

Karl, a former Navy Seal, stood just over six feet tall, had dark hair he kept cut to military standards, hazel eyes, a trim, fit body, and a firm-set jaw. He was a straight shooting, no nonsense type guy that could be counted on to get the job done, irrespective of how challenging the circumstances.

Former Coast Guard Rescue Swimmer Michael Sommers was the opposite of Karl in nearly every way. Standing five-eight, his well-muscled body moved with the grace of a dancer, his round, boyish face and twinkling blue eyes made his unruly blond curls an endearment rather than an eyesore, and his outgoing personality meant he knew no strangers and had few enemies.

Though very different, Marcus knew that both men were dedicated professionals who would give everything they had, and then some, to save lives and complete a mission successfully. That was why he included them on this mission, the Itinerant's first.

She was a brand-new, uniquely designed and built research and rescue submarine, developed privately in combination with Woods Hole Oceanographic Institute, Massachusetts Institute of Technology, and Ben Johnson, a Navy Admiral working on this project in his own time.

For this mission, due to the urgency, the Itinerant was not yet fully set up with all the research equipment she would eventually carry. She had, however passed her sea trials and was capable of a rescue mission. What remained to be seen was if she was suitable for *this* mission. However, it was a risk they had to take; there was no other marine rescue vehicle that could even attempt to undertake this mission.

Admiral Johnson met with Marcus the day before, advising that the navy had a sub in trouble and requested help. His thoughts returned to the conversation.

"I'm more than a little surprised you're bringing this to me, Ben. Why isn't the Navy responding to aid one of their own?"

Johnson sighed. "What I'm about to tell you is beyond top-secret. Aside from our late President Campbell, our current President Daniel Rossler, Secretary of Defense Willis, and myself, no one knows about her mission. So, before I go any further, I need your word that this information won't leave this office – need-to-know and face-to-face only."

Marcus whistled quietly and leaned back in his chair. "It must be some mission."

"It is. The lives of everyone on the sub, and anyone who goes after her, are at risk if word of the mission gets out. Are you with me?"

Marcus nodded slowly. "I understand. You have my word that I'll keep it secret, and you've got your rescue sub."

"All right let me bring you up to speed. As you know, Brideaux and his council members disappeared before they could be transferred to the Navy's Joint Regional Correctional Facility in Chesapeake, Virginia where they were to be held pending trial."

"Bloody brilliant!" Marcus interrupted; his British accent thick in his excitement. "They're on that sub!"

Johnson smiled and nodded. There was a reason the man had risen through the ranks of the Royal Navy so quickly. "That's correct. Several hours before the planned move, President Campbell ordered the prisoners secretly transferred to the *USS Trepang*."

Marcus frowned. "Wait, you don't have a sub designated 'Trepang' anymore. There have only been two – a Balao Class during World War Two, and a Sturgeon Class that was decommissioned in 2000."

This guy is sharp. I like it. "Right again. The name is part of the security measures—a decoy. She's actually one of our Virginia class subs under the command of Captain Reese Locklin.

"Captain Locklin's orders were to proceed under the polar ice cap to Bangor Naval Base in Washington State, where the prisoners were to be secretly transferred to the Northwest Joint Regional Correctional Facility near Fort Lewis.

"While she was under the ice cap, we lost contact with her. Earlier today, she made contact, advising there was an incident, and they have sustained some damage."

"Not good," Marcus said with a frown of concern.

"No, it isn't," Johnson replied, placing a map on the desk. "She's here, making repairs," he said, placing his index finger on the coordinates on the map.

"The Chukchi Sea over the continental shelf – any sign of the Russians?" Marcus asked.

"Nothing definite, only a couple of intermittent blips on a damaged sonar is all they've reported so far."

"But you can bet they're out there."

"Definitely."

"Yeah, they're lurking out there somewhere."

Marcus was brought out of his reverie when he realized Michael was waving a hand before his face.

"Knock, knock. Anybody home? Marcus, buddy, you there?"

"Yeah, yeah, I'm here. Sorry, got sidetracked."

"Sonya just reported a contact on the sonar—could be our sub."

"Great! Let's go see!"

Onboard the *USS Trepang* in the Chukchi Sea

"But Captain, you really should be in bed resting! Your knee is in no shape for you to be moving about."

"Corpsman Gibbs, I am still Captain of this boat, and it is *my* knee, therefore I will move about *my* boat with *my* knee as I see fit—with or without your assistance. Is that clear?"

Captain Reese Locklin was not a man to second guess. He was an outstanding leader, a tough but fair man, respected by his subordinates and superiors alike – and he ran a tight ship. His reputation as the best captain in the fleet was well earned.

"Yes, sir," Gibbs said dejectedly.

"Good. Then do what you have to but get me to the control room."

Gibbs prepared and delivered a morphine injection before assisting the Captain to a seat in the control room and making him as comfortable as possible.

"Thank you, Gibbs!"

Saluting, Gibbs replied, "You're welcome, sir!"

"Sonar, report. Any more of those intermittent blips?"

"Aye, sir. A few minutes ago—off to starboard, and we have a new contact just coming into range from astern."

"Is the stern contact steady?"

"Aye, sir, and moving straight for us."

"Could be the Itinerant. Keep an eye on it for the signal."

"Aye, sir."

Locklin picked up his hand mic, changed the communication dial setting to 'Trunk', and thumbed the mic switch.

"Has Lieutenant Larson come back aboard yet?"

"Aye, sir. We're draining the trunk now."

"Very good. As soon as he is able, have him report to me in the control room."

"Aye, sir!"

Within fifteen minutes, a still damp Lieutenant Gary Larson stood before the Captain.

"The last of the repair crew just came aboard, sir," he reported. "We've done as much as we can. We can be underway as soon as you give the word."

"Can she make it to Bangor?" Locklin asked.

"It won't be a fun trip, but as long as nothing else happens, I believe she can."

"The Bering Strait is fairly shallow. Normally it isn't a problem, but in our current condition, I'm concerned it could still be a bit of a challenge. Do we have enough control to stay shallow?"

"As with getting here, it will take a team effort, but we have the finest helmsmen in the Navy, they'll get us through!" Larson replied.

"Fair enough. As you know, my Executive Officer was killed by Brideaux. I'm promoting you to acting XO for the duration of this mission."

Larson suppressed a grin. "I'm honored, sir, thank you!"

Locklin let his steely gaze scrutinize the man. "Thank me later, Larson. Others will tell you that serving as my XO is no picnic. I'm not the easiest person to get along with, and I hold my XO to a higher standard than the rest of the crew."

Larson knew Captain Locklin was tough as nails, but he also knew the man cared deeply about the men on his crew. Serving Locklin didn't bother him. However, taking on the XO position meant he was the second-in-command. He would be responsible for administration, maintenance, and logistics, freeing Locklin to concentrate on tactical and operational matters. It also meant if Locklin was unable to perform his duties as commander, he would be in command, and he wasn't sure he was ready for that kind of responsibility yet. But his captain was in pain, their boat was in trouble, the crew was in danger, and he was an officer. Captain Locklin had confidence in him. He was not going to disappoint this fine man. Larson swallowed hard and replied, "Yes, sir."

"Captain!" the sonar officer interrupted excitedly. "The stern contact is maneuvering according to the signal pattern as she approaches!"

Termination

"It's about time something went right! Send the response ping sequence as required. Stations everyone! Set course for the Bering Strait, best speed."

"Aye, Captain!" came a chorus of excited voices.

Chapter Two

The Admiralty Building, Saint Petersburg, Russia

Fire crackled in the stone fireplace spreading the warmth through the room. A comforting haven away from the cold, pouring rain outside. Water dripped from the windows of the multi-story Empire Style building. Firelight played on the polished wood walls of the richly decorated room.

Shelves lined with old books, crystal chandeliers, turn of the century style furniture, and an ornately decorated wool rug covering nearly the entire wooden floor, were just a few of the many treasures to be found in this room, inside the Admiralty building of Saint Petersburg. Above the mantel hung an allegorical painting, artwork related to what was known as 'The Great Patriotic War'.

A tall trim man with sprinkles of gray in his dark brown hair stood looking at the oil painting, the four stars on the epaulettes of his uniform jacket flashed in the firelight.

"Do you know this painting, comrade?" he asked the

man sitting comfortably in the chair before the old, ornate desk.

"Yes, comrade, I do – it is called 'The Triumph of the People'."

"Not quite. 'The Conquering People', comrade. The Triumph of the Conquering People. It was painted by Mikhail Khmelko in 1949 after the war, as a tribute to the leadership of Stalin," he said, raising his cup of tea in tribute to the scene.

"Did you know that we almost lost that war?" As the other man shook his head, he continued. "Yes, indeed we did. As is so often done, history has been written in the most favorable context and our near-defeat quietly forgotten.

"The impact of the disastrous decisions made early in the invasion were borne by the people, and it is they who turned the tide and ultimately brought us to victory."

"I was not aware of that," his guest replied.

Turning, the man scrutinized his comrade. The man had worked for many years to earn the two stars displayed on the shoulders of his uniform jacket –just as he did to earn the four on his. The two had been comrades for many years, and he trusted the short, stocky man whose bald head gleamed in the firelight. "There are not many who are aware of that piece of history, and those of us who are, share it very selectively." As he strode to his desk and sat down, he continued, "The Russian people were almost defeated then, but as this painting shows, they rose up and conquered Germany, burning the captured flags at the feet, so to speak, of Stalin.

"The recent debacle with Brideaux almost defeated the world. But we, the people of Russia, are rising again and will conquer the devastation that the mongrel brought, and we will conquer the nation that spawned him."

"You are in a reflective mood this morning, comrade. What is it that has you so pensive?"

Glancing first at the many rows of ribbon bars on his left chest and the four stripes on the cuff of his uniform jacket, he looked about the room. "Time, comrade. Time."

The only items in the room that gave a hint of the current time period were electric lights, a telephone on the desk, and a television on the wall. The television was the focus of attention for the two men drinking a traditional cup of morning tea.

They watched and listened intently to the man on the screen. The man, although young, projected an aura of power and decision, his words were articulate and thoughtful.

"My fellow Americans, I'm here tonight to tell you that the illegal Presidency of General Thomas Hayden has come to an end.

"He, his advisors, and his militia leaders are all in custody where they will remain until they appear before courts of justice."

Admiral of the fleet, Yegor Fedorin, of the Russian Navy leaned back in the high-backed leather chair and stretched his legs, resting his feet on his desk.

"On behalf of myself and my fellow officers that served in …"

He sipped his tea and spoke over the words of the other man whose voice now came through the television, *"… want to apologize to …"*

"So, the Americans have settled their Presidential squabble."

"So, it would seem," agreed Vice-Admiral Gavriil Semenov.

"He is inexperienced; I think it unlikely that he will last, but let's hear what he has to say," Yegor said, returning their focus to the television.

"Civil unrest is running rampant in our country; violence and crime levels are reaching new record levels daily. People are starving and disillusioned, and in their despair, are being driven to rebellion and crime. I have the deepest sympathy for the people's suffering.

"This is not what I want for the people of America – this is not what the people of America want for themselves.

"Many millions of our fellow countrymen are without food, water, electricity, and other basic needs. They have had no choice but to return to the way they survived during John Brideaux's reign—stealing, looting, and killing—literally being forced to do whatever it takes to survive.

"As this country's situation became increasingly desperate, law enforcement agencies, left understaffed by Brideaux's new world order, are unable to maintain law and order, and have become the target of the very people they have sworn to protect. Many of them have been killed.

"These are not the actions of a true American. My fellow Americans, please, let us lay down our weapons and stop the fighting immediately."

"The late President Laurie Campbell promised you ..."

Yegor took another slow sip of his tea. "This man, this Daniel Rossler is no fool. He is a skillful orator."

"He is, but can he back his words with action?"

"We will watch and see. If he can't, the Americans will eat him alive. They may not be as calculating and cunning as we are, but they can be vicious."

"Indeed."

"Over the course of the next few days, my team will release all the evidence of General Hayden's meetings, plans, and actions, which we were able to collect. And you will be able to judge for yourself. Nothing will be withheld.

"America is a country founded on democracy. America is a country that has thrived because of democracy. America will continue as a democracy!"

"American democracy – bah! They think too much of themselves," Yegor exclaimed.

"In spite of the desperate circumstances this country finds itself in right now, let the record show, for all of history, that I am proud; very proud to serve the noble citizens of this honorable and great country.

"We will all come through this difficult time together by supporting and helping one another because this is who we are as Americans! Let's start now; this very moment. Let every one of us reach out to our neighbor, share what you have with those that don't. Share your food, your shelter, your kindness.

"If we do this, we will turn the tide of violence and hopelessness. Start now, and tomorrow will be better than today. Remember this, my fellow Americans, this is the low point, from here-on we are building a bright new future."

"A bright new future – the man is delusional. The world has no bright new future. John Brideaux took care of that. Damned Americans, they blow the world up, shoot themselves in the foot, and think they will have a 'bright new future.' Worthless, worse than worthless, those imbeciles will be the end of us all someday."

"… there is no reason why general meetings should preclude American citizens. The website you see displayed at the bottom of your screen has been set up for the public to see and hear what is happening in the Oval Office and in the Cabinet meeting room. This real-time, live feed will be accessible 24 hours a day, seven days a week, 365 days a year. My staff and I will be making arrangements so that in the future, several journalists will be allowed to be present at all meetings …"

"Ah, good for you, Mister President Daniel Rossler, and while you're disclosing your meetings to your people, see if you can find and deliver our wretched, traitorous countryman to us, eh! Let us put him to death along with all of Brideaux's other dastardly council leaders!" Yegor steamed.

"… *God bless you and may God bless America.*"

"God bless America," Yegor sneered. "Turn that thing off. I've heard enough!"

Gavriil complied with the Admirals request and sat down across from him, waiting for him to speak.

Yegor swirled the remaining tea in his cup. "So, Gavriil, my old friend, what brings you to my office so early in the morning?"

"Our sub, Knyaz Pozharskiy, under the command of Captain Ruslan Petrov, has been following an American sub through the Arctic Ocean. She attempted to surface through the ice near the pole and was damaged but sent no distress signal." Gavriil pulled a map from his briefcase, opened it on the desk, and indicated a position. "Captain Petrov has continued to follow her. She's here, over the continental shelf in the Chukchi Sea, making repairs."

"Crazy Americans! They know the ice is too thick at the pole to surface! What are they doing?"

"We don't know yet. Captain Petrov is holding position just outside their detection range, keeping an eye on them."

"Hmm." Yegor got up and began to pace. "I don't like it. The Knyaz Vladimir is due to put into port at Vilyuchinsk later today, isn't it?"

"Yes, at last report she is on schedule."

"Divert her. Send her to back up the Pozharskiy."

"Yes, Sir."

Onboard the *Itinerant*

"It's definitely our damaged sub, Captain, "Sonya Takahashi reported from the Sonar station aboard the Itinerant. "She responded to our maneuvering pattern with the ping sequence, and she's getting underway."

"That's good news, Taka," Marcus said, calling the young Asian Sonar Technician by her nickname. The small, black-haired, young woman had naturally tan-looking skin, a brilliant smile, and exotic eyes that a man could get lost in. She also graduated top of her class at Massachusetts Institute of Technology – MIT.

The sonar equipment on the Itinerant was Sonya's graduate project. Marcus still didn't understand how she did it, but her equipment could gather information at nearly twice the range of standard sonar. It was seventy-five percent more accurate, and with the algorithms she programmed into it, the sonar would be able to identify and differentiate between various types of targets: fish, rocks, ships, etcetera.

"Do we have an update on the damage she sustained?" Marcus asked with concern.

A voice spoke from the communications station. "It seems someone took temporary control of the sub and tried to surface near the pole by breaking through the ice."

Marcus swore. Mutiny? On a US Navy boat?

"Internal circuits and systems were damaged but have mostly been restored. She's lost both bow planes, the number one sonar array, most of the sail masts, and took on water in the upper bow compartment. They managed to repair the mast antenna and were able to temporarily seal the leak in the bow and remove most of the water."

Marcus whistled. "That's quite a bit of damage."

"Yes, sir. It is."

"Any sign of other ships or boats?" Marcus asked.

"Like the Russians?" Taka grinned at him. "Yes, there is a Russian sub staying just out of the Trepang's sonar range, starboard side and taking position astern."

"Are you certain it's Russian?"

"Absolutely. Borei II Class probably."

"Probably?"

"Well, the Borei II Class subs are fairly new, and we don't have a lot of information about them, but the sound isn't quite right for the old Borei Class, so I'm betting it's a Borei II."

"Do they know we're here?"

"Since we're staying far to Trepang's port side, we're still too far out of range for their sonars—the sonar technology we know about anyway. I'd say they haven't detected us yet."

"Good. Bill," he said, speaking to his electronics technician and helmsman, "follow the Trepang, work with Taka, and make sure we stay out of sight of the Russians."

"You got it, Capt'n!"

Chapter Three

Washington, D.C.

Daniel was deep in brown study at his desk in the Oval Office—replaying the activities of the previous night in his mind. To his relief, they had re-taken the White House without loss of life. His biggest concern had been that General Hayden's troops would open fire on the throng of protesters. Thanks to Roy's heat ray drones repelling the crowd with a burning sensation to their skin, none of them came into firing range.

There had been many injuries in the initial stampede toward the White House, several of them serious, and many were being treated for minor burns caused by the heat rays, but Daniel could live with that. No one was killed. The wounds would heal in time, as would the nation; that was his deepest hope.

With a sigh and a brief, tight smile, he reached for his cup and picked up the documents before him, reviewing each one as he sipped the hot coffee.

He had decided to retain those cabinet members Laurie had appointed. Among them were Secretary of State Bill Simms and Secretary of Defense Cliff Willis. Both men had proved their loyalty to his predecessor, Laurie Campbell, and to him during their escape from the White House, the crash of Air Force One, the time in exile, and in retaking the White House last night.

After careful consideration and much discussion with Nigel Harper, a personal friend, and former president, the most popular ever, Daniel was ready to nominate the people to fill the remaining eight positions of his cabinet.

For Secretary of Homeland Security, there was only ever going to be one person who Daniel wanted for that job —Salome James, former FBI profiler, a brilliant mind and one of the main players in the Rossler Foundation leadership team. She was married to Roy James, the Rossler Foundation's nanotechnology genius who played a big part in the foundation's successes of the past.

As part of his plan to get bipartisan buy-in, he included in his nominations, four people of the minority party. He knew this gesture might, once the dust settled and politics were back in play, bite him in the back, but for the sake of bringing the people together, it was a risk he was willing to take. If it worked, and he hoped it would, it was going to pay off big time.

Everything in the nomination documents appeared to be in order, ready for submission to the Senate. He signed them, placed them in an envelope with his personal letter requesting a quick approval, for the sake of the nation, and had them delivered immediately.

Daniel stretched as he stepped off the monorail car onto the platform in the dimly lit alcove. It had already been a long day, and he still had this one meeting to attend. He looked around at the solid rock walls, still marveling at the structure.

Raven Rock, who would have thought.

The abandoned Cold War military installation, a hidden cave chiseled into a mountain of solid granite, had been the perfect hiding place for the Rossler Foundation team while they plotted and orchestrated Operation Winnow – the unceremonious ousting of the dictator, General Hayden, from the White House.

Two secret service agents accompanied him through the dark passageway once used by military vehicles to reach the main cave. The eerie glow of hand-held pocket flashlights illuminated their way, and echoes of their quick footsteps attended them on their short trek to the Control Center.

Although he and Sarah had handed over their duties as joint CEOs of The Rossler Foundation to the team known as 'The Musketeers,' Daniel had called a meeting of the Foundation members to discuss what to do about the top-secret files on world leaders, government officials, and terrorist groups that had been stolen by Brideaux. JR and his team recovered them when they captured Brideaux. He also needed to table former President Nigel Harper's thoughts on the future of sharing the information in the Tenth Cycle Libraries.

The libraries. Daniel shook his head. *Are they more trouble than they're worth? We were so excited to translate the code etched into the walls of The Great Pyramid at Giza and discover the existence of an advanced civilization before our own! And then to discover there were nine other* civilization cycles before that—each lasting approximately twenty-six-thousand years—was astounding!

The advanced technology and medical treatments, all the good we hoped to share with the world, and then the discovery of the eighth-cycle library in the Grand Canyon and the fiasco with John Brideaux with his megalomaniac ideas.

It's true the nanotechnology of the eighth cycle and its possibilities are phenomenal, but so many people have died. There is so much knowledge that could be abused! Dare we share it outside the Foundation as we originally agreed we would not? If we share it, how long before people with nefarious intentions get their hands on it and destroy our way of life? Maybe forever this time.

Before the overthrow of Hayden, Nigel and others of the Rossler Foundation leadership had come to the conclusion that, due to its democracy, brainpower, infrastructure, technological advances, and industrious nature, the United States would most likely be the first of the world's nations to overcome the chaos and turmoil emerging as world leader again.

Under John Brideaux's One World Government, every country's military and security forces had been all but demolished- military arsenals were destroyed along with all nuclear weapons. Nuclear power stations were ordered to shut down. The 'playing fields' of the world were once again level—no one country had the where-with-all to dominate or control another. And therein lurked the danger —it was the ideal setting for a new arms race. It could give rise to a new Cold War if not an all-out World War as the former world powers tried to become the top dog. In the past, it was the doctrine of MAD, mutual assured destruction, that kept the super powers from the full-scale use of nuclear weapons which would've caused the complete annihilation of both the attacker and the defender. Now there were no nuclear weapons, and therein lay the risk.

Greeting his fellow Rosslerites captured his attention when he arrived, and it took him several minutes to work his way to the conference room. Taking his seat at the large table, he greeted his younger brother Aaron, Aaron's wife, Cyndi, his long-time friend from his working days at the New York Times, Raj Sankaran, and Raj's wife, Sushma.

Luke Clarke and the rest of the founding members of the Rossler Foundation joined the meeting via satellite from the Rabbit Hole, the Foundation's hideaway in the Gallatin Mountains of Montana.

Daniel was comforted to see the face of his beautiful wife, Sarah, along with her parents, Ryan and Emma Clarke. They were joined by her Aunt and Uncle, Sally and Luke Clarke.

His parents, Ben and Nancy Rossler were there as well, along with his grandmother, Bess. A shadow of longing crossed his face as he thought of his grandfather, Nicholas, who was no longer with them.

Sinclair and Martha O'Reilly, their head translator and his horticulturist wife were just taking seats. He was grateful that Sinclair had accepted the position as the new CEO of the foundation.

"Thank you all for joining this meeting," Sinclair said. "Daniel asked me to call the meeting to discuss something which he said was very important. I don't know what the topic is, so, the floor is yours, Daniel."

Daniel nodded. "We have a great deal to discuss and decisions to make. First, I want to address the issue of the top-secret files that Brideaux acquired.

"As you all know, those files contain damning information, in some cases possibly deadly, on every member of every government and every influential person spanning the globe. They also contain information on terrorist cells and organizations. In the wrong hands, most, if not all, of this information could be used to control governments and nations.

"Thanks to the recovery efforts by our team, the Rossler Foundation now holds this information. The question is, what are we going to do with it?"

Martha was the first to speak up. "It seems to me that kind of information is trash and trouble. No one should have access to it; it should be destroyed."

"Including the information on the terrorist groups?" Ryan asked.

"Well," Martha hesitated. "Maybe not that part of it, but definitely the other dirty laundry."

Several chuckled at her choice of expression. Luke, being a former CIA field agent, knew the value and use of that type of information. "I don't think we should let it go so easily. There is a time and a place for that kind of information."

"At what time and place would that kind of filth possibly be useful for anything except blackmailing someone into doing something illegal?" Martha fired back.

Knowing of several situations where 'that kind' of information had saved several lives and prevented wars, Luke was hard put not to answer that question. "I just think we should consider things carefully before taking any action that is permanent. What you're suggesting is irreversible. I'd rather be safe than sorry."

"Luke is right." Ryan, having worked with electronic surveillance, was all too aware of the value of information

—dirty or clean. "I think we would be wise not to make any hasty decisions regarding it."

"Ben, Sinclair, you're both being awfully quiet, and so are you, Aaron and Raj. Ladies? What do you think?" Martha asked, managing to put everyone on the spot at once.

Sally and Emma looked at one another with slight shrugs. "I think the less we all know about what's in those files the better off we all are," Sally said finally. Emma nodded in silent agreement.

"Ben?"

Scratching his head for a moment before speaking, Ben stated, "I don't know about the information on the government people, but I sure would like to see our country get its hands on that terrorist information and wipe them off the face of the planet. The sooner the better."

Raj cleared his throat. "I have a recommendation. What if the information concerning *all* government members is separated out and stored in a secure vault at the Rabbit Hole? We would be the only ones who know it exists. After a period of time, ten years for example, if there hasn't been a good reason to use it, we can destroy it. In the meantime, the information on terrorist cells and organizations could be used by Foundation security to monitor activities and offer unofficial intelligence to those who would appreciate the information."

Silence hung in the air while everyone considered Raj's suggestion. "I think that sounds like a very equitable solution," Sinclair said. "What do the rest of you think?"

Slowly, indications of agreement came from all in attendance, even Martha. "Very well, then. Raj, would you please see to the implementation of both solutions?"

"Certainly."

Turning back to Daniel, Sinclair continued, "Okay, Daniel, what's next on your agenda?"

Daniel made eye contact with each individual as he brought up the next issue. "We are the original members of the team that found and broke the code of the Tenth Cycle Library and the founding members of the Rossler Foundation. As such, I've decided to keep this initial discussion among us. We will decide together if we want, or need, to bring the rest of the membership in."

With that said, Daniel got right to the point. "Because of the destruction of conventional and nuclear armaments around the globe, we are facing a new arms race. It has been suggested that the only way to stem the tide is to use the technological advances available to us, the United States, in the Tenth Cycle Library to get us to the front of the race and keep us there."

"That sounds like you want to turn the library over to the government and use it to establish the United States as *the* World Leader," Sinclair said, with a hint of apprehension in his tone.

Murmurs spread around the table before Luke spoke. "Let's hear it, Daniel."

Clearing his throat for silence, Daniel continued. "The Foundation was established to keep the library out of the hands of the government. In the early days after our discovery of the library, when Nigel was still president, he tried to coax us into relinquishing control to the government. We refused, and we remained steadfast. Nigel eventually came around to our viewpoint. Our philosophy has always been to share the knowledge of the Tenth Cycle for the benefit of *all* of humanity, not just one government.

"However, as you all know, it didn't take us long to discover that there is too much information on technology in the library that could be used for malevolent purposes. Furthermore, it also became clear that our civilization has not reached a level of maturity that would allow the knowledge to be shared equally and used responsibly by everyone. Therefore, that knowledge which was considered dangerous was withheld, and only trusted countries were given access to the remainder of the information.

"But as you know, the library became the ultimate prize for various groups and individuals with evil intent. Thus far, by the grace of God, we've been able to keep it out of their hands. However, I don't have to tell you how close we came to losing control of it on at least two occasions.

"In light of the present circumstances, perhaps it is time to reconsider our stance about our exclusive guardianship of the library. To establish the United States ahead of those countries who will be contriving to become the new world power, we'll have to put extensive effort and resources into getting everything possible out of the library and using it to our advantage. Doing this might require accepting the government as a partner.

"We also need to keep in mind that regardless of whether the Foundation or the government has possession of the library, there will always be those who will want the information it contains. These people will make every effort to obtain it without regard for the cost, effort, or lives.

"Sarah and I believe the final decision has to be made by the Rossler Foundation leadership, possibly even the entire membership. Though, as founding members, we wanted to discuss this with you first.

"The topic is now open for discussion."

Silence reigned as the people stared at each other and shifted uncomfortably in their chairs.

"Daniel," spoke Martha. "After all we've been through

to protect the information and use it wisely for the benefit of all people, I can't believe that you are actually considering using the information for the sole benefit of our country, let alone using it to develop weapons to ensure our dominance over the world!" She hid her shaking hands beneath the table and took a breath to calm her voice.

Sinclair joined his wife. "Not too long ago you made the late Laurie Campbell promise that the US government won't lay claim to the library. What has changed?"

The unexpected antagonism evident in the group gave Daniel pause.

He held his hands up in surrender. "I've been clear about it Martha. I am putting the idea forward for discussion. I am not going to make a decision about this without this group's support. If you shoot it down here tonight, I'm not going to take it any further. As far as I am concerned, although Sarah and I own the controlling shares, and are in a position to make the call, we won't do it—ever.

"To answer your question Sinclair; what has changed is our understanding of the global political situation and perils we'll soon find ourselves in if we don't become the most powerful country again—very quickly."

Sarah nodded her agreement with her husband.

Several bodies sat back in their chairs, arms folded across their chests, frowns of concern on their faces.

Grumbles and muttering began, the air seemed to grow thick and chilled around them.

Sinclair was about to bring the meeting to order, but Daniel signaled to him to let it go. He didn't want to inhibit them from airing their views.

Bess rose quietly to her feet and silence fell across the room. At ninety-two, the matriarch was in remarkable mental and physical condition. She was still doing Pilates every day. Everyone loved and respected her and quietly wished that they would be able to age as gracefully as she did.

"Daniel," she spoke firmly but gently. "You have brought an extremely serious matter before us. We have all been through a lot over the past few years." She paused and looked at those gathered one by one. "I think we would all benefit from a bit of time to consider the suggestion and the possible consequences and opportunities that could come with it.

"I suggest we adjourn for tonight and come back to this in a few days when we've had time to think. We can then discuss it with clear minds instead of our emotions."

Ben nodded in agreement to what his mother was saying. Taking their lead, the others began to acquiesce.

"Thank you, Grandma," Daniel said with a slight grin of relief. His grandma's suggestion couldn't have come at a better time. It got him out of a very uncomfortable situation. "I think yours is very wise counsel. I agree, and if everyone else agrees, I'm happy to meet again in a few days. All I ask is that you keep it among the members of this group, let's not upset anyone else yet."

They all agreed.

"Good night everyone," Daniel said.

Several 'good-nights' were heard before the satellite transmission was cut.

Aaron shook his head at his brother. "You sure know how to stir up trouble."

Chapter Four

Onboard the *Trepang*

Lieutenant Larson wasn't kidding when he said the trip ahead of the Trepang wouldn't be fun, but it was easier than the trip to the Chukchi Sea. "We're able to maintain half speed and have just passed Point Hope. We'll reach the Bering Strait in about ten hours."

Captain Locklin lay on his bunk with his leg elevated. Once they were underway, and it became clear that the sub could limp along safely, the corpsman had insisted he rest, and this time he didn't argue.

"What else?"

"That intermittent sonar contact has reappeared and is following us, not trying to hide anymore."

"The Russians?"

"Most likely."

"What about the Itinerant? Is she maintaining position?"

"She's staying at the edge of our port sonar range; I doubt the Russians know she's here."

"That's odd. It's almost like she knows the Russians are following us, and she's trying to hide from them ... well, the longer we can keep her presence a secret, the better off we are. We sure don't want the Russians becoming nervous by thinking we're ganging up on them."

"That's for darn sure! We've taken enough damage. I've threatened to keel-haul the first man who sneezes!"

Locklin laughed. "I'll help you!"

"How is Ensign Littleton?" Larson asked.

The Captain's eyes darkened; a shadow of sadness mixed with anger passed over his face when he thought of the young man Brideaux had tortured in order to gain control of the submarine.

Locklin had always considered himself an emotionally strong man and held the belief that there was no way he would ever be forced into anything, especially relinquishing his command.

He was trained to withstand torture, trained to endure watching others being tortured. But nothing could've prepared him to endure watching one of his own men being taken apart piece by piece – skinned alive.

"He's in critical condition. Corpsman Gibbs is doing all he can but ..."

"I'm sorry, sir," Larson said, then stepped to the cabin door. "Try to get some rest, Captain. I'll let you know when we approach the strait."

Locklin raised his hand in acknowledgement.

Termination

Onboard the Russian submarine *Knyaz Pozharskiy*

Seaman Grigory Shulga watched the sonar screen before him intently. Fresh out of sonar technician training, this was his first tour aboard the Knyaz Pozharskiy, and he wanted to make a good impression on Captain Petrov.

He had discovered the American submarine when she foolishly tried to break through the ice near the North Pole. The Captain was pleased with the report of his discovery and his careful tracking of the boat as they followed her to the Chukchi Sea off the Northeast coast of Russia.

Grigory was not going to jeopardize his good standing with the Captain by letting his guard down for one minute.

"Captain! The Americans are holding at fifteen knots, still heading for the Bering Strait."

"Very good, Shulga. Any other contacts in the area?"

"Negative, sir. The scope is clear."

"Steady as she goes, stay with the Americans. How long until she enters the Strait."

"Calculating now, sir ... about eight hours."

"Tupolev," Petrov said, addressing his Weapons officer. "I want a check on all torpedoes. Make sure they are ready to fire if we need them. Run some drills."

"Yes, Captain!"

"I'll be in my quarters, Commander, keep me informed," he said as he left the Command Center.

Commander Roman Luski gave a salute. "Yes, Captain."

Onboard the *Itinerant*

Ed Mulligan, Culinary specialist and logistics officer aboard the Itinerant was just serving dinner when Brenda Hunte entered the lounge. The lounge was the crew's designation for the small compartment where they dined, watched movies, and played cards or board games.

Like Sonya Takahashi, the dark beauty from Barbados was also an MIT graduate monitoring the results of her new electrical design project that was part of this new research sub. She had developed smaller, more powerful batteries for submarines, and had a new space-saving design for the electricity-generation and distribution equipment deployed on board the Itinerant.

As she joined Captain Marcus, the engineer, 'Gus' Aquino and two of the six divers they brought along, she gave her report.

"We're entering the Strait, Captain. Bill and Taka are minding the store." By which she meant they were guiding the sub.

"All right," Marcus responded. "I'll check in with them when I've finished eating."

"Hi, boys!" she greeted Karl and Michael. "Are you bored yet?" she teased.

Ever the serious Navy Seal, Karl replied, "The down time has been useful for planning and reviewing rescue scenarios."

Michael and Brenda looked at each other and laughed, then Brenda slapped Karl on the shoulder. "C'mon Dunlap, lighten up." She laughed again. "You need to learn how to relax! Ever been on a date? Taken a vacation?"

"Hey, Hunte, wanna go out with *me* tonight?" Michael

asked, waggling his eyebrows and grinning at her. "I'll take ya to a movie!"

"I'd like that just fine, sugar!" she teased back. "I'll even let you buy me popcorn –if Ed here brought any!"

"Of course, I did! What's a movie without popcorn?" Ed responded.

Continuing to eat, Karl ignored them, and they settled down to eat as well.

As Marcus got up to leave, the remaining four divers entered the lounge, and the good-natured teasing and fun began again. Laughter echoed behind him as he made his way down the passageway.

Entering the bridge, he stepped to the sonar station. "How are our two contacts, Taka?" he inquired.

"Holding steady at fifteen knots. The Strait is narrowing and will force us all closer together. It won't be long before the Russians know we're here."

"Well, they were bound to find out sooner or later. Let's just stay on our toes and hope we don't unnerve them. Bill, anything going on I should hear about?"

"The rescue ship has arrived in the Bearing Sea and will be waiting for us when we exit the Strait. There's also an updated report on the damage to the Trepang."

"Let's hope they've been able to repair its damage and we won't be needed. But something tells me it's not going to be that easy."

"If your wish is granted, this will at least have been a good shake-down cruise for the Itinerant."

"What do we know about the rescue ship that's being sent?"

"She's the Mystic Sea, a privately-owned research vessel."

"Privately owned? There're over one hundred people on that sub. How many souls can she hold?"

"She's twelve-thousand-five-hundred gross tons, three-hundred feet long, with a total capacity for two-hundred souls."

Marcus shook his head in wonderment. "Who owns her, Jacque Cousteau's grandson or something?"

"No sir, a former Oceanographic professor from Oregon State University, a Doctor Dean Griffith."

"Humph. Well, she's big enough if we need her, and I hope we don't. I'm going to review that report on the Trepang and get a few hours of rest, as is Brenda when she's done eating. We'll be back to relieve you in six. Wake me if anything happens before then."

"You got it!"

Chapter Five

Onboard the *Knyaz Pozharskiy*

Shulga's eyes widened as a new contact blip suddenly appeared on the sonar screen. He ran through the identification sequence, but nothing came up. Double checking the information, he realized that the contact was smaller than any of the military class subs he was familiar with, yet too big to be a privately-owned scientific research or rescue sub.

This is an unknown.

"Captain! New sonar contact, just coming into range, port side."

"American?"

"Unknown, sir. It's not in our data banks—too small for military, too big for private."

"Heading?"

"She's pacing the Americans, sir," Shulga reported.

"I don't like this," Petrov growled as he began to pace the confines of the Command Center.

Five minutes passed. "Sonar report on new contact."

"Still pacing the Americans, sir. Like us, she's moving in closer as the Strait narrows."

Petrov took a few more steps, considering his position and options. "Bring us to the starboard edge of the American's baffles; we'll give them an escort out of our territory."

Turning to his weapons officer, he ordered, "Load tubes one and two – I want to be ready if they so much as twitch wrong."

Washington, D.C.

Chief of Staff, Glenn Baier, knocked on the door to the Oval Office and entered at Daniel's bidding. "Mister President, the Head of Maintenance has the damage report and is ready to meet with you as you requested."

He stopped short when he saw Attorney General, Scott Jenkins and a man he didn't know sitting on the couch across from the President. "Sorry, sir," he said a little puzzled, as he normally arranged the President's schedule and meetings. "I didn't realize you were in a meeting."

Daniel smiled, recognizing the man's consternation. "Don't worry, Glenn, you haven't been replaced, and this isn't a formal meeting. You already know Mister Jenkins. This is my friend Raj Sankaran—we worked together at the New York Times."

"Nice to meet you, Mister Sankaran," Glenn said, shaking Raj's hand.

"Send in Mister..." Daniel paused as he realized he didn't know the maintenance man's name.

"Seymour MacDougle," Glenn finished for him. "But

don't call him that or mister—he hates it. Call him 'Morey', and you'll get along fine."

"All right, 'Morey' it is, and thanks for the tip!"

Glenn opened the door to admit a small, grey-haired, hunchback man who walked with a limp.

Hiding his surprise, Daniel greeted him, "Good day, Mister ... ah, Morey. Please, have a seat," Daniel invited, indicating a place on the couch. "You have the damage report ready, I'm told."

"Yes, sir, I do." Morey handed Daniel a folder. "The residence didn't receive too much damage—mostly bullet holes in the drywall and doors on the ground and first floors and stairwells in-between. The second and third floors didn't receive any damage except for some scratched paint on one of the bedrooms' windowsills.

"Hayden and his damn fools had no respect for the historical value of this place and its contents," he said indignantly. "—if you'll forgive my language.

"Since the property is open for public tours, I suggest repairing the damage to the residence first."

"That sounds reasonable," Daniel said, opening the folder to inspect the meticulous notes and ledgers.

"The majority of the damage is in the lower levels of the East Wing," Morey continued. "The repairs there will be much more extensive. The entrance to the Presidential Emergency Operations Center and surrounding area will need to be completely gutted and restored to remove all the damage and ... blood stains."

Daniel remembered the bloodbath they went through to escape during Hayden's coup. "This is very thorough, Morey. You must have been doing this work for quite some time."

"I started working here as a grounds keeper when I was

a boy, raking leaves and trimming grass. In seventy years, except for a tour of duty in the Marines, I've never left. I've been head of maintenance for the past twenty years—there's nothing I don't know about how this place operates."

Stunned at the man's commitment to his job and obvious devotion to the property, Daniel was momentarily speechless. He finally found his tongue again. "All right, Morey, you are clearly well qualified to make the decisions on what needs to be done and when. I'll leave this in your capable hands. You may begin the work at your earliest convenience. My door is open, just let me know if you need my help with anything."

As the man got up to leave, Daniel stood with him and shook his hand. "And Morey, thank you for your dedication and service—to this country and to this office."

Morey grinned, and his grip tightened slightly. "You're welcome Mister President."

As the door closed behind the humble old man, Jenkins spoke up. "All these years. I had no idea."

Daniel shook his head. "That's about the most amazing tale of commitment to a job I've ever heard." Daniel smiled, and in a fake accent added, "Der ain't many o' his kind walkin the earth no more."

The three of them enjoyed a laugh before returning to their earlier discussion.

"So, Scott," Daniel addressed the man he hoped to keep as Attorney General. "Can we legally release the information and recordings we have on Hayden?"

"Yes, I believe we can. A few years before the debacle with Brideaux, a law went into effect that, on a national level, allows the public dissemination of this kind of information to the American people in the event they have been deceived by the leadership of the country.

"It was intended as a sort of 'spotlight' on government officials, to keep them honest, letting them know the American people were watching."

"That would certainly seem to apply in this case," Daniel said. "Raj, what do we have in place to accomplish this?"

"We have already established the website that allows public viewing of the Oval Office and Cabinet meeting room. I recommend we utilize it.

"Roy and I looked through the recordings of both Hayden's actions and ours. Neither of us see any reason why all of it shouldn't be accessible to the public. We can put it up to show as a single program and also have it indexed by time, date, location, person, and topic."

"That sounds perfect," Daniel said. "How soon can you have it active?"

"It's ready now. All we have to do is upload it to the site."

"Scott? Any last-minute reservations about the legality of this?" Daniel asked.

"No. I feel we're on solid ground."

"Ok, Raj, get it uploaded. Inform the news channels and have them announce it on the news tonight while running the web address along the bottom of the screen."

"You got it!" Raj was enthusiastic. At last, he was going to expose Hayden!

Chapter Six

Re'an headquarters Tunguska, Russia

Viktor strode briskly into the conference room, head held high, and quickly took his seat at the table. He had long planned for and awaited this day. The time had come for the Re'an to rise up and take control of the world.

Deszik, the 'son' he had chosen in order to control his mother, sat to his right; his Second-In-Command, Soltan, to his left. Stonash, Ama'ru, and Petya, his best commanders were also gathered for the meeting.

Looking at the four commanders before him, his mind drifted back more than one-hundred years, to the turn of the previous century, when he first awoke in the sleep pod here, in the cavern at Tunguska.

With the failure of his commander's pod, as second-in-command, it had fallen on him to lead the B'ran soldiers to victory in conquering the L'gundo people. To aid him in his endeavor, he had promoted Soltan to be his Second.

Together they had awakened Stonash and the rest of

the B'ran soldiers, along with the few remaining L'gundo scientists, and survived the explosive damage, caused by a pressure buildup of the volcanic gases that powered the facility.

It had taken years to repair and rebuild the facility, but the time was not wasted. Among the L'gundo scientists were their lead re-animation scientist, Dekka, and two of his assistants, Tellek and Baynor.

He used Deszik to control his mother, Telestra, and eventually took her as his wife. She was not a willing party in the marriage—she did it to protect her son. Telestra was also the leader of the rest of the L'gundo, so he gained control over them through her.

Petya had been a young boy when his soldiers found him wandering outside the facility after the Tunguska explosion, he'd been searching for the source of the powerful event.

Ama'ru was a young man from Petya's village who had been searching for him when he went missing. Viktor's men captured him not too far away from the facility.

Viktor had killed and reanimated them both, to the horror of the L'gundo scientists.

Thus, had begun the compulsory work of Dekka and his team to use the re-animation technology to build a new and powerful race called the Re'an. Petya and Ama'ru were two of the first three to be transformed.

Over the years, they had captured, killed and reanimated many more people. The process of the restoration of life by placing a computer chip in the brain and re-animating the body had become much more sophisticated. Now, they were able to program the mind, change the personality, substitute identities, and control almost every aspect of the person.

They had also developed techniques to augment anatomy and improve the senses, intelligence, strength, endurance, vision, and hearing. The Re'an were now a race of 'Super Soldiers.' With more training and enhancements than any of the others, Deszik, Stonash, Ama'ru, and Petya were the best of them all.

Viktor began. "Today is a day we will remember with pride. This day has been in the making for more than a century. Today we set in motion our plans to establish the reign of the Re'an across the world."

The men raised their morning drinks in salute.

"The four of you," Viktor gestured to Deszik, Stonash, Ama'ru, and Petya, "will each lead a team of six—including yourselves—to the canyon site in the United States and recover our base there.

"Deszik will be in command of this operation. Each of you will choose five of your best men from your regiment to accompany you. You will use commercial airlines to fly to a location near the canyon, and the teams will assemble in Flagstaff before descending into the canyon together.

"Teams One and Two will fly out of Yemelyanovo airport near Krasnoyarsk. Teams Three and Four will fly out of Yakutsk airport. Team leaders will fly out in six days. Three members from each team will depart the next day, and the final two on the third day.

"You will meet your team members and then have two days to reach Flagstaff. Join the other groups going down in the canyon and meet up at dusk, the following day. I expect you to reach and enter the canyon site by dawn the next morning.

"Team One will be yours, Deszik. You will fly into Phoenix, Arizona. Team Two will be Petya's, flying into Las Vegas, Nevada. Stonash, you have Team Three flying into

Albuquerque, New Mexico, and Ama'ru will be in charge of Team Four which will fly into Denver, Colorado.

"Soltan has your travel documents and itineraries. Everyone should be ready to leave Tunguska for their designated departure airports in four days. Any questions?"

There were none, so he dismissed them. "Petya," he called, stopping the man as he reached the door.

"Yes, sir?" He turned back to face Viktor.

Viktor looked around to be sure the room was clear, and no one was in the hallway near the door. "You have been with me for a long time Petya, grown up under my command, earned my respect and trust."

Petya listened without response.

"I have some ... concern about Deszik and have a special mission for you. I want you to be prepared to take command of this operation should he fail to meet our ... expectations. Do you understand?"

In other words, kill him if he steps out of line.

"Yes, sir – I will be watchful and address any ... situation that might arise."

"Thank you, Petya. You may go now."

Onboard the *Itinerant*

"Good morning, Captain, Dunlap," Taka greeted as Marcus and Karl Dunlap stepped onto the bridge.

"Good morning, Taka! You're up bright and early."

"Keeping an eye on Ivan"

"Good thinking. And what's he up to?"

"Like us, pacing the Trepang, except that he's moved in close – nearly into her starboard baffles."

"When did he move in?"

"Almost the instant we were in sonar range."

"Hmmm. I'd say our presence makes him nervous. Any attempt at contact or signs of aggression?"

"No, sir, unless you consider his change in proximity aggressive."

"It could be. Continue monitoring. What's our position?"

"We'll be exiting the strait in about thirty minutes."

"How is the Trepang doing?" Dunlap wanted to know.

"She's held a steady speed of 15 knots, a little slow, but she's holding together."

"I sure am glad I'm not aboard. With all her damage, that has to be one hell of a rough ride," Bill interjected.

"Let's hope she continues to 'hold together'," Dunlap replied. "I'm happy to rescue people, but I'm happier if they don't need it — it's *much* better for them!"

"Why don't you two get some breakfast? Gus and Brenda will be here in a few minutes, and I'll watch the store in the meantime."

The two excitedly left the bridge. Ed's breakfasts were to die for.

Onboard the *Trepang*

Locklin hobbled into the Command Information Center (CIC), with the help of Corpsman Gibbs. "Report," he barked before he even sat down. The pain in his shattered knee was wearing him down, making him feel like a wounded lion, and he spoke more harshly than he intended, but he didn't apologize. With the Russians this close and the boat's damage, he needed his crew on their toes.

"Sir!" responded Seaman Yoder from the number one sonar station. "We're clear of the strait and the Russians continue to pace us just outside our starboard baffles. The Itinerant is pacing to the port."

"Depth is one-hundred-twenty-five feet, speed holding at fifteen knots, sir!" barked the helmsman.

"It's shallow here, watch the bottom. Steady as she goes," Locklin ordered, settling back in his chair with a frown.

"Steady as she goes, aye, sir."

"Larson," Locklin addressed his exec. "How are the repairs holding?"

"The number one sonar array remains inoperative. A leak has developed in one of the vertical launch tubes as a result of the dent, and a couple of the welds in the bow are also leaking. I have a team looking at the launch tube to see if it can be repaired, but a diver will have to be sent out to repair the leaking welds."

"And that can't be done while we're underway," Locklin said bitterly. Again, he cursed Brideaux and his stupidity.

Should we stop for repairs?

"So, we either stop for repairs and let the Russians circle us like a hungry shark, or we stay shallow and hope to God we don't have to go deep."

"That's it in a nutshell, sir."

Damn you Brideaux.

Onboard the *Knyaz Pozharskiy*

"What are the Americans doing?" Petrov asked.

"They are slowing and going to the surface, Captain," Shulga answered in surprise.

"What about the other sub?"

"It is slowing but holding at one-hundred-twenty-five feet off to port."

"Surface. Bring us in behind the Americans. I want to stop that sub from joining them if they try."

"Aye, sir."

"As soon as we are on the surface, send a signal to the Americans. Ask if they need assistance."

"Sir?"

"Just do it!"

"Aye, sir."

Several tense minutes passed before the answer came.

"Sir, the Americans respectfully decline."

"Govno! I *want* to talk to them. Change to an open frequency and send it to them. Let's see if they will speak."

"Aye, sir."

"Tupolev! Make sure those torpedoes are ready!"

"They are ready, sir!"

Onboard the *Trepang*

Ensign Schmidt blinked as he read the message from the Russians. "Sir! They sent a message on an open radio frequency. I think they want to talk."

"Just what I need, a conversation with Ivan while we're in the middle of repairs. Larson!" Locklin called the exec to his side. "Can Hunter get out there, repair those leaks, and get back in here in five minutes?"

"He was on deck the moment we surfaced, but I don't think he can make the repairs that fast, but ... maybe. He can try."

"Tell him to hurry, we don't have much time."

"Aye, sir," Larson said and moved away to notify Hunter to get the job done and get back inside pronto.

"All right, let's see what Ivan wants to talk about."

When the Ensign signaled the Captain that the radio frequency was open, Locklin addressed the Russians.

"This is the Captain of the Trepang. How can we assist you?"

"It is not we who need the assistance, Trepang. This is the Captain of the Pozharskiy offering assistance to you."

"That's very kind Pozharskiy, but we are not in need of assistance at this time."

"Really, Captain? I find that hard to believe. Your boat has been limping along for nearly a week, and I see you have a man on deck making repairs."

"Oh, that," he said nonchalantly, "well, we've been cruising slowly, making better maps of the bottom, noting hazards. We're trying to increase safety for submarines in the Arctic. I'm surprised your government wasn't made aware of our mapping project. As for the man on deck, he is cleaning the surface of one of our sonars."

"We know all about your mapping project," Petrov lied. "It is simply of no interest to us because we already have highly detailed maps that identify the sub-marine hazards in the Arctic. As usual, you Americans are woefully behind us."

Locklin heard the snickers around the CIC at the Russians attempted bravado. "It seems like he knows more about our 'mapping project' than we do since it doesn't exist," Yoder muttered from the sonar station.

"Well, Captain, that is good news. To know that we won't have to come to the rescue of a Russian sub in trouble out here, will free us up for other duties."

"Yes, like repairing your ineptly built submarines. It looks to me like your man is attempting to weld places on the hull."

"As I said, he's cleaning the surface on one of our sonars. Amazing how much it looks like welding, isn't it?"

"Let us not play these games, Captain. We know about the unfortunate incident of trying to surface through the ice that damaged your boat. Now, what are you doing out here? Why didn't you signal for assistance from your government at the time of the incident? What is it that you are hiding?"

Turning to his exec, Locklin ordered him to have Hunter return immediately, finished or not.

"You must be misinformed. We have not attempted to surface until now, to clean our sonar. We certainly haven't had need of signaling for any assistance. As for what I'm hiding, why don't we start with you telling me what you're hiding?"

A long silence followed. "Now, if you'll excuse me, our sonar is clean, we'll be on our way," Locklin said. "Hope you have a good journey, let us know if we can be of any assistance."

Drawing his index finger across his neck Locklin ordered the radio connection severed. "Get us out of here, now!" he said. "Dive! And get Hunter up here – I want to know about the repairs he made."

Chapter Seven

Onboard the *Knyaz Pozharskiy*

"Message headquarters the name of the sub, her sail number, and that we're continuing to pace them – they're hiding something. Then take us down and put us back in their starboard baffles," Petrov ordered.

"What is their heading?"

"173.5 degrees south, sir."

"They're heading for the Aleutian Islands and then probably on to their submarine base in Washington State. Send that to headquarters as well."

"Yes, Captain."

Signaling to his executive officer, Commander Roman Luski, to follow him, the Captain left the Command Center. He didn't speak until they were in his quarters.

"What are your thoughts on this matter, Commander?"

"Like you, I believe the Americans are hiding something, but I've got no idea what it could be. Why would they've tried to surface through the ice knowing how thick it is?"

"You think they knew it was too thick to get through?"

"Yes sir, I do. They can't be *that* stupid. If they had truly wanted to surface, they would have put as much speed behind her as possible. But, had they done that, their boat wouldn't still be operational; it would be on the bottom of the ocean. From what I saw, the damage isn't consistent with a high-speed impact. My only conclusion then is that it was unintentional – perhaps a mechanical malfunction."

Petrov rubbed his thick beard, his fingers disappearing in the salt and pepper hair under his chin. "I can't see a mechanical malfunction being unnoticed long enough to create that scenario – as you've said, the Americans are no fools. Why would they start to surface through the ice and then abort? We're missing something."

"There is also the other sub to consider. Whose is it? Why is it here? And what does it have to do with the Americans and their damaged sub?"

"Good questions but with no obvious answers."

The two men sat in silence for several minutes, each considering the possibilities.

Petrov stood, intending to leave, and then sat back down. "Oh, and one other thing, I don't recall the Americans having a submarine identified as the Trepang. She must be a new sub, perhaps a prototype."

"If that's true, she could be on sea trials and carrying new, sophisticated equipment and armaments. Maybe some new icebreaking or ramming technology?"

"Now *that* would give any Captain plenty to hide," Petrov said.

He thought for a moment and made his decision. "Tell navigation to back off the Americans as far as they can without losing them. Surface and relay this information to Command and ask for instructions. If we could capture a new type of American submarine and bring it home intact…"

"Yes, sir!" Luski said as he got up and left the cabin.

Washington, D.C.

Secretary of Defense, Cliff Willis, and Admiral Ben Johnson waited impatiently outside the Oval Office, grateful to be invited in after only a few minutes.

"Mister Secretary, Admiral." Daniel greeted them hesitantly. The two of them wanting to see him probably meant something to do with the Trepang. "What brings you here?"

"It's the Trepang," Cliff answered. "I'll let Admiral Johnson fill you in."

"Please, have a seat," Daniel invited, gesturing to the two couches in the room.

Before stepping over to join them, he pressed a button on his desk and ordered coffee.

He noticed the worried frowns on the two men's faces as he sat and inquired, "What's the trouble, gentlemen?"

"The Trepang has cleared the Bering Strait, and is making her way across the Bering Sea."

"That is good news," Daniel interrupted.

"Yes. That *is* good news. Unfortunately, she had to surface to try to make some additional repairs, but then a Russian sub showed up and made contact. The Russian captain wanted to know what the Trepang was doing there, if they needed help, et cetera. Captain Locklin told the Russian the Trepang was mapping the bottom of the ocean. The Russian didn't believe him, but Locklin managed to cut the conversation short and they submerged again."

Daniel's head tilted forward slightly, and his eyes opened wider. *Are the Russians already jockeying for world leader?* "Yes, and…?"

"They are aware of the Itinerant's presence and have been maneuvering in a way that indicates they will try to keep the two boats apart."

"How did they find out about the Itinerant?"

"She had no choice but to come into sonar range of the Russian boat, as the channel in which they were traveling through the strait, narrowed."

"Regardless, if the Russians are going to cause trouble, the Trepang is in no shape to fight. Although the Itinerant carries a few weapons for defense, they are not capable of fending off an attack from that Russian sub."

"What could we do to help them?" Daniel asked.

Willis stood and paced the room. "The Admiral thinks we should send in an armed escort."

"Yes," Johnson added, "but there could be consequences."

"Such as?"

"Well, Mister President, the Russians have not shown any aggression; not yet. So, sending an armed escort in could create the impression of aggression from our side and quickly escalate what is currently a peaceful situation."

"After everything this world has been through in the past three years, do you really think the Russians would try to start a scrap with us? Haven't they seen enough death and destruction for at least one lifetime?" Daniel asked, but he already knew the answer.

"I wouldn't put it past them, Mister President," Johnson

replied. "I don't trust them, and I've made it my life's motto never to trust, nor to underestimate them."

Daniel nodded.

At that moment Elize brought in a tray of coffee and refreshments. Daniel had wasted no time in seeing that she and her mother were back on staff at the White House.

"Thank you, Elize," Daniel said, appreciating not only the refreshments, but also the additional thinking time the brief interruption provided him.

"You're welcome, sir," she replied, nodded, and quietly left the office.

"All right, Admiral," Daniel said. "Let's hear what you have in mind."

"Sir, the sub following the Trepang is the Knyaz Pozharskiy or Prince Pozharskiy, captained by Ruslan Petrov. The Pozharskiy is a relatively new boat, a Borei II Class Submarine based out of Polyarny and assigned to the Northern Fleet. Captain Petrov is an experienced mariner, patient, shrewd, and calculating – not someone to trifle with.

"I believe he is still analyzing his exchange with Captain Locklin, and when he is finished, he will take action; what action will of course depend upon what he believes Locklin is doing or hiding."

"I see why you're concerned," Daniel acknowledged.

"That's not all I'm concerned about. Our sources in the Russian Admiralty advised us that Admiral Fedorin diverted the Knyaz Vladimir, another Borei Class sub, that was due to put into port at Vilyuchinsk. Instead, he sent her to back up the Pozharskiy.

"The Vladimir is captained by, Kazimir Yuditsky. He is a younger man. Less experienced than Petrov and known to be somewhat of a 'hot-head.' He tends to act first and think later. Rumor has it he is in jeopardy of losing his command, because of his reckless behavior – a rogue captain, if you will."

"This Yuditsky sounds like just the kind of man we need to start a war. But, if they've already sent another sub, under command of a reprobate captain to the scene, they're the ones escalating the situation. We will just respond in kind. Or am I missing something?" Daniel asked.

Johnson grinned. "I agree, Mister President."

"What do you need me to do?"

"Authorize me to send an armed escort—ships and subs—military, of course."

"You have it."

"Mister President, in anticipation of your desire to bring the Trepang in safely, I've put two Destroyers, three submarines, and an aircraft carrier on alert status. The aircraft carrier and two of the subs are already at sea in the North Pacific. The other three vessels are at our bases in Washington State."

Daniel raised his eyebrows. "That's a lot of fire-power."

"Yes, sir. I'm hoping if we show up with an overwhelming force, we won't need any of it. Deterrent power."

"Good point." Daniel nodded.

"All right send them out – but tell them they are not authorized to throw the first punch. Understand?"

Johnson smiled. "Yes, sir. I'll make sure they get the order."

He started to leave, but Daniel stopped him.

"Admiral, would you list the ships for me? I'd like to know."

"I thought you would." Johnson handed Daniel a piece of paper as he left the office.

Daniel read the printed list:

Termination

Everett, Washington
DDG-86   USS Shoup   Destroyer   Arleigh Burke Class
DDG-122 USS Basilone Destroyer Arleigh Burke Class
Bangor, Washington
SSN-799 USS Idaho Attack submarine Virginia Class
SSN-801 USS Utah Attack submarine Virginia Class
Bremerton, Washington
SSN-21 USS Seawolf Attack submarine Seawolf Class
CVN-80 USS Enterprise Aircraft carrier Gerald R. Ford class

If those Russians know what's good for them, they'll behave themselves. Or they'll be in for a nasty surprise.

Chapter Eight

Onboard the *Trepang*

Captain Locklin lay on the bunk in his darkened quarters — sleep was out of the question. The Russian sub trailing them made him uneasy, their ace-in-the-hole, the Itinerant, was now known to the Russians. The Trepang continued to limp along at half speed, and Ensign Hunter hadn't been able to complete the needed repairs to the sub in the limited time they'd been on the surface.

The repairs he'd made were holding, but the boat was slowly taking on water through the remaining leaks. It wasn't the slowly dripping water that bothered him — they would reach Bangor port long before that would be a problem. The problem was the Russians, and whether they would force him to have to dive deep. Drippy leaks at one-hundred-twenty-five feet were mildly concerning, the question was, would they rupture at five-hundred or one-thousand feet?

Locklin didn't want to find out, but he had a nasty

feeling he was going to. He thought of his wife and family, and their home in Virginia. The faces of his crew members drifted before his mind's eye, and he thought of their families.

Will any of us see home again?

Silently, he said a prayer asking God that all would come right.

His intercom sounded. *"Captain to the CIC."* It was followed by a quick rap on his door. "Captain?"

"Come in, Doc," he invited, knowing his XO had notified the young man he would need assistance.

"How's the knee, Captain?"

"Would you believe me if I said, 'just fine'?"

"Not for a minute. I brought more morphine."

"Isn't there something else you can do or give me to ease the pain? I can't afford to have that stuff messing with my brains at a time like this."

"I suppose I could try numbing the leg just above the knee with local anesthetics, but I don't know how effective it would be, and you probably wouldn't be able to walk."

"I can't walk anyway, Doc, what difference does it make?"

"Having a deadened limb can affect your balance as you hobble about. You could injure yourself in a fall."

"I'll take my chances. I need my brain to function properly more than I need my leg to function. Get me to the CIC, strap me to my chair if you have to, and numb the leg – just keep my head clear."

"Yes, Captain."

That settled, the two made their awkward trip down the passageway and to the CIC. Once Locklin was settled in, without being strapped in his chair, the Doc injected the medication that numbed the leg.

"Is that helping, Captain?"

Relief showed on Locklin's face as numbness spread through his knee and lower leg. There was still some pain, but it was manageable now. "Yes, thanks, Doc."

"Let me know when it starts to wear off."

Locklin nodded, and the young man left.

"Report," he barked.

Lieutenant Copeland, Officer of the Deck, approached Locklin. "Sir, we are entering the Amukta Pass, transferring to the North Pacific. Depth is one-hundred-twenty-five feet. The Russians remain off our starboard stern, and the Itinerant slightly behind her off our port stern. System status is stable, hull integrity remains unchanged."

The Amukta Pass provided a deep channel connecting the Bering Sea and the North Pacific Ocean. It was a wide strait in the Aleutian Islands of Alaska passing between Seguam Island on the west and Amukta Island, its namesake, on the east.

"All right, steady as she goes. Advise me immediately of any changes in the Russians' movements."

"Yes, sir."

For the next few hours, as the Trepang navigated through the Amukta Pass, the quiet sounds of the CIC, under standard operation, implied a semblance of normalcy.

Locklin watched the interactions of the crew, proud of their teamwork. Simple, concise communication between the stations allowed for timely course corrections keeping the sub on a safe path through the Pass.

A mistake or miscommunication between any of them could kill us all – we literally hold one another's lives in our hands.

Copeland interrupted Locklin's musings. "Preparing to exit Amukta Pass."

"Very good," Locklin responded. "Adjust course to ..."

"Captain!" Yoder spoke urgently from sonar one. "Two new contacts; one is closing fast."

"Bearing?"

"Contact Alpha One sub-surface, one-hundred-fifty degrees south-south-east, moving at thirty-five knots, estimate intercept in twenty-seven minutes. Contact Bravo One, surface, ninety-one degrees east, moving at five knots, estimate intercept in seventy-four minutes."

"Can you identify the contacts?"

"Sir, Bravo One is not a known military contact. Alpha One is ... stand by ..."

Come on Yoder, we don't have all day.

"Captain!" Yoder's voice was tight. "She's Russian ... Borei Class."

"Helm, hard about to sixty-one degrees," Locklin ordered. Grabbing the mic and thumbing the switch, he called the maneuvering room. "We need speed!"

"Hard about to sixty-one degrees. Aye, Captain!" the helmsman replied.

"Captain!" Lieutenant Larson fairly leapt to his side. "She can't handle any more speed!"

"She has to! We have to get away from that sub." Locklin felt a new vibration in the deck plates as they increased speed.

"Captain, please!" Larson urged.

"I think we were too conservative in our estimates. We must chance more speed. If we can make it to the Islands of Four Mountains, we might be able to lose her."

Larson considered the idea for a moment. "A good idea. May I respectfully suggest we not exceed twenty knots?"

Locklin's jaw muscles worked as he considered his XO through narrowed eyes. Finally, with a nod he ordered, "Helm, hold our speed at twenty knots."

"Twenty knots! Aye, Sir!"

Yoder made a new set of calculations. "New time to intercept is ... thirty-two minutes, mark. The Pozharskiy is adjusting course and speed to maintain position in our starboard baffles."

Locklin felt the boat coming about, the deck plates vibrating as she increased speed.

"Contact Alpha One adjusting course and speed to overtake. Now at thirty-eight knots. New time to intercept ... twenty-five minutes ... mark." Yoder reported. "Itinerant adjusting course and speed to match us."

"What's Bravo One doing?"

"No change in contact, Bravo One."

Locklin rubbed his forehead with the index finger and thumb of his left hand. It felt like the Trepang herself was holding her breath, while he quickly considered his options.

"Helm, increase speed to twenty-five knots." He keyed the mic to let the maneuvering room know they needed more power.

"New time to intercept ... thirty-two minutes ... mark," Yoder called.

Larson and Copeland exchanged glances, the question clear in both men's eyes – *will the Russians get us or will it be the failure of the Trepang's systems?*

The minutes passed with painful slowness as the crew endured ever increasing vibrations throughout the boat as she struggled to maintain speed. Their muscles were tight, jaws clenched, and in the air, the tang of sweat.

"Time to intercept?" Locklin inquired.

"Intercept now at fifteen minutes, sir," Yoder responded

without delay. He kept his eyes glued to the sonar screen and knew by the second, exactly how far apart they were. "Pozharskiy adjusting course, moving to our port. Looks like she's trying to force the Itinerant to move away."

We need more speed! "Helm, do we have more speed?"

"Under normal circumstances we should, sir, but with this damage we are lucky to be holding at twenty-five knots."

"Try."

"Aye, sir."

After five minutes and much communication between the helm and the maneuvering room, it became clear that they were moving as fast as they could.

"Sorry, sir. That's the best she can do," the helmsman reported.

"Captain! Alpha One is firing!" Yoder exclaimed. "Time to impact one-minute twenty-four seconds," he added, removing his sonar headphones to protect his ears from the coming explosion.

Damn! "Full reverse!"

"But Captain…!"

"Full reverse! Hard to starboard!"

The sub was sluggish and tremulous. Locklin hoped against hope that the Russian's firing calculations were wrong. He held his breath. The sound of the CIC electronic equipment was deafening in the silence – no one breathed, no one moved.

Time slowed to a crawl as seconds stretched into years – every man thinking of loved ones, praying to return home.

The adage, 'there are no atheists in foxholes,' rang true as the Trepang became their foxhole.

A collective sigh swept through the CIC as the Russian torpedo passed over them within a hairs-breath.

"That missed us by inches, Captain," Yoder confirmed just as they were rocked by an explosion.

Onboard the *Itinerant*

The crew of the Itinerant had been tracking the newly arrived Russian sub for nearly thirty minutes, watching as she slowly overtook the Trepang – and them.

Now, the Pozharskiy worked her way toward them, forcing them to break away from pacing the Trepang.

"New sonar contact, bearing sixty-eight degrees moving at thirty-five knots," Taka reported.

"What now?"

"Correction, *four*, repeat *four*, new contacts, at that bearing. Three surface vessels, one submarine."

"Whose are they?"

After a brief pause, Taka sprung out of her seat, "Submarine is Seawolf Class; she's ours!"

"Bloody hell! Get us out of here; put us on the roof!" Marcus said. "We don't want to get caught in the cross-fire!"

Onboard the *Knyaz Pozharskiy* and *Knyaz Vladimir*

"*Chyort! What are you doing?*" Captain Petrov screamed over the speaker in the Command Center.

"Orders from the Admiralty, Petrov, get out of the way," Captain Yuditsky of the Knyaz Vladimir replied.

"No! Don't destroy her, we need to capture her, she's testing new technology, you fool!"

Termination

"You're the fool, Petrov. The information you called in has been examined and analyzed. The Americans haven't had a sub identified as Trepang since 2000. Her sail number identifies her as the USS Montana. Records show she is in dry-dock for a refit, but she disappeared the same time as Brideaux and his council members. The Admiralty believes they are on that sub. My orders are to sink her, and I will do it. Clear the area, *now*!" he said, signaling his communication officer to cut the link.

"Ivanov, report!" he demanded addressing his weapons officer.

Lieutenant Neven Ivanov checked the torpedo status board once again before replying, "Two torpedoes are loaded and standing by."

"Fire one!" Yuditsky ordered.

"Firing one!" Ivanov replied.

"Captain! The Pozharskiy! She's too close!" Sonar technician Radul Gurkovsky objected.

"*Po hooy!* I warned her away, she shouldn't be trailing the Americans so close."

Gurkovsky pulled the headphones from his head and watched in dismay as the blip showing the torpedo moved over the Trepang and stopped at the next blip – the Pozharskiy.

Onboard the *Itinerant*

"Thew new Russian sub has fired on the Trepang!" Taka ripped the sonar earphones off her head to avoid hearing-damage when the torpedo exploded.

"What?" Marcus jumped from his chair as if ejected. "Bloody hell! Did they get her?"

"Damn, it's moving fast. Time to impact one minute twenty-four seconds," Taka replied.

Please God! Marcus prayed.

"Time to impact, thirty seconds," Taka updated.

After an interminable wait, she put her earphones back on, listened briefly, and shook her head. "The Trepang changed course in full reverse; she turned away, they missed her, she's– *shit!*" she exclaimed as they were all thrown to the deck and the lights dimmed.

Stunned by the impact with the deck, Marcus struggled to his feet, making his way toward the helm.

"Taka? Brenda? You two okay?" he asked.

Taka answered from the deck, "I'm all right, I think Brenda's hurt, though."

"It's just a sprained wrist and a bit of a headache," Brenda objected.

"She's right, Marcus. Her left wrist has a ninety-degree sprain and the headache is just a drippy one," Taka answered, holding a hastily torn piece of shirt to a nasty gash on Brenda's head.

Marcus smiled despite the situation. "I thought you said they missed her!"

Bill groaned as he regained consciousness. "What happened?"

The lights resumed their normal illumination, and Taka shook her head as if to clear water from her ears. "That wasn't the Trepang."

"What do you mean?"

"The Trepang dove to get out of the way."

Marcus jumped toward the sonar. "Is the Trepang okay?"

"I don't know. If we can get someone to help Brenda, I'll take a look."

Marcus thumbed the intercom requesting Sean Nicholson, the rescue team's medic, to come to the bridge.

"Here, let me help Brenda until he gets here."

"What the hell are those things?" Hunte asked. "They're faster than anything I've ever seen—or heard of for that matter."

"They're Shkval's," Taka answered. "Jet-propelled torpedoes."

Dunlap, just arriving on the bridge with Nicholson, added, "Russian VA-111 Shkval super-cavitating torpedoes. They're extremely fast, two-hundred-thirty miles-per-hour or more. They seldom miss. Locklin was extremely lucky."

"The Trepang was just outside the optimum firing range – the Russian Captain was impatient. He won't miss again."

"The Russians are firing again!" Taka yelled.

Onboard the *Knyaz Vladimir*

"Report!" Yuditsky barked.

"Sir, we missed the Trepang and hit the Pozharskiy," Gurkovsky reported with dread.

"Confirmed," Ivanov said flatly.

"Govno!" Yuditsky swore. "Sooka sin! Adjust course, prepare to fire number two. Chyort!"

The Vladimir glided smoothly through the water as the helmsman adjusted course to line up on the perfect heading, and another torpedo left her starboard bow tube en route to the Trepang.

"Number two away," reported Ivanov. "Impact in forty-two seconds."

Chapter Nine

Washington, D.C.

Papers shuffling, pens clicking, briefcase locks snapping, and the general murmur of voices signaled the conclusion of Daniel's first meeting with his Cabinet members.

The brief meeting was mostly an introduction and overview of expectations. Everyone already understood the general chaotic status of the nation and the world and had a firm grasp of the mammoth task ahead of them.

Daniel's goals had been to establish a timeline for receiving status reports, from each department, and their plans for stabilizing the country. New members were given time to meet with their staff, gather information, and prepare an up-to-date report for the next meeting to take place in three days.

Daniel made his way toward the door.

"Mister Jenkins," Daniel addressed the Attorney General. "I wanted to thank you for agreeing to stay on and let you know how much I appreciate your support."

"Thank you, Mister President. I am grateful to you and your team for protecting me and my family during General Hayden's ... occupation."

"You're very welcome. I'm glad everyone is all right," Daniel said, and then noticed Secretary Willis answering his cell phone and saw the color drain from his face.

The Trepang.

"Please excuse me, there is a matter I must attend to," Daniel said.

Daniel caught Willis's eye and nodded slightly toward the Oval Office. Willis immediately followed him.

Without preamble, Daniel asked, "What happened?"

"The Vladimir joined the Pozharskiy and fired on the Trepang! Our ships are just coming into range. Admiral Johnson is requesting authorization to engage."

Daniel held out his hand for Willis's phone. "Admiral, full engagement is authorized. Keep me appraised."

As soon as Willis ended the call, Daniel ordered, "Get the situation room set up, and get the joint chiefs in here right away, please. Let Salome, our new Head of Homeland Security, and the head of the National Security Council know they are needed as well and have Admiral Johnson join us too."

"Right away, sir."

Onboard the *Trepang*

"Status!" Locklin yelled, struggling to raise himself from the deck without the use of his injured leg. "Larson! Copeland! Report!"

Termination

"Yoder here, sir," a voice said weakly from near the sonar station. "The Pozharskiy didn't get clear in time."

No shit. "Yoder..."

"They're adjusting heading, lining up for another shot."

"Helm! Get us out of here!"

"Helmsman is dead, Captain," Copeland spoke groggily. "I'm attempting to move us now."

"The Russians have fired again – impact in forty-two seconds."

Grabbing the intercom mic, Locklin thumbed it. "Maneuvering! Give me full speed *now!*"

No one answered, but a violent quiver ran through the deck plates and the sub lunged forward.

"Impact in thirty seconds," Yoder reported.

"Take us down! Dive! Dive!" Locklin roared.

"I can't! Without the bow-planes, we have to adjust the ballast and we don't have time!" Copeland responded, sweat and blood pouring down his face. His hands gripping the dive control were white and his arm muscles bunched in tight knots as if he could force the sub down himself.

"Time to clear torpedo?" Locklin yelled.

"Sixty-three seconds to clear, twenty seconds to impact."

"More speed!" Locklin screamed into the mic still in his hand. "Sound collision! Seal all hatches!"

The klaxon blared seconds later, the giant sub convulsed violently and went dark.

Onboard the *Itinerant*

Taka stood silently at her station, tears welling in her eyes. They'd all heard the explosion.

The radio crackled. "Itinerant, this is Seawolf. Continue to the surface and remain there until further notice."

Marcus nodded to Bill to respond. "Understood, Seawolf. We will comply. Itinerant out."

"Taka," Marcus said gently. "Here, sit down." He eased her back into her station chair. "I need to know what the Vladimir is doing."

Nodding, she wiped her eyes and took a deep, shaky breath. She closed her eyes and took another deep breath, a little sturdier this time, before she turned her attention back to the sonar screen.

She made some adjustments to the equipment. "The Vladimir is changing course – my God! She's going to fire on the Trepang again!"

They watched the blip on the sonar in silence. A silent killer on the move, stalking her wounded prey.

"The Trepang is continuing to sink—coming up on nine-hundred feet. The Vladimir coming about, going deep," Taka reported softly, watching the deadly dance play out on the screen.

"She's going to come up from below the Trepang and take her out," Marcus said in a surprisingly calm tone.

"She's breaking off! She's spotted the Seawolf and is turning to engage!"

A silent cheer of hope filled the bridge as they watched several small blips leave from the Seawolf.

"Tell me those are torpedoes, Taka," Bill begged.

"Damn straight, they are!" she responded excitedly. "The Vladimir is firing back!"

"Can the Seawolf get clear?" Marcus demanded.

Taka made a few quick calculations. "She's already clear —the Vladimir's Captain fired randomly."

"Can they lock onto her? Look! They're changing course, heading right for her!" Bill shouted.

Within moments, though, the two torpedoes seemed to lose their course. "Seawolf must have launched countermeasures."

"Where are those torpedoes going now?" Brenda whispered.

"Toward whatever they lock onto next," Taka answered.

"Shit! That could be any of us," Bill squawked.

"New contact in the water — correction two new contacts — they're tracking enemy torpedoes!" Taka exclaimed, grinding her fingernails into the edge of the sonar screen's housing.

"Where'd they come from?" Bill asked.

Dunlap spoke up. "Ship launched ATTDS."

"What's that?" someone asked.

"Anti-Torpedo Defense System. They're designed to detect, track, and destroy incoming torpedoes."

The next moment, the two directionless torpedoes connected with the ATTDS's and exploded.

A collective sigh of relief ran through the room just as another explosion confirmed that the Seawolf's aim had been true.

The Vladimir was no more.

High-fives were given but came to an abrupt halt when Marcus spoke. "Where's the Trepang?"

Taka returned her attention to the sonar, studied it for a moment, and replied, "She's at fifteen-hundred feet and still dropping."

"Where's the bottom and what's her crush depth?"

"We're near the Aleutian Trench—it's over twenty-thousand feet deep," Taka answered grimly.

"Her crush depth is probably about two-thousand feet, maybe a little more," Dunlap added.

"Stay with her, Taka, we need to know what is happening."

Chapter Ten

Washington, D.C.

Daniel signaled his Chief of Staff to join him at the head of the large conference table in the situation room. "Glenn, I want to talk to the Russian President, or whoever is in charge over there, *immediately*."

"Yes, sir."

Admiral Johnson was speaking with Captain Wiekelan aboard the Aircraft Carrier, Enterprise.

Daniel listened in dismay, hearing the blow-by-blow account of the action taking place in the North Pacific. His stomach churned. He leaned forward, elbows on the table, and covered his face with his hands, when the report of the strike to the Trepang came in.

At a tap on his shoulder he brought his head up, pinching the bridge of his nose and clearing his throat.

"Mister President, I have the call to Russian President Genrikh Mikhaulov connected for you."

"Thank you."

Picking up the phone nearest Daniel, Glenn spoke to his counterpart in Russia, "I'm handing the phone to President Rossler now."

Daniel accepted the phone. "President Mikhaulov, we can introduce ourselves at a later stage. But now I want to get right to the point. Two of your submarines attacked one of ours."

Mikhaulov shot back immediately. "I am unaware of any such act and have not authorized an attack."

"That doesn't really matter, Mister President. The fact is, we lost our sub in the attack, and I authorized engagement to stop your subs from attacking ours. I'm hoping that you and I can agree to end the confrontation right now."

"President Rossler, I can assure you that armed conflict is the last thing we want, and I'm sure you feel the same way."

"I sure do. There's been enough conflict in the world, the past few years, to last many lifetimes. But please, Mister President, don't confuse my equanimity with weakness."

If it was a video call, Daniel would have seen the shocking surprise on the Russian's face—and his hesitation. He was obviously not prepared for what he heard.

"I will look into this matter immediately. But I am not pleased that you authorized engagement, and I trust that no permanent damage was done by your ships."

"President Mikhaulov, your sub shot at ours without any provocation. My order to defend our vessels and its personnel stands. I suggest you look into the matter without delay and order your commanders to disengage—unless you want to take responsibility for the consequences."

The line went quiet.

In Moscow, President Mikhaulov glared at his advisors. They had assured him that this new American president was a youngster with no experience—a walkover for a veteran politician like himself. It was obvious by the expressions of angst on their faces they made a gross error of judgement.

"President Mikhaulov, I take it you need a little time to investigate. Let's talk again in, say, an hour?"

"One hour," Mikhaulov replied abruptly. The connection was severed.

The room had gone silent while Daniel spoke with Mikhaulov and no one moved as he put the phone down. There were more than a few smiles around the table. If anyone doubted the young president's courage and tenacity before they walked into the Situation Room, it was resolved in one short phone call—he had the respect of everyone in the room.

"All right, what's the situation?" Daniel asked without a hint of anxiety.

Admiral Johnson began the report—Daniel was aware of the sequence of events and didn't want the details again.

"Wait." He held up his hand. "Just give me the status of our ships that engaged the Russians and the outcome."

"According to the report from the Itinerant, the Pozharskiy was destroyed by the Vladimir—she was too close to the Trepang and couldn't get clear of the torpedo; in the wrong place at the wrong time."

Daniel's eyebrows rose, and there were several sounds of quiet amusement and astonishment around the table.

"The Itinerant also reports that the Vladimir has been destroyed—a direct hit by the Seawolf. The Trepang is resting on a ledge of the Aleutian Trench at nearly twenty-two-hundred feet, her crush depth is twenty-four hundred.

"At this point, we can't tell if there are any survivors. The Itinerant has been cleared by the Seawolf, and Captain

Wiekelan, to investigate and let us know if a rescue is possible and needed."

"Keep me posted." He turned to address everyone gathered. "All right, ladies and gentlemen, let's get down to business before I speak with President Mikhaulov again.

"He isn't going to be happy about the situation, and I'm not sure he will believe that the Vladimir destroyed the Pozharskiy. We may get blamed for both."

"Excuse me," Admiral Johnson interrupted as he put his cell phone down. "We've just received an update from our Russian informants. Two hours ago, three ships and another submarine were dispatched from the base at Vilyuchinsk, and two ships on patrol in the North Pacific were ordered to change course. They are all headed for the Aleutian Islands and the vicinity of the current situation."

"I need a plan for dealing with this and bringing it to a peaceful resolution—if possible." Daniel settled back in his chair to hear the advice and recommendations from his Joint Chiefs and watched Salome evaluating the points in the discussion.

By the time the meeting concluded, Daniel was ready for another round with his Russian counterpart.

Five-thousand miles away in Moscow, the atmosphere around their President was very different. After the quick investigation, Mikhaulov took twenty minutes to give his advisors an ass-chewing of epic proportions, and more than one would be seeking a new position by the end of the day.

Right on time, Glenn placed the call to Russia and handed the phone to Daniel.

"President Mikhaulov," Daniel greeted neutrally.

"President Rossler. I've investigated, and as I told you before, I was unaware of, and did not authorize, an attack on your sub. However, Admiral Fedorin informs me that you were sheltering Brideaux and his Council Members onboard that sub."

"President Mikhaulov, you're digressing from the issue. I hope that is not deliberate. One of your subs fired a torpedo on one of ours without reason. That's the subject of our discussion, not who is or was onboard that sub."

"Mister President, I'll take that as confirmation that Brideaux and his Council Members were in fact onboard that sub."

"Mister President." Daniel had a slight grin. "In that case, I'll have to take your response as confirmation that you are prepared to let the situation escalate and face the inevitable consequences."

"I haven't said that!" Mikhaulov exclaimed.

"President Mikhaulov, I'm very much aware that you currently have five ships and a submarine on headings that will bring them into close proximity of the current situation. So, what's it going to be, Mister President? Are you going to order your commanders to stand down and turn back, or are you going to make a bad situation worse?"

The line went quiet. Mikhaulov was punch-drunk. His advisors had it wrong yet again. They thought the mention of Brideaux and his cronies being on board that sub would catch Daniel off-guard.

The line became live again.

"President Rossler, the attack on your sub was not authorized by me or the Admiralty. The Vladimir was sent to investigate the possibility of the prisoners being onboard —that is all.

"Captain Yuditsky acted on his own. He was an inherent recreant and was to be relieved of his command when he put in.

"I've issued orders to my navy commanders to turn back immediately."

Daniel smiled as he said, "Thank you, Mister President. I appreciate your understanding and cooperation in this matter. I'm sure we're going to have a very good working relationship." Daniel handed the phone back to Glenn as applause broke out in the Situation Room.

In Russia, heads were about to roll as an embarrassed President Mikhaulov replaced the receiver of the phone and started looking around the room at his advisors.

Chapter Eleven

Onboard the *Itinerant*

The Itinerant descended slowly through the dark, briny water above the Aleutian Trench.

With the Russian subs destroyed and the Mystic Sea standing by, the Navy had given permission for Marcus to take the rescue sub down to investigate the condition of the Trepang.

It pleased him to have the knowledge that the Navy was continuing to patrol the area. He didn't want to be surprised by more unwelcome guests.

"Passing two-thousand feet," Taka reported.

"Hit the floods and get the cameras online. Let's see what's left," Marcus ordered grimly.

The brilliant radiance of the floodlights illuminated the barren sub-marine landscape along the edge of the trench. Rocks projecting from the steep slope of the trench disappeared into the murky depths.

Taka whistled, "And to think, that trench is four times as deep and forty times as long as the Grand Canyon."

Bill grinned despite the seriousness of the occasion. "Yeah, watch that first step!"

"No kidding."

Within minutes they found the Trepang.

"Looks like they took it in the seat of the pants," Dunlap remarked. "That's the propulsor duct and part of the shaft over here," he said, pointing to an area further away from the ledge.

"That looks like what's left of the main turbine just in front of it," Marcus said. As they came up to the main body of the sub, he had Bill slow down while he examined the wreckage carefully. "I'd say the torpedo hit the engineering section, but it looks like the nuclear reactor was spared. Move us forward, slowly."

"Most of the main body looks intact, Marcus," Dunlap commented, as they passed the sail. "It doesn't look like anything in front of the sail survived though. From the looks of things, I'd say the repairs they made after colliding with the ice failed at depth."

"Sure looks that way," Marcus agreed. "What's her angle, Taka?"

"She's resting tail down at twenty-one-hundred-eighty-four feet listing twenty-two degrees to port on a negative incline of eighteen percent."

Marcus looked at Dunlap. "Well, it's your team—your call. She appears to be stable for the moment, and the lockout trunk is accessible. But you know the drill—if she shifts, I can't sacrifice this sub trying to get your men out."

Dunlap nodded. "I know. Let's put her down skin to skin and hammer an SOS, see if we get a response."

"Bill, set us down about halfway back from the sail. Let's give it a try."

When the *Itinerant* was in position, Dunlap took a two-pound hammer from the engineer's toolbox and pounded out the SOS on the hull, then waited.

When he got no response, he moved a few feet further down the sub and tried again. Still no response. He repeated the procedure several more times with no answer. Disheartened, he was just about to give up when Hunte shouted, "Listen!"

Tap-tap-tap. Tap-tap-tap. Tap-tap-tap. Silence. Tap-tap-tap. Tap-tap-tap. Tap-tap-tap.

"They're alive!" Taka shrieked.

The rescue team whooped.

"All right! Let's do what we came to do!" Dunlap shouted with enthusiasm.

Marcus agreed, his heart racing as he gave the order to mate with the Trepang's lockout trunk. Once the watertight seal between the subs was confirmed, Dunlap opened the outer hatch on the Itinerant and pounded the SOS on the Trepang's hatch. He was relieved when the reply came immediately—had the lockout trunk access been flooded, there would have been no way to reach the survivors.

He knocked again, and the hatch began to open.

An unashamedly tear-streaked face appeared before them. "You're really here!" the young man cried, and then turned to shout back into the depths of the sub, "they're really here!"

They heard a chorus of cheers echoing from somewhere behind him.

"Boy, are we glad to see you! Come on down," he said, stepping away from the ladder. "I'm Ensign Hunter, welcome aboard."

Dunlap was impressed the young man had the ability to grant such courtesies under the circumstances and shook his hand. "Thank you, Ensign. Where's Captain Locklin?"

"In the CIC, sir, he's injured."

The other five members of the team had boarded, and he turned to them. "Nicholson, you're with me to the CIC. Sommers and Nelson, work your way aft, Kidd and Nelson work your way forward. I need a head and body count, and general status of survivors."

"Aye, sir," they chorused and spread out.

Onboard the *Trepang*

Reese Locklin shook his head. "I'll not leave ahead of my men," he said firmly.

"But sir, you're injured."

"Yes, I'm injured, but I'm still in command of this boat, and I'm not leaving until my crew has been rescued first. Now get on with it before you have to be removed with the injured."

Dunlap scratched his jaw. There was a slight twinkle in Locklin's eyes despite the implied threat, but he wasn't sure how far he could push the man. "All right, Captain. Have it your way."

"Thank you. I will," Locklin responded with a satisfied grin. "And while we're on the subject, Littleton goes first."

"The ensign is in critical condition," Dunlap nodded. "He's being transferred as we speak."

Locklin nodded his thanks. "Good. Now go do your job and let me get on with mine. I'll see you on the next trip. Oh, and by the way—those damned prisoners go last."

"Yes, sir," Dunlap saluted and left the CIC.

Nearly every Trepang crew member had one or more injuries, so it was by severity of injury, with the exception of the crusty Captain, that they sorted them into transfer groups.

Since the Itinerant could only take fifty at a time, they would need to make three trips. One-hundred crew members would be taken off in the first two loads. That left fifteen crew members, the Captain, the prisoners, and twenty bodies to wait for the final run.

Rather than ordering some of his crew to stay behind, Locklin asked for fifteen volunteers—and got them.

"We're ready to go, sir," Sommers advised Dunlap.

"Very good. Nicholson and I are going to remain here and help. Don't take your time going, and definitely hurry back."

"Aye, sir!" Sommers grinned as Dunlap helped him secure the hatch.

Washington, D.C.

Daniel and Nigel strolled through the dimly lit corridors and rooms of the main White House structure. Until now, in the quietness of this evening, events requiring Daniel's attention had prevented him from 'exploring' his new residence.

As they entered the ground floor, they looked briefly in the Map Room, used by President Franklin Roosevelt as a situation room during World War II. It was decorated in the Chippendale style, popular in the latter half of the 18th Century, its furnishings from the mid to late 1700s. Two maps hung on the walls; one, a rare French version of a map charted by colonial surveyors in 1755, and the last map, prepared in the room for President Roosevelt on April 3, 1945.

In his mind's-eye, Daniel could almost see President Roosevelt bent over one of the tables, studying a new map and asking for updates on troop movement.

Moving on, Daniel realized there was still a myriad of pressing matters to attend to, but he was glad Nigel had suggested the stroll— stretching his legs and taking a break from the 'worries-of-the-world' as he and Sarah called them, was good for body and mind.

Some rooms they bypassed, others they entered, and Nigel told Daniel a brief history of the room or something in it. In some cases, he shared a story about an occurrence or memory there from his time serving as President.

There were vestiges of restoration work in the Center Hall. The beautiful deep-red rugs had been rolled up and stored neatly to one side, revealing the rich brown and beige tiles laid in diamond patterns beneath.

The vaulted ceiling was undamaged, as were the chandeliers that illuminated the one-hundred-sixty-one-foot windowless passageway. Daniel noted that the bullet riddled doors to the Diplomatic Reception Room had been removed and the door jambs replaced. *Just waiting for the new doors to be delivered.*

Both shook their heads as they passed the China Room where the china used by each serving President was on display—in chronological order of term.

"It's a woman thing." Daniel shrugged. "Had to have been thought up by the First Ladies."

"Undoubtedly," Nigel said. "There *are* a couple of sidechairs in there that belonged to George Washington."

"Now that's worth putting on display!" Daniel laughed.

They turned left, crossing the hall, and climbed the wide staircase to the First Floor, also known as the 'State Floor', where they entered the Red Room.

"During the Madison administration, this was called the Yellow Drawing Room," Nigel informed Daniel. "Dolly Madison held her ever-popular, high-fashion, Wednesday night receptions here, and it was Mrs. Lincoln's favorite sitting room."

Daniel wandered through the room, taking in the abundance of ormolu work, vases, and various other items on display. "Beautiful pieces," he said admiringly.

"Yes. Most of it was brought in during the Monroe and Madison administrations."

Moving on, they saw that repair work on this floor had presumably been completed. The deep-red rugs matching those on the ground floor had been spread through the Cross Hall again, muffling the footsteps of all who tread their path.

They entered the oval Blue Room, the place where presidents traditionally, formally received guests, and Nigel let his gaze travel over the French Empire style decor of the room. "The business of democracy, the social graces of diplomacy, and the entertaining of kings has taken place in this room," he said almost reverently.

"I remember reading somewhere that Grover Cleveland and Frances Folsum got married in this room—the only president ever to be wed in the White House," Daniel said, breathing in the historical atmosphere.

I can almost feel the power of the men who have attended this room.

"Yes," Nigel agreed. "That's true. Did you know the idea of the oval rooms in the White House goes back to

George Washington? He preferred rooms where no one could get stuck in a corner," Nigel smiled. "And the circle has become a symbol of democracy."

Daniel let his fingers trail across the coolness of the marble-top center table as he left the room. "I'm glad most of the damage was in the lower, modern levels and that all this history remains intact—this is a monument of national treasures."

The East Room was easily recognized, as it was frequently the location of press conferences and bill-signings. Daniel had been sworn in as Vice-President, in this room, at the same time the late Laurie Campbell was sworn in as President. The memories of all that transpired since that day flashed through Daniel's mind making his throat tighten and eyes sting briefly.

Sensing his mood shift, Nigel nudged Daniel saying, "Did you know that young Tad Lincoln once harnessed a pair of goats to a kitchen chair and had them pull him through this room?"

Daniel eyed him, his expression clearly stating he didn't believe the story.

"It's true! Check the White House museum records if you don't believe me. And the Roosevelt children used it as a roller-skating rink!"

"As I recall, both Lincoln and Kennedy lay in state in this room, after their assassinations," Daniel said flatly.

"True, true," Nigel agreed. "And Nixon gathered his staff here to announce his resignation. But here's something I'll bet you'd never guess." Nigel leaned toward Daniel and lowered his voice as if sharing a conspiracy. "Before this room was completed, Abigail Adams hung laundry out to dry in this very place."

Daniel tried to keep a straight face, but it was no use. He

burst out laughing, "Oh what a scandal that would cause nowadays! Can you just imagine?"

Nigel joined him in laughter, and they left the room with images of sheets, bloomers, and long underwear blowing in the breeze.

As they meandered into the Green Room, Daniel felt some of the tension drain from his body and mind.

"After hanging laundry in the East Room, I'm almost too afraid to ask, but what is the grand history of this room?"

"Nothing as scandalous as that!" Nigel laughed. "During the Monroe administration, it was a card room, and the nation's first declaration of war was signed by President James Madison here.

Daniel surveyed the room, appreciating the antique furnishings and carefully choreographed decor. "There is something truly soothing about the color green," he sighed.

"Umm-hmm. This was the favorite room of President Taft's wife, Helen," Nigel said as they took seats on the green and cream striped couch.

Their conversation transitioned to a light-hearted visit, and Nigel had Daniel roaring in laughter when Secretary Willis strolled easily into the room.

"Excuse me, gentlemen," he said with a smile. "May I interrupt to bring you good tidings?"

Laughing, Nigel teased, "If it is truly good tidings, then yes. Otherwise, go away!"

Willis laughed and pulled up the chair when Daniel indicated.

"I just spoke with Admiral Johnson and wanted to let you know that the Itinerant has returned from the Trepang with fifty survivors, and there are more to come!"

Daniel's grin could've illuminated the room, and his eyes

shone. "*That* is the best news I've heard in a very long time!"

"Yes, sir, it sure is!" Willis agreed, setting a bottle of whiskey and three glasses on the table. "I think this deserves a toast!"

The two of them agreed, and as Daniel took a sip of the amber liquid, he asked the most burning question on his mind. "Between the crew and the prisoners, there were one-hundred-forty-eight people on the Trepang, how many more are there to be rescued?"

"Seventy-nine."

"One-hundred-twenty-nine survivors—that is a miracle." Daniel paused a moment. "And Brideaux? Is he among the survivors?"

"No, Mister President. He was killed by one of his council members, Rafael Martinez, who assisted the crew in retaking the ship," Willis informed him.

"Martinez is also the one who assisted us in bringing Brideaux down," Daniel said.

"Yes, sir." Willis then summarized the events aboard the Trepang as they had been told to him, including the rescue and the condition of the survivors.

"Six killed by Brideaux and thirteen by the Russian attack," Daniel shook his head. "That is nineteen too many."

Nigel and Willis nodded in agreement—words seemed inadequate.

"The young Ensign—Littleton—will he live?" Daniel asked quietly. The story of the young man's torture infuriated him.

I'd raise Brideaux from the dead and kill him myself if I could.

"He's in critical condition and was airlifted to a hospital in Anchorage. It's too soon to know."

"I see, and the others?"

"The fifty that have been rescued are all crew. The injured were brought up first. There were two with head wounds that went to Anchorage with Littleton, the rest have mostly bumps and bruises, minor cuts, and a few with broken bones.

"They are being treated by the doctor aboard the Mystic Sea. Her captain has provided cabins for them and ordered his galley to serve them 'meals fit for a king,' I believe were the words he used. They will be well cared for and comfortable on the trip to Bangor." Willis smiled. "It seems the Captain had the forethought to have an assortment of clothing, personal items—even jackets—brought aboard in addition to the extra medical supplies. The men are being provided with everything they need from socks and underwear to toothbrushes and aftershave."

"God bless that man," Daniel said with a grateful sheen to his eyes.

Chapter Twelve

Re'an headquarters Tunguska, Russia

Viktor caught a glimpse of the fiery storm in Telestra's eyes before she hid them from him. He grinned and leaned back easily on the couch. "What, nothing to say? I'm sending your son on a warrior's mission to the other side of the planet and you aren't objecting?"

Telestra sighed. She was weary of these skirmishes with Viktor, weary of the manipulation, and frustrated that after nearly one-hundred years he could still provoke her to anger. "You have made your decision, and nothing I say will change it, so why should I bother?"

He missed the fiery, scathing words she once had for him when she was displeased. To him, there was nothing in the world more pleasing than Telestra when she was angry —especially if it involved Deszik. "Oh, I just thought you might beg me not to send him, the way you once begged me to wake him from the deep sleep," he taunted.

Her face flushed at the memory from so long ago.

Termination

"Deszik is a man; he will choose his own path. And you, if it makes you happy to hear me say it, can go to hell."

The words were there, but not the energy that was once behind them. "You are a waste of my time, woman," he snarled, rising from the couch and lunging at her simultaneously.

She didn't flinch. "So you say."

Shoving her against the wall in exasperation, Viktor stormed from their quarters.

Picking herself up, Telestra also left their quarters.

It is time.

As usual, she found Dekka in one of the science labs. Viktor had forced Dekka to create enhancements for the soldiers and develop more powerful weapons. She had watched Dekka die by inches inside, with each success, and wondered about his ability to continue working.

Then one day, many years ago, she had entered the lab to find a seemingly 'new' Dekka—he was happy and energized.

"I am going to atone for all that was incumbent upon me to do. It will take years, but I will do it," he had told her.

He was secretly developing technology that could be used against Viktor, without his knowledge.

The first thing Dekka developed was a way to make infinitesimal adjustments to Deszik's chip that would gradually allow him to become free of Viktor's control.

Eventually, she and Dekka had been able to feed the history of the B'ran, the L'gundo, and the past one-hundred years into Deszik's chip and allow him to draw his own conclusions.

As they had hoped, once he was free from Viktor's influence, he quickly came around to supporting his mother's and Dekka's views. And it pleased the two of them that the boy was eager to do what he could to help them work against 'the tyrant' as Deszik called Viktor. He trained harder than ever and worked diligently to earn Viktor's trust and respect so that when the time came, he would be able to act for his own people, the L'gundo.

Dekka had also developed and deployed, to their chips, a unique enhancement that allowed only the three of them to communicate collusively via chip to chip transmissions without having to utter a single word. They could be talking about the weather while discussing the application of Dekka's latest secret invention at the same time, with no one being the wiser. The only drawback was it required proximity—they had to be within twelve to fifteen feet of one another. Dekka had been working tirelessly to solve the limitation.

"*Dekka*," she spoke with her mind as she approached. *"It is time."* Out loud she said, "Hello Dekka! How are you today?"

"Ah, Telestra! Hello! *Yes, I know.* I am well, and you?"

"I'm well." They continued a friendly, simple conversation about a colleague's experiment while covertly discussing the integral parts of a plan long in the making that was starting to come together.

"Deszik will be leaving in two days."

"It is as we expected. However, I have solved the limitation factor of the communication enhancement."

Telestra almost squealed aloud in her excitement over that announcement and had a difficult time maintaining her casual presence at the lab table.

"Dekka! That's wonderful news! Is it difficult to do?"

"No, not at all. In fact, the change can be transmitted—there is no need to connect to the computer for an adjustment. I have already made mine."

He glanced at an instrument on the table next to him and then appeared to check some calculations he was making before looking back at the instrument.

"There! Your adjustment is complete!"

"I didn't feel a thing. Are you sure?"

"I'm sure! We will be able to communicate anywhere we go now."

"What about Deszik? Will the range increase be enough to reach him where he is going?"

"I believe so."

"But, that's ... so ... incredible! How does it work? No, wait. Don't tell me, quantum-something-or-other."

He grinned and looked at her. "*Correct. Let Deszik know I need to see him.* If you could have a look at these findings, and let me know what you think, I would be most appreciative," he said handing her a notebook, wrapping up the secondary conversation.

"I'll be happy to. I'll send him to you this evening."

"Thank you, Telestra," he called after her as she passed into the corridor.

Chapter Thirteen

Onboard the *Itinerant*

With the first fifty crew members settling in and receiving care aboard the Mystic Sea, the crew of the Itinerant was anxious to make its second run to the Trepang.

"Is everything cleaned and sealed up and ready to go?" Marcus asked.

"Everything is ship-shape," Taka replied.

"All right let's go get them. Bill, take us down."

"We're on our way!"

In contrast to the dismal, fearful, first trip into the unknown, this time the knowledge that they were going to retrieve survivors made the time pass quickly.

As they approached the spot where they expected the Trepang to be, Taka noticed it first. "Marcus, something's wrong. The Trepang isn't where she should be."

"What? There's no way she had the ability to move."

"No, that's not what I mean. She's slipped further down the incline toward the trench."

"Shit. Where is she now?"

"Five-hundred yards from where she was and three-hundred-eighty-four feet deeper."

A chill ran down Marcus' spine. "But that's one-hundred-sixty-eight feet below her crush depth," he said dejectedly. "Bill, see if you can raise them."

Bill quickly got on the radio. "Trepang, Trepang, this is Itinerant, come in."

"Itinerant, this is Trepang, we read you. I hope you guys are on the way, we've shifted below our crush depth and, although we're holding together, we sure would like to get out of here."

"Affirmative, Trepang. We see you. Hang tight, we're about to dock. Trepang out."

"They're listing another ten degrees—thirty degrees total, but the hatch is clear, we can still dock."

"Let's get moving, we're running out of time. Bill, contact the Seawolf—see if she will monitor us and the Trepang until we get everyone off."

They docked quickly, and Marcus boarded the Trepang to speak with Captain Locklin while the next group loaded. He knew there might not be another trip if the Trepang shifted again.

As they finished their conversation and returned to the group, they caught the tail end of a conversation between the XO and Ensign Hunter.

"Thank you, Ensign, that's kind of you, and I appreciate the offer, but my place is here with the Captain." He turned to check on the progress of the men boarding the Itinerant.

"With all due respect, *sir*," Hunter spat. "You are wrong, and you're being a damn fool."

By now, the loading process had halted to watch the

scene.

Larson slowly turned back around, eyes narrowed, jaw clenched, and spoke in a low voice. "Are you addressing *me*, Ensign Hunter?"

"Yes, sir. I am."

Taking a step toward him, Larson eyed him coldly. "Because of our circumstances, I'm going to assume you are under duress, and I'm going to forget what I just heard. I suggest you hold your tongue from now on."

"Yes, sir," Hunter responded.

Lieutenant Larson turned back toward the group and never saw the ensign's swing.

While Nicholson examined the unconscious XO, Locklin and Marcus held Hunter between them.

"Striking a superior officer is a court martial offense, Hunter," Locklin said.

"Yes, sir, I know."

"But why? You had a promising career ahead of you."

"Permission to speak freely, Captain?"

"Granted."

"Lieutenant Larson has two little boys back home, and his wife is pregnant. They need their husband and father. I'm single. I will take his place among the third group to leave, just in case."

Locklin shook his head. "Nicholson? Is he going to be all right?"

"I believe so, sir."

"And I suppose that blow to his head is serious and requires the immediate attention of a doctor, so he needs to be in this next group to go?"

Nicholson cocked his head in thought for a moment before cottoning-on. "Oh yes, sir. Extremely serious. He should be placed aboard the Itinerant without delay."

"See that it's done now," Locklin ordered.

Turning to the rest of the group he said, "I don't suppose anyone here saw how Larson was injured?"

Silence filled the compartment briefly and then Yoder spoke up, "I'm not positive, Captain, with everything that's been happening, but it's likely the Lieutenant was struck by a piece of overhead pipe that broke loose—or it could have been a piece of equipment ..."

"Anybody see anything different?"

When no one else answered, Locklin looked at Hunter long and hard. "Well, it's good we were able to find him and get him on board the Itinerant then."

Marcus shook Locklin's hand and followed the last of the fifty crewmen to board the Itinerant. "I promise we'll be back," he said as Copeland prepared to help him seal the hatch. *I just hope I can keep that promise.*

For a moment, the unspoken truth lay heavy between them. "We know. We'll be ready. God speed," he replied as he closed and sealed the hatch.

Nearby, in the murky depths, the Seawolf cruised slowly, the motionless blip like a ghost on her radar screen.

Chapter Fourteen

Re'an headquarters Tunguska, Russia

Telestra went about her daily routine of checking the readings and equipment in the control room, the heart of the facility. Here, computers monitored and controlled the ingenious equipment created by the L'gundo ancestors. The equipment harnessed the power of a forming volcano, by using the highly volatile hot gasses released by magma from the planet's mantle, to provide the facility with all the power they needed to live comfortably.

As usual, everything was in perfect working order, all readings within the expected safety spectrum.

The new communication adjustment to her chip was working perfectly, and she relished the ability to conspire with Dekka as they went about their daily tasks.

"Deszik's adjustment last night went perfectly," Dekka reported.

"He will be leaving tomorrow. It is time to finalize our plans."

"Yes. We have been working for this day for more than a century. It is time."

Leaving the control room, Telestra headed for the fissure access area and her weekly inspection of its equipment. *"Have you completed the work on the medical program?"*

"I have a few more adjustments to make, but yes, it is ready."

"Are you sure Viktor will not know what is happening?"

"There are two-thousand sleep pods occupied currently," he said referring to the people Viktor had captured, killed, re-animated, and put into the Deep Sleep as reserve soldiers. They were sustained in pods that provided their bodies with a highly oxygenated liquid for breathing, nutrient-rich artificial 'blood' for sustenance, and micro electrical stimulation to support the brain.

When the subjects were needed, the breathable liquid and chemical blood were removed, replaced with air and their original blood, their hearts re-started, and the brain stimulated until they regained consciousness.

"This program," he continued, "is designed to work undetected. I've adjusted the nutrients just enough so that the proteins break down in a way that prevents them from forming amino acids, and thus cannot be absorbed by the body which will create a starvation condition within a few days. This will force their bodies into gluconeogenesis—a process that occurs under starvation conditions where the body draws glucose first from stored sources in fat, then from lean tissue and muscle to support life."

"So, they will 'starve' to death without knowing it, and Viktor will never know. That is ingenious, Dekka—diabolical, but ingenious."

"At least they will not consciously suffer."

"What will happen if Viktor tries to awaken any of them before the process is complete?"

"He will find them physically weak at the least. If the process has progressed far enough, the effort to restart their hearts will kill them. In any case, the chip in the brain is dependent on glucose for its source of energy, similar to a battery, and the low levels of glucose available to the chip will render it inoperable, irreparably damaged."

"It would seem you have thought of everything."

"Let's hope. How are your plans coming?"

"I've written the computer program that, when loaded, will feed the monitoring equipment false information so that all the instruments record normal levels of activity in the fissures. It will also override the normal functioning of the control programs so that no action will be taken by the automatic adjustment system to prevent the build-up of pressure."

"When we are ready to proceed, during my weekly equipment check, I will make the adjustments to the flow regulators which will allow the gas pressure to build in the four natural fissure vents. I will see to it that Jezza is assigned to monitor the fissures and the access area after I've made the changes. No one else will see the pressure building, and she will be able to let us know when it's time to leave."

"And have you figured out a way for us to escape? I don't mind dying for a noble cause, but I would rather live."

"I believe so, but it will be risky."

When Telestra didn't elaborate, Dekka probed, *"Well, what's the plan?"*

"Several years ago, while she was inspecting fissure four, Jezza discovered a side channel that opens on the surface. We will climb out through it."

Silence followed her statement. *"Dekka?"*

"Dear Lord! You're going to have us crawl through the belly of a fire breathing dragon and out through its mouth, hoping it doesn't sneeze?"

"Something like that," she agreed. "I know it sounds crazy, but that's exactly what I hope they will think if they discover us missing. It's unlikely they will look for us there."

"Let's hope and pray that's how it will work out for us," Dekka replied.

Chapter Fifteen

Onboard the *Itinerant*

The Itinerant broke the surface and Marcus ordered the hatches opened even before they pulled alongside the Mystic Sea. The crew was all on deck anxious to clear the sub as swiftly as possible, so she could return for their remaining crewmates and captain of the ill-fated Trepang. They all knew time was growing short for those left behind.

As the last man boarded the Mystic Sea, Captain Dean Griffith hollered to Marcus, "Anything you need?"

"A miracle!" Marcus replied. He heard the Captain wish him Godspeed as he closed the hatch, water spilling in around him as the Itinerant submerged rapidly.

As he entered the bridge, he caught the tail-end of a message. *"Better hurry, you guys are out of time. Seawolf out."*

"What's up, Bill?"

"The Trepang slipped again, not far, only about ten-feet this time. But the Seawolf reports there are increasing submarine seaquakes in the area, at the moment, and she could go over the edge any time."

"Great. That's all we need," Marcus mumbled. He paced the bridge restlessly as they descended. "Can we still mate up?" he demanded as soon as they approached.

"Yes," Taka replied. "Her angle hasn't changed."

"Thank God. All right, here's how this is going to work—we'll get the remaining crew onboard first, then the prisoners, then the bodies of the deceased, if we have time. Let's get this done and get out of here," he said as the hatch to the Trepang opened revealing Nicholson's smiling face.

"Glad you're back. Now get out of the way, we'd like to get out of here!"

Marcus laughed in spite of himself. "Come on!"

Nicholson disappeared, and the crew of the Trepang began to board. Within minutes, the last of the prisoners were boarding, and Dunlap and Sommers were preparing to hand up the first body, under the supervision of Locklin who refused to leave until *all* of his crew was rescued.

Nicholson had argued endlessly with Locklin while waiting for the return of the Itinerant and now muttered something that sounded a lot like *'damn fool'* under his breath while he and Sommers tried to load the bodies double-time.

They'd just passed the body of the last deceased crew member up and were picking up Brideaux's body, when they felt a tingling in their feet and then the sub began to shake.

"Seaquake!" Marcus yelled down the hatch. "Get up here, *NOW!*"

The men grabbed Locklin and unceremoniously lifted him through the hatch where he was hoisted roughly aboard the Itinerant. "I can climb a ladder myself, dammit,

I don't need your ... ouch ... hey ... ow!" they heard him protesting.

His feet disappeared, and Nicholson started up the ladder. The sub lurched violently, throwing him off the ladder and Sommers to the floor. They felt the sub sliding and heard the groaning of metal as she reached the limit of her depth tolerance.

"C'mon, c'mon, c'mon!" Marcus shouted.

The two men, hearts racing, scrambled for the ladder and climbed, almost as one body, toward the Itinerant. As they reached the hatch, they were grabbed by their hands and shoulders, hauled swiftly the rest of the way, and dumped abruptly on the deck on top of one another.

The hatch slammed closed and was just being sealed behind them when they were all jarred by a sudden impact and the sub's forward motion ceased.

"What happened?" Marcus yelled.

"We've hit a rock!" Taka said loudly, her voice trembling.

"Are we clear of the Trepang?"

"No, we haven't fully disengaged the clamps yet."

"Get us loose!" he shouted.

"Trying, Marcus, trying, but they're stuck."

"Bill, get the Seawolf. See if she can tell us what's happening."

"Itinerant, this is Seawolf, go ahead," they answered almost immediately.

"Can you see what's happening? We can't disengage from the Trepang."

"Itinerant, it looks like you've come into contact with another large object, probably a rock, and have become an anchor holding the Trepang in place. We can't tell more than that with our sonars."

"The Mystic Sea has a mini-sub with a Remote Operated Vehicle on board. See if they can send it down for a look."

"Will do Itinerant, stand by."

Several long minutes passed before the Seawolf radioed again. "They're prepping it for launch now."

For each and every one of the souls on the Itinerant it became the longest wait of their lives as they felt every tremor of the seaquakes rattling through the body of the Itinerant, and their own.

One of them summed up what all of them felt—"So this is what eternity feels like."

Shortly after, Mystic Two, the mini sub, reached depth and launched the ROV. Those aboard the Itinerant still held their breaths—they had no idea what their situation was. Would they be able to get out of there? No one knew. They had to wait. The sour scent of fear grew with every tremor of the seaquakes.

"Itinerant, this is Mystic Two, do you read?"

"We read you, Mystic Two," Bill responded.

Marcus sighed with relief. He looked at his watch. It had been twenty-five minutes. But it might as well have been twenty-five hours, twenty-five years, or twenty-five decades.

"Itinerant, we've sent the ROV out, and we're receiving visual now. Looks like there was a mudslide. The Trepang appears to have rolled as she slid. You're wedged on the bottom between a large rock formation and the sail, partially covered in sediment."

"Our docking clamps won't release from the Trepang – they're jammed or something. Can you make out what the problem is?"

"Standby Itinerant, repositioning to check it out."

Taka sat at her station, arms crossed, biting her lower

lip, while Bill spun nervously side to side in his chair. Marcus stood frozen in place, greeting Dunlap and Sommers with a nod as they joined the bridge.

"Itinerant, this is Mystic Two. There's a lot of sediment covering the area, but it looks as if the impact with the rock twisted the docking seals. I'm sorry to tell you, but I don't think they can be released. It looks pretty bad."

"Just great," Marcus muttered. "Now what?" He paced the deck, *we're too deep to send out divers – below Seawolf's crush depth – shit!*" He scratched his head, spun around, and started pacing in the opposite direction, stopped, spun around, stopped, and spun slowly yet again. "Taka, the Trepang is sliding tail-first, isn't she?"

"Yes, she is."

"Which direction did she roll? It feels like we are nose down."

"That's correct, Marcus. We docked with our nose to Trepang's starboard side and she rolled to starboard."

"Bill," Marcus said, motioning for Bill to pass him the radio mic. "Mystic Two, this is Itinerant."

"Itinerant, Mystic Two, go ahead."

"If we push with our starboard engine, from your vantage point, can you tell if that turn would be enough for us to escape?"

A long moment of silence passed before the Mystic Two answered. "Negative, Itinerant, you're nose down against the bottom. You'd only push yourself deeper into the mud."

"Well, so much for that idea," Marcus said. "I'm open to suggestions people."

At that moment, the Seawolf broke in, "Mystic Two, get clear! Itinerant, hang on, a large seaquake just occurred, arriving in ten seconds!"

They barely had time to grab hold of something solid

before violent tremors shook the sub, and her metal hull began to moan as the Trepang slid again, dragging her into the deep trench with it.

The last thing Marcus heard was Bill yelling, "C'mon!" as the sub spun upside down and the lights went out.

Washington, D.C.

Daniel, Salome, Scott, and Bill waited patiently as the other Cabinet members left the room. "Thank you for staying," Daniel said. "We need to discuss the prisoners."

Bill and Scott, not being privy to the knowledge that the prisoners were on the Trepang, looked surprised.

"Have they been located?" Scott asked.

"We believe so," Daniel answered carefully. "I need your counsel, Scott, on our international legal position, and input from all of you on the best way to handle this situation."

"As discussed with the late President Campbell, the crimes they committed were against humanity which puts them under the jurisdiction of the International Criminal Court—the ICC," Scott said.

"That's right," Daniel said. "The court in The Hague in the Netherlands."

"Correct."

"Do we know if the treaties that apply are still in place and if the ICC is functioning?" Daniel asked, turning to Bill.

"We don't know at this time, sir. They were never officially recalled by Brideaux, and it is debatable if he did, that it would have been valid. However, I would like to suggest that this is an excellent opportunity to re-establish those treaties. It would go a long way in easing the hostile feelings toward our country if we support and assist with the restoration of the ICC and turn the prisoners over to them.

"If we set the example of following International Law, we put ourselves on par with all nations and encourage them to support and follow International Law as well."

"I agreed with Bill," Scott said. "If the United States were to do otherwise, it would encourage other countries to defy what was once established and could, in the worst-case scenario, eventually lead to another world war."

A knock sounded on the door, and the Chief of Staff stepped in. "Excuse me, Mister President, there is an urgent call for you from Admiral Johnson."

"Thank you, Glenn, I'll take it in my office in just a moment."

"Yes, sir."

Daniel turned back to the three. "You've been very helpful, thank you. Please work together on this matter and keep me updated. Salome, I will leave it to you to make the arrangements for the transportation of the prisoners to the Netherlands when the time comes."

Daniel stood, indicating that Salome was to follow him, went to his office, and pushed the button for speakerphone. "Yes Admiral, what can I do for you?"

"Mister President, I'm afraid I have some very bad news. We've lost the Trepang and the Itinerant."

"Dear God, what happened?"

"There was a severe seaquake that caused a sub-marine landslide. It carried the Trepang into the Aleutian Trench. The Itinerant was docked with her in the process of completing the last rescue dive and was unable to release her docking clamps. Unfortunately, she was dragged into the trench along with the Trepang."

"Is there any chance at all that the Itinerant survived?"

"The ROV they were using was damaged in the slide as well. It has been retrieved and is being repaired as we speak, but it will be several hours before we can send it down again.

"The Seawolf is searching the area but is officially at the limit of her operating depth."

"Officially? Then that means she *can* go deeper?"

There was silence for a moment before Johnson continued. "Yes, sir, she can go a little deeper, but she isn't supposed to. However, unofficially, she has already passed her operating and crush depths in the search for the Itinerant without result. She has truly gone as deep as she dares, and we're damn lucky we didn't lose her too."

"I see. Please give the Captain of the Seawolf my sincere thanks for his efforts and initiative in this search, and do not reprimand him for his actions."

"I will. I suggest that Secretary Willis and I convene at your office within the hour for updates on the situation as they come in."

"I'd appreciate that, yes. I'll see you shortly."

Chapter Sixteen

Washington, D.C.

Daniel, Salome, Admiral Johnson, and Secretary of Defense Cliff Willis gathered in the Situation Room once again, to monitor the activities in the North Pacific.

Over the last two hours, the USS Seawolf, USS Idaho, and USS Utah submarines were working a search grid trying to locate any sign of the Itinerant. "She's either lost completely or too deep for them to detect," Johnson reported.

Daniel shook his head miserably. "How long until they can launch the ROV again?"

"They're preparing her for launch now, and the Mystic Two is standing by to depart as soon as the ROV is ready to go."

"Will we have a live feed from the Mystic Two?"

"Yes, we'll be able to see and hear what is happening as it happens. Captain Wiekelan, aboard the Enterprise, will also be updating us as needed."

Daniel nodded. The wait seemed inordinately long, but at last, the Mystic Two was ready to depart.

"Mystic Two proceeding with all due haste."

Those gathered in the Situation Room listened to the smooth interaction of the three-man crew aboard the Mystic Two as she descended into the depths and returned to the last known coordinates of the Trepang and Itinerant.

"All right, that's as deep as we can go. Send out Bendoth."

"He's on his way!"

"Bendoth?" Daniel inquired curiously.

Johnson laughed. "It's the nickname of their ROV – an acronym for 'Been There Done That.' Apparently, they use it quite a bit and have had several ... what they call, 'adventures' with it."

"Sounds more like nightmares to me." Daniel smiled half-heartedly.

"The water is still very murky with all the suspended sediment particles in it. It's going to be difficult to see anything in this mess."

"Understood, Mystic Two, just do your best," came the voice of Captain Wiekelan.

"Let's follow the slide path and see what we find," suggested one of the Mystic Two's crew.

To give Daniel a better understanding of what he was hearing, Admiral Johnson pulled out a nautical chart of the Alaska Peninsula and Aleutian Islands to Seguam Pass. "She was laying here on this slope at 364 fathoms—2,184 feet.

"As you can see here," his finger drew a line down the points where a series of closely spaced curved lines came together, "this is a steep ravine that drops down to more than 3,500 feet before falling off into the Aleutian Trench."

"There's no way the Trepang could survive that, is there?"

"No, Mister President, there isn't. She was already below crush depth when she first came to rest on the bottom."

"What about the Itinerant?"

"Her crush depth is 4,000 feet. There's a possibility she's still in one piece—if she was able to break away from the Trepang in time."

"How deep can that ROV go?"

"Ordinarily, private vessels that carry an ROV have either micro or mini class that have very shallow limits within a few hundred feet. Mystic Sea's ROV is a custom design. It can reach depths of nearly 23,000 feet. If there's anything to find, this ROV has a good chance of doing so."

"And all we can do in the meantime is sit here and wait," Daniel said glumly.

"Unfortunately, yes, Mister President," Johnson confirmed as the Mystic Two reported they had begun the grid search pattern of the slide area—they had to be sure the subs didn't get buried under the slide.

It took hours for the little ROV to complete the grid; hours that passed with an agonizing lack of information.

"That's it for the ravine. We've completed the grid and found nothing."

"If they've gone into the trench, there's nothing we can do for them. There are a couple of shelves on the west side of the ravine—check them before proceeding into the trench," Wiekelan ordered.

"Copy, Enterprise. Proceeding to check the shelves on the west side."

The little ROV made its way south-west along the ledge

at the bottom of the ravine until it came to a slightly wider area where the ledge turned back toward the north. From there it began a slow ascent, shining its blindingly bright lights over the surface of the ledge.

"Starting search at 6,000 feet. The area isn't too large, this won't take long."

Thirty minutes seemed a long time to Daniel, but at last, the Mystic Two reported, "Nothing here, coming to 5,900 feet to search the next ledge. At least a lot of the sediment particles have settled out, visibility is a lot better than when we started."

Evidently, this ledge was smaller than the last because within fifteen minutes another negative contact report came through, and ten minutes after that, yet another one.

Daniel was losing hope – everyone was losing hope. The Situation Room was heavy with despair and silent in the growing sense of grief.

"Ascending to the next shelf at 4,200 feet ... *Stop!*"

The excited voice brought everyone in the room to the edge of their seats.

"There she is! The Itinerant!"

Cheers rang out from on board the Mystic Two and around the Situation Room. Everyone turned to the large monitors on the walls to see the live feed from the ROV.

To their dismay, it showed the Itinerant lying 'lifelessly' on her side on the shelf, partially buried under sediment.

Onboard the *Itinerant*

Marcus came to with a headache, the likes of which he'd

never had before. He tried to sit up and groaned as pain shot through his ribs.

"Easy Captain, you've got a nasty concussion, some broken ribs, and a back injury," Nicholson said.

Marcus groaned again. "What happened?"

"A sub-marine landslide washed the Trepang into the Aleutian Trench. If it weren't for you and Bill, we'd have gone with her.

"Bill said he heard your idea about pushing with the starboard engine to break us loose, but we couldn't because we were nosed into the bottom. The landslide shifted the Trepang, lifting us off the bottom, so he applied the engine the way you suggested, and we broke free. We were still caught in the landslide, but we didn't go over the edge into the trench."

"Thank heavens for that. What's our status, and how long have I been out?" Marcus looked around carefully in the dim light—it hurt to move his head—and noticed the angle of the sub didn't look right.

Nicholson saw the look of puzzlement on Marcus' face. "We're lying on our side on the bottom, about 150 feet below crush depth. While you've been unconscious for the past four hours, the crew has been making repairs to the systems that were damaged.

"Gus says he should have the engines working again in about an hour. We're operating on battery power right now, that's why the lights are dim. Bill says the radio is out until we can reach the surface and replace the antenna."

"Any injuries to the crew? What about our guests?"

"No life-threatening injuries—cuts and bruises mostly, a few broken bones, and concussions. I believe everyone will recover."

"Thanks for the update. Help me up, will you?"

Termination

"No, I won't. You have broken ribs and if you move the wrong way or fall, you could wind up with a punctured lung. You're on bedrest until you're in an environment where it's easier and safer to move around."

"But ..."

"No 'buts'– that's the way it is. Period. End of discussion."

Marcus was stewing, but every time he started to move, the pain in his head and ribs convinced him being quiet really was the best thing he could do.

Nicholson returned with three crewmen from the Trepang and a backboard. "Ok, Captain, Gus is ready to start the engines and try to get us out of here. We're going to support you with the backboard and shift you as the sub comes upright."

Thinking about what it would feel like to fall onto the floor, he decided not to argue. "Thank you, men, I appreciate that."

It hurt more than he cared to admit when they slid the backboard under him, but he was grateful to Nicholson for thinking ahead and preventing something much more painful.

A few minutes later, he felt the vibration of the engines, and shortly after that, the scraping of the sub as she slid along the bottom.

"What the hell? Why didn't we rise before trying to move forward?" Marcus asked.

"We tried, but we have too much sediment on top of us. We're hoping we can wiggle out from under it so we can rise."

The crewman had barely finished speaking when they all felt the sub begin to shift.

Washington, D.C.

Daniel was on his feet, mesmerized by the image from the ROV.

Have we lost them both?

"Is there any way to tell if they're alive, or to bring the sub up?"

Johnson shook his head. "The Navy isn't equipped for salvage operations like this. We can bring in someone who is though. I don't know how fast we can get them here, and if there's anyone alive onboard, we don't know how much time they have."

Deep sorrow drove Daniel back into his chair uttering a heavy sigh. He continued to watch as the ROV moved in close to the stricken sub for investigation. Following the length of the sub revealed it was resting on the bottom, but clear of obstructions against it. Moving up and over, revealed a moderate amount of sediment covering nearly three-quarters of her surface.

"If she were clear of that sediment, she might come upright."

They listened as the crew of the Mystic Two discussed how to assist the Itinerant.

As he analyzed the images, Admiral Johnson muttered to himself, "If only she had power, she might be able to …"

"To what?" Daniel asked.

"Move away, move away!"

Daniel looked back to the screen to see what new calamity awaited them.

"Look at that! She's moving! They're alive!"

From the Situation Room they watched as the Itinerant began to push itself along the bottom. The bow began to rise. In something like a slow-motion display, the sediment fell away, the Itinerant rolled upright and began to rise toward the surface.

The cheers aboard the Mystic Two were drowned out by the celebratory remarks in the Situation Room. When the excitement quieted, they listened to the voices from the Mystic Sea again.

"Her radio must be damaged, or she would have contacted us by now. We'll have to wait until she reaches the surface."

Heading for Bangor

When the Intinerant broke the surface and turned to dock with the Mystic Sea, there wasn't a dry eye in the Situation Room when the report came that all souls from the Trepang had been rescued and no major injuries had been sustained.

"Mister President," Johnson said. "Captain Wiekelan, aboard the Enterprise, is standing by to take possession of the prisoners and escort everyone to Bangor Naval Base. The Itinerant can make repairs there."

Daniel nodded. "Do it!"

Excited chatter flowed around Daniel as he leaned back in his chair smiling.

Finally! Something in this dreadful situation has gone right!

Johnson approached Daniel with the report that the prisoners had been transferred to the Enterprise, and the small fleet was underway on the three-day trip to Bangor Base, Washington State.

Five miles below the departing Enterprise, the sectional remains of the imploded Trepang rested in the heart of the Aleutian Trench. The failed reactors aboard that had started to melt down were cooled by the frigid deep-ocean water and lay benign on a ledge one hundred feet above the floor of the trench.

A few hundred yards to the west, the mid-section containing the crew quarters lay scattered in large pieces, and three hundred yards beyond that, the sail and missile section rested on top of a geothermal vent.

The conditions the sub was subjected to at such great depth, combined with the unusual and unexpected heat from the geothermal vent, caused the safety mechanisms on the Tomahawk missiles and Mark 48 torpedoes to fail. Several exploded, opening the vent and allowing the wreckage to drop further down the vent where the remaining weapons exploded.

One thousand miles to the northwest at the Alaska Volcano Observatory in Fairbanks, Alaska, seismographs recorded a sudden and violent event deep in the Aleutian Trench.

Umnak Island experienced a violent earthquake, and the other Fox Islands shook to a lesser extent.

The accompanying large sub-marine landslide triggered alarms at The Pacific Tsunami Warning Centers at Ford Island, Hawaii, and Palmer, Alaska.

Termination

Tsunami Watch Bulletins went out to the coastal areas and islands surrounding and throughout the Pacific Ocean, warning of the sub-marine earthquake, possible tsunami, and advising an alert status be maintained while further data was collected.

On Bogoslof Island, just north of the Fox Islands, the Bogoslof Volcano began to steam.

Chapter Seventeen

Re'an headquarters Tunguska, Russia

Telestra ate her dinner silently, having tuned-out most of Viktor's babbling about the mission to the canyon. He'd bragged about his plans to her so often she felt like she could run the mission herself.

Her thoughts turned to the mission leader, her son Deszik, and she reached out to him through the chip link Dekka made.

"Deszik? How are you?"

"Good evening, Mother. I am well."

"Are you ready to go tomorrow?"

"Just about. I'm completing my final preparations and checks now."

"I hate it that Viktor is making you do this!"

"I know, mother. I too regret his interference in our lives, but there isn't anything we can do about it at this time."

"No, not now, but soon."

"Have you and Dekka formed a plan?"

"Yes. Contact him, and we will tell you."

A few moments later, Dekka was in conference with them.

"Hello Telestra, Deszik tells me he's ready to hear our plan."

"Yes, as he is leaving in the morning, it seems appropriate to tell him now."

"I agree. I'm sure you have much to do this evening, Deszik, so I will keep this short.

"Your mother and I are going to work in tandem to destroy Viktor and this site. That will leave you to deal with the Re'an accompanying you."

"I'm ready and will take care of the others."

"Very well. I have created a program that will slowly shut down the soldiers that are currently in the pods, so Viktor won't notice. If he awakens any of them before they are dead, he will find them weak and brain-damaged. I activated the routine today."

"And I," Telestra added, "have written a program to show normal status with the facility after I adjust the flow regulators to allow pressure to build in the fissures. Dekka, I, and a few others will escape before the place explodes."

"And with our ability to communicate over long distances, I will be able to locate and join you once I am free of the canyon," Deszik concluded. "Excellent plan."

"Depending on what you find at the canyon site, we may join you there."

"What do you mean, mother?"

"My sister, Siasha, was in love with a B'ran soldier who was an L'gundo sympathizer—he was one of the commanders at the Canyon Control Center. She and a small team of L'gundo lived in secret tunnels connected to the canyon site, working with the B'ran sympathizers and providing intelligence to us.

"Before the Healer turned against the people, we were hoping to overthrow the soldiers there and take possession of the site ourselves.

"There has been no contact with the canyon site despite the fact we know it is operational. Something has changed at the site. It's possible it is under the control of L'Gundo sympathizers, or even the L'Gundo team we sent. If that is true, we will join you there."

"I have a few early memories of Siasha from when I was a boy. I liked her. It would be great to see her again."

"I hope you get the chance, son. Safe journey. I love you."

"I love you too, Mother. And Dekka? You have been like a father to me despite Viktor's interference. I have never said it before, but I love you too. Please take care of yourself, and my mother."

"I will. I have always thought of you as the son I never had. Safe journey."

An unaccustomed tightness filled Deszik's throat as he left the conversation. He had always wished that Dekka could be his father, but never knew that Dekka felt the same about him. He was touched and felt honored that the man he respected so much considered him as a son.

In a lab in another part of the facility, Dekka squeezed his eyes with his fingers. The last exchange with Deszik had been both heart-warming and heart-breaking. He smiled as he remembered Deszik's words—'… like a father to me … I love you too'—Dekka would never forget them, no matter what happened.

Telestra, now alone in her quarters, grieved silently for the family that was and yet had never been.

Chapter Eighteen

Washington, D.C.

As promised, Owen arrived with the Metroliner late that afternoon and was greeted warmly by everyone. He had a special 'package' to deliver to Daniel, and arrangements were made for him to visit the White House.

The Secret Service agents smiled when they saw the 'package' and quickly led him to the Oval Office, where Daniel was just finishing up a meeting with his Chief of Staff.

The Special Agent knocked on the open door as Glenn left the office. "Excuse me, Mister President. There's a Mister Owen Bell here to see you."

"Send him in!" Daniel said and started to get up.

At that moment, a small, fast-moving body hurled through the door yelling "Daddy! Daddy!" and launched himself at Daniel.

Opening his arms in delighted surprise, Daniel bent to

catch the boy in his arms and swung him around in circles, making them both laugh. "Nicholas! My boy. What a big surprise!"

Daniel stopped spinning and locked eyes with his lovely wife, Sarah. Shifting Nicholas to his hip, he stepped to embrace Sarah and held them both tightly for a long moment whispering loving endearments.

He finally pulled away saying, "I'm so glad you're here!" and turned to Owen. "Thank you for bringing them."

"Don't thank me. When Sarah found out I was flying out here, wild horses couldn't have stopped her. Truth be told, she threatened to skin me alive if I even *thought* about coming out here without them!" Owen grinned. "It's good to see you though."

The rest of the afternoon Daniel spent giving Owen, Sarah, and Nicholas a grand tour of the White House. It was early evening when the tour ended, and Owen excused himself saying he'd planned to spend some time with Roy and Raj that evening.

As soon as he had seen Owen and his 'package' to the Oval Office, the agent had let the kitchen staff know that the First Lady had arrived, and they prepared a special dinner for the family.

That evening, Nicholas fell asleep in his chair during dinner—the day had been so full of excitement and adventures that he just couldn't keep his eyes open. Daniel picked him up, and he and Sarah tucked him into bed in the Blue Room, on the Second Floor across the hall from their room.

Daniel led Sarah through the door to the living room and closed it quietly behind them. Gathering her in his arms he kissed her deeply and held her close for several minutes, enjoying the warmth of her body against his, the softness of her lips, the scent of her hair, and just the simple feeling of oneness he shared with her.

"I've missed you terribly," she whispered.

"I've missed you too. I'm glad it's over, and I pray that our country and the world will now have peace."

Chapter Nineteen

Washington, D.C.

Daniel awoke the next morning with Sarah curled close to his side. "Good morning, Mister President," she said smiling.

Drawing her closer, he kissed the top of her head. "It's so good to have you here beside me. I'm very glad you insisted on coming out with Owen."

"Me too," she said and nipped his shoulder.

"Ow! Hey! You can get arrested for that."

"What, for biting the President of the United States? I'll plead not guilty. I'll go to court and tell my story so the whole world can hear that the President turned his back on me when we got into bed."

"Just what I need—more bad publicity. Okay, I won't press charges." Daniel chuckled.

After sharing breakfast with Sarah and Nicholas, where Nicholas spent most of his time in his father's lap, Daniel went to the Oval Office. It had been difficult to tear himself away from his family; they'd been apart for so long he didn't want to let them out of his sight.

Reminding himself that this was only the first of many such mornings, he'd managed to leave the table and whistled cheerily as he walked to his office. His step was jauntier and lighter than it had been in many weeks, and he felt a new sense of self-confidence and positivity.

"Good morning, Mister President," Glenn greeted as Daniel stepped into the Oval Office.

"Good morning, Glenn," he responded. "How are you this fine morning; and what's on the agenda today?"

"Just fine, sir, thank you for asking." Noting Daniel's tranquil, happy attitude he added, "Having your family here seems to be very agreeable with you, I wish I could say the day was free for you to spend with them."

"I'm sure those days will come once things settle down some."

"Yes, sir. So, here we go, your schedule for the day. You have a meeting in fifteen minutes with Admiral Johnson and Secretary of Defense Willis to discuss the prisoner transfer."

"Speak of the devil," said a voice from the doorway."

Daniel looked up to see Cliff Willis standing on the threshold with a grin, holding two cups of coffee. With a smile, Daniel beckoned him to enter while Glenn continued a summary of Daniel's schedule for the day.

"After that is a meeting with the Head of Homeland Security, the Attorney General and Secretary of State Simms, about the prisoners and pending the outcome of *that* meeting, I have tentatively scheduled a call with world leaders this afternoon to discuss the issue."

"Sounds like a busy day," Daniel commented.

"More of a headache than busy," Willis offered. "Dealing with world leaders is always a headache—too many of them are pompous asses."

Daniel laughed. "I guess I'm about to find out who they are and to what degree."

"Exactly."

Just then Admiral Johnson knocked on the open door and stepped in when Daniel waved for him to come in.

Johnson closed the door and took a seat beside Willis.

"What's the news?" Daniel asked.

"The Enterprise is two days from port. Incidentally, there was a significant earthquake near the site where the Trepang went down. It caused some damage on Umnak Island and the other Fox Island group. There was also an associated tsunami, but it was fortunately fairly small—some minor flooding on the islands in the immediate vicinity, and unusually high tides along the west coast of North America and the Hawaiian Islands, but no real damage."

Daniel frowned. "Were there any lives lost?"

"No sir, a few mild to moderate injuries, but none of them life-threatening."

"More good news." Daniel nodded, pleased. "So, how are we going to transfer the prisoners?"

"We thought we'd slow the Enterprise, so she arrives after dark. The prisoners, dressed as sailors, with about fifty crewmembers will disembark as if going on shore leave. Some crewmembers will be going on shore leave while the rest escort the prisoners to Fort Lewis.

"Once there, the prisoners will be confined to the brig, and the crew will have a few days unofficial 'shore leave' before returning to the Enterprise."

"Sounds simple enough, I like it," approved Daniel. "Willis, do you see any problems with that plan?"

"Not at all—simple and low key, it's a good plan."

"Excellent! Well then, gentlemen, if you'll excuse me, I'll see to making it happen!" Johnson said.

"Thank you, Admiral, that would be most appreciated," Daniel replied as Johnson stood to leave.

Turning back to Willis, Daniel inquired about the status of the injured Trepang crew.

"The doctor aboard the Mystic Sea has taken good care of them and reports they are recovering well. They're all going to be just fine."

"What about the ones that were air-lifted to Anchorage with the young Ensign, that Brideaux had tortured?"

Willis had a sad expression on his face when he said, "The two with head injuries are going to be just fine. Unfortunately, Ensign Littleton is the exception, sir. I'm told that his condition has stabilized and has been upgraded from 'critical' to 'guarded.' He will recover, physically, in time, but it's going to be a long, hard road. Psychologically—well, you never know – some people handle traumas like this better than others. He had to have shown a strong psyche in order to qualify for sub duty, so we're hoping he will be able to cope with what Brideaux did to him."

"It's just unbelievable that he's still alive. I thought I had an idea of how sick and twisted Brideaux was, but it's obvious, I didn't. Pulling the boy's nails out, cutting off his toes, skinning him alive…" Daniel shuddered. "There is no description that can begin to describe the evilness of that man."

Willis nodded.

"I want him to have the best treatment available,"

Daniel growled through clenched teeth. "What isn't covered by whatever benefits he has, I will personally pay for—just see to it that he gets the best." *Brideaux will not have the last say in this.*

"Yes, sir."

The men were silent for a few moments before Daniel spoke again. "What about his family? Is there anything we can do for them?"

"I'm afraid the boy was an orphan. His entire life he'd been bounced from children's home to children's home. He joined the Navy as soon as he graduated high school."

"Talk about a hard life," Daniel muttered. "All right, just see that he gets the best—and Willis…"

"Yes, sir?"

"I'd appreciate it and consider it a personal favor if you would keep an eye on this personally and keep me updated."

Willis nodded. "Absolutely, sir. I'll take care of it."

"Thanks."

Almost on the heels of Willis' departure, Salome, Scott Jenkins, and Bill Simms arrived. When they were all seated, Daniel dove right into the issue of the prisoners.

"They will be transferred to the brig at Fort Lewis in two days. I've been thinking about how to transfer them to the ICC, International Criminal Court, safely and at the same time appease leaders of their respective countries who desire to settle the matter themselves.

"I don't know if it's legal, but what if we invite the ICC to convene here? Try the prisoners according to International Law and get them to agree to let the individual countries carry out the punishment under the ICC's supervision—that is if the ICC exists, I forgot to ask about that. Secretary Simms?"

"I've been able to confirm that part of the ICC does still exist, and there is great interest in getting it re-established—quickly. A few of the members will be new due to death or incapacitation of previous members by the Beast."

"How soon could they be ready to start the trial?"

"Probably within a few weeks."

"Mister Jenkins, you've been awfully quiet. Could this work?"

"I believe it could, if all parties are agreeable to it," Jenkins answered thoughtfully.

"Salome? Any concerns on the Homeland Security front?"

"Given the nature of the crimes, this is going to be nothing *but* a security issue. I think trying to move them to The Hague in the Netherlands would be a disaster and probably get a lot of innocent people killed. In fact, I would recommend clearing Fort Lewis of all non-essential personnel. Once their location is known, it could be attacked."

"Ok, I'll let Secretary Willis know."

Salome added, "I would also recommend you postpone your meeting with world leaders until the prisoners are safely under lock and key at Fort Lewis. That way we won't be putting the Enterprise at risk of becoming a target."

"Good idea," Daniel agreed. "Bill let's see if we can have the ICC on board with our idea in the next two days. I want that in place before I let the others know we have the prisoners secured."

"Yes, sir."

"Salome, I will leave it to you to choose the location of the trial and set up whatever security arrangements you deem necessary."

"You got it, Mister President!"

"Thank you all for being here. Unless there is anything else, I think we're done for the moment."

With the afternoon freed up, Daniel left in search of Sarah and Nicholas.

Chapter Twenty

Washington, D.C.

Daniel and Sarah, enjoying a quiet morning together, sat next to each other on the couch in the living room of their White House home. Sarah sipped a mocha latte and worked a crossword puzzle while Daniel drank his coffee, read the morning newspaper, and listened to the news on the television.

"And in other news, scientists at the Alaska Volcano Observatory in Anchorage are observing what they say is unusual increased seismic activity along the Aleutian Trench near the Fox Islands."

Daniel looked up from the paper to focus on the newscaster's report.

"The Fox Islands are part of the Aleutian Island Chain that extends West into the Pacific Ocean from the Alaskan Peninsula. Observatory scientists also report slight increases in minor, non-eruptive activity in four of the volcanoes in the area: Kanaga, Bogoslof, Cleveland, and Pavlof.

"Although all four of these volcanoes have been active this century, two of them as recently at 2017, scientists say there is nothing to be concerned about at this point, but they will continue to monitor the area closely."

The reporter paused to change subjects, and Daniel's mind strayed from the newscast. "That's odd," he murmured.

"What's odd?" Sarah asked.

"The area he was just talking about is very near where we lost the submarine the prisoners were on."

"I can't see how that could have anything to do with the seismic activities they're talking about."

"Maybe. It still seems strange to me, though."

Nicholas wandered sleepily into the room and Daniel, pushing the matter from his mind, helped his son climb into his lap for some morning cuddling.

"And how is my favorite young man this morning?" Daniel asked, brushing the boy's bangs away from his eyes.

Nicholas rubbed his face against Daniel's shoulder and pulled his little arms in close to his body as if to make himself into a ball.

"Are you okay, Nicholas?" Daniel asked

The boy nodded silently.

Daniel laughed and gently tickled his belly. "Oh, I see—you're not awake yet!"

Giggling, Nicholas objected half-heartedly, "Daddy!"

Sarah looked at the pair and smiled at their antics.

"Did you sleep well?" Daniel continued to engage his son.

Nicholas shook his head. "I had a scary dream."

"Do you want to tell me about it?"

"Big, big mountains, giant explosions," he said, flinging his arms in the air.

"You dreamt of mountains that exploded?"

Nicholas nodded solemnly.

"Did anyone get hurt?"

Thinking for a moment, he finally shook his head.

"Well, everything is all right then, isn't it?"

His little sleepy-eyed face broke into a sunny smile. Nicholas nodded again and relaxed in his father's arms.

Chapter Twenty-One

Private airstrip, Washington, D.C.

Peter Scott, member of the Rossler Foundation and former CIA operative, piloted the Baron 58 to a smooth touchdown in the light of the setting sun at the private airstrip in D.C.

Raj was present to meet him and his passengers.

"Welcome back," Raj's greeting died on his lips when he saw the tall, brown-haired man. "Robert?" He breathed wide-eyed. His heart raced, a cool moisture broke out on his skin, and the ground seemed to spin.

Oblivious to Raj's state, JR asked, "Is the leadership assembled?"

Raj slowly turned to look at JR, incomprehension on his face.

Impatient, JR repeated the question only to receive no answer again, just the continuing dazed look from Raj. Suddenly realizing the problem, he took Raj by both arms and shook him gently. "Raj, buddy, look at me." To help, he patted Raj lightly on one cheek and saw his eyes begin to focus again. "You're okay, Raj. This really is Robert."

"He's dead," Raj whispered as terror washed over his face.

"Yes, he was killed by Brideaux at the canyon."

"We buried him."

"That's right, we did. But through a miracle of 8th cycle technology, he is alive again."

"Miracle?"

"Miracle, yes."

"Oh, okay," Raj responded flatly. Obviously, his brain had decided to shut down rather than try to process this 'miracle'.

Rebecca saw Raj's shock and bewilderment and said, "JR, I think you better drive."

"Yeah, I think you're right," he agreed. "Come on."

Peter grabbed a blanket out of the plane and helped Rebecca wrap it around Raj, who was now shaking like a leaf in the wind. He looked like he was in urgent need of a lot of sugar water, or a stiff drink.

"Get Sam on the phone," JR said. "We need to know where the meeting is taking place."

Peter made the call and put Sam on speakerphone. "Sam, Peter here. What is the location of the meeting?"

"Didn't Raj tell you? He's supposed to pick you up; he should be there."

"Oh, he's here – in a manner of speaking – he's ... indisposed at the moment."

"Do I want to know why?"

"No, not now."

A heavy sigh followed. "The meeting's at Raven Rock. Catch the monorail at Camp David. The Foundation leadership, as well as Roy, Salome, James, Sarah, and Daniel will be there by the time you arrive. Do you want to tell me what's going on?"

"We'll tell everyone at the meeting; it's a long story and we don't want to have to tell it twice."

"Suit yourself. We'll see you there."

"Cheers."

The rest of the trip was made in silence, each lost in their own thoughts—Raj didn't say a word – he just stared at Robert. The three from the canyon wondered how much time they had.

Raven Rock meeting room

The leadership of the Rossler Foundation gathered in perplexity. When Daniel accepted the appointment to the Vice-Presidency, he and Sarah had stepped down as the leaders of the Foundation, handing the reins over to a team who had been dubbed 'The Musketeers'. From an original group of three, their membership had grown to seven and included: Daniel's father, Ben Rossler; John Mendenhall, Rebecca's father, a retired college dean; Luke Clarke, Sarah's uncle and retired CIA field agent; Nigel Harper, a former US president; Ryan Clarke, Sarah's father, an electronics engineer; Sam Lewis, retired head of the CIA under Nigel Harper; and Sinclair O'Reilly, the Foundation's chief translator and now head of the Foundation.

Except for Nigel who was in D.C. assisting Daniel with his transition to the Presidency, the rest of the leadership was at the Rabbit Hole.

When JR requested the meeting, Sam had discussed it

with Daniel, and both agreed they smelled trouble. As a result, Daniel suggested including Raj Sankaran, their computer expert and Daniel's friend from working at the New York Times; Roy James, their nanotechnology expert; Salome James, Roy's wife and the head of security for the Foundation; and Jack Symonds, a former Special Forces operator and one of Sam's former CIA Special Agents.

When the team from the canyon, accompanied by a still partially dazed Raj, arrived at Raven Rock and walked into the conference room, a stunned silence fell as the attendees recognized Robert.

Daniel, blindsided at the juncture, sat in slack-jawed astonishment but was the first to find his voice, "What the hell …!"

JR heard whispered exclamations begin to drift around the room and saw the same on the big screen linked up with those at the Rabbit Hole.

"Robert?"

"This is impossible!"

"Oh, my God!"

"How can this be?"

"This can't be happening."

Robert didn't say a word. He stood against the wall and just looked at everyone in the room and the faces on the screen.

It was surreal, unearthly—impossible. Yet, there he was, Robert Cartwright, the Australian, their friend who was killed by John Brideaux. The same Robert Cartwright whom they'd buried in the Grand Canyon, the same Robert Cartwright after whom they'd named the meeting hall at the Rabbit Hole. But this Robert Cartwright was alive and breathing, right in front of their eyes.

JR realized that mass hysteria and chaos were threatening to erupt, and he'd better do something, quickly. "Everyone," JR started. "Please be calm, take a seat, and take a few deep breaths while I explain.

"There is a logic... ah... well maybe not logical to us, but there *is* an explanation – and impossible as it might sound, it's true." He paused a moment to let the sundry remarks die down. "This man *is* indeed Robert Cartwright, and through a miracle of eighth-cycle technology, which I don't understand, he is alive and well.

"For reasons that will be explained shortly, we don't have a lot of time, so I will provide you with a brief explanation before we move on to why I requested this meeting.

"When Robert and I initially entered the installation at the Grand Canyon, the first time, and discovered the Eighth Cycle headquarters, we unknowingly triggered an activation sequence in a part of the facility that was never discovered by us or any of our later teams. This activation sequence 'awoke' three people from the Eighth Cycle who were in a cryonic state they call 'Deep Sleep.'

"They, the Eighth Cycle people, have the technology to put humans in this 'Deep Sleep' for up to one hundred thousand years, awakening them whenever they want. They also have the technology to revive, repair, and restore the dead within twelve hours of death, using a microchip inserted in the brain and some advanced repair and revival techniques.

"This technology is how Robert is alive."

Mindful of his own and Rebecca's reactions and incredulity when Robert 'visited' them in their room a few days ago, JR paused to let what he told them sink in. He understood all too well how impossible it was to come to grips with the entire concept.

Some were silent and motionless, some were silent but shaking their heads, and some were murmuring, "don't believe it," "impossible," "rubbish," "next we'll get a visit from aliens," "JR's playing a prank on us," "a hoax."

JR held his hand up for silence.

"In addition to this 're-animation' technology as they call it, they have the ability to place another person's mind, memories, or whatever you want to call it, into a revived body."

"The hell you say!" shouted Sinclair in the silence that followed.

Stunned expressions around the table gave way to pale faces, blank stares, appalled horror, and chilled distress punctuated by more commentary of shock and disbelief.

JR continued, "Robert was initially implanted with the memory of a soldier from the Eighth Cycle. After a time, because of the information we are going to provide to you momentarily, his Eighth Cycle persona was joined with his original Robert Cartwright memories. It was the first time the Eighth Cycle scientists were able to do so successfully..."

"So, what you're saying is the person we're seeing there," Sam pointed to Robert, "is actually two people. C'mon JR, you can end the joke now. You've had your fun, you had all of us. Let's get serious now. Tell us why we're really here."

"Sam, Daniel, all of you, please listen to us." He pointed to Rebecca, Peter, and himself. "We went through the same ordeal a few days ago when Robert made contact with us. We've been at the canyon site the last few days. What I'm telling you has been verified by the three of us. You *must* listen to me now. We're in trouble, I'm not talking about us only, our civilization, the entire world is on the brink of an unimaginable tragedy, and apart from a handful of people, no one knows about it. That's why Robert has been reanimated so that he could contact us and warn us of the danger that is fast approaching."

Daniel's shoulders dropped. He looked at Nigel for support, but Nigel was clearly still in shock, just staring at Robert.

What else can go wrong? When will we ever have peace and stability? Are we destined to stumble from one crisis to another?

"Not *another* calamity," Roy blurted. "But what's wrong with Robert, can't he talk?"

"Yes, he can. I was about to let him explain." JR nodded to Robert.

Robert stood, and for a moment had to fight down the personality of Tawndo threatening to take over. He needed to communicate with the group, not order them. "Hello everyone, it is good to see you all again. I know most of you and have heard about the rest of you. Let me first put your minds at ease, I *am* real, I am really Robert Cartwright, your friend, and colleague. I *was* killed by John Brideaux, and I *have* been brought back to life by the Eighth Cycle technology that JR spoke about earlier. It is correct that the body you see in front of you hosts two personalities. I know it is an all but impossible concept to understand, and it has not been without its challenges for me, but I'd like to suggest we talk about that later.

"I'm here as Robert Cartwright for one reason, and that's to tell you that the world is in grave danger."

The audience had gone quiet and listened intently as Robert stepped them through the basic history of the conflict between the war-like B'ran and the peaceful

L'gundo, the transformation of The Healer into The Beast that ended the Eighth Cycle, and the information gathered since his reanimation.

"Using links to the twelve global satellite sites, still intact from the days of the Eighth Cycle, I was able to connect to the regional control center at one of our other sites in Tunguska, Russia and access their data storage units.

"I discovered that the B'ran were successful in their takeover of the L'gundo site but were stranded there when the Beast destroyed everyone who was chipped. That was the event that ended the Eighth Cycle.

"The Eighth Cycle scientists knew, as we did, that reanimated beings are incapable of reproduction but that there would be some survivors who were hiding, remaining unchipped and whose descendants would repopulate the planet. They decided, as we did, to enter the Deep Sleep and await the future.

"People who were placed in Deep Sleep, in the last days of the Eighth Cycle at the Tunguska site, about forty-thousand years ago, were awakened in 1908 to a problem with the volcanic gasses used to power the facility and were unable to stop an explosion that severely damaged the facility. Nevertheless, some of them, some B'ran and some L'gundo, survived. The B'ran were in the majority and forced the L'gundo survivors to work for them.

"Over the next forty-five years, while they repaired the facility, Viktor, the B'ran commander, captured and killed people outside the facility and coerced the L'gundo scientists to reanimate them as soldiers. His goal—to create a new powerful race called the Re'an."

"Then, in 1954, the Russians tested a nuclear bomb near the facility that caused a secondary explosion inside, which killed many of them and severely damaged the site again.

"But since then, the Re'an at the Tunguska site have been building an army for the sole purpose of conquering the world.

"According to their records, they have seventeen-hundred active soldiers and another two-thousand in Deep Sleep, which very recently they started waking up and training."

"So, let's say there are four-thousand of them; that's hardly a force that could take over the world," Salome interjected.

Robert held his hand up. "Yes, that doesn't sound like much, does it? But, in addition to the re-animation, over the years they have made astounding enhancements to anatomy, senses, intelligence, strength, endurance, vision, and hearing. They have created super soldiers. The soldiers are equipped with handheld particle-beam weapons that can destroy targets up to two miles or more away. Their weapons can destroy the best armored vehicles and tanks available today. Their larger, long-range weapons can take out targets in the air and on land, even if they're thousands of miles away.

"Ultra-lightweight liquid armor that doesn't restrict movement protects the bodies of these soldiers. It will repel any projectile of Eleventh Cycle technology.

In short, their technology is advanced and beyond the comprehension of Eleventh Cycle scientists. With their weaponry, they can destroy anything any of the militaries of the Eleventh Cycle can throw at them. They could probably take over the world with a thousand of their soldiers or less. Nothing short of a nuclear weapon can stop them.

"I could tell you much more, but I think you've got the

picture. Each of these soldiers is a one-man, unstoppable army, capable of unimaginable death and destruction.

"My friends and I, at the canyon site, Linkola, Korda, and Siasha can't stop them by ourselves. We have the technology, and we understand theirs, but you have the people. We need your help, and you need ours; we need to work together to find a way to stop them."

"If they have all these extraordinary weapons and soldiers, what's holding them back? Why haven't they made their move for world domination yet?" Daniel asked.

"From the data I've been able to collect, I've discovered that their plans are to retake the canyon installation first—it was their Eighth Cycle Head Quarters. Once they have conquered it, I suspect they will attack the US and then the rest of the world.

"I don't know how much time we have, but I can tell you it is counted in days—not weeks—they are mobilizing."

Robert sat down in the petrified silence that followed his presentation.

After a few moments, Daniel cleared his throat. "Why the canyon site? What does it have that the Tunguska site doesn't?"

"As the headquarters site, it is linked to eleven other locations across the globe. In those locations are thousands more B'ran in Deep Sleep awaiting the awakening cycles.

"I believe Viktor also wants the technology of The Healer, or rather 'The Beast' as it has become known."

"That technology has been removed and destroyed," Daniel replied.

"*We* know that. Viktor doesn't. According to what I found in their data banks, they don't know anyone has been to the canyon site. He believes it remains hidden and that you developed your own 'Beast.'"

At this point, Daniel said, "Robert, I'm sure we all have hundreds more questions, I know I have. But if we're facing the dangers of which you told us, and if it's as urgent as you've said, there's no time for all of that. However, before we make any decisions, I'd like to give everyone the opportunity to have their say. For that part, I trust you'd take no offense if I ask you to wait outside?"

Robert nodded. "No problem, maybe one of the guards can show me where I can get something to eat and some coffee in this place?"

Daniel stood and accompanied Robert to the door where he asked one of his security guards to arrange for Robert to be taken to the restaurant.

Raven Rock meeting room

Back in his seat, Daniel said, "The floor is open. I'd say the first thing we'd have to decide is if we believe any of this?"

It quickly became evident there were three groups of thought. The first group rejected the whole thing as some kind of prank played by JR, who was well-known for his practical jokes. Who this man was, who looked and spoke and acted like Robert Cartwright, they could not explain.

It was not surprising to Daniel that the majority of this group consisted of the older Rosslerites, which included the Musketeers.

The second group was ambivalent, they neither believed nor rejected it, Daniel and Sarah found themselves in this group.

The third group consisted mostly of the younger and

more tech-savvy Rosslerites, such as Raj and Roy. They accepted everything and wanted to take action.

Daniel was, however, very surprised to find his ninety-two-year-old grandmother in the latter group.

He had to ask. "Grandma, I am pleasantly surprised to see you have no issues with what you've heard. What was it that convinced you?"

Bess grinned. "Son, I know Robert Cartwright, that man who stood here earlier is him, it was not an imposter. Besides, the way I see it, we don't have much of a choice. If we don't believe him and do nothing, and those people from Russia are real and they take over the world, we would have a lot to be sorry about and nothing we could do about it. But, if we choose to believe him and send some of our people to help him, as he requested, all we stand to lose is a bit of our time."

Daniel smiled. That was his grandma Bess, coolheaded and wise. He looked at Sarah, and the expression on her face told him she'd just joined the third group, and as Daniel's gaze shifted around the table, he found more of them nodding. There was no arguing with Bess's logic.

"It seems Grandma Bess has provided the answer. It's not a matter of *if* we believe this to be true or not, it's just that it's better to be safe than sorry.

"Everyone onboard with that?"

The Rosslerites have dealt with scary and weird situations in the few years of their existence. This was by far the most way-out thing anyone of them had ever heard. But Bess's reasoning was correct, and Daniel's summary thereof, 'better to be safe than sorry', soon had everyone in agreement.

Getting the nod from everyone, Daniel invited suggestions of what to do next.

Raj spoke with unfocused eyes. "I don't know who these people are, but they have to be stopped," he almost whispered.

All eyes focused on Raj. "Raj?" Sam inquired.

Speaking slowly and softly, eyes still unfocused, Raj responded, "These people at the canyon brought Robert back to life and ... loaded another person into him ..." he shivered. "He says the people at the canyon site are friendly. If they are friendly and *can* do this, and this Viktor person is killing people just so he can re-animate them, he has to be stopped. He can't have access to *anything* at the canyon site – who knows what he would do with it."

"I believe Raj is right," Luke stated. "He needs to be stopped, and the sooner the better."

Within minutes, no one seemed to have reservations; they participated as if they were all believers.

"The question is, do we go after him in Tunguska, or wait for him to come to the canyon?" Jack asked.

"I didn't know we'd decided to get involved in this at all yet," Sinclair said, bringing the meeting back to focus.

Roy looked at him incredulously. "Sinclair! We can't let them just take over the planet!"

"Who said anything about letting them take over anything? I just want to know if we are united in the decision to do something about this threat."

A chorus of "hell yes," and "damn straight," followed Sinclair's statement.

Roy stood up, drawing everyone's attention. "We're gonna nano-nuke 'em!"

Luke said, "Roy, I'm starting to worry just a little bit about you and those nano-nukes—you're awfully enthusiastic about using them."

Salome started a 'nan-no-nuke, nan-no-nuke' chant,

and the others joined in and then started laughing as Luke shook his head in defeat. The comic relief eased the terror of Robert's report and the tension from moments before, even Raj looked more himself.

Daniel let the laughter and teasing flow around him for a bit and then nodded to Sinclair who understood, that as leader of the Rossler Foundation, he was now in charge of the meeting.

Chapter Twenty-Two

Yemelyanovo airport near Krasnoyarsk, Russia

Six thousand miles away, in a green valley surrounded by rolling hills covered in a dense pine forest, Deszik watched from a third level window as the Airbus A320 descended against the backdrop of a beautiful blue sky and touched down on the single runway. His eyes followed it as it taxied to the gate, and the boarding ramp rolled out to meet it, sealing gently against the side of the aircraft.

Shifting his gaze, he scanned the terminal for Petya. He'd found it odd that Viktor paired him with Petya on this mission when he was normally paired with Ama'ru. Something wasn't right, and his internal sense of wariness had been triggered.

Watch your back.

Petya's flight wouldn't leave for several hours yet, and he had no reason to be at the airport this early, but Deszik couldn't shake the feeling that he would show up early.

Getting up, he meandered across the terminal and peered out the windows toward the passenger arrival area.

There he is!

Deszik watched as Petya made his way toward the four-story glass atrium entrance to terminal two. Returning to his gate area, Deszik settled into a seat where he would be able to watch the gate-area entrance without Petya being aware of his scrutiny.

Within a few minutes, he watched Petya enter, scan the area, identify him, and then make his way to a seat perfect for observing Deszik covertly. A hard knot formed in Deszik's stomach.

I was right! He is watching me.

"Dekka?" Deszik reached out on their secured communication link. *"Can you still hear me this far away?"*

"Yes. I'm here Deszik."

"Is there a way to modify my chip so I can detect the others when they are near me?"

"I'm not sure, especially over this distance. Why?"

"Petya is following me, and I'm not sure why. I'd like to be able to know when any of the others are near."

"I see. Let me give it some thought and see what I can come up with."

"Thanks, Dekka!"

"You're welcome."

"First boarding call for Aeroflot-Russian Airlines flight 7456 with service to Moscow," the overhead speakers announced.

"That's my flight; I have to go."

"Safe journey."

Deszik moved with a sense of unease as he got up and joined the boarding line. Just before he stepped into the boarding tunnel and lost sight of him, he noted Petya raising his cell phone to his ear. Thanks to his enhanced hearing – enhanced more than Viktor knew thanks to Dekka, Deszik faintly heard Petya's report.

"Yes, sir, he's boarding now."

While Deszik settled into his seat in the aircraft, Petya made his way to a restaurant and ordered breakfast.

A thousand miles to the northeast, Stonash and Ama'ru arrived separately at the Yakutsk airport. Each aware of the other's presence but acting as strangers, they waited at separate gates. Stonash departed first, Ama'ru an hour later. They would meet again in Flagstaff.

Chapter Twenty-Three

Raven Rock

It was 1:00 a.m. when Robert was called back into the room and told that they'd unanimously decided to help.

Robert nodded and thanked them.

"All right everyone, let's settle down and talk this through. Robert, what exactly do you want us to do?" Sinclair asked.

"We need to keep Viktor and his men out of the canyon site—they can't be allowed access to the technology and connections there."

"Do you want us to raise an army? Move the equipment? Or something else? What do you have in mind?"

Sinclair didn't wait for Robert's answer. He looked at Daniel and said, "I suppose you won't authorize a few bombers to go over to Russia and nuke the Tunguska site?"

Daniel shivered when he heard that and shook his head. He couldn't tell them how strained the relations with the Russians were and the reasons for it. "Nope, not an option for now. Nor would be the option to bring the Russians into the fold and get them to do the bombing. They might just want to capture the technology for themselves."

"Yep, that's precisely what you can expect from them," Sam commented.

Daniel nodded. "I'm afraid we're on our own."

"Sorry, Robert, please continue," Sinclair said.

"Actually, we hoped your team would have some ideas. We don't have time to raise an army or move the equipment."

"A small force of commandos could engage them in the confines of the canyon, but it doesn't sound as if they would stand much of a chance," Jack said.

Roy started to say something, but Sinclair cut him off. "Roy, we don't want to nuke the Grand Canyon if we can keep from it."

Frowning at Sinclair, Roy replied, "Believe it or not, that wasn't what I was thinking," and he turned to Robert. "You said Viktor and these soldiers are all re-animated people with chips in their heads. Right?"

Nodding, Robert agreed, "That's right."

"Do you have access to their technology and medical records through their database?"

Robert nodded.

"Then I suggest we let them in and find a way to kill them using their chips against them. If the Beast could kill through a chip, why can't we?"

"The chips that were tied to the Beast had a specific design with a trigger to kill that could be activated. We have to find out if these chips have the same feature," Rebecca said.

"They wouldn't necessarily need a 'trigger', just a vulnerability," Roy responded. "Isn't that right, Raj?"

Raj, deep in thought, nodded. "That's true, and maybe we could relocate the headquarters to another part of the facility or canyon to hide it from the soldiers and leave it looking like it's still operational. Then we could kill them when we know how to do it."

"There are some hidden tunnels and areas within the canyon," Robert said. "It is possible that could work. I suggest we contact my colleagues at the canyon and bring them into this discussion."

"Let's bring them in then," Sinclair agreed.

Within moments, the life-like holographic images of the three canyon dwellers appeared in the meeting room at Raven Rock and the war room in the Rabbit Hole, and Robert introduced them.

"Linkola, Korda, Siasha, it is a great pleasure to meet you," Daniel said. "I only wish this were in person."

"I'm sure there will be time for that in the future, Mister President," Linkola said. "In the meantime, since you've contacted us, I assume an agreement has been reached for us to work together against the Re'an."

"Correct. I will turn this discussion back to Sinclair who is head of the Rossler Foundation and who will be in charge of this effort."

"Thank you," Sinclair said. "It is nice to meet you three! This is Roy, our resident nano-technology expert." He motioned to Roy and Raj to stand up. "And this is Raj, our computer expert, and Information Technology guru. I'll let them bring you up to speed on what we have been discussing."

Roy took the lead, giving them a quick summary of the discussion leading up to contacting them.

Linkola thought for a moment as Roy's summary drew to a close. "I think there is a very good chance that a vulnerability could be found in the chip. Nothing is ever perfect. I would be happy to assist you in researching that. However, we must remember that all of us, here at the canyon, also have a chip implanted, so we must find something different about theirs, or a way to shield us."

Roy hadn't thought that far ahead. "Good point."

"What do you think about moving the headquarters?" Raj asked.

"I believe Tawndo will be better able to answer that question."

"Tawndo?"

"Forgive me, the man you know as Robert."

All eyes turned to Robert. "The name of the B'ran officer who also inhabits my mind," he said by way of simple explanation. "Linkola, I have already suggested that perhaps we could relocate it to another part of the facility. Do you know if Viktor, or his people, would know about that secret lab of yours?"

"I doubt it. Knowledge of its existence and use was restricted to a few of our top scientists. It requires a special implant under the skin to be able to access it."

"Then I suggest we augment the equipment there with whatever we need to move the headquarters control programming to the lab. That way it can remain hidden and secure," Robert offered.

"Sounds good," Linkola agreed.

With that settled, Sinclair took the lead again. "Raj, how many people and what equipment do you need to make this happen—and quickly?"

Sinclair waited, amused at the myriad of expressions that crossed Raj's face while he considered the question. "I think between, Roy, Robert, one or two of you, and me, we might be able to do it. As for equipment, I'd have to think about that for a while longer."

"I can help too," Korda said.

"Great!" Raj acknowledged. "Let's just add Max to the team then—that should do it." Max Ellis, a former Marine buddy of Daniel's had joined the Rossler team early on and proved to be an excellent asset. The fact that he was also a medic *and* knew his way around a computer added to his value on field teams.

"Sinclair, I think it would be wise to have some trained soldiers on site with them—just in case."

"I agree, Jack. Good thinking! Would you put a team together?"

"Sure. I'd like to take six with me. Do you mind if I include some Tectus members?"

"Who do you have in mind?"

Jack had been one of Sam's CIA Special Agents after serving as a Delta Force member and had been instrumental in bringing Brideaux down. "Raj already called Max, but he can double as our team medic. I think Doug and Mark would be good," he said referring to the two former Marines.

"They've been more than helpful and very professional," Sinclair said. "I have no objection. Comments?" he invited.

"Sounds reasonable," Sam said.

Nigel nodded and everyone else gave similar expressions of agreement.

"Okay," Sinclair said. "Who else do you have in mind?"

"Dennis, Eric, Mouse, and Kerinski," Jack named the Tectus members without hesitation.

Dennis McMahon, leader of Tectus, was a former Navy Seal and had been another asset in bringing Brideaux down. He had arranged contact with Tectus cells worldwide to assist the Rosslers in gaining surveillance, safe houses, and various other supports as needed. As second-in-command of Tectus, Eric Winchester, previously a Marine Colonel had assisted as well.

Mouse, a former Marine Special Forces officer, and Kerinski, a computer technologist had come to the attention of the Foundation during the recent overthrow of General Hayden. The two worked well together and had been responsible for deploying the spy equipment in the White House and for capturing most of Hayden's top advisors.

"That sounds like a top-notch team, Jack. Approved," Sinclair said. "Get your teams and equipment together, guys. I'm sending Owen out with the Metroliner—you're going to need more space than you've got in the Baron."

"That's perfect, Sinclair," JR said. "I was going to ask about that."

"How soon can you be ready to go?"

Raj looked at his watch, it was 4:15 a.m. "I can be ready in twenty-four hours."

"Me too," Jack nodded.

Bremerton, Washington State

It was just after midnight when the Enterprise maneuvered quietly into her home port in Bremerton, Washington State.

Despite the late hour, seventy-two sailors disembarked, all carried duffels for shore leave. The Captain released them in groups of twelve, and in the darkness, no one noticed that two sailors in each group seemed slightly out of place; they were too old, wore slightly ill-fitting uniforms, lacked military posture, and wore expressions of dull resignation.

"I'm glad to be rid of those scumbags," Captain Wiekelan said to his Second-in-command. "I would like to have keel-hauled them."

"You and the rest of the crew with you, sir."

"Where are the buses?"

"Arriving now, sir," the officer responded, pointing to headlights turning a corner a quarter mile away.

"Good. The sooner those prisoners are under lock and key, the better."

They watched in silence as the two Navy buses pulled up close to the gangway and the sailors boarded. The boarding seemed to be random, but Wiekelan knew that the security officers made sure the prisoners got on board the bus going to Fort Lewis while the rest of the sailors boarded the one heading to town and three days of R&R.

Chapter Twenty-Four

Various airports in the USA

Two jets touched down, minutes apart, in the southwest of the desert—one in Phoenix, and one in Las Vegas—a man on each plane disembarked with the rest of the passengers, deliberately losing himself in the crowd.

Deszik quickly made his way to the car rental counter and was soon entering the busy traffic leaving Sky Harbor Airport. The freeways around Phoenix were clogged with heavy traffic, and the planned two-hour drive was quickly extending toward the three-hour mark. The sky was a beautiful blue the likes of which he had never seen before, but the bright sun gave him a headache.

Gazing across the flat landscape he saw nothing but buildings, palm trees, roads, and vehicles for miles in every direction. It was a relief when he reached the outskirts of Phoenix and headed north up Interstate 17 toward Flagstaff. The change from city to rolling hills of cactus covered desert to the climbing foothills covered in brush, helped him relax, and soon he was enjoying the drive. He planned to use the two days to survey the canyon area before the others arrived.

He was just entering the pine-filled forest south of Flagstaff when Dekka contacted him.

"Deszik?"

"Yes, Dekka, I am here!" he answered with excitement at the discovery that their communication was still working at this great distance.

"I'm sending an encoded signal that will alter your chip to detect the identity codes of the others. It will alert you of their presence, identity, and general location when they are within a quarter mile, updating every fifteen seconds. If they are within 100 yards, you will be able to follow their movements in real time.

"It's not much, but it's the best I could do on short notice."

"It's more than I expected, Dekka, thank you!" he said sincerely.

In Las Vegas, 300 miles away, Petya boarded an interterminal shuttle at the McCarran International Airport, disembarking at the terminal exit where he caught a taxi and headed south toward Henderson Executive Airport. Interstate 215 was busy and, like Deszik, everywhere Petya looked was concrete, buildings, and traffic.

He had learned on the flight to Las Vegas that he could charter a plane at the General Aviation Airport that would fly him direct to Grand Canyon Airport. He intended to arrive well before Deszik, scout the area, and prepare to keep Deszik under surveillance until the others arrived. Not knowing exactly what Viktor suspected of Deszik, Petya wanted to be ready for anything.

Once airborne again, in the little Cessna, Petya was

amazed at the barren landscape that passed below him—varying shades of tan marked the desert terrain. Sparsely located shades of darker brown and green showed where mountains of exposed rock and vegetation rose above their desolate surroundings.

Stonash deplaned to much the same desert scenery at the Albuquerque Sunport, rented a car, and headed west with an eight-hour drive ahead of him.

After crossing the Rio Grande and passing over the surrounding *bosque*, the word the locals used to describe the woods that grow along a riverbank, on Interstate 40, he watched Sandia Mountain disappear from view as he crested Nine-mile Hill. Except for a few towns along the way, the rest of the trip was filled with sandy scenery broken by reddish hewed desert rock and the occasional glimpse of mountains far in the distance to the north.

Ama'ru arrived to a slightly different view. With flat plains to the east he looked out on emptiness, but to the west was the city of Denver and beyond that, the Rocky Mountains.

The plan was to travel south out of Denver down Interstate 25 and turn west onto Interstate 40 at Albuquerque. However, he studied maps on the flight to Denver and realized it would take him less than an hour longer to cut through part of the Rocky Mountains. Thus, he decided to head southwest out of Denver on Highway 285 and work his way through Cortez and on over to Grand Canyon National Park.

He was thrilled with the drive through the rocky crags and evergreen forest. Beautiful streams flowed through narrow ravines, cascading over rocks and fallen trees, and slowed to gently transverse peaceful, grass-filled meadows.

Termination

After the beautiful and uplifting scenery of the mountains, he felt a little tired and drained as he descended into Cortez and continued into the miles of empty desert before reaching the Grand Canyon.

Chapter Twenty-Five

En route to the Eighth Cycle Site, Grand Canyon, USA

A thin glow was just appearing in the eastern sky as the Metroliner rolled down the runway, picking up speed. Owen adjusted the controls; the nose of the sleek plane lifted, and the wings caught air sending a familiar thrill through his body as the plane became airborne.

"I expected you to have half-a-ton of equipment," Jack said to Raj.

"Only if you want to be the pack mule to carry it in," Raj grinned.

"Oh, yeah, there is that. When you put it that way, I'm glad to see you *don't* have half-a-ton of equipment!"

"Mostly, I just need data transfer capabilities which won't be a problem with the links we have." Turning to Robert, Raj continued, "I've made arrangements to transfer all the data and programs to storage drives at the Rabbit Hole as a backup safety measure."

A look Raj couldn't read, but could have been anger,

passed across Robert's face. He really wasn't quite the same 'Robert' Raj remembered.

Raj added, "... just in case ... that is, if you are all in agreement with that."

Nodding, Robert responded stiffly, "I will speak with Linkola about it."

"Good, good," Raj said nervously and returned to the conversation with Jack. "So ... um ... we each have two hard drives in our backpacks, some cabling, and other stuff to expedite the transfer."

Jack raised an eyebrow at the exchange between Robert and Raj, but responded simply, "Sounds like you have everything under control." *That guy is going to bear watching.*

The cabin was silent except for the sound of the engines for a few minutes until Jack spoke again.

"You guys who have been to the site before – why don't you give me and the rest of the new team members a rundown? What it's like, what we should expect, what the terrain is like, etcetera? We'll need to plan a defense, and the more we know going in, the better."

"You need to hang on to your skivvies when you enter the damn place," JR quipped.

Robert laughed out loud.

The others looked around in bemused curiosity—it was the first time they'd seen him in a friendly mood. Then they related their first adventure to the canyon site and shared their experiences, reactions, and thoughts about the place.

Soon Raj joined in helping to tell the story, and then Max, Doug, and Mark added what they had found upon their arrival.

This opened a discussion on strategic planning and ideas that carried on for several hours until they arrived in

Page, Arizona where a helicopter was waiting to transport them to the drop-off point near the canyon site.

Eighth Cycle Site, Grand Canyon, USA

"All right everyone," Robert said. "We'll go down in two groups. Owen, Raj, and Max, you come with me. I'll need three more. Rebecca, you bring the second group."

"Come on," JR beckoned, addressing Dennis and Jack who had never visited the site before, "and hang on to your… hats… for a wild ride!"

The doors to the elevator closed, sealing the six of them inside. Outside the doors, the members of the second group heard a faint yelp of surprise echo through the small side canyon as one or more of the newcomers experienced the heart-stopping drop of the descent into the facility.

Doug and Mark grinned at each other, remembering the unforgettable experience of their first trip down.

"Are you sure this thing is safe?" Eric asked while Mouse and Kerinski looked apprehensively at one another.

"It's one hell of a ride," Mark quipped.

Rebecca smiled at the others. "Don't worry, it's safe. It's just… startling the first time you experience it."

A few minutes later, they all stepped a little shakily from the elevator.

"Startling my ass!" Kerinski exclaimed. "I might need a change of underwear!"

"Pansy," Mouse teased his friend and received a shaky but playful shove in return.

"I saw you tense up, tough guy, so don't 'pansy' me!"

They all quickly sobered up for introductions to Linkola, Korda, and Siasha who were waiting to welcome them.

After the general introductions, Korda took Jack and his security team on a tour of the facility to help them get their bearings and start strategizing their defense tactics.

Robert and Linkola led Raj and Max into the hidden lab while Siasha beckoned JR and Rebecca to follow her.

"I wanted to show you something before all the work gets started," she explained, opening the entrance to their oasis.

JR and Rebecca were stunned by the beautiful valley the Eighth cyclers had created in the cave. They stood in awe looking over the crystal-clear lake surrounded by trees and shrubs, and a grassy slope leading down to its banks. With the simulated blue sky, the sun shining on their faces, and the gentle simulated breeze brushing their hair, they quickly accepted the illusion that they were outside.

"This is so beautiful – stunning," Rebecca breathed.

"Yes. We come here to relax. You and your team are welcome to come here as well. Please let them know that they are free to use it at any time."

"We will and thank you!" JR said appreciatively.

"Good! Now, let's get back and see if they have figured out how we're going to rearrange this place!" Siasha replied.

"If I know Raj," JR replied, "he will already have it half-way disassembled by the time we get there!"

Raj didn't have anything torn apart yet, but the three guys were just leaving the lab following behind Robert like ducklings after their mother. Without thinking, they had arranged themselves in order by height with the shortest at the back of the line.

Rebecca laughed at the sight.

JR elbowed her and asked them, "Where are you guys off to?"

"I've seen what I need to know about the lab, now we're going to the command center to see what we're going to have to do there," Raj replied.

Taking Rebecca by the hand, JR fell in line with the 'ducklings,' with Siasha bringing up the rear.

When they crossed the threshold into the command center, Raj gave a low whistle. "This is some place."

Chapter Twenty-Six

Eighth Cycle Site, Grand Canyon, USA

While the technical team was busy examining the guts of the technology that ran the facility, the security team, with Owen tagging along, enjoyed Korda's grand tour.

Beginning in the large room that JR and Robert had initially visited, he let them all try the self-adjusting chair and tables to which each had a unique but delighted reaction. "This room, our Great Hall, was where our young people studied and learned—our version of school.

"But it's huge!" Kerinski said. "They weren't all the same age, were they? How'd you teach different levels?"

Korda smiled. "The children's interests and abilities were identified when they were very young, and each child's curriculum was tailored for their unique talents and interests. The lessons were then made available through the computer, and each child studied at their own pace from one of the stations in this room. Teachers were available in person or via holographic communications for the children to approach with questions."

Kerinski frowned. "So, the children were set on a path when they were little and that was it? They had no choice later if they decided to do or try something else?"

"Not at all." Korda grinned. "No offense, but you 11th cyclers are very narrow-minded. We discovered long ago that children learn best when they are interested in what they are learning. Forcing them to learn things they don't want to know slows them down and is a waste of time. What are your children interested in at the age of three?"

Everyone laughed and Kerinski shrugged. "Playing?"

"Exactly!" Korda replied. "As were ours. We started our children at the age of three, playing the games they enjoyed the most…"

"Three!" Kerinski interrupted appalled. "You sent your kids to school at the age of *three?*"

"Yes, but you misunderstand. Their school was *play*. For instance, children that enjoyed building with blocks were encouraged to build anything they wanted. As the children aged, different kinds of building materials were introduced to allow their creativity to grow. Through their interest, they learned to read and write because they had to identify products and learn how to obtain them. They learned math by learning how to count and then estimate how many more items they would need, and later to calculate angles, weights, and volumes.

"This facility, for example, is the result of a young boy who enjoyed exploring caves and wanted to live underground.

"As a su'tien, or student as you call them, he became friends with another young man that enjoyed designing family dwellings. Together they branched out, one learning about the earth structure and materials, the other about building, and together they used their knowledge to design and build this facility when they became adults.

"This also required them to bring in others with knowledge in areas such as electronics, computer technology, environments, horticulture, power systems, waste disposal, craftsmanship, and all the areas that would form an operational system.

"The su'tien learned much more than just their own subject of interest, they also learned to work as a team. Most of them stayed in their field of interest, but the young man who was interested in caves and living underground became one of our best *kolte'ahr*, most knowledgeable, planet scientists. The one that wanted to design family dwellings did so, but he branched out into larger structures and became one of our most well-known designers of buildings and family dwellings that complimented the surroundings of the environment they were in.

"Some children stayed with their initial interest of choice, others branched out into other related fields, and many of them mastered a variety of fields. All learning was encouraged."

The group was dumbfounded at the simplicity of the solution of a subject that troubled the modern world's school systems whose curriculums were set and soon outdated.

While they marveled at the concept, Korda moved through the room, showing them the three long hallways that housed the dormitories. "These were for the older children when they were ready to leave their parents' homes, usually by the age of twelve or thirteen. There are large labs at the end of each hall where the children gained hands-on practice with what they learned on the computer in the great hall.

"This," he said stopping at the next hallway, "is the recreation wing where the children participated in physical exercise and games."

The next hallway he identified as the kitchen and laundry areas. "Serving one another was also taught to our children. All the children took turns working in the kitchen and laundry. They learned that serving is a requirement of life, for without it, one is hungry and unclean."

"What does that mean?" Kerinski asked. "It sounds like if they didn't participate, they didn't eat or have clean clothes."

"Precisely," Korda replied grinning. "Any child that refused to serve was denied meals and access to the laundry —in our way of life, laundry includes personal hygiene as well."

"You let them starve?"

"No, they were denied meals, but they could choose to take a nutritional supplement instead of serving."

"That doesn't sound too bad."

Korda smiled. "In our culture, nutritional supplements were not enhanced with flavorings to make them palatable. The supplement was a powder of vitamins and protein, nothing else."

Wrinkling her nose, Kerinski responded, "Yuck."

"Exactly. A few of those meals, and most of them decided that serving wasn't such a bad idea."

As the group moved through the multi-level facility, they continued to be amazed by what they saw.

Each level had the same layout – a large central room with five spokes leading off it. Below the educational level, as Korda referred to it, was the family level. The large room seemed to be a general gathering area, and Korda explained that it was also used as an art museum with statues, sculptures, paintings, pictures, and various other forms of art. All of which still exist as it had been removed and hidden in an unknown location in the last days of the Eighth Cycle. Four of the spokes held apartments suitable for family dwellings with the fifth spoke being used purely for recreation.

Below the family level, they were surprised to find a farming level. "Before the end of our cycle, these gardens were rich with fruit and vegetables. All our sustenance came from here," Korda said sadly. "The gardens were beautiful."

"So, you are vegetarians?" Eric asked.

"No, not at all," Korda responded. "Come this way," and he led them toward one of the spokes.

Upon entering, they saw the hallway consisted of glass walls containing a large amount of water behind them. "I believe you would call these aquariums," Korda said. "This side," he said indicating the wall to the left, "contained freshwater fish, and the other, ocean fish. In the last third of this hallway we kept an aviary for meat and eggs."

"Amazing," Jack commented. "All this underground."

On the next level down, Korda showed them an entire hospital, medical facility, and research laboratory. Underneath that, was the room with all the Eighth Cycle deep sleep pods. Here was the secret lab of Linkola and Korda.

Returning to the lift, Korda took them up past the educational level. "This is where our soldiers stayed," he said stepping out of the lift. "Their housing, training, medical, and recreational facilities were all on this level. Between this level and the educational level below is a storage level. Above this level are the Command Center and other military type facilities.

Stepping back into the lift, they ascended one level and joined the others in the Command Center.

"How's it going?" Jack asked.

"Fairly well," Raj replied. "Max and Robert are setting up the portable drives to transfer the data. I'm going to have to write a program that simulates the satellite input so that the B'ran think they are seeing real data even though the actual transmission will be re-routed to the hidden lab."

Looking a little bemused at how easy Raj made it sound, Jake replied, "Sure – sounds simple enough when you explain it like that."

"Well, maybe not *simple*, but doable." Raj laughed. "If you all have some time, Robert and I could use some help moving some equipment from storage to the lab."

"Sure!" Jake replied. "Then we need to raid your spyder and fly collection and place them in strategic locations."

"All right Robert, we've got our help!" Raj exclaimed.

"Great!" Robert replied standing up. "These are set to run on their own, and we can set up downstairs while they transfer the data."

Following him out the door, they all headed for the storage level and the required equipment.

Washington, D.C.

Daniel stood fidgeting behind the curtain waiting to take the stage for his address to the nation. His mind was occupied with the new danger that was hanging like a dark cloud over the world but which only a few knew about. Suddenly he felt tired, emotionally spent. It felt like a never-ending saga since discovering the existence of the Tenth Cycle. Every time they have discovered an earlier cycle the world had been thrown into turmoil and people died in their thousands and millions.

"I hate giving speeches," he said with a deep sigh.

"But you do it all the time, and I've never seen it bother you before," Sarah objected, straightening his tie.

"No, I talk in front of people—that's easy—I just … talk … to them. This is different, it's a speech."

"Daniel, this is no different. You're just talking to the people, telling them what you know. It's only different in your mind," she reassured him.

"It feels different, Sarah." He shrugged and sighed again. "I'm afraid this new threat we're facing is not going to end well for us. Not you and me but our civilization."

A somber look had settled on Sarah's face. "It's worrying, but so far God has protected us and always provided an outcome. He will not forsake us."

He leaned forward and kissed her lightly on the cheek. "You're right. You're my pillar of strength. I don't know what I'd do without you."

Sarah smiled and whispered, "I love you Daniel."

The Chief of Staff approached Daniel. "We're ready, Mister President."

With a final kiss, Daniel parted from Sarah, stepped from behind the curtain, and took his place at the podium in the East Room of the White House.

The blinding strobe of flashing cameras and stage lighting disoriented Daniel for an instant as he raised his right hand to greet and silence the clapping, cheering crowd.

The news that night carried clips of Daniel's speech, showing cheering crowds as he relayed an update on the Nation's progress toward stabilization. From fully operational military bases to the completely restored power grid, to FEMA shelters, food trucks, and the lifting of Martial Law in many areas, the news was good, the nation was recovering.

When he announced the re-establishment of the pledge of allegiance, footage showed a few of his military advisors with tears shining in their eyes.

Watching the broadcast from the White House with Sarah, Daniel's eyes stung too, just as they had during the speech.

The story concluded with Daniel's final words. "In short, the government has been living and operating for its own benefit at the expense of the people, and it is time for control of this country to be returned to the people for their benefit."

"That was some ending," Sarah said grinning.

Twenty-three hundred miles away, in the western third of the United States, three men stepped off a plane in the desert heat. Moving through the deplaning crowd they went their separate ways knowing they would meet again in Flagstaff.

Throughout the evening, nine more of the Re'an soldiers would arrive in three other towns and make their way to Flagstaff as well.

"Salome told me that the phone meeting with the world leaders went well," Sarah said.

Daniel smiled. "Yes, I think it did go fairly well. We have

a good start on some valuable trade negotiations, and I think they will be amenable to the prisoner situation."

"What have you decided to do about that?"

"We still have to get a couple of countries to agree, but we plan on holding the trials in Washington near where the prisoners are being held.

"The problem is the punishment if they are found guilty. Under normal circumstances, the ICC would carry out the punishment, but in this case, the represented countries are out for blood. Most of them have the death penalty and want it applied immediately—and they want to be the ones to apply it, their way."

"Can't we allow them to carry out punishment here?"

"Some of their forms of execution are rather... gruesome."

"And Brideaux's methods weren't?"

"I see your point."

Chapter Twenty-Seven

Eighth Cycle Site, Grand Canyon, USA

While Jack and the two Tectus leaders went through the facility again, strategically placing Roy's technology-enhanced spyders and spy flies, Jack and the others were helping Robert move and rearrange equipment between the command center and the lab.

After working with Raj and getting to know him a little better, Linkola had agreed that transferring the command center data to the Rabbit Hole as a backup in case of the destruction of the canyon site was a good idea.

Raj set up the transfer and contacted his computer-tech helper at the Rabbit Hole. "Okay, Stuart, I'm ready to send."

"Everything is set here, ready to receive," Stuart confirmed.

"Transmitting."

A brief pause was followed by, "It's coming through now."

"Ok. There're many terabytes of data here; it's going to take some time. Just let it run, and I'll check back with you in about six hours to see where we are."

"Sounds good, I'll talk to you later."

Raj checked the transmission equipment one more time before turning back to Linkola. "Let's see if we can give the others a hand."

When they arrived in the lab, the team was just bringing in the last of the items that had been requested from storage, and Max and Robert had the place torn apart.

Linkola looked in horror and dismay at the mess. "Oh, no!" he groaned.

Siasha stepped to his side, patting his shoulder. "It will be ok, Linkola. It's worse than it looks."

Linkola did a double take. "What?"

She laughed. "I'm just kidding. This is mostly boxes and storage crates of equipment. Once it's installed and the packing is removed it will look as good as new, I promise. They haven't touched any of the lab equipment."

"We're going to install everything over on this wall," Robert said indicating the one bare wall in the room.

"Where are all the charts that were on that wall?"

"I carefully took them down, rolled them up, and stored them in the room over there, Linkola," Siasha said and pointed to a room adjacent to the lab. Linkola still looked unconvinced and seemed stunned. "Why don't we leave them to it and go to the kitchen for a cup of tea?" she suggested.

He nodded, and together they left the lab.

"I just wasn't expecting it to be so... messy," they all heard him say in bewilderment as the door closed behind him.

The men got back to work, and Rebecca took Kerinski

by the arm saying, "Let's see what we can find to fix for dinner!"

"But I can help with the computers," Kerinski objected.

"I know you can, and would rather, but there are plenty of them, and I need some help."

Looking back into the lab she locked eyes with Korda, saw him blush, and then motion for her to go with Rebecca. With a grin, she shrugged and said, "Sure, okay."

Re'an headquarters Tunguska, Russia

Viktor's gaze moved over the group of well-disciplined soldiers gathered in the small hall. They were of varying ages, backgrounds, skin-tone, hair and eye color, but they all had several things in common; every one of them was a Re'an soldier with an enhanced body and senses, strong, highly trained, and known for fierceness in battle; each had earned the respect not only of their team members, but of Viktor. They were one hundred and twenty-five of his best team leaders.

Pacing slowly before them, he began the instructions for the coming deployment to the United States.

"Twenty-five of America's largest cities have been identified as targets for this operation." He moved to a large map displayed on the wall in front of them where twenty-five red circles across the image of the United States glowed clearly.

"We've divided the country into five regions and selected the target cities from those regions." Identifying each city with a laser pointer as he called them out, he worked his way across the map from left to right.

"On the west coast our targets are Seattle, Portland, San Francisco, Los Angeles, and we have included Phoenix.

"In the Mid-West will be Denver, Albuquerque, Houston, Dallas, and Kansas City.

"Up North, as they call it, are Minneapolis, Milwaukee, Detroit, Chicago, Indianapolis, and Columbus.

"Boston, New York City, Philadelphia, Baltimore, and Washington, D.C. comprise the Northeast region with Memphis, Charlotte, Jacksonville, and Atlanta being the Southeast.

"Each of you will be taking a team of five other members to one of these cities; there will be five teams assigned to each city. With your special training and sophisticated weaponry, you should be more than adequate for the task at hand.

"I'm holding another one hundred and twenty-five teams here so that once America has been subdued, they can be deployed to other countries to perform the same task.

"Starting tomorrow, teams will depart for their designated city. By the end of the week, you will all be on site and ready to implement our plans once the canyon team has seized control of our central command center.

"When Deszik is in command of the canyon site, your teams will begin a systematic purge of the cities. Those unfit for reanimation will be killed—they will be of no use to us. As soon as we can set up reanimation facilities, those in their prime will become soldiers.

"The young will be breeding stock until they reach their prime, then they will become soldiers. The children will be allowed to grow until they come of age and can be of use.

"If there are no questions, this meeting is adjourned."

As the determined-looking soldiers filed out past him,

Viktor grinned thinking of the glory to come when he ruled the world.

Eighth Cycle Site, Grand Canyon, USA

Robert walked quietly down the dimly lit corridor toward the sanctuary. It had been a very long day, and he was tired, yet sleep eluded him.

The conversion of the lab had been successful. All the necessary equipment was installed and powered. To Linkola's relief, the 'mess' had been cleared away.

Tomorrow they would begin transferring all the operational programs and data from the computers in the command center to the control center, as Raj had started calling the secret lab. They would also transfer the satellite transmission and monitoring systems.

It will be another busy day.

Reaching the door to the Sanctuary, he opened it and stepped inside. The imitation moon, reflecting the lunar cycle on the outside, was full tonight, its light shimmering serenely off the still water of the lake.

Walking to his favorite spot, he sat down beneath the tree stretching his legs out in front of him, leaning back to relax and think. He'd barely crossed his ankles in front of him when he saw the figure walking along the shore. He tensed.

Siasha!

The crux of his problem. Siasha. The woman Tawndo loved with every fiber of his being. Robert felt his body react to her just as if he were Tawndo, but his mind was his own. Wasn't it?

Do I have a responsibility to Tawndo?
No!
The man hi-jacked my body!
I... am... Robert!

At the same time, he had to admit that as Robert he liked Siasha. She was kind, considerate, intelligent, fun to be around, and very beautiful. He could fall for her.

But she belongs to another man!

If she did come to me, would it be me or Tawndo that she was responding to?

Pulling his knees up, he wrapped his arms around them and rested his head on his knees.

It is all so confusing... so frustrating!

Walking along the shore, Siasha had seen Robert enter and move to Tawndo's favorite place.

Tawndo! How can I live without you?

Oh, how she missed him. She'd learned to accept him in Robert's body, but now Robert was back, keeping Tawndo tightly under control, and she hated him for it.

No, that wasn't exactly true. At times she liked Robert, found him intriguing and fun. But every so often he would say or do something or exhibit a mannerism that was so like Tawndo, and the longing for the man she loved would flare, stirring the feelings of hatred for Robert.

She left the Sanctuary without looking back, returning to her quarters, and fell asleep, cheeks and pillow wet with tears.

While Roy lay awake in his bunk, wondering if there was a way to interfere with the Re'an soldier's chips, ten members of Victor's canyon team arrived at their designated airports and started on their journey to Flagstaff.

Deciding he would seek out Robert the next morning and ask for data on the Re'an, Roy turned over and went to sleep at last.

Chapter Twenty-Eight

Eighth Cycle Site, Grand Canyon, USA

Despite a sleepless night, Robert was already hard at work in the command center early the next morning, removing evidence of tampering and generally cleaning the area up, when Roy found him.

Raj, having arrived a few minutes ahead of Roy, was busy checking the data transfer equipment.

"Good morning, Robert!" Roy greeted. "Sleep well?"

Not particularly. "Good morning. Yeah, I slept great!" he lied.

"Hey, Raj!"

Deep in concentration, Raj simply waved.

Looking back to Robert, Roy continued, "I was thinking last night about how we can stop the Re'an, and I'm wondering if you have any data on their physiology, the microchip, and how they interact?"

Robert paused, and Roy saw Raj's head come up at the question.

"Actually, yes," Robert replied. "I have all the files from the L'gundo site in Tunguska. You'll have to sort through them, though. I haven't the time and don't know what you'll need anyway."

"He'll need the medical and technology files specifically related to the re-animation process and the chip. I can help him with that," Raj offered.

"You're busy—and needed —to work on this command center relocation," Robert reminded brusquely.

"It won't take long to write a simple search parameter program for him, and then he can work on his own," Raj assured.

"That would be great!" Roy grinned. "Robert?"

Reluctantly, Robert nodded his approval and went back to work. "I'll make the information available to you when you're ready."

"Why don't we all meet in the new control center in thirty minutes?" Raj suggested.

The others agreed, and he returned to finish what he was doing.

Realizing he could use help with the research, Roy brought Rebecca, Linkola, and Siasha with him to the meeting in the lab. The three had readily agreed to help him, and they were all eager to get started.

Robert made the data files available to Raj who created a new file folder on the hard drive and set a pre-loaded program to run.

Raising his eyebrows, Robert inquired, "What is that and where did it come from?"

Grinning proudly, Raj explained. "It's a search program I wrote for the Eighth Cycle library when we were dissecting that nasty chip of Brideaux's—had a feeling it might come in handy and brought it with me.

"I loaded it yesterday in case we needed it. After I finished with the satellite transmission review earlier, I modified it for Roy's needs. It's ready to go!"

Roy whistled appreciatively, and Robert managed to look both impressed and irritated at the same time. He wasn't happy that Raj could penetrate and manipulate the command computer so easily.

"All the relevant data will feed into this folder," he said indicating the new folder to Roy.

"Great! How long will it take?" Roy asked.

"About... five minutes... and you should be good to go."

"Excellent!"

"I assume you gentlemen will be continuing to work in this part of the lab throughout the day," Linkola inquired.

Robert nodded. "On and off, yes."

"Why don't the four of us work in my office? It's big enough, we can bring some portable computers, and we'll be out of the way there," Linkola added.

"Sounds like a plan," Rebecca agreed.

As the four followed Linkola to his office, picking up laptops on the way, Roy looked over his shoulder back at Raj. "Thanks! I owe you one!"

"Find a way to stop these guys and we'll be even!" he replied. "Let me know if you need anything else!"

"Will do!"

Jack entered the lab in time to hear the last bit of the exchange between Roy and Raj. "What are you two up to now?" he inquired.

Raj explained while Robert continued to work on transferring the satellite link to the lab.

At the conclusion of Raj's summary, Jack turned to

Robert. "It might be helpful to know what Viktor and his soldiers are up to right now. Can you find out?"

Robert turned from the display panel he was adjusting to face Jack. "I'm not sure I can obtain that information without tipping them off to my presence in their systems. So far, I've only been accessing information stored in their backup systems, I haven't been in their live system."

Raj interjected, "Maybe I can help."

"Okay, between the two of us, maybe we could sneak in," Robert replied. "Let's give it a try."

With Jack looking over their shoulders, the two got to work hacking into the L'gundo's live system.

Minutes later, Raj exclaimed jubilantly, "We're in!"

"Are they aware of us?" Robert asked, concerned.

Double-checking a few items on the computer screen, Raj replied, "No, I don't think so. Now, you're familiar with their system, where do I need to go?"

"See if they have a file called *World Conquest Plans*," Jack wise cracked.

"Yeah right," Raj retorted.

Robert looked at Jack momentarily, thoughtfully, before speaking. "Try '*World Ruler*'," he suggested.

Shrugging, Raj entered the search and was instantly rewarded with a hit. He looked at Robert, impressed. "Wow! How did you come up with that?"

"Tawndo knows Viktor very well and finds his tactics and methods… predictable. Open the file; let's see what he's up to," Robert said.

"One moment, it's encrypted and flagged to notify him of unauthorized access."

Within minutes, Raj had safe access to the file and said, "Here we go."

Information filled the screen at his touch of the 'enter'

button: weapons specifications, battle tactics, files on individual soldiers, unit orders, deployments, and travel documents.

A warning flashed on the screen. "Shit!" Raj exclaimed.

"What?" Jack asked, alarmed.

"Viktor has another flag set," Raj replied, typing furiously on the keyboard. "I've got fifteen seconds to get out before it triggers an alarm and he becomes aware of our intrusion!" The screen went blank just as he finished speaking.

"The screen is blank! Did you do that? Did you get out in time?" Robert asked, anxiously.

"Yes, with a second to spare," Raj replied flopping back in his chair and blowing air between his lips with puffed cheeks.

"That was close… too close," Jack said.

"Can you get back in again?" Robert wanted to know. "We need that information."

"Yeah, I can," Raj replied. "But I don't know if it would do any good. Even if I do, fifteen seconds isn't enough time to download that much information."

"We don't need all of it. Tawndo is only interested in three files: deployments, travel documents, and unit orders – in that priority. Can you get those?"

"I can try," Raj said preparing to access the system again.

The three of them held their breath as the files were downloading and sighed with relief when it completed after ten seconds. Raj exited with three seconds to spare.

"All right let's take a look at the data and see what has Tawndo all riled up," Robert directed.

It took mere moments of reviewing the deployment file to understand Tawndo's agitation.

"My God!" Jack blurted in a voice mixed with awe and anxiety. "They're here! They're already in the States."

Robert nodded. "Yes, this is what Tawndo feared."

"I need to get in touch with Daniel immediately," Jack said. "Please contact JR, Dennis, and Eric. Let them know I need them on the surface immediately," he added on his way out the door.

On the surface outside the Eighth Cycle Site, Grand Canyon, USA

Jack barely had time to settle himself on a rock and place the call to Daniel on his mirror phone, when the three men stepped from the elevator.

"What's up? What's so urgent?" JR asked.

Holding his hand up for silence, Jack said, "I'm calling Daniel. I'll put him on speaker, then I don't have to say it twice."

When Daniel answered, Jack appraised him of who was present before saying, "I'd like to put you on speaker phone so everyone can hear this discussion. Is that okay?"

"Sure, go ahead. This sounds important."

Pressing the button to engage the speaker, Jack got down to business. "Raj and Robert were able to break into Viktor's live system and track down some information about his plans that you need to be aware of.

"Viktor has already deployed his troops to America..."

"What?" Daniel exclaimed. "How many? Where? When?"

"He has twenty-four of his soldiers, four teams of six each, heading for us here in the canyon and seven-hundred-fifty dispersing throughout twenty-five U. S. cities across the country."

"Do we know which cities?"

"Yes, I'll have Raj send you the relevant information shortly. In the meantime, Roy and some of the others have already started reviewing the re-animation process and chip technology to see if they can find a way to stop these soldiers."

"That's good. Will your team be ready for them at the canyon?"

"Yes sir, we're nearly finished with the change in command locations, and our surveillance insects are already in place."

"Good work. Keep me posted. And may God protect us all."

"Raj will send you a secure file named 'Jack Daniels'– watch for it."

The other three men stared at Jack, stunned.

"We have work to do, gentlemen," Jack said heading for the elevator. "JR give Robert's team a hand in finishing up their work and then have them join Roy and the others. Guys," he said turning to Dennis and Eric, "let's get the rest of the team together; we're out of time."

Chapter Twenty-Nine

Eighth Cycle Site, Grand Canyon, USA

Hours later, the sixteen people at the canyon site gathered around a large table in the dining area for a working dinner.

"We're expecting company in the next day or two," Jack started. "According to the information in Viktor's files, they should be arriving in Flagstaff tomorrow and making their way into the canyon the next day.

"My team is as ready as we can be. We've placed some spyders a half mile up the canyon where they will be able to detect and monitor activity.

"Roy's holographic emitters are in place concealing the elevator entrance, but we aren't sure that will fool these guys with their enhanced vision. The elevator is temporarily shut down, but again, it's probably just a delaying tactic.

"Robert has removed access to the command center and pod room levels from the main elevator system—they now require a special code to access. He's also providing all of us with Eighth Cycle hand weapons and making some additional, more powerful weapons, available to my team.

"Again, with the enhancements made to these 'super-soldiers', we don't know how effective the weapons will be." He paused briefly. "Raj, what's the status of the Command Center relocation?"

Clearing his throat, Raj replied, "The relocation is complete. All systems have been transferred to the Lab Control Center and are functioning perfectly.

"The data transfer to the Rabbit Hole completed without any problems. Stuart has set everything up in my lab, control can be transferred there with the push of a button."

"Excellent work, Raj, well done!" Jack praised. "What about the command center here? What will happen if and when they gain access to it?"

"I've put old data on the computers and satellite processors. Everything will appear to be functioning normally. If they try to manipulate it – I've programmed a couple of surprises for them."

"Surprises?"

"Yeah," Raj said with an evil grin.

JR laughed. "Don't ask, Jack. The last person who tried to hijack a computer of Raj's got screens showing 'the middle finger', boxes of toilet paper, and enough movies and games to last for years."

Jack's eyebrows raised and he grinned. "I want to hear that story sometime!"

"Yeah, well, there is that, but this time if they persist in messing with it, the satellites will appear to blow-up," Raj informed them.

"That'll work!" Jack said. "Roy, how is the research going?"

"We've discovered that the microchips have a unique identifying code—it's similar to the Media Access Control, MAC, number on all our modern-day electronic hardware.

"If we could match the soldiers with their chips, we could locate them and track their movements. We're still working on that. We are also investigating the possibility that Raj could hack into the chips which might give us the opportunity to re-program them or just shut them down."

"Keep at it, Roy. It sounds like any of those options could give us the upper hand," Jack said.

Roy nodded.

Raj, do you think you could download those individual soldier files?" Jack asked.

"I'm already on it, but I'm limited to fifteen seconds access at a time."

"What?"

Raj explained the access limitation and added thoughtfully, "But I might be able to circumvent that second flag. I'm going to give it a try."

As Raj got up to leave, Roy joined him announcing, "I'm coming with you!"

"Me too," agreed Robert.

A few minutes later, the three were gathered at a computer station in the lab. Raj made a few adjustments to the settings on the computer, accessed the L'gundo system, made a few more adjustments, then said, "Here we go."

Taking a deep, calming breath, Raj punched the 'enter' key. As soon as the file displayed, he accessed it and started the download.

"Damn," he said when the forty-five seconds remaining dialog box appeared.

Robert tensed. "Can you get it? Were you able to get around the flag?"

"We'll know in about five seconds."

When the five seconds passed, Roy looked at Raj. "Well?"

"Well, what?" Raj asked.

"Did you get around the flag?"

"It would appear so." Raj was smiling.

The download completed without further incident, and Raj exited the system, transferring the file to Roy's research folder. "There you go, it's all yours!"

Roy took over the seat as Raj got up. At that moment an ear-piercing alarm sounded, making them all jump.

"What's that?" Roy yelled with his hands over his ears.

Robert had already stepped up to an equipment panel and tapped a blinking light. "Hi-temp alarm in server room two." Entering a code on the keyboard shut the audible alarm off, but the light continued to flash.

"I was wondering about that," Raj said. "We added quite a bit of equipment in there. What can we do to cool it down? We don't want the servers shutting down just when we need them the most."

"Linkola isn't using most of the equipment in the lab. I can shut it down instead of leaving it on standby—that should help reduce the load. We can add some auxiliary power to help the cooling units run more efficiently as well," Robert replied.

"Good idea. I'll help," Raj said.

As Robert began making the adjustments, Raj noticed Roy standing frozen in place.

"Roy? Are you all right?"

Roy waved his hand for silence. Robert and Raj exchanged puzzled glances.

After a moment, Roy asked. "Don't these soldiers have enhanced hearing?"

"Yes, they do," Robert replied. "Why?"

"I remember reading somewhere about how high-pitched sounds can affect the brain. Maybe these chips would be vulnerable to certain sound frequencies," Roy said.

They all looked at one another. "It's... possible," Raj stated slowly.

Roy laughed.

"What's so funny?" Raj asked.

"You," Roy answered. "I can almost see the smoke coming out your ears, your mind is working so fast."

Looking to Robert, Raj asked, "What do you think? Are these chips likely to be vulnerable to high-pitched sound waves?"

"I'm not sure. I hadn't considered the possibility. How would you test it?"

Roy and Raj looked at each other. "I think we need to investigate those chips further," Roy said. "Do you need our help here, Robert?"

"No, I'm nearly done."

Raj and Roy left to return to Linkola's lab and review the data again.

In the wee hours of the morning, they emerged, along with Linkola and Rebecca who had joined them. They looked exhausted but were all grinning broadly.

"Let's get a few hours of sleep before we join the others for breakfast and give them the good news!" Rebecca suggested.

Chapter Thirty

The Rabbit Hole

The seven men, Ben Rossler, John Mendenhall, Luke Clarke, Nigel Harper, Ryan Clarke, Sam Lewis, and Sinclair O'Reilly, known as the Musketeers, sat comfortably in their lair at the Rabbit Hole. Daniel had apprised them of Jack's report about the Re'an soldiers heading for the twenty-five US cities, and they had been deep in discussion about the matter since dinner.

"I really don't see how else this can be handled… somewhat quietly," Luke said.

"I don't either," Nigel added. "I think Tectus is our best bet, but I'm concerned about civilians getting hurt or killed in the process.

"If what Robert reported is true, we have a war on our hands, and it will be the civilians who suffer as a result."

"Agreed," Ryan said. "But what other option do we have?"

"Why don't we give our boys at the canyon site a little

time to see what they come up with?" Sinclair asked. "I don't have to remind you how inventive those youngsters can be. They have access to that chip information – I'm sure they'll find something—they always have in the past."

"I'm hoping they do," Luke said. "But in the meantime, we need to be working on a solution, as well."

Speaking for the first time in a while, Sam added, "I think it's likely that our tech geniuses will have a solution for us, but they still may need our help. It seems logical to mobilize Tectus and put teams in those cities on alert and have them ready to move at a moment's notice when the time comes."

Swirling the last of the liquid in his glass, Sinclair agreed. "Sam, I think you should let Daniel know what we'd like to do and see if he can get Dennis and Eric on board with the idea. Any orders to Tectus will have to come from them."

"Will do," Sam agreed and dialed Daniel's mirror phone. Within minutes, he had Daniel's undivided attention.

"What we want to do is activate the Tectus groups in each of the twenty-five cities and have them prepared to intercept and possibly take out these soldiers."

"Wait a minute," Daniel said. "Let me get Dennis and Eric on this call."

Sam waited and was soon repeating the Musketeers idea to Dennis and Eric.

"You want to do what?" exclaimed Dennis. "Are you out of your minds? That's going to take a lot of manpower… and time… I don't think we have the time to set up an operation like that!"

"We may not. All we want to do is start organizing it."

"I'm not sending my people out on a half-baked plan."

"We're not asking you to. Let me give you the details before you decide," Sam said.

Dennis and Eric looked at one another for a moment before Eric gave a slight nod and Dennis agreed to let Sam continue.

"We're hoping that the tech team at the canyon will be able to come up with a plan, but in the meantime, we want to have our own plan in place as a backup.

"After considering the situation, we think that a small team of top operators should be assigned to surveillance on the Re'an – two or three Tectus people per team in each city.

"You all have a supply of Roy's spyflys; once the Re'an teams are located, the technology could be used to supply the information we need. From that, it may be possible to put together a plan to safely intercept and stop the soldiers.

"We aren't asking them to go out and battle these super soldiers; just to watch, listen, and report."

Dennis chewed the corner of his bottom lip deep in thought.

"It could work," Eric said.

"Mmmh. Yes, it could," Dennis agreed. "Let me talk this over with the rest of the leadership team and get back to you tomorrow."

"Sounds good," Sam replied.

Chapter Thirty-One

Re'an headquarters Tunguska, Russia

Viktor entered the fissure maintenance chamber, just as Telestra exited Fissure One.

"I didn't realize it was time for fissure maintenance," he stated.

"Not maintenance – repair," she replied smoothly despite her racing heart. *Does he suspect?* She had been setting the equipment in the fissures in preparation for the upcoming failure she had planned.

"Is there a problem?" he asked with concern.

"Not anymore. One of the valve seals we replaced last month must have been bad. I just put a new one in it; should be fine now. I'll watch it closely for a few days to make sure there isn't some other problem though."

"I see. I'm glad you're so diligent," he said looking around the cavern. The place unnerved him; had ever since he first entered it during the earthquakes that nearly destroyed the site.

Termination

"What brings you down here?"

"Does a man need a reason to see his wife?"

"Most men don't. You, on the other hand, always have an ulterior motive. What do you want?"

He sighed slightly and began to walk around the room with a smile. "Oh, I thought you'd be interested in knowing that all the members of the canyon team have arrived safely and will be meeting in Flagstaff tomorrow, before descending into the Grand Canyon. They should reach the canyon facility in the next forty-eight hours.

"And the twenty-five US Team Three members are on their way with Team Four already at the airports and waiting. Then there will just be one more team to deploy, and all will be in place."

Telestra frowned. "You mean you've come here to gloat and rub my nose in the fact that you've turned my son into a warrior and sent him into harm's way?"

"Well, I thought you'd want to know how *our* son performs on his first major assignment."

"He is *my* son, not yours, and you are taking great pleasure in trying to torment me with the knowledge that you have sent him into a dangerous situation. *My* son can take care of himself and will be fine."

"I hope for *his* sake you are right."

"What's that supposed to mean?"

Viktor stopped and turned to face her. "It means that the instant he hesitates or fails to do his duty, in this matter, he *will* be killed."

In spite of her determination not to be provoked, she felt her muscles tense, her heart rate increase, and a flush spread over her body.

Turning away from him to place her protective suit and equipment back in the locker she replied, "Then I have nothing to worry about; Deszik will follow the orders he's been given. What reason would he have to do otherwise?"

Viktor stepped next to her, grabbed her by the arm, and spun her around. "I don't know. Why don't *you* tell me?"

"Tell you what?"

"What Deszik is up to."

"What I know is that my son has been sent half-way across the globe, to the Grand Canyon of the United States, to take control of the Eighth Cycle facility so that some egotistical maniac can use it to take control of the world."

Viktor flushed with anger and slapped her, knocking her to the ground. "He is up to something and will not come back alive," he said as he stormed from the room.

Rising slowly, shaking with rage and fear, Telestra got to her feet, took a deep breath, and reached in her mind for Deszik.

Deszik! Can you hear me?

Yes, mother.

Are you all right?

I am safe.

Be careful. Viktor has sent someone along to kill you if you hesitate or fail to complete your mission.

I know, mother – or at least I suspected. Thank you for confirming that for me. I have already asked Dekka to give me some enhancements to help me keep track of everyone in the group.

Dekka knows and didn't tell me?

No. He only knows that I suspect I am being followed. I asked him not to tell you because I wasn't sure, and I didn't want you to worry.

He still should have told me.

Don't blame him, mother. It was my doing.

Termination

Just be careful, Deszik. I love you.
I will, mother. I love you too.

Chapter Thirty-Two

Washington, D.C.

Daniel's mind was pre-occupied with the new looming danger, when he stepped into the Cabinet room and took his place at the giant table. He would've preferred not to have the meeting at all, but there was no way out of it. A few members came in behind him and found their seats.

"Good morning, everyone," he greeted in a friendly tone trying, as best he could, to hide the nervous tension that'd besieged him the last few days. "I'd like to keep this meeting short, if possible, so please keep your updates as brief as you can.

"Secretary Simms, why don't you start us off?"

Clearing his throat, Bill Simms began. "The fighting along the European borders has diminished…"

Daniel listened to the Cabinet members one by one, each report bringing proof that the Nation was continuing to recover.

Peter Scott, Secretary of Treasury, brought the most

hopeful report. The Nation's financial system was close to being re-established, as was a plan for a free nation-wide insurance program.

Forty-five minutes later, as the other Cabinet members filed out, Daniel motioned to Salome to join him in the Oval Office.

Once they were seated, he placed a call to Jack and Dennis at the canyon and conferenced in the Musketeers at the Rabbit Hole.

"All right, Dennis, what have you come up with?" Daniel asked without preamble.

"After discussing this among the Tectus leaders in the twenty-five cities where the Re'an are headed, we've decided that a surveillance mission is warranted and, with Roy's gadgets, shouldn't be too hard to implement."

"That is good news!" Sam said excitedly.

"Take it easy, Sam," Dennis warned. "We're agreeing to surveillance, nothing else at this time. We will watch, listen, and report. That's all we're willing and able to do for now."

"That's good enough for us," Sam said.

"What's your plan, and will it work separately or in conjunction with what is happening at the canyon?" Daniel asked.

"For that, I will have to let Raj and Roy bring you up to speed."

Roy started. "With the help of Rebecca and the canyon dwellers, Raj and I were able to identify and test the possibility of shutting down the chips using ultra-high frequency sound.

"It works at short range, the closer to the source, the more effective it will be. The problem is that we must be sure the Eighth Cycle canyon dwellers are shielded from it, since they also have chips; we don't want to harm them.

"We're going to set up a two-phase process. All the rooms where the soldiers are likely to be will have a device set to emit a high-frequency sound that will knock them unconscious, then we can deal with them. The Eighth Cycle people who are with us, if accidentally exposed, will obviously also be rendered unconscious but won't be hurt.

"To eliminate the Re'an soldiers, I've programmed nanites that will be injected into them while unconscious. These nanites will make their way to the chip and set off a localized ultra-high frequency sound that will destroy it.

"Fantastic!" Daniel exclaimed. "You and Raj never cease to amaze us."

Sam laughed. "Yes, I think the world should be glad those two are on the good side!"

"Agreed," Daniel said. Seeing the grin on Salome's face, he added, "Judging from the proud smile on your wife's face, Roy, she agrees as well!"

Roy blushed but looked pleased as Raj gave him a friendly punch on the shoulder.

After a thoughtful pause, Sam inquired, "I understand how your plan will work in the confines of the canyon site, but how will this work for the teams of Re'an soldiers descending upon our cities?"

Rebecca responded, "There we have a bit more of a challenge, Sam. The first problem is that Roy's ultra-high frequency sound is only effective up to five or so yards. Unless we can herd those soldiers into small spaces and get close enough to them, it won't work. The second problem is, if we manage to overcome the distance issue and kill them, we'd have to remove and destroy those chips. I guess I don't have to spell out the danger we'd find ourselves in if those chips are discovered during autopsies and someone reverse engineered them."

"Oh," Sam replied.

The rest of the audience nodded as they grasped the dilemma Rebecca alluded to.

"I've been working on a way to interfere with the chips' signal," Raj said. "I'm hoping it may be possible to take control of the chips and order the Re'an to go to a specific place, or maybe even return to Tunguska."

"Keep working on it, Raj," Daniel encouraged. "I'm sure you can find a way!"

Chapter Thirty-Three

Flagstaff, Arizona, USA

Deszik had altered his plans for investigating the canyon, prior to the arrival of the others. Instead of spending his days along the canyon rim as a tourist, he remained at the Flagstaff hotel until the proximity monitor in his chip announced Petya's arrival.

Although Petya's room was in another part of the hotel, it was within the one-hundred-yard radius that allowed Deszik to monitor his movements, in real time, in accordance with Dekka's promise.

Deszik had made a point of moving about the hotel, nearby restaurants, and shops. Although Deszik never actually saw him, Petya was like a constant shadow remaining at a distance of about sixty or seventy yards, no matter where he went.

After returning to his room early on the evening he arrived in Flagstaff, Deszik contacted Dekka requesting to be advised when Petya was asleep.

He showered and dressed in the black clothing of the soldiers, filled his backpack, and watched TV for an hour before turning out the lights and lying down on the bed.

At 11:30 that night, Dekka let him know that Petya had been asleep for nearly thirty minutes.

Deszik opened his window, removed the screen, and climbed out onto the landing outside his room. He closed the window and carefully replaced the screen, noting the tiny sensor on his door that would no doubt have awakened Petya had he opened it.

Walking away from the hotel and around the block, his chip confirmed that Petya was not moving, so he caught a cab to the airport where he rented another car and headed toward the town of Tusayan. From there, he took one of the fire roads to Rowe Well Road, a dirt-road back entrance to Grand Canyon Village, and followed it to just before the Kennels.

Pulling off the road behind some high desert brush, he hid the car as best he could and set out on foot for the canyon rim, which he reached in less than fifteen minutes. Another hour would see him at the bottom of the canyon and well away from the reservation. With care, Petya wouldn't find him until he was ready to be found, and then it would only be a matter of time until no one would ever find Petya.

Grand Canyon, USA

By the time the rest of the team arrived, several days later, Deszik was ready and met them at the rendezvous coordinates, at dusk.

He noticed Petya's frown but ignored it. The man was obviously frustrated at his lack of ability to locate him after he disappeared. This pleased Deszik as it showed his caution had been well worth the trouble.

"We have twelve hours to reach the facility," he addressed the group. "With our enhanced vision, we shouldn't have any trouble traveling at speed in the dark, even in here."

Dividing the group of twenty-four soldiers into their respective teams and instructing them to move in two's, they spread out slightly and headed for the facility.

As Deszik expected, Petya stayed close to him, and over the next two hours, he carefully worked his way along the river toward an area he'd discovered the day before.

Approaching the banks of the mighty Colorado they came to a division in the path. Ordering Petya to check the fork that went toward the riverbank, Deszik continued on the path they had been following.

Petya paused with a frown, suspicious. "Wait!" he shouted. "Why do you want me to check the riverbank? I think I'd rather check the trail ahead."

Deszik shrugged. He started down the path to the riverbank.

"Hang on a minute," Petya said. "What are you up to?"

Looking at Petya with a puzzled expression, Deszik responded, "What's your problem?"

"Why do you want *me* to take the path we were on instead of checking the riverbank?"

"Petya, make up your mind. I asked you to check the riverbank, and you said you'd rather check the path ahead. I agreed, and now you've got a problem with *that*. I don't care which path you check. Both have to be checked. Which one is it?"

"I don't trust you."

"Trust me? What's trust got to do with anything? We're supposed to check the canyon as we move toward the site. One of us has to check the main trail while the other checks by the river."

Petya made no reply, he just glowered at Deszik.

"Fine, you don't trust me. The feeling is mutual. You choose which path you want to check. We need to get moving so we can meet up with the others on time."

Petya responded after a long silence. "I'll check the riverbank path."

Deszik moved swiftly ahead and stepped off the trail at the marker he'd placed the day before. He climbed up into a cleft in the rocks, moving along it to where he could see the river trail.

As he got into position, he saw Petya come around a slight curve in the trail. Five steps later, he stepped on the false bridge Deszik had created and fell into a deep, water-filled hole between the rocks.

Deszik ran to the site, already knowing what he would find. As he reached the side, he caught the last glimpse of Petya being sucked down into the churning water.

The river undercut the bank along this section and had created an inescapable underground channel that, according to the tracking devices he has released there, rejoined the main river nearly four miles downstream. The trip took hours; even with his enhanced body, Petya wouldn't be able to hold his breath that long. Besides, there were many narrow places that his body might not be able to pass through. It was likely his body would never complete the transit in one piece.

Dekka? Mother?

I'm here, son.

What is it, Deszik? Are you all right?

I am safe. I wanted to let you know that Petya has been eliminated and is no longer a threat.

I'm glad you're safe, my son. Thank you for letting me know.

I am sorry that was necessary, but I'm glad you are all right.

Thank you. I'll be in touch again, soon.

He lay on the ground and placed his arms in the hole where Petya had fallen, then dragged them across the sharp rocks along the edge, cutting the backs and undersides of his arms. Satisfied that he was safe from his executioner, Deszik continued to the rendezvous.

"Where is Petya?" one of his team members asked.

"He slipped into a chasm along the river. I tried to get him out, but he was sucked under. I waited nearly half an hour and looked along the banks downstream, but he never resurfaced."

"What happened to your arms?"

Deszik looked at the dried blood and shrugged. "The rocks along the edge of the hole were sharp and Petya's weight, while I was trying to drag him out, caused the rocks to cut into me."

The others looked at him for a moment before he saw acceptance in their eyes.

"Come on, it's an hour before sun-up, and we still have to reach the site."

Chapter Thirty-Four

Eighth Cycle Site, Grand Canyon, USA

Robert was alone in the new control room, watching as the dark clothed figures made their way through the canyon. They'd triggered the first proximity sensor a few minutes ago. It was time to wake the others and get Jack's team outside.

As he was standing to leave the room, Jack walked in.

"Good morning, Robert! What are you doing up so early?"

"Keeping an eye on the Re'an soldiers," he said pointing to the monitors. "They arrived at the first monitoring station a few minutes ago. I was just about to wake everyone."

Jack stepped up to the station where Robert had been sitting. "They're a little earlier than I expected. I'll keep watch while you wake the others."

Robert nodded and left the room. As he made his way

toward the rooms where the others slept, he pondered the news reports he'd been monitoring the night before.

In recent days, seismic monitoring stations in Anchorage, Alaska were recording a substantial increase in submarine earthquake activity along the Aleutian Trench in the North Pacific. Additionally, several of the volcanoes along the Aleutian Island chain were showing suspicious activity - earthquakes, deformation—or swelling, and increasing levels of sulfur dioxide in the steam they released. The volcanoes Kanaga, Bogoslof, Cleveland, and Pavlof were growing restless.

The fact that a helicopter had been sent out to measure sulfur dioxide levels told the geologist in Robert that scientists were concerned.

Time will tell.

After waking the others, they all gathered in the new control room. "Roy, do you have the high-frequency sound devices set up in all major areas as planned?" Jack asked.

"Yes, I'm still working on the nanites, though. I need at least another day to have them all ready," Roy answered. "As soon as they're done, I've modified a few spyders for several areas on each level to deliver the nanites."

"Good. The sooner you can have them ready, the better!"

"Jack," Robert said. "I think it would be wise to have someone here to greet the soldiers. I suspect they might know there are people here and finding no one might make them suspicious."

Linkola nodded. "He's right. Korda and I should be here to greet them."

"I was actually thinking of myself," Robert said wryly.

"I'm sure you were, but your skills are needed elsewhere. Korda and I will meet them."

"I will join you," Siasha said.

"Why should we risk you as well?" Korda protested.

Pointing to one of the monitors, Siasha replied, "This man here – he… has a slight resemblance to my sister's son. I'm not sure it's him, but if it is, and there is trouble, I might be able to intercede through him."

"Are you sure you want to put yourself in that position?" Robert asked. "If it isn't him, or he turns out to be not the person you remember, it could be dangerous."

"I'll take the risk."

"Ok," Jack said. "I suggest you let them find you in the farming or family dwelling level. You're not military and aren't supposed to know anything about the control room, so stay away from here."

They agreed.

"At their current speed, we should still have an hour or so before they arrive. Once they get here, we don't know how long it will take them to gain access, or what they are likely to do, so we all need to stay on our toes," Jack said.

"Dennis let's get our teams in place outside. Mouse, you and Kerinski take care of the rest of the foundation team in the new control room as well as keeping your eyes on the Eighth Cycle people here."

"If no one has questions, let's move!" Jack said.

They scattered to their respective assignments.

Chapter Thirty-Five

Eighth Cycle Site, Grand Canyon, USA

Deszik and the other teams made their way along the main trail and carefully picked their way into the side canyon, unaware that they were under the watchful eyes of the Tectus and Rossler Foundation teams.

The teams and monitoring equipment were well hidden, Jack had seen to that. He had conducted drills under different lighting conditions. Wearing night vision goggles, he had moved about the canyon carefully observing the team member locations and equipment placement, until he was sure it was undetectable.

His diligence payed off. The Re'an team members were unaware they were being monitored.

Deszik paused after reaching the side canyon and began scanning the cliff for the entrance.

It took him a while before he finally noticed a holographic distortion in one area and climbed up to investigate.

Reaching through what appeared to be solid rock, he touched the smooth surface of the lift doors.

"Up here!" he called into his throat mic and was soon joined by the rest of the team.

"Viktor didn't say anything about the door being hidden by holographic technology," the youngest of the soldiers observed.

"No, he didn't," Deszik said. "He may have forgotten, didn't know, or we have a surprise waiting inside. We will proceed with caution. Eight of us can descend at a time."

He quickly divided the group into three teams and proceeded to give the orders. "I will take the first team down. Stonash, you follow as soon as the lift returns. Ama'ru, wait two minutes before making your descent; I want to have our own surprise in case we are surprised upon arrival."

The rapid descent caught the Re'an off guard, and those on the Rossler team watching from the new control room laughed at their reactions.

"Watch that first step, boys; it's a doozy!" JR whispered with a grin.

As programmed, the lift stopped at level four, the education facility. The Re'an tumbled out of the lift, quickly took up cover positions, and waited for the second team to arrive.

When team two arrived, they spread out, investigating the central area of the level. With the arrival of the third team, they split up in groups of five, four soldiers to check each of the five hallways, and four to remain holding the central area secure.

It took time, but Deszik had the soldiers check every dorm room in the three hallways. Once he was satisfied the level was clear, he left two soldiers as guards in the central room and took the rest down one level to the gathering room and museum on the fifth level.

"Same drill here," Deszik ordered. "One of you stay behind to guard the central area, the rest of you break into teams of four and check every room."

Shortly after starting the search with his team, Deszik received a message from Ama'ru asking him to come back to the central area as they had captured three prisoners.

Ama'ru reported first. "I found him reading a book in the tenth apartment on the left in hallway one. He says his name is Linkola."

A stern-looking soldier spoke next, shoving a nervous-looking man forward, "This one says his name is Korda."

Deszik's eyes shifted to the third prisoner, a woman, Stonash was tugging forward by her arm. "This one calls herself Siasha."

He identified her immediately as his mother's sister. Without showing any sign of recognition, he turned to speak with Linkola. "How many of you are here?"

"Only the three of us," Linkola answered calmly.

"You better not be lying to me."

"Why are you here?" Linkola asked.

"Do you know who we are?"

Linkola shook his head and said, "No. Should I?"

"We are the Re'an."

"Never heard of you."

"No, I suppose you haven't. We are… a new race, descendants of the B'ran and the L'gundo of the Eighth cycle."

Linkola fixed a look of severe skepticism on his face. "Not possible… unless… well, unless you found a solution to the infertility problem. Did you?"

"In a manner of speaking."

Linkola smirked. "Really? Interesting. I would like..."

"Where is the main control center of this facility?" Deszik interrupted.

"Level one. I'm not sure it's operational. I was up there some time ago and it had power, but I don't know anything about it."

"Aren't you a soldier?"

"No. I'm a scientist, and so is she," he pointed to Siasha. "And Korda is our assistant. None of us are military, or know anything about the command center, other than where it is."

"Take me there," Deszik demanded bluntly.

Choosing four of his men to accompany them, Deszik directed Ama'ru and Stonash to take the remaining soldiers and complete a search of the site.

As they rode the lift to level one, he reached out to Dekka.

Dekka?

No answer.

Dekka!

What! Sorry, I was asleep.

I've found my mother's sister, and I need to know if you can alter her chip so I can speak to her by mind as I do with you and mother.

I'm sorry, Deszik, but I can't. I made many adjustments to our chips over the years to give us this ability. Her chip won't have the supporting systems in place that make this possible.

Ok. I'll find another way.

Good luck!

Deszik inspected the control room carefully.

Everything appears to be operational, yet some of the readings aren't quite right. These controls have been tampered with... but when? Did these three do it? Have the systems degraded over time? Or, was it done at the shut-down of the facility?

He studied Linkola for several minutes, watching the subtle movements of his body and eyes and his breathing.

He knows!

He studied the other two.

They all know!

Clearing his throat, he said to his soldiers, "Everything appears to be in order here. You," he said pointing to three of his men in turn. "Guard these stations. I'll send two more up to help you.

"You," he said speaking to the fourth man, a burly soldier on his team. "Take the woman back to her room and keep her there under guard." He let his eyes rake cruelly down her body, and he brushed his fingers down her cheek and neck.

He saw the look of hurt and loathing cross her face before it sparked with anger, and she slapped him across the face.

I think she has recognized me.

The burly soldier shoved her up against the wall and drew his arm back to strike, but Deszik intervened. "Leave her! We will not hurt the prisoners." He looked around the room at his men. Is that understood?"

"Yes, sir!" They replied in chorus.

Deszik stepped closer to Siasha, and with a grin on his face he again ran his hand across her cheek and neck and said, "But I'll definitely want to have a quiet word with her a bit later."

The soldier grabbed Siasha's arm and led her away.

Korda started toward Deszik, shouting, "You leave her alone!"

Linkola managed to grab Korda by the back of his shirt and pulled him back. Two of the soldiers moved quickly—one punched Korda in the face and the second drew his weapon.

Once again Deszik intervened. "Stop! I told you, we will not hurt them. They're not soldiers. If you must subdue them, you'll do it with the least amount of violence to overcome their aggression."

The angry soldier looked at Korda with disgust before holstering his weapon and returning to his station.

Speaking into his throat mic again, Deszik called six more soldiers to the control room. While he waited, he contacted his mother.

Mother! Your sister is alive!

Siasha lives?

Yes! And I think she recognized me. Do you think she will help us?

If you can convince her of who you are and your truthfulness, I'm sure she will.

How can I convince her quickly?

Tell her about our plans if you must.

I will.

When the six stolid looking soldiers arrived, he set two of them to additional stations in the control room.

"Take these two back to their rooms and keep them there. I want two of you outside their doors at all times," Deszik ordered.

Chapter Thirty-Six

Eighth Cycle Site, Grand Canyon, USA

Deszik followed the group to the family level and then headed to Siasha's room.

The guard opened the door for him as he approached. Once inside, he closed and locked the door behind him, and just as he was about to turn to Siasha, he sensed danger, something hurtling through the air toward his head. He ducked, and the glass vase shattered against the wall where his head was a split second earlier.

Deszik approached Siasha standing in the corner of the room, from where she was screaming insults and throwing any moveable objects within her reach at him. He continued calmly, dodging the flying objects with ease until he caught her and pinned her arms down.

"Stop it!" he hissed. "I'm not going to hurt you! Be quiet."

She fought against his grip, kicking and screaming as he pulled her to the bedroom. Pushing her down on the bed on her back, he straddled her and pinned her down with his legs, covering her mouth with his hand - which she bit, drawing blood.

He removed his hand, shook his head and whispered in an urgent voice, "Stop it! Listen to me. I am not going to hurt you."

But she refused and kept on yelling and wriggling to get away from him.

He grabbed a pillow and forced it over her face. Leaning as close as he dared to her ear he whispered loudly, "Sister of my mother, stop! I promise I will not harm you. I need to talk to you privately and this was the only way I could do it."

Gradually her body grew still beneath him. "I'm going to remove the pillow so we can talk. Please trust me and don't do anything foolish."

Feeling her head nod, he carefully took the pillow away from her face and helped her to sit up.

She moved away from him still wide-eyed with shock and disgust.

"I'm sorry, Siasha. I didn't want to frighten you. Please forgive me."

She remained silent and slowly seemed to calm down and collect herself. She stared at Deszik for a while longer before stuttering, "Is… is… my sister… is… Telestra alive?"

"Yes, she is, and she misses you very much. She can't wait to see you again."

"How… I mean… how could that even be possible?"

"That's why I am here. There might be a way, but we don't have much time. You'll have to work with me."

Siasha didn't respond. It was clear she still didn't trust him. And he couldn't blame her for it.

"Siasha, I'd say from the looks of things in the control room that you knew we were coming. Is that so?"

Getting no answer, he shrugged and continued. "I don't blame you for not trusting me. I know you were part of the Liberty Movement and sent here to spy on the B'ran. Are Linkola and Korda L'gundo sympathizers?"

Still no comment.

"Let me tell you what is happening. Perhaps that will convince you to trust me." He proceeded to summarize Viktor's plans, as well as those of Dekka and his mother.

When he finished, she cautiously approached him, sitting next to him on the bed. "Deszik, I'm so sorry for slapping you."

"Forget about it. Let's talk about what's important now."

"Linkola and Korda are L'gundo sympathizers. They saved my life after I was caught," she started.

"What about the soldier you were… involved with? Is he alive? Is he here, or was he sent to Tunguska with the others?"

"He was here. He was killed, but he has been reanimated - in a manner of speaking. It is a long story…"

Deszik held his hand up to stop her and said, "We can talk about that at another time. For now, the most important thing is to stop Viktor."

"Mother and Dekka have already set their plan into motion at Tunguska, but apart from the twenty-two others with me, Viktor has sent seven-hundred and fifty Re'an soldiers to twenty-five American cities. They're just waiting for word from us, that we have taken over this facility, before they will launch their attacks and take over those cities."

"We know about that as well. We're working on a way to stop them all."

"You must have gained access to Viktor's files at the

Tunguska site then. But the three of you won't be able to stop him."

Siasha hesitated a moment before she said, "There are others."

Deszik nodded slowly. "I see. That's why the control room seems 'off'. They've changed it somehow?"

"Yes. And we've found a way to ...," Her hand flew to her mouth the moment the words had left her mouth.

"What is it?"

"Oh no. Oh no..." Tears welled up in her eyes.

"What is it, Siasha. You *have* to tell me."

"They... they... found a way to kill all of you. I... I... must stop them... before they execute their plan. I need to talk to them to find a way to spare you. Deszik we have to act *now*."

"Wait. I need to know how they're going to do it and when."

Siasha wiped the tears from her eyes and said, "Deszik, I can't tell you that. It is now your turn to trust me."

He stared at her for a long while. A battle was raging in his mind.

She trusted me by telling me about their plans.

She cared enough to tell me that my life is in danger.

But why is she not prepared to give me the details?

Deszik shook his head. "Siasha, I've trusted you, I told you what's going to happen here and in the rest of the country, I told you about Viktor's plans. Why can't you tell me?"

"It would be a betrayal. I won't do it. I already told you more than I should have. All I can say is that I need to talk to the others and explain what your role is and ask them to help me save you."

Deszik saw the look of determination on her face and

knew he wouldn't persuade her to change her mind. He had to accept it and trust that she would manage to keep him alive. "I don't like it, but I have no choice, I will trust you."

"Thank you, Deszik. I want you to tell your men that you are putting me into the deep sleep. Tell them that Linkola will help you do it, he is the only one here that knows how.

"I will ask Linkola to play along with everything. Once inside the pod room, I can contact the others when I'm alone. You'll have to let me cue Linkola in or he might not be willing to help."

"The three of you will be allowed to eat your next meal together. Tell him then."

She nodded.

"After I leave here you will have to treat me as if you hate me as long as the others are around. We must keep up the charade I started. Whatever I say, I won't harm you."

"And whatever cruel thing I might say, I don't mean it," Siasha replied.

"I know. It's good to see you again, Siasha. I have missed you, sister of my mother."

"And it's good to see you too. You've become a fine man, Deszik."

"Thank you. Now, I want you to rip my shirt and attack me."

"What?"

"We have to make this look real. Rip my shirt like you were trying to fight me off; scratch my face."

By the time Deszik knocked for the guard to let him out, he looked a little worse for wear but put a big, satisfied grin on his face and pretended to be tucking his torn shirt back in and fastening his belt.

The guard looked in astonishment at Deszik's torn shirt, bloody cheek and hand, and the grin on his face.

As he stepped through the doorway, a glass shattered against the wall near his head and he heard Siasha screaming, "You filthy pig! I'll kill you if I get the chance!"

"Whew! She's a wild one!" Deszik exclaimed with a wink.

"Yes, sir." The guard replied casually, but Deszik saw the twinkle in his eyes.

"When she has calmed down and cleaned up, please escort her and the other two to get something to eat. Afterward, they are all to be returned to their rooms and kept under guard. I'll be in the control center."

"Yes, sir!"

Chapter Thirty-Seven

Re'an headquarters, Tunguska, Russia

Siasha is alive! Telestra rejoiced.

This is all going to be over soon. Entering the control room, she accessed the fissure monitoring system and activated the program she had written. It would provide false readings, showing a normal pressure status even though they would be building up pressure.

Verifying the program was working properly, she made her way to the fissure access room where she donned the protective gear and entered the first fissure.

Slowly and carefully, she made the adjustments to the control valves and other equipment that would allow the pressure to build up slowly over the next two days. She also sabotaged the valves, so they couldn't be adjusted again in the event the problem was discovered.

Repeating the process in the remaining three fissures took most of the day. By the time she finished, she knew that the days of the Tunguska site were very limited indeed.

Even if the pressure build-up was discovered, the only choice would be to seal the room off and hope the facility survived. The explosion would set them back to square one, just like it did the first time, more than one hundred years ago.

Stopping by the control room again, she checked the monitors to verify that the program was indeed working as expected.

All readings were normal.

Just as they should be.

Dekka?

Here, Telestra.

It is done. The fissure equipment is set. The pressure is building, and the monitoring equipment is altered to ignore it and show normal levels.

Good! I've confirmed that several of those in the pods have died and others continue to deteriorate. I will get word to the others that we will leave in two days.

Very good!

I'm glad to hear about Siasha. I hope we are able to complete our work here successfully and meet her.

Me too!

Chapter Thirty-Eight

Eighth Cycle Site, Grand Canyon, USA

While Deszik's men searched the site for The Beast, Linkola, Korda, and Siasha were having dinner under the watchful eyes of their guards.

Siasha noted that neither of the men looked directly at her, and it took her a few minutes to figure out why.

"You can quit feeling ashamed for me," she whispered. "He didn't hurt me. He *is* my sister's son, and what you think happened didn't. It was a ruse to talk to me where his men couldn't hear."

Linkola looked up in surprise, Korda in relief.

"I don't have time to explain everything now. He is going to announce that he is putting me into the deep sleep, and you have to help him, Linkola."

"I *will* not!" Linkola exploded.

Their three guards looked over and two of them started toward the table.

"Shhh," Siasha tried to quiet him.

Termination

"What's going on over here?" The tallest guard asked.

"I was telling my friends to cooperate with you because your leader threatened to kill all of us if they don't," Siasha lied.

"At least one of you has some brains," He retorted. "You two should listen to her; she's right."

"Tell your leader I won't cooperate. He might as well kill me right now." Linkola exploded.

The guard slapped him with an open hand against the side of the head which sent him sprawling on the floor.

Siasha jumped between the two. "Please! Stop it. Don't hurt him. Just give me a chance to convince them. They *will* cooperate, I promise."

"Very well," the guard said. "But things better remain calm, or I'll be back."

She nodded and reached to help Linkola up without breaking eye contact with the guard.

Linkola sat back down at the table without another word and Siasha spoke to the guard. "See? Calm. Nothing to worry about, just as I promised."

The guard looked them over harshly and walked away, the other one joining him.

"I won't…" Linkola began in a furious whisper.

"Listen," Siasha interrupted with urgency in her voice. "It's another ruse to allow me to hide in the pod room so I can join the others and let them know the plan."

"What plan?" Korda asked quietly.

"The Tunguska site is going to be destroyed."

"When? How?" Linkola asked.

"In a matter of days. I don't have time to explain. Just don't argue when you're asked to put me into the deep sleep. You won't actually have to do it. You'll have to make it look as if you're putting me into the pod. I will hide inside the pod room and when everyone is out, I will contact Tawn... ah... Robert and the others and tell them..."

Before she could explain it all, Deszik appeared. "I hear there was some commotion down here." Looking at Siasha who lowered her head, he said, "Didn't you tell them I'll kill you all if they don't cooperate? I'm surprised; I thought you and your colleagues wanted to live."

She cowered. "Please don't hurt me. I did tell them, and I've explained. They'll cooperate. Won't you guys?"

Linkola and Korda nodded glumly.

"I don't trust you," Deszik said, pointing at Siasha. "I can see you're a troublemaker, and I don't have time for distractions right now." Turning to Linkola he said, "So, I've decided to put her into the deep sleep. You will do that."

"The hell I will!" Linkola responded defiantly.

Deszik and Siasha both looked surprised. It was not the response either of them had expected.

"Excuse me?" Deszik said, "I thought you'd agreed to cooperate?"

Linkola gave him an odd look, as though inviting him to fight. "I won't help you. There is no reason to put her into the deep sleep."

Deszik looked him over for a moment before realizing he was playing the game, trying to make the situation look genuine.

"It's either that or..." he drew his weapon and pointed it at her head. "I kill her, here and now." He paused a moment. "What's it going to be?"

Hanging his head as if in defeat, Linkola said, "Fine, I'll do it. Just don't hurt her."

Deszik laughed cruelly. "You see how easily the weak are manipulated?"

The three guards laughed along with him.

"Come on," he said grabbing Siasha roughly by her arm, hauling her to her feet. "You've had plenty of time to eat. It's time for your nap."

"You don't have to be so rough with her," Korda muttered.

Deszik frowned and said to Korda's guard, "Take him back to his room and keep him under guard."

"You," he said to Linkola's guard. "Come with us." And he headed toward the lift.

Chapter Thirty-Nine

Eighth Cycle Site, Grand Canyon, USA

"What the hell?" Robert exploded as he watched two Re'an soldiers enter the pod chamber with Siasha and Linkola. "Isn't the one on the left the guy Siasha said was her nephew?"

Roy and JR came over and stood beside him, looking at the screen.

"She said she *thought* he might be," Roy corrected. "Maybe he isn't."

"Can we hear what they are saying?" Robert asked.

Raj joined them and flipped a switch on the control panel.

"It will take me a few minutes to prepare the pod," they heard Linkola say.

"Fine," the leader responded. Turning to the other soldier he said, "We'll only be a few minutes. Go to the control room and get an updated report on the search for

The Beast. I'll bring him with me." He jerked his head in Linkola's direction. "Then you can take him back to his quarters."

"Yes, sir," the soldier responded and left.

"This doesn't look right," Roy said.

"What?" Robert asked.

"Look at the settings Linkola is entering in the controls for the pod. He's filling it with liquid already. From the way I understand the process, it's too early for this step."

"You're right. What's he doing?"

"I don't know."

The leader looked around the chamber before looking back at Siasha and holstering his weapon. "All right, it's time to contact your friends; I want to meet them."

Siasha looked shocked; this wasn't part of the agreement. "I thought…"

"We don't have time to argue about it, Siasha, I need to speak with them directly."

"She told him we're here!" JR exclaimed. "Now what?"

"Siasha wouldn't do that without good reason. She is a trained infiltration specialist," Robert replied.

"I think we should talk to him," Roy said.

"What! Why?" JR retorted.

"Because, things aren't adding up," Roy explained. "Why would Linkola make it look like he was putting someone in the pod and then not do it?"

"And why did that one send the other guard away and leave himself outnumbered?" Raj added, deep in thought.

Linkola and Siasha stood looking at one another in silence.

"Well?" Deszik inquired. "Where are they?"

"I'm sure they're confused by what is going on. They

will reveal themselves if they choose to do so," Siasha said. "But this is not what you and I agreed."

"Don't you know where they are?" Deszik asked.

"Of course, I do, but I won't reveal their location."

"Siasha! I'm not the enemy!"

"*I* know that - they don't."

"I don't have time - *we* don't have time for this."

"You have all the time you need," Robert said from behind Deszik, who whirled around to find himself staring at the business end of a 9-millimeter Glock 17 pistol.

Siasha had managed to maneuver Deszik into a position allowing Robert to slip quietly into the pod chamber from the new control room behind him.

Deszik knew the weapon was no match for the weapon he carried, and his body armor would protect him against anything that gun would spit out. The problem was the gun was pointing at his face—an area not protected by his body armor. A bullet from that gun would kill him just as effectively as any of the Re'an weapons.

He assessed his situation. His only option was to try and cover the gap between him and the gunman and disarm him. A quick calculation showed it would take him eight-hundred and fifty-four milliseconds to cover the distance.

Enough time for the man to pull the trigger and kill me.

Slowly he raised his hands. "I'm not going to resist. I think we're on the same side."

"I suggest you don't resist. I know this weapon is archaic compared to yours, but I also know a bullet between the eyes would blow your brains and your chip out—both of which you need to be alive."

Deszik nodded calmly.

Robert indicated to Siasha to take Deszik's weapon from him, which she did.

"So, you think we're on the same side? I highly doubt that," Robert said. "You are a race bent on the conquest of the world."

"I didn't say all of us are on the same side," replied Deszik. "The Re'an are on a mission to take over the world. I, however, and a few other L'gundo back at the Tunguska site, want to stop them."

"Of course, you do, and you expect us to take your word for it," Robert replied sarcastically.

"He's telling the truth," Siasha said softly. "He is my sister's son. He told me about their plan to thwart Viktor's plans. My sister..."

Robert looked at Siasha. "You don't know what that maniac, Viktor, has turned him into since he took over the Tunguska site."

"No, she doesn't," Deszik interrupted. "But I can tell you he has turned me into someone that hates everything to do with him and the Re'an."

Robert kept the gun pointed at Deszik's face and sat down on a nearby bench, motioning for Siasha and Linkola to join him. Sighing, he said, "What's your name?"

Siasha took up introductions. "Robert, this is my sister's son, Deszik. Deszik, this is Robert, he is also Tawndo, my lover from the Eighth Cycle."

Deszik's eyebrows shot up, "What?"

"He has been merged. Tawndo's body was destroyed at the end of the Eighth Cycle. Robert was killed in the Eleventh Cycle during the abduction of the Beast technology. Robert was re-animated as Tawndo, but it became necessary to bring Robert back as well, and the two were merged."

"But that's never been done successfully," exclaimed Deszik.

"He's the first," Siasha said. "I'll tell you about it later, if we all survive this."

"What do you have to tell us, Deszik?" Robert interrupted.

For the next few minutes, Deszik told them all he knew about Dekka and Telestra's plans to destroy the Tunguska site, ending with, "She started the pressure build up early this morning, and some of the soldiers in the pods have already died.

"Now it's your turn. Siasha tells me you plan to kill all the Re'an here and elsewhere in the United States. How?"

Robert paused a moment considering how much information to trust him with.

"We'll use high-frequency sound waves to destroy the chips you and your men carry inside your brains. We're not sure yet about the others in the twenty-five cities."

"I see," Deszik responded in a whisper.

"Are there any other of your soldiers who share your views that we should be aware of?" Robert asked.

"No. I am the only one."

The unexpected sound of the lift coming to a stop caused Robert and Siasha to drop to the floor behind the bench they had been sitting on.

Deszik stood and, followed by Linkola, approached the lift as the doors opened.

"Sir," the young soldier spoke. "We have searched the entire facility. The Beast technology is not here."

"What do you mean it isn't here?" Deszik spoke harshly. "It has to be here somewhere; it couldn't have just gotten up and walked away!"

"I'm sorry, sir, we've searched everywhere."

"Obviously you haven't searched where it is or you would have found it," Deszik snapped. Nodding toward

Linkola, he continued as the three of them stepped back into the lift. "Take him back to his quarters and have him held there under guard."

He saw no sign of Robert or Siasha as the doors closed on the pod room.

Will they spare me or kill me?

Chapter Forty

Eighth Cycle Site, Grand Canyon, USA

A dark figure made its way slowly through the canyon, stealthily moving from rock, to bush, to outcropping, making sure to remain hidden from the figures shrouded in the canyon walls. He had no doubt that they were not his men.

Making his way carefully into the side canyon, his enhanced night vision allowed him to find dusty footprints, which he followed up a slope to exactly what he'd hoped to find, the door to the lift that would take him down into the B'ran facility.

With a last look around him to be sure he remained undetected, he turned to trigger the opening to the lift. As he reached out, a body fell on him from the rock above, forcing him to the ground.

Hidden in the side canyon above the entrance to the facility, Jack had silently watched the man approach with the caution of a stalking cat. When the moment came, he was ready and launched himself from his hiding place in the cliff-face onto the man, knocking him to the ground.

Rolling sideways, the man penned his attacker between himself and the rock face, shoving his elbow behind him into Jack's gut and raising his other arm to remove the arm that was choking him.

He heard the grunt that told him his elbow struck solidly, and in another moment, he was sitting on top of his assailant, twisting his arm behind his back until he heard the snap of breaking bone.

Leaning forward, he ordered the man to be still, just as the rock-face shattered above him. The bullet narrowly missed, scattering dust, dirt, and fragments over him.

A quick shoulder roll placed him behind a rock, and he dragged his opponent in front of him, putting a slight twist on the broken arm for control. "You will help me get to the lift," he said.

The prisoner shook his head, stepped back and performed a perfect shoulder throw, putting the man down hard, back first, on the ground. Any other man would have been stunned long enough for Jack to secure him. The man wasn't even fazed, he regained his feet before the impact fully registered, driving his fist into the left of Jack's jaw.

Stars obscuring his vision, Jack felt his body hit the ground, and a weight dropping on his chest. Jack used his best moves and nearly all his strength to fight the man off, but every attempt was met with a brutal blow from the man's fists.

Jack was a highly trained Special Forces soldier, an expert at hand-to-hand combat, but he soon realized he was outclassed. Whatever tactic and maneuver he tried; this man blocked with ease. With inhuman strength and lightning-fast movements, he was quickly taking Jack apart.

Finally, near the edge of unconsciousness, the man grabbed Jack and his gun, twisted his broken arm painfully behind his back, and using him as a human shield, shoved him to the lift doors and stepped inside.

Jack found himself pinned against the lift wall his body and head throbbing in pain. He tried to free himself but heard another crack followed immediately with more pain in his arm, and then the blessed blackness of oblivion.

The man hoisted his unconscious attacker over his shoulder, peered carefully out the doors of the elevator, and made his way stealthily into the corridor. Moving silently, he rapidly made his way toward the area where he knew the command center was located.

When he was near the door's automatic opening trigger radius, he re-adjusted his hold on the man on his shoulder, leveled the gun, and stepped quickly into the sensor area, through the doorway, and into the command center.

After working through the rooms and areas his soldiers had already examined, Deszik was forced to agree that The Beast was gone and headed toward the command center to contact Viktor and inform him.

Stepping into the command center, Deszik stopped in his tracks when he faced half a dozen weapons pointed directly at him.

"What is the meaning of this?"

"These men are now following *my* commands, not yours, Deszik," said a voice that he thought he would never hear again, from the other side of the room."

A chair slowly spun around, and Petya came into view.

"Surprised to see me, old friend?" Petya asked with a grin.

"Yes! Of course, I am surprised. I thought you were dead!" Deszik responded.

"I might have believed you, except that the men tell me you tried to pull me out, but I slipped from your hands."

"You did," Deszik said. "I tried to save you Petya, don't you remember?"

"No, I don't remember, because it never happened. You tried to kill me!"

"It seems to me you're suffering from memory loss. Can you remember how you fell in that hole in the first place?"

Petya made no reply.

"But if you've made up your mind that I tried to kill you, it won't do me any good to argue with you then, will it?"

"No. It won't."

"So, what now? You think I tried to kill you, The Beast is gone, and our mission has failed."

"*Your* mission has failed," Petya corrected. "I think I'll watch while you try to explain all this to Viktor. But first, tell me what you have found so far."

"Nothing, other than a couple of scientists and their assistant."

"And where are they now?"

Sighing, Deszik answered, "One scientist is in his quarters under guard, so is the assistant. The third one, a woman, I had her put into the deep sleep; she was a trouble-maker."

"I see. Were there any others?"

"I already told you. No."

"What about people outside in the canyon?"

"What people outside? I am not aware of there being

any." He looked around at his men. "Anyone of you aware of people on the outside?" They were shaking their heads.

"Really? How interesting ...," Petya said. He nodded to one of the men who bent down and dragged an unconscious man before them. "How do you explain him then? He was waiting for me at the entrance."

Deszik winced internally as he recognized some of the marks B'ran torture methods left scattered over Jack's body and was relieved to notice that he was still breathing. "Since I've never seen him before, there's nothing I can explain."

"You're lying, Deszik. What are you up to?"

"You were in Viktor's leadership meeting with me when we received our orders for this mission. You know my orders as well as I do, Petya. I see no point in this discussion."

Petya paced the room slowly, considering Deszik, finally coming to a stop when he reached the unconscious man.

"We'll do this my way." He signaled to a burly looking soldier who approached and picked Jack up effortlessly. "Prepare him," Petya ordered.

Turning back to Deszik he said, "We don't know how much of our... interrogation methods these weakling humans can withstand. We thought he was as good as dead when we finished last time. You can watch and see how much longer he survives."

"Isn't that a waste of time? He's obviously near death as it is."

"The fact that you think it would be a waste of my time tells me it isn't. So, all you have to do is tell me who else is here and maybe he can recover."

"We're out of time," Robert said as he watched the scene unfolding in the command center.

"Yes, we have to do something, quickly," Siasha replied.

"Are all the soldiers in areas where the sound waves will reach them?" Robert asked Roy.

Turning from his research on the Re'an chips, Roy replied, "Yes. We can knock them all out, any time we want."

"Do it," Robert said.

"What about Siasha's nephew?" Roy asked.

Robert spoke through clenched teeth. "His fate will be no different than his comrades. Kill him." Clearly, Tawndo was in control now.

"No!" Siasha cried, grabbing Robert by the shoulder. "You *can't*... we need him."

"You mean you want him spared for your sister's sake," Robert snapped. "It's him or all of us and your sister."

"Robert, think! We *need* him to keep us informed on the escape of the L'gundo from the destruction of the Tunguska site. Tawndo, don't let your hate for the B'ran blind your judgment."

"I am *not* Tawndo!"

Siasha cringed. "I'm sorry... Robert." In a quieter voice, she added, "We really do need him to help us."

Robert turned from her abruptly and walked to the edge of the room where he stood quietly with his back to them. After a moment he turned. He was calm again, in control. "You trust him with our lives, Siasha?"

"Yes, I do."

Robert frowned and looked at the rest of them. "What do the rest of you think?"

Raj spoke first. "She hasn't steered us wrong yet. She *is* on our side, Robert."

The muscles in Robert's jaw bulged. "Fine. Roy, work your magic and knock them out, but hold back on releasing the nanobots until we've removed Siasha's nephew."

"You got it!" he said, working the controls at his station. "Sorry Siasha, but your nephew is going to wake up with a bit of a headache," he added.

They watched the soldiers in the control room collapse to the floor in sync as if in a choreographed act when the high-pitched ultrasonic tone reached their chips rendering them unconscious.

"You better move and get Siasha's nephew and Jack out of there. I have no idea how long they'll be knocked out. I'd say we've only got a few minutes," Roy told them. "And someone needs to get Linkola and Korda from their rooms."

Robert, Raj, Siasha, and JR scrambled out of the room. Less than a minute later, Roy saw Siasha and Raj rushing into the command center. Siasha ran straight to Deszik, grabbed him by his feet, and started dragging him toward the door while Raj went for Jack. JR and Robert sped to Linkola's and Korda's rooms.

Within two minutes, JR and Robert had their charges over their shoulders and were heading for the lift. When the doors opened on the command center level, JR grabbed one of Deszik's feet to help Siasha drag him to the lift. She kept the door open while JR went back to help Raj move Jack inside.

When they stepped back into the control room with the limp bodies of the four unconscious men, Roy said, "Deploying the spyders with the nanites now."

"How long before they're dead?" JR asked.

"Just a few minutes."

Just a slight twitch of their bodies as the nanites activated was the only indication of death throes of the dark cladded Re'an soldiers.

"How long before they regain consciousness," Siasha asked, concern in her voice as she pointed to the four on the floor.

"I can't say about Jack. He would not have been impacted by the ultrasonic tone. The rest of them should start to come around soon, minutes maybe," Roy replied. "They'll have one hell of a headache though, but otherwise, they should be fine."

"How long do we have to wait before the nanobots would self-destruct and not be a threat to us?" Robert asked.

"Give it ten more minutes and it'll be safe," Roy said.

Ten minutes later, Linkola, Korda, and Deszik were still on the floor curled into a fetal position holding their heads in their hands moaning and groaning in pain. There was not much anyone could do for them.

"Sorry guys," Roy said. "You'll just have to tough it out."

Nevertheless, Siasha and JR tried to comfort them until Rebecca and Max arrived to provide medical assistance. It didn't even look as if they were aware of anything going on around them.

"It's time. Let's get those bodies out of the command center. Get Jack's team in here and have them help us move the bodies to the Chasm of Marwolaeth. Toss them in it to join Nator," Robert growled, referring to the B'ran who tried to kill him.

"Chasm of Mar-what?" Raj inquired.

"Marwolaeth," Siasha answered. "It's a very deep chasm in one of the hidden tunnels the Liberty Movement used. I'll show you."

"Actually," Roy said, "I'd like Raj to stay here and work

with me on this chip research, I think I may be on to something and would like his input."

"Just one more thing," JR said. "We must strip those bodies naked, collect all their clothes, body armor, and weapons. We might want to use those against the other horde of Re'an who's invading our country."

By then, Dennis, Eric, Doug, Rebecca, and the others had arrived.

"Good thinking, JR," Dennis said. "But I've got a strange feeling that the body armor and weapons could be personalized, meaning that they won't work unless the owner operates them. Maybe they're activated with a fingerprint or retina scan or God forbid, the chips in their brains, which we've just destroyed."

"Come to think of it," JR said, "in the movies, they always say the retina can only be read by those scanners for ten to fifteen minutes after death, so we…"

"Relax, JR." Rebecca smiled. "You should know better than believing all the stuff you see in movies. Eyes can be used for biometric identification for many hours, even days after death. So, unless the Re'an found a way to distinguish between the iris of a dead and live person, we should be okay."

"Phew!" Doug blew out a sigh of relief. "One less thing to worry about, if it comes down to retina scans."

"I see," JR mumbled then started speaking more clearly. "Well, I guess then we go in, strip them of everything, and remove it, but leave the bodies there until Deszik comes around so we can ask him?"

"Agreed," Dennis replied and turned to Roy and Robert. "Any issues with that?"

"Nope, makes sense to me," Roy replied, and Robert also agreed.

Chapter Forty-One

Alaska Volcano Observatory, Anchorage, Alaska

Twenty-year-old Andrew Smyth bent over a series of reports scattered across his desk at the Alaska Volcano Observatory—AVO—in Anchorage, Alaska. His head moved from side to side as if he was watching a tennis match, moving from one report to the next, comparing statistics, measurements, and satellite photos.

"How many times are you going to go over those reports, kid?"

Andrew looked up frowning slightly. The head seismologist at AVO, Bud Winthrop, had referred to him as 'kid' ever since he'd arrived for his internship two months ago. It bothered him. *No time like the present.*

"Excuse me, sir, my name is Andrew."

Winthrop grinned. "Sure, Andrew. I'm sorry, didn't mean any offense. You're about my son's age, and I forget sometimes."

Andrew nodded, accepting the apology.

"So, Andrew, what has piqued your interest in those reports?"

"Well, sir..."

"Hang on there. If I can't call you 'kid', then you have to stop calling me 'sir', like I'm your grandfather or something. Call me Bud, like everyone else. Okay... Andrew?"

It was Andrew's turn to grin. "Yes, sir, er, thank you... Bud."

"Carry on then."

"Well, Bud, I'm fascinated and concerned by the increase in seismic activity and signs of volcanic activity along the Aleutian Trench and Islands.

"At first it was just some earthquakes along the trench, then some minor activity began at these four volcanoes," he said, indicating Kanga, Bogoslof, Cleveland, and Pavlof. "And now," he continued, pointing to an area on the map slightly to the right of the four volcanoes, "there are signs indicating we might see some minor volcanic activity in these six volcanoes: Trident, Snowy, Katmai, Augustine, Redoubt, and Spurr.

"Based on the readings I'm seeing at the first four, and some predictive calculations I've made, I'd say both Bogoslof and Cleveland will see major eruptive events within five to six days, followed by Kanaga and Pavlof in another ten to twelve days."

Winthrop raised his eyebrows. "What calculations are you using?"

"Some of my own predictive algorithms, based on certain current readings and historical data. The mathematics is part of my thesis to see if it is possible to more accurately predict an eruption."

"Really? That's very interesting! Let's see what you've got!"

The two sat down, and Andrew took him step-by-step through the information and his calculations. When he finished, Winthrop leaned back in his chair and eyed the young man with renewed respect.

"Young man, sorry... Andrew, what you've shown me is incredible. If your calculations prove to be accurate, this could be one of the biggest breakthroughs in the study of volcanoes in a century."

"What do we do with the information now?"

"We wait and see if your predictions are correct."

"But don't we need to let someone know?"

"Not for these volcanoes; they are far enough away from populated areas to not cause problems in the event of an eruption.

"Let's get your information officially recorded, if it's correct, we don't want to miss the chance to be able to prove it."

Chapter Forty-Two

Eighth Cycle Site, Grand Canyon, USA

Deszik came to with a headache like he'd never experienced before. After a moment, he hung his head over the side of the bed and relieved his stomach of its contents. The movement and retching sent a sharp stab of pain through his head like a hot dagger slicing through it. Retching again, he saw stars and momentarily feared he would pass out and fall off the bed.

"Easy does it, son," a male voice said near him. Very slowly and carefully he turned his head and saw a tall, muscular man speaking to him from beside another bed nearby. He was in a hospital room.

"What happened?" Deszik asked quietly to keep the pain in his head to a minimum.

"You were subjected to a high-pitched sound wave that interfered with your chip causing you to lose consciousness," the man replied stepping next to Deszik's bed. "My name's Max."

"They decided to spare me then," Deszik stated flatly.

"Yes."

"And the others?"

"They have all been destroyed."

"Help me up."

"I suggest you stay on your back quietly for a while until your headache goes away."

"You don't understand, Victor is expecting a report. How long have I been out?"

"About two hours."

"We're running out of time," Deszik groaned as he tried to sit up. He immediately regretted it. His head pounded, and he retched again and then managed to stand weakly beside his bed.

"Sit back down, and at least let me give you something for the pain."

"Make it fast."

Max was already retrieving the medication and returned to Deszik's side quickly, giving him the injection almost before he stopped moving. "Now give that a minute or two to work through your system and you should start feeling better."

"Thanks," Deszik said standing and making his way to the door.

"Hey! I said give it a minute or two!" Max objected.

"It'll have a minute or two on my way to the command center. I have to report to Viktor," he said as the door closed behind him.

Shaking his head, Max returned to the bed where Jack lay unconscious. He didn't know what instruments had been used to torture Jack, but he knew he was fortunate to still be alive and unconscious.

Stepping through the doorway, Rebecca inquired, "How is he?"

"Not good."

She reviewed his vitals before examining his injuries.

"The external damage is minimal compared to the internal damage," she said after a while.

"What the hell did they do to him?"

"I don't know, and I don't think I want to know. I'm fairly certain he will recover," she said checking the IV's. "We'll just have to keep a close eye on him."

"Why are they still unconscious?" she asked indicating the figures of Linkola and Korda on the other beds.

"With the headache that Deszik woke up with, I thought it was better to let them sleep a while longer. So, I injected them with morphine. Hopefully, that will help them wake up a lot happier than Deszik."

"That bad, huh?"

"Yep," he said nodding to the area on the floor next to Deszik's bed displaying the contents of his stomach.

Robert and Siasha literally ran into Deszik stepping through the doorway.

"Sorry," Deszik exclaimed reaching to steady Robert on his feet.

Shrugging Deszik's hand from his arm Robert said, "No problem. Where are you going in such a hurry?"

"To the command center, I must report to Viktor."

"We'll go with you," Robert stated.

Siasha trailed along behind them in silence hoping Robert would come to realize that Deszik was on their side.

Reaching the command center, Deszik started to open

the communication channel to Viktor when Robert leveled a gun at him saying, "One wrong word, and it will be your last."

Deszik nodded.

"Ah, Deszik, my son!" Viktor's voice came over the speaker. "What have you to report?"

"Sir!" Deszik started, "I regret to inform you that The Beast is no longer here."

"What?" Viktor yelled. "You idiot, clearly you've overlooked it!"

"No, sir. It is not here. The team has searched the entire place three times, and then I personally searched it as well. When we entered the site, we found a B'ran scientist that was awakened when the Rossler's entered the site a few years ago. I… questioned him extensively, and he told us where the Rossler's hid it, but then Brideaux apparently found it and removed it."

"*You* questioned him?" Viktor sneered. "I would like to speak with him myself."

"I'm afraid that won't be possible."

"And why not?"

"Because he succumbed to the methods used during the extensive questioning."

"*You* tortured him? I didn't think you had it in you."

Deszik didn't comment on that. Instead he said, "He had considerable resistance, but in the end, he told us the truth and gave us the location of a hidden vault where we would find it."

"Where is it?" Viktor demanded.

"He said it's in a side canyon not far from here. Apparently, there is a hidden hallway leading to it. I've sent two teams to investigate and report back."

Viktor leaned forward and said in a low, tight voice

emphasizing each word, "I want that equipment found. Is that clear?"

"Very clear, sir."

The call ended without another word.

"Well, Deszik," Robert spoke lowering his gun. "I see that you are an experienced liar."

Deszik made no reply. He just looked at Robert to continue.

"I have to wonder, are you lying to us too?"

"Robert, I don't know what I have to do to convince you that I am on your side. That I am as eager as you are if not more to destroy Viktor. I have lived with him for more than a hundred years. I know how deranged the man is. But I can't make you believe me. As far as I am concerned, you have to get over yourself, and we will then be able to start to work together to stop Viktor and his Re'an."

Robert stared at him for a while longer, then without saying a word, got up and left the room.

Siasha touched Deszik's arm and said, "Don't mind him. He's having a hard time with the constant battle of the two personalities in one body."

"What do you mean two personalities in one body? That's…"

"I will explain later. We've got something very important to ask you first. Please come with me to see Raj and Roy," she said and took him by the arm to support him and led him out of the room.

Chapter Forty-Three

Naval Base Kitsap, Bremerton, Washington State

Daniel descended the stairs of Airforce One returning the salute of the soldiers lined up to greet him. Taking a few extra minutes, he stopped to shake hands with many of them.

"We should keep moving, sir," his agents urged.

Daniel continued shaking hands. "We're almost there."

Salome, who had joined him on the trip, grinned.

Still the Daniel Rossler I know! The presidency had not gone to his head.

As they entered the car, Bill Simms commented on the beauty and greenness of the area.

"That's Washington State for you," Scott Jenkins said. "All the rain keeps things green!"

The trip across the base to the courthouse where the trial was held only took a few minutes. Daniel used the time to review the status. He had been following the trial of the prisoners, as had most of the world, through the live broadcasts from the courtroom, but thought it best to complete a quick review before he arrived.

"Mister Jenkins," he said addressing the Attorney General. "Please refresh my memory on the history of the International Criminal Court and its processes."

Jenkins nodded. "In 1998, at a convention in Rome, a statute known as the Rome Statute of the International Criminal Court, or simply 'the Rome Statute', was adopted. It was the first, permanent, treaty-based international criminal court established. The countries that accept the rules of the Rome Statute are called States Parties.

"The ICC is independent of the United Nations and is not intended to, nor does it replace the existing national criminal justice systems of the member countries. It is intended to complement those systems. It is preferred that the individual States maintain their own oversight of those who commit international crimes."

"Then why did we involve them in this?" Daniel asked.

"Many of the most atrocious crimes committed during the twentieth century - especially during World War Two - went unpunished for lack of a court like this. It was the establishment of the Nuremberg and Tokyo tribunals, along with the adoption of the Convention on the Prevention and Punishment of the Crime of Genocide, that made the United Nations realize a permanent International Court was needed. The ICC only deals with those who, based on the evidence, carry the most responsibility for the crimes that are committed."

"Given the worldwide impact of the actions of Brideaux and the Supreme Council, this was the only agreement that could be reached for the trial and punishment of the accused. None of the countries involved could agree on who could be trusted with the trial, and what was acceptable punishment, but they did all agree to abide by the ICC's decisions."

Daniel nodded. "I see. Please continue."

"The ICC is divided into four components: The Presidency, or the Head of the Court; the Chambers which is responsible for ensuring fair trials; the Office of the Prosecutor which handles investigation and prosecution, and the Registry which provides administrative support for the court.

"The Chambers is further divided into three sections. The first is the Pre-Trial Chambers. Among other things, they ensure the integrity of the investigation, preserve the rights of all involved, and make the determination to confirm bringing charges against the accused.

"The second is the Trial Chambers which is composed of three judges who try the case, render the verdict, and in the case of a finding of guilt, sets the sentence of anything from making reparations to life in prison."

"They don't have the authority to invoke the death penalty?"

"Yes, that's correct. However, in this case, they have been endowed with that power, I think due to the number of Americans accused and the fear that they will escape true punishment through the appeals process. The American Justice System has so many checks, balances, loop-holes, and other red tape that it would take years, if ever before a death sentence would be carried out."

"Doesn't the ICC have an appeals process?"

"Yes, the Appeals Chamber is the third in the division. Again, in this case, an exception has been made; all countries have agreed there will be no appeals granted. I believe this was done to prevent the issue from being dragged out further."

"So, the verdict and sentencing we hear today are final?"

"Yes, sir."

"What is the expected outcome?"

"There is little doubt that they will be found guilty."

"What are the likely sentences?"

"The prosecutors have been pushing hard for the death penalty for all of them except Rafael Martinez. His lawyer had been arguing that his client was instrumental in ending the carnage and bringing Brideaux down. They argued that his actions clearly speak of deep remorse, and as you know, he was the one who killed Brideaux. The prosecutors seem to agree with Martinez's lawyer, and it is likely that *he* might escape the death penalty.

"However, I've heard from the lead prosecutor that Martinez has requested to address the court before his sentencing. None of the others did, despite being given the opportunity to do so.

"There is speculation that he might ask the court to impose the same penalty on him as on his fellow accused."

"Bizarre, I'd say."

Daniel shook his head. "Maybe not. I remember a short conversation I had with him after they were arrested in Brussels. The man was guilt-ridden about what happened, and his share in it. Even though he has changed course, he told me he felt he had the blood of countless innocent people on his hands and therefore was not exempt from the consequences."

"That's going to be a tough decision," Simms said.

Arriving at the courthouse, they quickly made their way inside and took seats in the right, front area of the gallery set aside for them.

The accused sat in metal chairs in a double row along

the left side of the room on the other side of the bar, while the prosecuting and defense teams sat in their usual spots along the bar in front of the bench.

The three judges walked in and took their seats facing the gallery. The small woman in the middle who was the presiding judge, from Sweden, ordered the defendants to rise.

She started by reading out the names of the thirteen accused which included the twelve prisoners rescued from the Trepang and, to Daniel's satisfaction, Barbara Cohen.

"You have been accused of genocide defined by the Rome Statute as acts that are committed with the intent to destroy, in whole or in part, a national, ethnical, racial, or religious group by killing, causing serious bodily or mental harm to members of the group, including imposing measures intended to prevent births within the group.

"In regard to the charge of genocide, based on testimony given and evidence presented here, the International Criminal Court unanimously finds you guilty."

"You are also accused of crimes against humanity," the Judge continued. As defined by the Rome Statute, this is knowingly committing acts as part of a widespread or systematic attack against civilian populations. These acts include but are not limited to: murder; extermination; enslavement; imprisonment; torture; and other similar inhumane acts that intentionally cause great suffering, serious bodily, or mental injury.

"In regard to the charge of crimes against humanity, based on testimony given and evidence presented here, the International Criminal Court unanimously finds you guilty."

The judge paused as sighs were heard throughout the

room. Daniel could almost feel the heavy atmosphere of gloom dissipating from the room.

No one moved.

The defendants were emotionless. It was obvious none of them expected different verdicts.

"As you have been made aware at the onset of this trial, because of the great extent and the brutality of the crimes committed, world leaders have unanimously agreed that the prohibition on invoking the death penalty be lifted and that no appeals be granted in this situation."

Turning her focus directly to Rafael Martinez, the judge spoke to him. "Mister Martinez, you were the only one who took up the offer to address the court before sentencing. You now have the opportunity to speak."

Martinez cleared his throat. "Your Honor, I don't have much to say. My crimes were severe, and this court has justly found me guilty. I am deeply ashamed of my actions, and although I saw the error of my ways before the others and set out to rectify my wrongdoing, it was too late. I am still responsible for immeasurable suffering and death of innocent people. I should suffer the same fate as the rest of them." He hung his head and with tears in his eyes, added, "I deserve to die. I beg of this court to grant me my wish."

Gasps and whispers could be heard from the public gallery which grew in intensity.

The Swedish judge looked at the rest of the panel of judges and mouthed the question, "Adjourn?" They all nodded, and she said, "The court will adjourn for half an hour."

Forty minutes later, the court was back in session.

The Swedish judge started by reading the names of twelve of the accused, leaving out the name of Rafael Martinez, following each name with, "You are hereby sentenced to death for your crimes against humanity and of genocide.

"These sentences will be carried out by a representative of, and in accordance with the laws of, each person's respective country of citizenship in two hours.

"May God have mercy on your souls."

In the gallery, people began to stir, some wept openly with the knowledge that justice had been served, the threat was finally over, and they could move on with their lives.

Turning her focus directly to Rafael Martinez, the judge said, Mister Martinez, this court has considered your request to receive the death penalty, like the others. We found it a very strange request, yet a noble gesture and proof of your deep remorse. However, the court has decided, unanimously, that given your actions once you came to comprehend the transgressions committed against humanity, and your role in ending the carnage, the death penalty is not appropriate. You are hereby sentenced to ten years in prison.

"It is the hope of this court that once you are released from prison, you will spend the rest of your life assisting humanity in their efforts to recover from the terrible suffering caused by the Supreme Council of John Brideaux."

Martinez just nodded his head in disbelief.

"This court is adjourned."

Two hours later, the twelve prisoners were executed, and Martinez was transferred to a prison in Brazil to commence his ten-year sentence.

As Air Force One took off from the runway, Daniel leaned back in his chair and sighed.

Salome looked at him with a slight frown.

"John Brideaux is dead and so are his cohorts, I should be relieved, but I'm not. The Eighth Cycle and all the evil it left behind is still haunting us."

Salome nodded. "Yes, that is indeed true. But I'm confident we're not too far away from eradicating it for good. Eliminating the group that tried to take control of the canyon site was a big victory."

"That's true, but it was only one battle in the war. We still don't have a solution to deal with the seven-hundred and fifty who are now in our cities."

"We'll find a way, Daniel. The Rosslerites always do."

Chapter Forty-Four

Eighth Cycle Site, Grand Canyon, USA

Later that evening, as they gathered for an evening meal, Raj and Roy arrived last looking tired, downcast, and frustrated. Their occasional comments to one another made it clear that they were far from defeated.

"What's got you two so perplexed?" JR asked.

Roy managed a tight smile. "We're still trying to find a way to deal with the army of soldiers Viktor has dispersed to the cities. But the solution evades us."

"Maybe it will help if you explain to us what you've tried so far and what you're thinking," Dennis suggested. "Not that many of us understand geek-speak, but maybe if you simplify it for us, it will help you ignore the forest and see the trees. Who knows, maybe one of us could have a lightbulb moment and be able to trigger a few of your brain cells."

Roy started, "Well, it's not all bad. One of the issues

kind of resolved itself. That's the one we have about removing or destroying the chips after killing these soldiers."

Everyone was looking at Roy in anticipation when he paused for a breath.

"Early on in Viktor's Re'an program, the scientists developed a chip that disintegrates upon the death of the host. That was to keep their technology from being discovered should one of their soldiers fall into the hands of their enemy. Their chips are made of some kind of organic material that disintegrates and disperses into the brain upon death. So, that's one less thing to worry about."

"That's good news; it solves part of our problem. All we have to do now is find a way to kill these super soldiers," Doug said.

"Yes, but it still leaves us with a fire-fight on our hands. And our weapons are so inferior to theirs, we might as well attack them with pitchforks," interjected Eric.

"Not necessarily," Robert said. "We have an arsenal of Eighth Cycle weapons. It won't match their particle-beam weapons, but they are certainly a lot more advanced than the weapons you have now."

"Let's get back to that in a moment," Dennis said and turned to Raj. "I got the impression you wanted to say something before we digressed?"

Raj nodded. "According to Deszik, his mother told him that the Tunguska site is going to be destroyed in the next day or two. He also told us that the Tunguska facility has an elaborate system that they use to control these chips remotely, upload enhancements, and issue orders."

JR asked, "So, what happens if that computer is turned off? Do they just drop dead—problem solved?"

Raj shook his head. "That would've been great,

wouldn't it? Unfortunately, that's not what happens. Dekka informed us that although there *is* a constant low-frequency tether between that computer and every chip, they've built a failsafe in that, if the connection is lost, the soldiers will continue to carry out their mission as per their last instructions."

"Damn! So, we're back to square one," Dennis said.

Raj nodded. "Yes, I'm afraid that's it… for now."

"What about Siasha and the others?" Korda asked. "Are they tethered as well, or is it just the soldiers?"

No one knew the answer.

Dennis looked at JR and Robert. "I guess we need to have a look at those Eighth Cycle weapons and start planning an old-fashioned assault."

"Yep, let's get on with it. We should give Daniel an update," JR said.

As Roy and Raj got to their feet to return to the lab, Siasha arrived with Deszik, steadying him as she led him up to the dining room table.

She said, "I brought Deszik over so that we could ask him about the Re'an weapons."

Roy and Raj sat down again.

Roy turned to Deszik and said, "Sorry, man, seems to me that ultra-high frequency sound had a much harsher effect on you than I anticipated."

"It's okay, I'll live," Deszik whispered, still labored with pain. "What can I help you with?"

"It's about the Re'an weapons and body armor. We have collected all from the dead soldiers. We thought we could use them against the seven-hundred and fifty who are about to attack our cities. We hope that you will be able to train some of our soldiers to use them."

Deszik nodded slightly and his face immediately contorted from the pain shooting through his head. He took a slow breath and said, "The body armor is not a problem, it can be used by anyone. It's stretchable, as you've probably already noticed; it fits tightly over the body like a second skin. However, it has been designed and developed specifically to protect against your Eleventh Cycle weapons. It offers no protection against the Re'an weapons."

Dennis was shaking his head. "Damn, there goes that idea. What about the weapons, will we be able to use them?"

Deszik started to shake his head but grimaced and stopped. "The weapons have been personalized; each soldier can only use his own. It's connected with the individual's chip which activates it and keeps it operational for as long as the connection is intact."

"A bit shortsighted, wouldn't you say?" JR interjected. "When a soldier is killed, his weapon becomes useless—to everyone."

"However," Deszik said, unfazed by JR's interruption, "another Re'an soldier can reactivate it with a retina scan which, if recognized by the weapon as an authorized one, will establish a connection between the new soldier's chip and the weapon and reactivate it."

"That means we need the combination of an active chip and a retina of a living Re'an?" Raj asked.

"Yes."

"Like yourself?" Roy said.

"Yes. But keep in mind that all those events; activation,

deactivation, and reactivation are registered on the control computers back at Tunguska."

Raj and Roy stared at each other in silence for a while as they processed the information.

"So," Raj said, "the control computers at Tunguska don't control the activation, deactivation, et cetera, it only registers when it happens?"

"Yes, that's correct. Those events happen only between the soldiers' chips and their weapons."

"And one soldier could have many activated weapons?" Raj said.

"Yes. There's no limit."

"So, all we need to do is wait until your mother and her team blow up the Tunguska site, and when we're certain the control computers are gone, we can activate the weapons we took off the twenty-four soldiers," Roy said.

"It's not quite that simple," Deszik replied.

"All we have established is that Deszik can activate all the weapons, but he's the only one that'll be able to use them. They'll still be useless to us," Roy stated flatly.

"Unless you and Raj and the other scientists can find a way to circumvent their authentication system," JR said.

A stunned silence followed as the group realized that they were presented with yet another challenge.

"Thanks, Deszik, that was very helpful," Roy said. "By the looks of you, it seems as if you could do with a bit more rest and medical attention."

"Absolutely," Siasha said on Deszik's behalf and stood to help him get to his feet. "I'm taking him back to Rebecca and Max, right now."

Deszik didn't protest as he was led away.

There was a protracted silence around the table before

Roy looked up and said in a firm voice, "We're not finished yet; there has to be a way!" He paused, stood up, and added, "And I swear to you, Raj and I *will* find it!" With that he left the table headed for his lab, his firm footsteps assuring everyone that he meant business.

Chapter Forty-Five

Washington, D.C.

Daniel managed to suppress a frown of concern as Dennis completed his report.

It was not so much the contents of the report, but the look of dejection on the faces of the people at the canyon site. And although he felt the same melancholy, he knew his best contribution now was to boost their morale.

He fixed a slight smile on his face and said, "We've not run out of time or ideas yet. In the past, in times like these, the Rosslerites have always managed to turn things around. I have always believed, and still do, that good always triumphs over evil in the end. You'll figure it out; keep working on it!"

"That you can bet on, Daniel," Dennis replied.

"One last thing," JR said.

"Shoot."

"As you know, Deszik's mother and six other L'gundo scientists at the Tunguska site are about to trigger a series of events that will destroy the place while they make their escape.

"They're planning to pull that off within the next twenty-four hours."

Daniel nodded.

"We need you to order the Itinerant to pick up the seven L'gundo scientists on the East Coast of Russia and rendezvous with the Mystic Sea to take them on to Kitsap Naval Base."

"What's the specific location?"

JR looked at Deszik.

"One moment," he responded and lowered his head as he contacted his mother.

Mother?

Yes?

The Americans are making arrangements to send a submarine to pick you up on the East Coast. Where shall I tell them to meet you?

The others waited quietly, it was still an eerie experience for them to watch while Deszik, in an almost trance-like state, conversed with his mother without uttering a single word.

At last Deszik scribbled some numbers on a notepad and replied, "They will be at these coordinates on the beach at Puyshariya Bay at 02:00 a.m. their time, the day after tomorrow, if it all works out as planned."

JR read the coordinates to Daniel.

Daniel replied hesitantly, "But how will we know that your mother and company were successful in their escape?"

Deszik smiled. "My mother and Dekka will stay in touch with me to provide updates."

"Yes, of course. I'm still trying to come to grips with this method of communications. You can tell her the sub will be there."

"Thank you, sir," Deszik replied.

"Anything else?" Daniel asked.

"Nope, that's it for now," Dennis said.

"Keep me posted. Until next time!" Daniel said closing the call.

Chapter Forty-Six

Eighth Cycle Site, Grand Canyon, USA

"How soon can I have the location of the soldiers?" Dennis asked Robert.

"The information Raj downloaded included the general locations each team was assigned to within the cities; I'll have that for you in a few minutes."

"My teams can work with that," Dennis confirmed. "Since the threat here is neutralized, I'll take the Tectus members with me and join the Phoenix forces."

"How soon can you be ready to leave?" Owen inquired. "I'll need to arrange for the helicopter to retrieve you."

"How fast can it get here?"

"I can have it here in two hours."

"Make it three, so we have time to hike to the rendezvous point."

"You got it!" Owen replied.

Dennis looked at Eric who had remained silent

throughout the call. "Let's split the list of cities and start contacting our cell leaders to assemble the teams."

"I'll set up a conference call with the team leaders of the twenty-five cities," Eric agreed looking at the list. "That will give you a little extra time to organize the team here."

"Thanks!" Dennis replied. "Make it in two hours."

Video conference

"We're ready to go," Eric greeted as Dennis stepped into the control room two hours later. "The Leaders and Seconds from all twenty-five cities have joined this conference call and are ready to hear what you have to say."

Dennis nodded, noting that the entire canyon team, as requested, was in attendance as well.

"Ladies and gentlemen," Dennis started. "I know you've already agreed to have two-man teams provide surveillance on the Re'an soldiers, and we appreciate that.

"There've been some new developments requiring us to change our operation from passive observation to active engagement. I want to reiterate that Tectus has always been a voluntary organization. No one has been forced to join or do anything they didn't want to do. Our only proviso has been that once you commit to a mission, you follow the orders you're given, or get out. I'm going to explain what needs doing, if anyone wants to opt out of this mission, you'll have the opportunity do so."

The audience listened in silence.

"We'll have to take these Re'an soldiers out ourselves.

"I would've preferred if it never came to this, but there's no alternative, unless we want to capitulate."

"And give up without a fight? Not likely," said the team leader from Atlanta, Georgia, a former Recon Marine lieutenant.

These were all former military men and women, many of them former Special Forces operators. Dennis knew they would not run from a fight. But he had an obligation to not mislead them.

"The scenario is all but rosy, and I'll understand if anyone prefers to opt out from this once you've heard what I've got to say."

"I ain't planning to run from no fight. But I'd certainly like to know what I'm getting into. So, I can't make that decision unless I've heard it all," one of them said, which from the nodding heads indicated he'd just summed up how everyone else felt.

Dennis proceeded. "It will have to be done quietly, without attracting any attention from civilians or authorities; we'll need to recover and secure every bit of the technology they have. We cannot, I repeat, can*not*, allow it to fall in the hands of anyone else.

"Ladies and gentlemen, we're up against a superior force."

"Seven-hundred and fifty Re'an foot soldiers is a superior force? Why?" a former Delta Force operator from Washington, D.C. interjected.

Before Dennis could answer, Steve Wilson – former Navy SEAL and the team leader of the Portland, Oregon cell, a tall dark-tanned man with raven-black hair said, "I agree, it would be good to know what we're going up against."

Dennis subdued a grin.

That's Special Forces operators for you. No question

about whether to do it or not—but rather how to do it most efficiently.

He replied, "Physically, these soldiers are superior to us. They have greatly enhanced strength, endurance, vision, and hearing. They are protected by lightweight, liquid body armor that fits like a second skin over their bodies and provides free range of motion. It will protect them against any projectile fired by a twenty-first century handgun or rifle."

He paused to let them digest the information for a moment before continuing. "As far as weaponry goes, they have particle-beam weapons that destroy targets by disrupting their atomic and molecular structure using high-energy beams of subatomic particles. These weapons can vaporize targets in the blink of an eye.

"The short-range version of these particle beam weapons is effective up to a mile, possibly more. The long-range version is capable of taking out armored targets, both airborne and surface, up to five miles away." He paused and added carefully, "Every soldier is equipped with both versions of the weapon."

He heard several whistles and various expletives in exclamation. He let them continue for a moment.

A former Army Ranger and leader of the Columbus, Ohio cell, a man of about five foot ten, broad shoulders and blond hair, spoke first. "Dennis, I know *you* well enough to tell you aren't kidding, no matter how far-fetched this sounds; but are you crazy? Not only does it sound like a suicide mission, but how the hell do you expect us to neutralize these supermen, let alone do it quietly and without drawing attention? By the sounds of it, we need nukes to kill these soldiers."

Everyone turned their eyes back to Dennis.

"The Re'an have had decades to perfect their weapons, but we're not going up against them with our conventional weapons. What we have aren't quite as advanced as theirs, but we believe in the right circumstances they'll be effective."

"What kind of weapons? What are the right circumstances?" Another leader asked.

"Hand-held laser weapons," Dennis replied.

Another round of unease among his listeners followed, and Dennis decided to nip it in the bud. "As I've said, not as advanced and capable as theirs, but a direct shot to the head will kill them.

"These weapons come in both close-quarter and long-range versions as well. Their range isn't the same as the enemy's and will require a direct hit to any unprotected part of the head."

"So, exactly which parts of their heads are unprotected?" One asked.

"The eyes."

More exclamations followed this statement.

"In other words, it requires a direct hit to the eye to take them down?"

Dennis nodded. "I wish I could've given you more than that. But I won't lie to you."

"Talk about having the deck stacked against you," Steve, the SEAL from Oregon, mumbled with enough clarity for everyone to hear.

"So," the Army Ranger said, "we have to sneak up on these guys, get close enough to shoot them in the eyes, and hope they don't get a chance to pull their Star Wars weapons and vaporize us? Not to mention not alerting the rest of their team."

"Beats trying to shoot them in the ass, I reckon,"

another former SEAL, the team leader of Dallas, Texas a giant of a man with a bushy black beard and shock of salt and pepper hair, remarked matter-of-factly.

Dennis smiled as everyone exploded in laughter. He welcomed the lighter moment and let it go for a minute before continuing.

"So, ladies and gents, there you have it. Now you know as much about the challenge we face as I do. The floor is open for discussion."

The team leader from Boston, Massachusetts, a blond-haired, athletically-built, woman with stunning green eyes, a former CIA field agent, said, "Dennis, you've told us about their physical attributes and weapons, and that sounds daunting enough, but what about their intelligence? Are they any smarter than us?"

Everyone turned their gazes at this woman. She had touched on something significant that none of them had considered.

Dennis looked at Linkola, Siasha, Korda, Deszik, and Robert questioningly.

The five of them moved closer to each other and conferred in a whispered tone for a few minutes, while everyone else watched in silence.

Finally, Linkola spoke. "No, they're not. We're in agreement. Our experience since encountering you people from the Eleventh Cycle, has been that your intelligence is not inferior to ours or the Re'an's. Our Eighth Cycle technology might be superior to yours, but over the last few days, you have proven that you are intelligent enough to quickly grasp the technology and overcome it. As far as we are concerned, your intelligence matches ours."

"Well, if that's the case," the former CIA agent said,

"then that's what we will have to use to level the playing field—outsmart them."

"Now we're cookin' with gas," the Dallas guy said in his deep baritone voice, eliciting another round of laughs.

Dennis smiled and nodded. "Thanks for that Tracey, you've certainly nailed it with that insight. We've been blinded by their physique and weapons and forgot the biblical account of David, the shepherd boy, who went up against Goliath. The giant was protected from head to toe in body armor and had superior weapons in his hands yet got defeated by a single stone propelled from a simple slingshot."

"Yep, one shot right between the eyes," said the team leader from Memphis, Tennessee, a former Navy fighter pilot, a woman with dark hair and deep brown eyes. "Come to think of it, we're one-hundred percent better off than David. We have two vulnerable spots where we can hit them —left or right eye."

"Now there's an attitude that I like," responded the Dallas guy with the opera voice again, to the amusement of everyone else.

When the laughter subsided, Dennis continued. "So far we have a few things going for us. One, they don't know that we know they're here and will be watching them. So, we will pick the time and place where we want to engage them. In other words, the element of surprise. Two, we know the terrain where we're going to do battle better than they do. And finally, these guys are semi-robots and probably rely heavily on very detailed orders and their enhanced body features to give them the upper hand. Therefore, they won't be as agile as we are to adapt to changing circumstances – we can outwit them."

Deszik motioned for Dennis to have a quick word in private.

Dennis, Eric, and the others at the canyon site had agreed prior to the meeting not to disclose the fact that Deszik was a Re'an soldier who switched allegiance. There was not enough time to deal with a new round of trust issues, especially not in a group as big as this one. Deszik would attend the meeting but only listen and remain quiet. Therefore, he was introduced as one of the Eighth Cycle group who lived at the canyon site. It was also agreed that no mention would be made of Deszik's group of twenty-four Re'an who'd been ambushed and killed three days before.

Dennis realized Deszik must have had something important to say. He asked Eric, his second in command, to take over the meeting while he and Deszik went out into the hallway.

Deszik told Dennis that they were on the right track with their thinking about the Re'an soldiers' lack of agility. That the Re'an operated on very elaborate orders, almost as if they are programmed, and therein lay the potential solution. In other words, they needed to devise a plan that would require the Re'an to operate outside the parameters of their original orders. With the Tunguska site demolished and the link between the control computers and the soldiers severed, they would individually attempt to complete their mission. As a group, they would quickly be in chaos if they were unable to get new orders when their circumstances changed.

"The seven-hundred and fifty were sent on their respective missions to attack and destroy all hospitals, old age, and nursing homes. They were to purge those cities of everyone who would be unfit to be reanimated as Re'an. That was the first stage of the plan after which they had to wait for the stage two orders," Deszik explained.

"And as you know, once the canyon site was secured and The Beast reactivated, Viktor planned to start awakening the people in deep sleep in the twelve other sites across the globe, implant them with the Re'an chips, and commence his quest to take control of the world."

Dennis nodded. "Well, thankfully *that* part of his plan will not come to fruition."

"Indeed, but he doesn't know that yet. He still thinks we have control of the canyon site and The Beast will be found and be operational soon."

"So, this means if your mother and her associates are successful in destroying the Tunguska site and killing everyone inside, including Viktor, we have the seven-hundred and fifty Re'an here in America practically isolated?"

"Exactly. But make no mistake, they *will* soon start to execute their current orders, and they *will* cause immense damage and loss of life. They are merciless, it has been programmed into their chips. We *have* to find a way to throw them off balance; that might be the only opportunity to stop them."

When they returned to the meeting, Eric brought Dennis up to speed with the discussion that took place while he and Deszik were out.

Dennis then said, "I think there are still a lot of questions and ideas, but before we continue with that, I think maybe this is a good time to ask who wants to be in or out of this operation? Hands up those who are staying."

There was a brief silence and then all hands went up. There was not a single one who wanted out.

Dennis and Eric looked at each other and smiled. They were a bit surprised, but not much; this was what they've come to expect of the Tectus members. Most of them were former military where they'd learned to never shy away from their duty to defend and protect.

"Thanks everyone," Dennis said. "I'm humbled by your commitment, and it's an honor to be part of this group.

"I'm sending you each information on the assigned locations of the soldiers in your individual cities. They are already there.

"Prepare your teams and start your surveillance, but don't interfere with them yet. I am relocating to Phoenix. I want each of you to choose five of your members including yourself, to meet me in Phoenix tomorrow. I will send the location to you after the meeting. The plan is to introduce you to the new weapons we're going to use and provide you with training. After that, we'll sit down and work out a strategy to take these terrorists out."

Chapter Forty-Seven

Video conference

When the meeting ended, and the video feeds had been severed, Dennis asked JR to establish a video conference with Daniel, Salome, and the leadership group at the Rabbit Hole so they could be given an update.

A few minutes later, Dennis welcomed them to the call and proceeded to give an overview of the meeting with the Tectus leadership group.

"Tectus is in, boots and all. I take it we don't have to belabor the point about the danger facing these men and women?"

"No need for that Dennis," Daniel said. "I think all of us understand the risks your people are prepared to take. As far as I'm concerned, and I think without fear of dissent from any one of us here, it was inspiring to see the motivation and determination of the Tectus group."

Dennis and Eric both nodded.

Dennis turned to Raj and Roy. "Guys, I hate to state the

obvious, but as you can see, we can really do with a bit of help from the technical side."

Raj said, "We're working on an idea to access these soldiers' individual chips to send them a message that would order them to disperse into smaller teams or even one-man outfits. That way your attack teams don't have to face a large group."

"That'll certainly go a long way to minimize risk for us," Eric said.

"But will you still be able to do it if the Tunguska site and the control computers are destroyed?" Daniel asked.

"No, not with the current setup. I'm trying to take over the functions of the control computers at Tunguska and transfer them to our computers here but have not been able to do so yet. We still have a bit of time before Deszik's mother blows up the site. I hope for a breakthrough before then."

"That would make things a lot simpler," Roy said.

"Damn, this is so complicated," JR said. "Too bad we can't just knock them all out in one go, turn them to ashes, and sweep it up with vacuum cleaners. But I guess that'd be too easy. We'll have to kill them the old-fashioned way, a bullet to the head, or in this case, a laser beam through the eye."

Seeing the meeting was drawing to an end, Daniel asked Dennis to pass along his thanks to the Tectus members for their commitment.

As Dennis closed the connection, Roy, seated on a nearby table, suddenly sat up straight and froze, his eyes unfocused, far away as if in another world.

"Roy?" Dennis asked when he saw Roy's sudden movement.

When Roy didn't respond, Dennis and several of the others became concerned and started calling his name.

His eyes remained unfocused, and he still didn't respond.

Korda said, "Hey all, stop talking. Roy's on to something."

After nearly a minute, Roy's eyes focused once more, he hopped down from the table. "I need to think," he mumbled and stepped into the hallway.

"Don't mind us, Roy," JR shouted. "You can let us in on your plan any time!"

Everyone who had known Roy for a while knew that he meant no offense. Usually, when he started acting like that, he was onto something big. Often, in the past, behavior like this produced the solution to their problems. They knew all they had to do was wait for him to work through it and he would tell them.

Chapter Forty-Eight

Eighth Cycle Site, Grand Canyon, USA

Robert found himself escaping to the Oasis for some quiet time. The Tectus teams were all being arranged, and the Eighth Cycle weapons had been packed for the trip to Phoenix. Dennis and Eric had departed near midnight. In the lab, Raj was working furiously on codes to send to the soldier's chips to make them disperse, while Roy studied the Re'an information yet again, looking for answers to ideas he was not ready to discuss with anyone yet.

For now, the only feasible option was the idea of splitting the soldiers off and eliminating them one at a time. It remained the most efficient way to deal with the threat of discovery... *if* Raj could gain access to the computers. It was a monumental task, but Raj assured them he would not give up until the Tunguska site was destroyed and he could no longer access the control computers.

Reaching the door to the secluded sanctuary, Robert opened it and stepped inside. Making his way to the shore, he wandered the edge enjoying the moonlight playing on the water.

His thoughts turned to Siasha and how he'd treated her when she asked for Deszik to be spared. He didn't like to admit it, but she was right; he had let his hatred of the B'ran cloud his judgment.

He had yelled at her, and he could feel Tawndo's anger over it. Having calmed down, he now had to admit to himself that he felt ashamed about it. He had been raised to respect others, and he knew he had treated her with disrespect.

His stomach clenched and his jaw tightened.

I'm not going to apologize.

I'm not going to care about her feelings.

He continued arguing with himself as he walked.

Growing tired, he finally returned to the doorway. Just as he reached to open it, the door slid aside, and there stood Siasha.

The emotional pain burned in her chest; the hurt rose in her throat. Recognizing the anger in his eyes, she glared at him.

As he moved to step past her, she called, "Robert! Please... wait."

He stopped and turned to face her but said nothing.

"I... I want to thank you... thank you for sparing Deszik's life."

"You're welcome," he replied stiffly, then added a little softer, "I'm sorry I yelled at you."

Why am I apologizing? I wasn't going to!

They stood in the doorway staring at one another for a long moment before Siasha said, "You're forgiven... and I'm sorry I called you by the wrong name and for the cruel things I said."

The silence lasted so long this time that Siasha thought he wasn't going to speak again.

"You... were right... I was blinded by my hate," Robert finally admitted.

Get a grip on yourself... you're losing it, man!

Again, the silence hung heavily between them. Robert felt a longing to take her in his arms but remained frozen. "Well, I'm glad we got that cleared up," he finally said. "I was just heading for bed. Good night."

For a moment she thought he might touch her and was surprised to find herself a little disappointed when he turned to walk away. "Good night," she replied to his retreating form.

Entering the Oasis, she found her and Tawndo's favorite spot and sat down to sort out her raging emotions.

Chapter Forty-Nine

Re'an headquarters Tunguska, Russia

Viktor paced the living room under Telestra's watchful eyes. It had been a day since his last contact with Deszik. Something wasn't right – he could *feel* it. He was sure that Deszik had planned to betray him – would have bet on it, yet the boy had proven himself more a soldier than Viktor would have expected.

Perhaps getting him away from his mother and giving him responsibility has changed him.

"Would you stop pacing? You're disturbing me," Telestra complained.

"Oh, shut up and go somewhere else if you don't like it," he snapped and continued pacing, still unable to ignore the feeling that something was very wrong. He had tried several times to reach Deszik again but to no avail. His agitation mounted by the minute. Suddenly, a call came through the intercom.

"Sir?" a voice queried.

"Viktor here; what is it?"

"Sir, there is a problem in the pod chamber. Could you come down here please?"

"What kind of problem?"

"S... sir, several of the soldiers have... died, sir."

Viktor frowned and glared at Telestra.

"I'm on my way," he said.

As Viktor left the room, Telestra contacted Dekka.

Dekka, it's begun!

I know. I'm in the pod room.

I'll alert the others.

Thank you. Tellek is here with me, and Baynor and Naamin have been sent for.

I'll contact Rauel and Jezza.

Be careful, Telestra!

You too!

Telestra broke the link and left her quarters in search of her two contacts.

Chapter Fifty

Phoenix, Arizona, USA

At an abandoned military site East of Phoenix, Eric, dressed in desert pattern fatigues, placed the last eighth-cycle weapon on the table before him.

As he viewed the seven rows of white, portable tables on either side of the center aisle, he imagined the reactions of the Tectus soldiers to the unfamiliar technology.

Each position held two weapons; one, a small cylinder, silver and black in color and about an inch in diameter. It was a weapon for use in close quarters. The second, larger weapon resembled a square-handled, short cane more than anything else. The deceptively elegant weapon held its lethal power in a black casing accented in silver. This was a long-range weapon.

Satisfied with the setup, Eric stepped into the hallway securing the door behind him. The short walk to the common room where the others were gathered gave him a chance to marvel once again at the fortune of having such a place available to them.

The 3,500 acres of desert had been purchased years ago by a local Tectus member, who made it available to the local cell. Few people knew it existed, and as most of the facility was underground, it provided a perfect, hidden base of operation and training for Tectus.

The common room hummed loudly with the voices of the assembled Tectus members.

"Dennis," he said approaching his leader. "Just how are our people going to get these weapons aboard commercial aircraft with security the way it is?"

Dennis grinned. "TSA won't know what they're looking at. Besides, our people will be traveling as air marshals and as such will be authorized to carry concealed weapons."

"Excellent!" Eric said. "How soon can we get started?"

"Just as soon as everyone is here. We're just waiting on two more people; and here they are," he said as a local Tectus member escorted two people into the room.

Dennis gave them a few minutes to get acquainted before inviting the one-hundred and twenty-five guests to join him in the spacious classroom.

As they entered, Dennis instructed them not to touch the items on the table until told to do so. Eric, filing in behind them, was not disappointed as he watched their reactions to the weapons.

Dennis began. "We're going to put you through a few quick training sessions so that you can go back to your cities and train the rest of your teams. We have enough of these weapons to arm every member of your teams.

"These innocent looking items you see on the table before you are advanced technology weapons."

Several eyebrows shot up, and many looks of surprise and doubt showed on the faces before him.

"I don't have time to go into the details of where they came from. Consider them to be beyond-top-secret and discuss them with no one except the members of your cell that you will train."

He paused to see nods of agreement from the participants.

"First, I'm going to tell you about these weapons, what they are capable of, and how to use them. Afterward, we'll go to the range for practice. Any questions?"

There were none, and he continued. "The first weapon we will talk about is the small cylinder. This weapon has several settings and can be adjusted to…," but he was interrupted by the sound of laughter coming from a tall dark haired young man in the back row.

Addressing the man, Dennis asked, "What's your name, son?"

The man stopped laughing. "Brandon, sir."

"Brandon, just what is it you find so funny?"

"Aw man, surely you're having us on! These aren't really weapons, are they? They look more like women's lipstick holders to me."

Remembering his own initial reaction when Robert demonstrated the weapons to him and Eric, Dennis knew there was just one way to nip any further antics in the bud.

He stepped over to the first row of tables, picked up one of the small cylinders, and after checking the setting, turned and fired it at the podium.

The solid wood lectern vanished immediately leaving behind a small heap of ashes in its place.

When he turned back to face the class, he was greeted

by wide-eyed slack-jawed expressions of astonishment and shock.

Damn. I'm going to have to replace that podium.

Without a word, Dennis replaced the weapon and returned to the front of the class. Everyone had gone quiet, and a sense of sharpened concentration had descended in the room.

Chapter Fifty-One

Re'an headquarters Tunguska, Russia

Viktor was fuming by the time he reached the pod room. "How did this happen?" he demanded.

Dekka faced him. "We are trying to determine that now."

"Is it a failure in the pods, or is it limited to these soldiers?"

"I've run a quick check on the other pods, but they appear to be functioning normally. I'll do a more thorough check when we are done here."

"I've never liked nor trusted you Dekka," Viktor snarled, "and I swear to you that if you have done something to these pods, you will die the most terrible and agonizing death you can imagine."

Dekka made no reply, he didn't even look at Viktor, he just continued to work frantically on the computer.

"Keep me informed," Viktor growled, "and send three of your specialists to acquire more soldiers."

Viktor stormed from the room nearly running Rauel down.

"What the hell are you doing here, Rauel?" Viktor asked angrily. "Never mind, don't answer that," he continued as the man opened his mouth to answer. "I need a pilot; Dekka will inform you of your passengers and mission."

"Yes, sir," Rauel said as he stepped aside to let Viktor pass, then continued to enter the pod chamber to step to Dekka's side. "Viktor says you have a mission and passengers for me."

Dekka turned to face him. "Yes; take Tellek, Baynor, and... let... me... see..." He pretended to think. "Naamin and bring back some new specimens for soldiers."

"Yes, sir, right away."

The three reanimation scientists fell in line behind Rauel and headed for the flight bay where the acquired helicopters were kept. Knowing this was the start of the planned escape, they each had to concentrate on walking normally and behaving as if this was just another acquisition mission.

Telestra and Jezza were in the fissure access room.

"... and I just informed Rauel," Telestra finished.

Jezza said, "The climbing gear is already in the fissure. We can begin as soon as Dekka gets here."

Dekka, are you on your way?

Almost. As soon as I get the recovery team dispatched. Go ahead and get ready.

"I'm sure he'll be here shortly; let's get ready," she told Jezza.

The two women crept into the fissure opening on the far left of the room and began donning their climbing gear.

Deszik?

I am here, Mother.
It's begun.
I understand. Be safe, all my hopes.

Eighth Cycle Site, Grand Canyon, USA

"Excuse me," Deszik interrupted the discussion at the dinner table. "It has begun. My mother and her colleagues are entering the fissure, and their recovery team has been dispatched. We have about two hours."

Jumping up from the table, Robert said, "I'll be in the control center monitoring the area for volcanic activity." Sprinting for the elevator he added, "JR, contact Dennis and tell him his time is up; the show's begun."

JR was on his feet and joined Robert in the sprint for the elevator. "I'm with you, Robert!"

"I'll inform Daniel," Rebecca shouted to them as they launched themselves through the door of the elevator. She caught a brief glimpse of a 'thumbs-up' sign from JR as the doors whisked shut.

The others were now on their feet making a mad dash for the elevator as well.

Within a few minutes, Daniel and Dennis were informed, and everyone at the canyon site gathered in the control room to hear what was going on.

"We won't be able to see anything, of course," Deszik was saying, "but I can keep you informed on the team's ascent out of the fissure."

"There aren't many seismographs or other monitoring equipment that I can access in the area," Robert said, frustrated. "But I'll let you know what I can do."

He tied into the Anchorage, Alaska Volcano Observatory, AVO, monitoring equipment and began studying it carefully.

For the next hour, quiet conversations and speculations carried on in various parts of the control room, and Deszik provided frequent updates on the climbers' progress.

Chapter Fifty-Two

Re'an headquarters Tunguska, Russia

Dekka paused on the narrow ledge, looked up at Telestra and Jezza, and looked at his watch. *I'm slowing them down too much; we'll never make it out of here in time.*

Are you all right, Dekka? Telestra asked.

Yes, I just need a break.

Telestra silently thanked Dekka for developing the chip-to-chip communication method. They had mics in their gas masks, but they were monitored by the command center, and the three escapees didn't dare activate and use them.

Telestra looked at her watch. They had been climbing for over an hour and should be near the top, but they were behind schedule.

We don't have much time, please make it quick, she told Dekka.

Dekka began to climb again. The heat and steam in the fissure made the temperature and humidity nearly unbearable and the surface of the rocks slick. Handholds and foot placement had to be done carefully. His clothes were dripping and sticking to his body, and he was miserable.

Telestra understated the conditions of this climb.

The next moment, the rocks supporting his weight gave way, and he fell.

"Dekka!" Telestra screamed before she could stop herself.

He bounced off the ledge he just left, spun, and slammed back first into the wall below it, the breath knocked out of his lungs.

Spinning again and falling sideways, his head struck a rocky outcropping, and he saw stars. He heard Telestra shouting his name in his head and threw out his hands desperately grabbing for handholds. He found one but screamed as the sudden jerk of his weight dislocated his shoulder, and he lost his grip.

His drop ceased abruptly as he reached the end of the rope tethering him to Jezza and Telestra. Telestra had insisted on the arrangement in case one of them fell, the other two could arrest the fall and help their comrade recover. At that moment he was very glad she had insisted.

Briefly, he lost consciousness and came to with Telestra's thought nudging his mind.

Dekka! Dekka! Are you all right?

He groaned, dazed but feeling sharp, intense pain in his left shoulder.

No, my shoulder is injured.

How bad?

He tried moving it and nearly screamed as dark unconsciousness approached again. He tried to relax against the pain and breathe slowly and deeply. Even that hurt like hell. He knew then he was a dead man; he couldn't climb one-handed.

It's dislocated, possibly broken.

You have to keep going.

I don't think I can.

Yes, you can! Try!

Fighting against the agonizing pain, Dekka managed to turn himself to face the rock wall. To his surprise, despite the dizzying pain, he quickly found footholds and a handhold, taking the weight off the rope and relieving the women from their burden.

He began climbing again, one-handed; it was beyond agony. With every shift upward, stars danced before his eyes and unconsciousness threated to engulf him.

I can't do this, Telestra. I'm already too slow, and this will make me slower. If you wait for me, we'll all be killed when this thing blows.

Looking up at Jezza paused above her, Telestra said, "Wait there!" and started back down the wall.

I'm not letting you give up, Dekka!

Telestra! Dekka objected in exasperation. Don't do this! There's no use!

Coming to a stop just below him, she said, I'm going to be your ledge; start climbing.

You can't.

I already am. Start climbing, damn you! I'm not leaving you behind!

Slowly, Dekka started up the wall again, Telestra supporting him from below, moving as he moved.

"What do you mean you can't find them!" Victor shouted. "Tear this place apart if you have to but find them!" He finished, shoving the short burly soldier out of his way.

Viktor was livid. Telestra and Dekka had disappeared, and now more of the pods held dead soldiers.

They're in this together, I know it! They've been working behind my back to destroy me! I'll kill them both when I find them! He paced his office angrily but stopped suddenly. *What else have they done?*

Calling his commanders to his office, he ordered, "Check the rest of the equipment, all the pods, the computers, then the reanimation equipment, the facility power..." He trailed off. His body tensed with fear, and he said in a low voice, "Check the fissures... make sure the equipment is functioning."

He waited impatiently for the reports to come in, pacing again. After what seemed like an hour, the intercom came to life.

"Sir, we have found more soldiers dead in the pods with more dying. There is a serious pod malfunction."

"The reanimation equipment appears to be functioning normally, but we won't know for sure until we attempt to reanimate someone, sir."

"You'll have more to reanimate when the team returns with our new recruits," Viktor replied.

"The facility power is stable; all monitors are working and reporting normal levels."

"Check the fissure equipment, you idiot!" Viktor screamed. "Don't trust the computers!"

Incompetent idiot!

"Yes, sir. Right away, sir!"

"No wait, I'll check it myself," he roared as he bolted from his office.

Chapter Fifty-Three

Re'an headquarters Tunguska, Russia

In the fissure, Dekka continued his agonizing climb up the rock wall. The heat from the rock that he felt on his face told him that the explosion was not far off.

We've almost reached the lateral tunnel, Telestra informed him. From there it isn't far to the surface!

I am glad to hear that!

He looked up just in time to see Jezza's feet disappear into the side of the wall a few yards above him. Gritting his teeth, he continued to climb, and minutes later, he felt his hand land on a ledge.

Pulling himself up, with the help of Telestra below him, he looked into a dark passage. Jezza sat at the opening and helped him onto the ledge. Telestra appeared moments later.

"Let's go!" she shouted inside her mask, indicating forward motion with her hand, and the three moved quickly into the cave.

They hadn't gone far when the rock floor beneath their feet began to tremble.

"Run!" Telestra screamed both vocally and in her mind.

They ran, stepping from rock to rock as quickly as they could, jumping when necessary, their headlamps lighting their way. The uneven, unpredictable surface made it difficult for them, but they were desperate and kept moving.

Suddenly, the earth shook violently throwing them down and saving them from the gust of hot steam passing over them where their bodies were a second or two before. Without their protective suits, they would have been severely blistered and burned.

Dekka was getting worried that it would never stop.

Mercifully, it subsided. They climbed to their feet and continued to make their way rapidly through the passageway. Just as they saw blue sky above them, the ground began to tremble again.

"Hurry!" Jezza screamed.

They hastened up the final twenty-foot incline to the opening, the outside world, and freedom.

When they looked up, they saw the helicopter waiting for them fifty yards away; its rotors were already spinning in a blur. Running toward it, they were again thrown to the ground when the earth shook—stronger than before.

Their friends in the helicopter were waving them on, and they hauled themselves back to their feet and continued to run as rocks and embers began raining down from the sky.

"Hurry!" Tellek yelled from the open door of the chopper.

The shaking ground made running difficult, but at last they were pulled through the doorway by those inside the helicopter. Jezza helped pull Dekka inside, and Tellek grabbed hold of Telestra and started shouting over his shoulder to the pilot, "Take off! Take off right now!" Telestra's feet were still on the landing skids but a few seconds later she was safely inside, and the door was closed.

Rauel applied more power to the rotors and lifted off, flying away to the east through a hail of volcanic debris.

Viktor reached the fissure chamber just in time to be thrown into the wall as a massive explosion tore through the facility, destroying everything in its path.

Eighth Cycle Site, Grand Canyon, USA

At the canyon site, JR leapt to his feet. "They did it! They did it!" he shouted. "The Tunguska site is exploding!"

Mother?

I'm here, Deszik; we made it... barely.

Everyone?

Yes, everyone. Dekka is injured, but he will be okay.

I am relieved to hear that, Deszik grinned. "They're safe! They all made it just in time!" he reported, and the control room was filled with cheers.

While the others cheered, Robert studied the AVO data. Within minutes, he began unconsciously tapping his heel on the ground. The more he watched, the more uneasy he became, the corners of his mouth turning down in a tight frown, the lines on his forehead creasing in concentration.

Despite the celebratory mood of the others, an uneasy feeling he couldn't explain continued growing in the pit of his stomach.

Something's wrong... but what?

Termination

He suddenly stiffened. At last, he saw it...
I have to warn Daniel!

Chapter Fifty-Four

Washington, D.C.

Daniel was behind his desk in the Oval Office when his mirror phone rang, and he noticed it was JR.

"JR! What's up?" I wasn't expecting to talk to you until later this evening."

"Daniel, sit down, I'm afraid this isn't a pleasant call."

Daniel, still reveling in the success of the Tunguska site destruction, felt his muscles tighten and a frown formed on his forehead. "What's the problem?"

"I will let Robert explain that to you; he's the expert."

There was a moment of ruffling sounds as the phone was presumably handed to Robert.

"Hi, Daniel," Robert's voice, with its Australian accent, came over the connection. "I'm afraid I have some very bad news. That new volcano that formed in Tunguska caused a massive submarine landslide. Islands in the North Pacific and the west coast of North America are going to be hit by a massive tsunami."

"What! How big?"

"I'm not sure, I don't have the instruments to measure it. I'm guesstimating the probable amount of displacement, and by those calculations, there will be coastal flooding and damage, especially in those locations that are closest. Alaska will get the worst of it, followed by Hawaii, and then the western coastline."

"How much time do we have?"

"The landslide occurred about thirty minutes ago. Given the speed of the waves through deep water, which can exceed five-hundred miles per hour, I'd say Alaska has about four to five hours depending on location. The islands furthest west will be hit first, of course.

"Hawaii may have seven or eight hours, and the west coast eight or nine, again depending on location.

"The Alaska Volcano Observatory and the National Oceanic and Atmospheric Administration must be tracking it, and I can only hope they will take appropriate action."

At that moment, Glenn knocked on the door and entered at Daniel's bidding. Secretary of Commerce, Ross Lewis, followed closely on his heels.

"I think they're on it," Daniel said, eyeing Lewis and beckoning him to sit down. "I'll talk to you later. Thanks for letting me know."

Putting the mirror phone back in his pocket, he invited Ross to sit down. "Glenn, please have Salome join us."

"Mister President let me get right to the point. A tsunami is headed for the west coast of the United States."

Daniel schooled himself to remain calm and not interrupt as Ross repeated everything Robert had just told him.

"We are sounding the alarms in all areas projected to be impacted and recommending evacuation of the entire coastline as far south as Mexico."

"Evacuation – how much water are you expecting?"

"Sir, there is no way of knowing exactly, but given the amount of displacement and the readings we've received so far, in the northern most areas the initial wave could be as high as one-hundred feet by the time it reaches land; that height will decrease moving south as the wave dissipates, but even San Diego could see a fifty-foot wave."

"That's going to cause a lot of damage in coastal areas."

"Yes, sir, absolutely."

A knock sounded on the door, and Salome entered. After inviting her to join them, Daniel filled her in on the situation with added comments from Ross.

"I need you to mobilize FEMA immediately to begin the evacuations. Work with other departments to open shelters and supply other needs."

"I'm on it," Salome replied. "Anything else?"

"I think that's enough for now. Let's hope we're overreacting. I'd rather be safe than sorry."

Chapter Fifty-Five

Re'an headquarters Tunguska, Russia

Everyone in the helicopter cringed when Dekka hollered as Naamin adjusted his dislocated shoulder. Dekka wasn't sure which hurt worse, dislocating it in the first place or having it put back. He was lucky it wasn't broken.

Telestra, assisting Naamin, cleaned the blood from his face and head.

"You guys cut that awfully close," Rauel said from the cockpit. "I didn't think you were going to make it."

"Telestra should have left me behind," Dekka said. "But she is stubborn – and I'm eternally grateful for that."

Telestra just frowned at him in mock anger.

For several minutes, they all watched the glow of the massive inferno in silence, thankful to be alive, grieving for those few friends left behind.

It had taken years for the seven of them to discover their mutual independence from Viktor. Dekka and Telestra had screened the others, using carefully constructed conversations and observation, but found only the five that accompanied them to be trustworthy.

Rauel broke the silence. "Are you sure the Americans will meet us as planned?"

"Yes. Deszik says they can be trusted. He has confirmed that the submarine will meet us after dark at the coordinates I provided to him, on the shoreline of Puyshariya Bay," Telestra said.

"What happens after we meet this submarine?"

The rest of the group sat up listening carefully. They had not been privy to the details of the entire escape plan; they only knew they were going to America to join their colleagues at the canyon site.

"We will be on the submarine for about a day, traveling toward America. A ship will meet us, and we will transfer to it for the remainder of the trip. It will take us a day or so to reach Washington where some people will meet us and help us get to the canyon site where Deszik and the others are."

"And then what?" Naamin asked as he applied the portable mendar to Dekka's shoulder.

Dekka sighed with relief as the healing stimulator began to restore the injured muscles and tendons. He knew it would only be a matter of hours, maybe a day, and his shoulder would be as good as new.

"Then we begin a new life where we can be who we truly are," Telestra responded and smiled at Dekka.

Eighth Cycle Site, Grand Canyon, USA

Raj's fingers had been flying ceaselessly over the keyboard for hours on end.

Termination

He hadn't seen his bed in more than two days. He'd been taking twenty-minute powernaps every four hours, sleeping on his arms in front of the computer. But the effectiveness of those had waned. Then about three hours ago, he made the breakthrough he'd been working on for so long; he finally managed to break into the main chip control computer at the Tunguska site. His adrenaline had spiked, and it blew new life and energy into him. Within another two hours, he was able to start copying the entire program including its data over to the canyon site's computers.

The copying was about sixty percent done when he got the news that Deszik's mother and her colleagues had activated the routine to destroy the Tunguska facility. He had no idea how much time he had, and he had no time to stop and ask. He just kept on working and mumbling inaudibly to himself, "Not now, not now. Just a few more hours. Don't blow it up yet. I'm almost there."

At the eighty percent mark, the sweat of anxiety was pearling on his forehead and eyebrows. "Go, go, go. Please, please don't stop now."

Then, just as the download indicator displayed ninety-one percent, the counter stopped, and a message appeared *'Resume Connection'*. Raj's scream of frustration, "Noooooo!" echoed through the lab and hallways.

When Roy entered Raj's computer lab, he found him shaking with rage and disappointment; his hands were locked behind his head and tears of utter frustration were streaming down his face.

Roy took one look at the screen, saw the message, and knew what had caused Raj's outburst. He grabbed him by the shoulders and said, "Hey buddy, you almost – almost made it. Let's check what you've downloaded, maybe you've got enough of it to get the program up and running and get into those chips."

Raj shook his head and dropped his head onto his arms.

Roy stood next to him in silence for a few minutes before he said, "Raj, snap out of it, let's see what you've got. It's not over yet."

Raj raised his head from the desk, sat up, looked at Roy, and said, "Okay."

For the next hour or more, the two of them tried every hack and technical trick they knew to get the program up and running, but without success. Finally, they agreed they were wasting valuable time; they had to move on to another task.

They went to the kitchen and made themselves coffee, and while they stood there sipping it, discussed what was next.

"With the control computers gone, I'd suggest you get hold of Deszik, Robert, JR, Dennis, et cetera and 'transfer' those weapons over to Deszik and start working on bypassing their authentication system."

"That sounds like a good idea," Raj said. "What are you working on?"

"It's still too early to say if it would work, but I'm experimenting with nanobots to see if I can perhaps program them to attack the soldiers, find their chips, and destroy them, or at least make them malfunction."

"That would be a neat solution. I'm off to get Deszik and the rest. Let me know if I can help with anything."

Roy nodded. "And the same for you."

For several hours the people at the canyon sat and watched in mesmerized shock at the news reports coming in and the scenes of destruction showing on the monitors.

Entire coastal towns had been swept away by the one-hundred- twenty-five-foot wave. Nearby towns further inland were flooded; rivers that emptied into the ocean swelled with the high tide, flooding homes, businesses, even entire towns along their banks.

Alaska's inside passage islands had become isolated mountain tops.

Trees, cars, airplanes, boats, bodies of people and animals floated in the water. Never in known history had the west coast seen such destruction, such loss of life. Nearly a mile-wide stretch of the entire coastline lay underwater.

"All those people," Rebecca whispered. "They didn't make it out, make it to safety."

"No," JR responded softly, wrapping his arms around her. "There wasn't enough time."

They watched as reporters in helicopters followed rescue boats trolling slowly through neighborhoods, where children once played. People huddled in blankets at FEMA shelters described harrowing rescues and chilling experiences.

In between reports, lists of survivors and their locations were broadcast in an attempt to reunite separated families or at least ease people's minds about their missing loved ones.

For some, the reports brought good news. For others, each report lacking the name they were looking for brought an ever downward-spiraling mood as their hopes were dashed again and again.

Many in the shelters sat, blankets hanging unnoticed from their shoulders, simply holding cups of hot coffee, unaware of their surroundings. They neither drank nor spoke; they merely stared into empty space in disbelief, eyes unfocused and absent of blinking. So frozen were they that even their breathing was hard to detect; it was as if they were dead.

When she could stand it no more, Rebecca buried her face in JR's shoulder and he held her tight, letting her sob out her grief. While he held her, he continued to watch the reports coming in. His eyes drifted to the tickertape along the bottom of the screen. FEMA shelters were filling up fast, and directions to alternate sites were being broadcast. His eyes flickered back to the scenes of destruction and rescue attempts to see a couple and two small boys on a mountain top surrounded by water.

At least they will be rescued.

Chapter Fifty-Six

Washington, D.C.

Leaning back in his office chair, Daniel closed his eyes and sighed deeply. He had never in his life sighed as often as he had since he became president. What made it worse was the fact that amid the Re'an crisis, one of the most challenging he had to deal with in the existence of the Rossler Foundation, he was on his own; separated from the rest of the Rosslerites, who always functioned at their best when they were together to tackle a problem. Salome was the only one close by who he could talk to.

The Tunguska site is gone.

Viktor is gone, and all of his Re'an with him, I hope.

That should have been the end of it, but no such luck, the curse of the Eighth Cycle is still haunting us.

Stretching each muscle-group, he attempted to release some of the tension in his body.

Sarah had long been asleep when he crawled into bed

beside her the night before, and she was still sleeping when he rose two hours later.

He opened his eyes just as Salome entered the office with a tray covered with a tea towel. "I hope you brought coffee and donuts."

Smiling, she placed the tray in front of him and removed the cloth. "Your favorite!"

"Have a seat on the couch – I'll join you over there – it's too early to be official," he said moving from behind his desk.

Seated on the couch across from her, she held out a cup of coffee and placed a donut on a napkin in front of him.

"You look tired and troubled Daniel."

He nodded. "Right on both counts. I feel like I've been on the merry-go-round from hell riding alongside the devil himself."

"I understand that. But if it's any conciliation, your address last night is getting favorable ratings.

"The people are pleased with your foresight to act immediately and the measures you are taking to aid and support the west coast states. They like that you didn't drag your feet and immediately sounded the alarm; a lot of people were saved because you didn't hesitate and wait for more information. You're being seen as a man of action, and they like it."

"Well, it's good to hear that we've acted in a timely manner," he said, then took a sip of his coffee and picked up the chocolate donut from the napkin. "I'm almost afraid to ask. What's the current death toll?"

Somberly Salome replied, "There are well over a thousand confirmed deaths, thousands are still missing. Officials are hoping the number will not reach the ten-thousand mark."

Hanging his head, Daniel whispered, "So many people... so many lives. How many more lives will the cursed Eighth Cycle claim before it's over? They were supposed to have disappeared more than seventy-thousand years ago, but it seems as if they just refuse to give up. First John Brideaux reactivating The Beast, then this madman Viktor wanted to control the world, as if we haven't had enough of those in the Eleventh Cycle already. And now we still have seven-hundred and fifty cyborgs on the loose with orders to wipe us out."

The silence grew heavy between them before Salome spoke softly. "The Tunguska scientists had no way of knowing that explosion would cause a massive submarine landslide. They didn't do this on purpose."

"I know," Daniel sighed. "I just wish it hadn't happened, that's all."

"Well, on a slightly happier note, you will be glad to know that the seven L'gundo scientists made it to the rendezvous with the Itinerant as planned and are on their way to rendezvous with the Mystic Sea.

"Since Raj couldn't get that control program copied over, I've been thinking... those L'gundo scientists know the Re'an technology inside out. I'm hoping that when they get to the canyon site, they can work with the team to find a way to overcome Viktor's cyborgs."

"I certainly hope so, Salome. We are now stuck with only one option since Tunguska has been destroyed; Tectus has to take these terrorists out, and they don't have much of a chance to succeed. Eighth Cycle laser weapons or not.

"And we can't send our police or military against them, they'd be decimated."

"Yes, that's true, and all the more reason to get the seven

L'gundo scientists to the canyon site as quickly as possible. Maybe we should airlift them?"

"That's a good idea," Daniel looked at his watch. "Ross Lewis will be here in about fifteen minutes, and we'll be busy for a while. Could you make arrangements to get those L'gundo scientists airlifted to the canyon?"

"No problem, I'll take care of it."

Daniel took a few more sips and another bite of the donut, sat back, and said, "Salome, one of my dilemmas is that we, no, not we, I, have been keeping all of this from my cabinet, the National Security Council, and the American people in the hope that we'll find a solution and stop the Re'an before they can even begin.

"Please understand, I am not worried about losing my job. I'm worried about the pandemonium that will follow, if we're forced to reveal it all. Can you even begin to imagine the disruption this would cause if people were to learn about all of this? For instance, reanimation of the dead? Technology and weapons that we can't even begin to comprehend.

"For starters, people's religious beliefs will be destroyed, and I am too scared to even think about the damage that would do to our social structures and orderly lives. And that is *if* we win this war. I just can't bring myself to imagine what life under these maniacs would be like if we lose. We might even miss the good old days when John Brideaux was the ruler."

"Those are spine chilling thoughts, Daniel; some of them had crossed my mind as well."

Daniel sighed again. "Humanly speaking, there is only one more card we have left up our sleeves."

"And that is?"

"That genius husband of yours."

Salome nodded slowly as she stared at Daniel. "I haven't spoken to him in days. The last time I saw him was on the conference call after the Tectus meeting, when he left the room without saying what he was up to. I can contact him and get an update if you want to."

"No, don't disturb him. You know better than I do, we need to let him be; he will show his face when he's ready."

"I can only pray to God to lead him to the answer."

Daniel nodded. "As will I, and I will ask all of the Rosslerites to do the same."

A knock on the door announced the arrival of Ross Lewis, and they agreed to continue their discussion later.

Salome asked to be excused and left. Daniel and Lewis spent the next several hours going over FEMA's progress and needs in the effort to bring relief and support to the disaster areas.

Throughout the meeting, Daniel was burning to leave it all in the hands of Lewis so that he could spend his time on helping find a solution to the looming war with the Re'an. But there was no way out of it. He had to sit through it and pretend there was nothing more important than the tsunami disaster relief effort, although the disaster that the Re'an was about to release on the country and the world would make the tsunami disaster pale in comparison.

Chapter Fifty-Seven

Tossing and turning, Robert muttered in his sleep as his dream escalated and his mumbling turned into a scream, which woke him.

What the hell?

Turning over he tried to return to sleep, but images from the strange dream immediately haunted him again.

A rainforest, a volcano, an honored choice; it didn't make sense.

In frustration, he got up and headed for the kitchen and a snack.

He found Siasha and Rebecca sitting at a table talking quietly over cups of hot tea.

Siasha. Why do I keep running into her? At least she's with Rebecca; I don't have to talk to her.

"Robert! Come join us insomniacs," Rebecca called.

Wincing inside, Robert replied, "Be right there." He couldn't refuse Rebecca's invitation without appearing rude. "Let me grab some coffee."

The girls continued to talk quietly until he joined them.

Termination

"So, you two can't sleep either, huh?" he said sitting down at the end of the table.

"No," Rebecca replied. "The tsunami and the terrible damage it's causing is making us ..."

"...anxious," Siasha finished for her.

"I can understand; I've been having crazy dreams, disturbing dreams."

"They are reporting minor activity in some of the volcanos in the Aleutian chain. Do you think those volcanos will erupt?" Rebecca asked.

"It's difficult to say at this point," Robert replied. "Predicting volcanic eruptions is a very inaccurate science at this point. We can monitor them and know that changes are taking place but predicting if and when a volcano will erupt is still just a guess."

"If they do erupt, will they create more tsunamis?"

Robert smiled slightly.

"What's funny?" Rebecca asked.

"Actually, 'tsunami" is both singular and plural, but the English language has added 'tsunamis'; it grates on those of us who are old school geologists."

Rebecca rolled her eyes and smiled. "Just answer the question, 'professor'."

"It would depend on the strength and type of eruption and whether or not there is an accompanying sub-sea displacement, along with other things; but yes, in some circumstances, they could create additional tsunami."

"How likely is that to happen?"

"It's impossible to tell."

They sat in silence, each considering the possibilities and consequences. Robert stared into his cup, mesmerized.

"It's no wonder we can't sleep," Siasha finally whispered, breaking the silence.

Robert agreed. "I just wish these nightmares would stop."

"Maybe if you talk about them it will help," Rebecca suggested.

Robert paused to consider the idea. "I guess it can't hurt. They are strange. Set in a rain forest, and there's a volcano erupting…"

Rebecca laughed. "Robert, I don't think one has to be clairvoyant to say your dreams are a result of what's been happening lately."

"Yeah, well, it gets weird. There are people gathered, and someone receives a great honor, and then I see someone fall into the volcano."

"That's terrible!" Rebecca exclaimed.

"The weird thing is that it seems familiar to me somehow, like I've been there or had the dream before, like I know something." Robert shook his head. "I don't get it."

"Robert," Siasha said softly. "Perhaps it's something Tawndo remembers."

"I'm *not* Tawndo," he snapped.

"I know that, Robert," she responded patiently. "However, you have Tawndo's memories buried inside you. I was going to suggest that you try to access them; they might help you understand."

"*No*," he responded firmly getting to his feet. "I am Robert, and Tawndo is gone; he no longer exists, and I won't do anything to bring him back," he finished, almost shouting the last few words.

"That is your choice," Siasha said quietly as he stalked off.

Robert found himself following the familiar path to the Oasis sanctuary and allowed himself to wander once he got there.

I am not Tawndo, and I won't let him interfere with me OR my dreams.

Unconsciously, his wandering took him to Tawndo's favorite tree. Recognizing where he was, he angrily started to walk away, but then he stopped.

Ah hell. Might as well.

He sat down under the tree, closed his eyes, and dreamed.

Chapter Fifty-Eight

Washington, D.C.

When Salome left the Oval Office, she got hold of Cliff Willis, the Secretary of Defense, and asked him if she could see him as a matter of urgency. He immediately cleared his schedule and invited her to come over.

On the way to his office, she had a bit of time to organize her thoughts and strategy.

Trustworthy as Willis was, there was no way she could give him a full brief about the looming Re'an threat. First of all, there was not enough time to explain it to him—it would take hours. Second, was the need-to-know principle; and for Willis to do what she wanted, he didn't need to know it all.

In fact, she thought as she stared out the window from the back seat of her official vehicle, he doesn't have to know anything. Which means I'd have to lie to him. But I guess the end might justify the means in this case.

She had her story ready when she walked into his office.

Over her second coffee of the morning, she told Willis that she was acting on Daniel's orders to retrieve seven scientists who had been working on a top-secret program for the Russians from a US Navy ship, en route to Kitsap Naval Base. She told him that Daniel had arranged for the Itinerant to pick them up at night on the East Coast of Russia, but due to the disaster caused by the tsunami, Daniel needed to give his full attention to that and asked her to step in for him.

When he prompted her for more details, she told him that she knew nothing of the details, of the work the scientists were doing, or how it came about that they'd decided to leave Russia in such an unorthodox manner.

"Maybe it shows how sensitive the program is that they've been working on," she said with a shrug.

She almost heaved a sigh of relief when Willis said, "I guess we'll be filled in with the details if and when the President thinks it necessary."

Within the hour, Willis called Salome to let her know that he had a CH 47 Chinook helicopter ready at Kitsap Naval Base, waiting for take-off instructions.

In the meantime, Salome had been in contact with the captain of the Mystic Sea to make the necessary arrangements for the airlifting of the scientists. The captain told her that they were about two hours from the rendezvous point and gave her the coordinates.

She then got in touch with Owen at the canyon site and arranged with him to fly the Metroliner up to Kitsap Naval Base, pick up Telestra and company, and transport them to the canyon site.

Two and a half hours later, she got the thumbs up from the captain of the Mystic Sea, and she asked Willis to dispatch the helicopter.

Then, she phoned Daniel on the mirror phone and filled him in on everything she'd done. She also warned him about the story she had spun to Willis which soon had Daniel chuckling.

"Salome, if I didn't hear it from your own mouth, I wouldn't believe it if anyone told me you are such an accomplished liar."

"Yeah, well I was in a tight spot, and of course I was under orders from the President of the United States."

Daniel was still smiling broadly when he said, "Thanks, Salome, you did great. Don't worry about Willis. It is as you've said, on a need-to-know basis, and for now, he doesn't need to know."

About three hours after the call to Daniel, Salome got word from Owen that he had collected the seven L'gundo scientists, they were all safe and about to take off to head back to the canyon.

Bremerton, Washington State to Eighth Cycle Site, Grand Canyon, USA

In the passenger area of the Metroliner, the L'gundo scientists were welcomed by Owen, Doug, JR, and Rebecca.

"Welcome to America. I am Rebecca Rossler, and this is my husband, Joshua Rossler, everyone calls him JR, and these are our friends Owen and Doug, the pilots," Rebecca said.

Telestra smiled and said, "Thank you. We are relieved to finally be here. I am Telestra, and these are my colleagues: Dekka, Rauel, Tellek, Baynor, Jezza, and Naamin."

Termination

"Get a seat and buckle up. Make sure you tighten those belts," Owen said as he and Doug started moving toward the cockpit after all the handshaking was over.

"If you are God-fearing people, now would be a good time to start praying because this is my first flight ever. I haven't even been a passenger on an airplane before.

"But I'm under orders from the President of this country to fly you to some place I've never even heard of. To tell you the truth, I am not even sure I know which country we're in and in which direction I should fly. That's if I can get us in the air to start with."

Several gasps of shock and bewilderment could be heard from the seven newcomers, who were staring at each other and at the cockpit door through which Owen and Doug had disappeared.

Rebecca immediately saw the consternation Owen had caused among their guests and realized that the L'gundo probably didn't have the same sense of humor as they had, not to mention Owen's sense of humor. He was a walking, never-ending string of pranks and jokes.

JR was laughing so hard he had doubled over, holding his stomach.

"JR, stop it!" Rebecca hissed into his ear. "Go up to that cockpit and tell Owen Bell he'd better stop clowning around or he'll find himself gagged and hogtied in the cargo area, and Doug will be flying this plane.

"These people think he's serious, they obviously don't understand his raillery."

JR stopped laughing and got out of his seat. "I guess over a period of seventy-thousand or so years, people's sense of humor might change a little."

The look in his wife's eyes made him lose the grin on his face and scurry to the front.

Rebecca got up, went to Telestra and company with a big smile on her face, and explained to them that Owen was a very good pilot, and an eternal jokester. She assured them they had nothing to fear and seeing Rebecca so relaxed and friendly quickly put them all at ease.

The rest of the flight happened without so much as a squeak out of the cockpit from Owen.

When they reached cruising altitude, Doug told them over the intercom they were welcome to unfasten their seatbelts and use the toilet or kitchen if they had need of it. Rebecca took over and played hostess to the guests, ordering JR to make the coffee and tea, get out the snacks, and serve them, which he did without any objection... even in his facial expressions.

"On the way from the ship in the helicopter, we were told there is some increasing seismic activity in the Pacific," Telestra said to Rebecca.

"Yes, scientists are monitoring an increase of minor earthquakes in the vicinity of the Aleutian Trench and increased pressure and some sub-surface volcanic activity along the Aleutian Islands as well. Our resident expert on volcanoes is Robert; you will meet him when we get to the canyon site, and he will be able to explain much better what has been happening.

Dekka looked at Telestra and spoke to her with his mind. *I wonder if the explosion of the site is to blame; if we have brought this turmoil on the world.*

I doubt it, she said.

How can you be sure?

I'm not. I'm going to discuss it with Jezza as soon as I get the chance. She is a geoscientist too, and we can evaluate it together.

Good idea.

Four hours later, shortly after dark, Rebecca, JR, Doug, and a very subdued Owen, led the seven L'gundo scientists into the canyon facility where they received a cheering welcome from everyone.

Deszik hugged his crying mother, who'd run to him the moment she saw him. A few seconds later, Siasha wormed herself into their hug and started crying when she put her arms around her sister's neck and whispered, "Telestra, Telestra, I thought we would never see each other again."

Dekka approached Deszik, laying his hand on the young man's shoulder. "You did very well. I'm proud of you!"

"Thank you, Dekka."

Dekka, smiling, turned to speak with Korda and Linkola.

"I've been told there's a welcome dinner waiting for us. I suggest we head that direction and continue getting acquainted and re-acquainted while we eat!" Rebecca said through the excited voices.

They talked late into the night as the newcomers were briefed on the events of the past few days, not only at the canyon site but also across America. Although Telestra and company celebrated their escape from Viktor and the destruction of the Tunguska site with their hosts, everyone knew it was not over yet. They would not be able to relax until the last of Viktor's Re'an were also eliminated.

When they finally adjourned in the early hours of the morning, Telestra entered her room and lay down on the unfamiliar bed.

After several minutes of trying to get comfortable, she was up, slowly pacing the room. *Why am I uneasy?* She continued moving about the room, first sitting on the couch, then in the chair at the desk. Finally, she identified the source of her uneasiness and left the room.

Knocking on the door of the room down from hers, she softly called his name, and Dekka opened the door.

Stepping inside, Telestra spoke. "I…" She didn't know how to finish the sentence.

"I'm glad you came," Dekka said. "I'm lonely too."

"I love you, Dekka. I always have. I've waited a long time to say that."

"I know," he replied. "I've always known. I love you too and am glad I can finally say it." He leaned to kiss her.

As she put her arms around his neck, she felt a quickening of her heart.

None of the canyon dwellers would have fallen asleep if they'd known that Viktor's taskforce was on their way to their first targets.

Thirty-five hundred miles to the northwest, pressure began building beneath the mountains of Alaska, and a small, almost undetectable earthquake rolled through northern Washington.

Chapter Fifty-Nine

Phoenix, Arizona, USA

About one-hundred and fifty miles to the south of the canyon site, in a suburb of Phoenix, Arizona, a lone figure moved carefully through the early morning darkness, his dark clothes concealing him in the shadows. Proud to be one of the first to receive an assignment, he was careful not to do anything to put his mission in jeopardy.

Few lights were illuminated in the large nursing home facility. Only the kitchen area was bustling with activity.

Looking back at the facility with his enhanced eyes, he checked the timers on the devices he had placed and activated fifteen minutes earlier.

Two minutes.

Entering his car, he spent the time thinking of his comrades in other cities across the nation who were carrying out similar missions at the same time.

The multiple targets varied in size, and thus the teams

dispatched varied in number. His target was small, requiring only one person to carry it out.

Although all teams reported losing contact with headquarters two days ago, and nothing had come through from Viktor since, their operational procedures had been laid down, *execute your orders*, and their orders were clear. Today they began, and over the next days and weeks, the same action would be taken in other cities as well. This was only the first wave of strikes, many more would follow in the days to come.

Ten seconds!

He adjusted his vision to protect his eyes just before an inferno erupted, consuming the Saguaro Sun nursing facility in Phoenix.

Knowing he was far enough away not to be associated with the site, he watched for a time while emergency vehicles arrived, contained the fire, and locked down the area. When he was satisfied that he'd done his job well, he started the car and drove away, returning to the rental house where the rest of his team awaited his return.

He arrived to find them all watching the news report covering the incident.

"Well done!" his commander said. "They are reporting that it appears to have been a gas explosion."

He smiled, knowing there were other cities where reporters were also going to be citing 'gas explosion' or other equipment malfunctions as an explanation for similar incidents.

He was right. That night, news reports in the targeted cities confirmed that officials had determined the cause of the disasters to be a gas explosion caused by failing equipment.

Footage of bodies in bags being carried from the

charred remains played as newscasters reported no survivors.

Turning the news off, the tall, muscular commander stood to address his team. "We have done well! Tonight, ten nursing homes, five hospitals, six homeless shelters, and four Head Start schools have been eliminated along with the aged, infirm, and undesirables in them."

After the team's cheers died down, he continued. "Tomorrow, more institutions will be eliminated, and the next day, and the next. We will continue until all those unfit to become Re'an have been eradicated!"

A big burly soldier exclaimed, "And then we will begin the assimilation process on the others!"

"Yeah!" shouted another. "We will build an army – an unstoppable, undefeatable army."

"...and rule the world!" a short broad-shouldered soldier finished for him.

Nodding, their leader added, "That we will. We most certainly will." Looking proudly at his team, he said, "Let's get busy; we want to be ready for tomorrow."

Moving as one, the team members scattered to various locations in the house and focused on assembling their destructive devices, packing them carefully for transportation to the destination sites.

Chapter Sixty

Washington, D.C.

Daniel was a bundle of nerves as he listened to the rants of various members of the National Security Council about the country-wide attacks. He was on the edge of the cliff of one of the biggest, if not *the* biggest, presidential transgressions in the existence of the republic. He had been withholding crucial information about national security, from the council and his cabinet. Sometimes presidents had to, in the interest of national security, withhold information from various persons, departments, and agencies, but Daniel's dilemma was that he might have withheld it for too long.

Since the news of the attacks broke in the early hours of the morning, Daniel had been doing a lot of soul-searching. Was it time to come clean? If he did, how would they respond? He had no illusions that he would immediately lose the bipartisan loyalty he had been able to build during his short tenure in office. It was this unprecedented cooperation between politicians from both sides of the aisle that was helping to get the country back on its feet after the mayhem caused, first by John Brideaux and his Supreme Council, and then the mercifully short dictatorship of General Thomas Hayden.

However, he had no doubt that he would be expected to step down as President immediately, and he was sure he would become the subject of an investigation. It would be a scandal of epic proportions.

He was brutally honest with himself when he asked himself the question; Is this about you and your presidency, or is it about what's in the best interest of the American people? He was relieved when he could honestly answer; It's not about me, it's about what's in the best interest of the American people, and nothing else.

He and Salome, the only member of the National Security Council who knew as much as he did, had been discussing the dilemma for hours before the meeting. They had concluded that there were only two options; either they tell the members what was really going on or they didn't.

"Daniel, if you tell them you knew what was going to happen, you'll have to step down; otherwise, you'll be investigated and impeached. If that happens, you'll very likely be the first President to go to jail. And it's not just you we're talking about. The rest of the Rosslerites will be made out as a secret government within the government and be charged with conspiracy. We'll *all* go to jail."

Daniel had nodded slowly, and said, "Salome, I will take the fall for all of us."

"That's very noble of you Daniel," she had interjected, "and I knew you were going to say that. But be assured they will be out for blood. They won't be satisfied to have just your head; they'll want the heads of each and every one of the Rosslerites. Just like you, I'm prepared to take the fall as

I'm sure many of the Rosslerites are, but that's not the main issue."

"What is?"

"They're going to confiscate the libraries of the Tenth and Eighth Cycles. They'll want to put it under government control. Do I have to…"

"We talked about doing that anyway."

Salome stared at him dumbfounded for a moment. "You did?"

"Yes." Daniel sighed and filled her in on the meeting of the Foundation Founders. "But a consensus was never reached, and then all this with the Re'an broke loose, and we never reconvened to settle the matter."

"Have you lost your ever-loving mind?" she asked incredulously. "That would be…"

Daniel shook his head. "No, Salome, I haven't lost my mind, and you don't have to tell me – it would be a disaster." He sat back in his chair. "I guess we can't do anything other than what we've already been doing—keep it quiet."

"Yes, hope and pray we can find a way, within the next day or two, to stop those Re'an terrorists and destroy every bit of technology we find on them."

Daniel nodded again. "I agree. But one thing we have to do once this is over, and if we survive, is to vet a group of National Security Council members and brief them fully."

"Agreed. Let's see how this morning's meeting goes. It might even be necessary to start briefing two or three of the most loyal and trustworthy members today, if we think it's necessary."

"A problem shared is a problem halved." Daniel looked at his watch, took the last sip of coffee from his mug, and said, "Time to face the music."

"These incidents were not accidents; this *has* to be the work of terrorists, Mister President!" Emory Lansing concluded his report. "There just isn't any other explanation!"

The council members were all nodding silently and started turning their attention to Daniel for his thoughts.

Salome started speaking. "I agree with Emory. We are obviously under attack. My teams are working over-time tracking down leads and conducting investigations."

"What have they come up with so far?" Daniel inquired.

"Not a lot, unfortunately," Salome said. "The attacks all seem to have the same modus operandi, but no group or individual is claiming responsibility yet.

"The attacks appear to have been carefully orchestrated and carried out by small groups of individuals and timed to occur simultaneously regardless of the time zone.

"No incendiary instruments, chemicals, or devices, that we know of, have been identified, but analysts agree, based on the timing, location, and force of the blasts, they were carefully planned and executed to cause the most amount of damage."

Secretary of State, Bill Simms added, "My teams haven't heard even a whisper or suggestion of who is responsible for these attacks.

"Ordinarily, there would be some suspects, but in this case, those on our watchlists seem to be as surprised as we are."

"Do we have the manpower to provide some protection for these types of facilities in other cities?" Daniel asked to no one in particular.

"I will meet with Salome after the meeting to get a list

of potential targets and make personnel available for that purpose," the Secretary of Defense, Cliff Willis said.

"Very well, please see to it, Cliff. Salome will provide you with an analysis."

"I don't want to borrow trouble, but I'm a little surprised they didn't try to hit our power facilities," Daniel said.

"It's probably only a matter of time," Ted Marks, Secretary of Energy, said. "I've already put every power facility, no matter how small, on high alert and asked them to bring on extra security.

"The largest power plants and all nuclear sites have been put on lock-down. They're shut up as tight as we can make them. They also have additional security and are using the highest security measures they have in place."

The meeting adjourned a few minutes later, and Daniel hurried back to the Oval Office to set up a conference call with the Rosslerites leadership team.

Chapter Sixty-One

Video conference

An hour after the National Security Council meeting, Daniel and Salome were in conference with the leadership at the Rabbit Hole and the team at the canyon site.

"Please tell me we have a way to stop these attacks," Daniel started.

"I'm sorry, Daniel," JR said. "We don't, but we are working on it non-stop."

"Do we have any specific or promising ideas we're working on now?"

JR said, "Raj is working with Deszik and two of the L'gundo scientists that arrived last night to override the authentication system of the Re'an weapons we captured. They've made some progress but no breakthrough yet.

"Roy is working with Robert, Linkola, and two more of the L'gundo scientists that arrived last night. They're trying to find a way to destroy or at least disable their chips, even if it's temporary. But as with Raj's group, some progress has been made but no breakthrough yet."

JR nodded for Dennis to continue the report.

"We are still on Plan A. Tectus members will have to launch attacks against these invaders. We have trained the leadership group and four additional members of each city. They've returned to their cities where they will equip the rest of their teams with Eighth Cycle laser weapons and train them. Unfortunately, they were too late to do anything about the attacks that happened this morning.

"Thanks to Roy's Spyflies and Spyders, the Tectus teams in all the target cities have identified the Re'an infiltrators and have been able to keep them under constant surveillance."

At this point Dennis paused for a long while. It was clear he had more to say, so no one interrupted.

Finally, he cleared his throat, getting rid of the emotion before he continued. "Daniel, this morning when the attacks began, we were watching, and we were powerless to do anything. I can't begin to tell you how difficult it was to stop my people from throwing caution to the wind and attack those villains with the weapons they had on them. If they had, they would've been slaughtered."

Daniel felt like crying, but he controlled his emotions and nodded for Dennis to continue.

"The teams are being trained as we speak, and we *will* be ready by the end of the day. We are studying the surveillance data gathered by the teams and are working on a strategy. We'll not stand by idly again."

"Thank you, Dennis. Let me and Salome know if there is anything, and I really mean anything, you need that we can do to help your teams," Daniel said.

Sinclair at the Rabbit Hole also reported, "We are

searching records from the Eighth, Ninth, and Tenth cycles in hopes of finding technology we can use, but so far there isn't anything that looks promising."

"Thank you, all. Keep at it, and keep me posted," was all Daniel said as his image vanished from the screen.

Chapter Sixty-Two

Eighth Cycle Site, Grand Canyon, USA

It was around mid-day when Roy and two of the L'gundo scientists, Dekka and Tellek headed out of the lab in search of coffee and something to eat.

In the common area, they found Siasha and Telestra enjoying a glass of juice, talking quietly.

He greeted them and headed for the coffee maker.

Roy started pouring coffee for him and his colleagues, when Raj walked in looking dejected. Roy poured another cup and handed it to Raj asking, "What's up with your team and those weapons?"

He shrugged. "Nothing that I'd call progress."

"And you?"

"Same story," Roy said. "I know the answer is there, right in front of me. It's going to be a simple one, and I'm going to kick myself when I get it."

Raj laughed. He could still remember how shy and introverted Roy was when he joined the Rossler Foundation.

Back then he was almost too shy to speak, especially when there were strangers around. But not anymore. Since he and Salome started dating and got married, and since his exposure to the good-humored Rosslerites, Roy had become much more of an extrovert. And from time-to-time, he could come out with the funniest sayings that had them cracking up with laughter.

A few minutes later, JR and Rebecca strolled in and joined them at the table.

Dekka said, "I am surprised that you all survived the invasion of Viktor's top troops. How did you do it?"

"We turned Raj and Roy loose on them!" JR replied with pride.

"Just the two of you?"

"We all had our part to do," Roy responded.

"That is modesty on his part," JR said to Dekka. "He and Raj are the reason we succeeded, although the rest of us *did* help—but only a little."

"How *did* you do it?" Telestra asked, now curious herself.

Neither Roy nor Raj seemed compelled to answer the question, so JR began the narrative of the sound waves used to knock out the soldiers and the nanites that killed them.

By the time JR concluded, Dekka was staring at the two men in astonishment. "You have accomplished quite a feat with your limited technological knowledge and equipment."

Roy shrugged as JR laughed aloud and slapped him on the shoulder. "Our Roy here doesn't like being limited; his mind operates in the future, way ahead of the rest of us!"

"Indeed, it seems it does," Dekka said.

Roy finally broke his silence. "I just wish it could be that easy with the soldiers that are attacking the cities. I've been experimenting with harmonics and distortion fields, but so far nothing has worked. It's close, but just doesn't produce an effect that would be helpful."

"Too bad we just can't hit them with an EMP, assuming they aren't shielded from such a thing," Raj quipped.

"Yeah," JR agreed. "That is the one draw-back to EMP attacks, the loud boom of the nuclear explosion that creates the effect."

"EMP attacks?" inquired Telestra.

"Electromagnetic pulse attacks," Roy answered. "They destroy electronics as a result of a nuclear blast. You see…"

"Please, no physics lessons, Roy," JR moaned.

"Although we were well aware of the concept of nuclear weapons, we never developed them," Dekka said. "They were too general, massive and messy; 'overkill' I believe is the expression you use. We focused our energy on developing the more precise particle beam weapons – much more direct, and leaves very little mess."

"That is a good way of describing it," Raj agreed nodding. "Way overkill."

None of them noticed that Roy had gone quiet, staring into the distance while they were talking.

Raj, the first to notice, held his hand up to silence everyone, put his finger on his lip, and pointed to Roy.

Everyone turned their gazes to Roy.

When Roy became aware of the silence and everyone staring at him, he started speaking excitedly. "If you didn't develop nuclear weapons, then does that mean your technology isn't shielded from the effects of it?"

Frowning in thought, Dekka replied hesitantly, "No… I don't think… that we… ever… even… considered the possibility that we might need to."

"Excuse me," Roy exclaimed jumping to his feet.

"Wait!" JR grabbed Roy's shirt. "What is going on in that head of yours?"

"Well, an EMP doesn't have to be large and massive like most people imagine. It can be a low-level contained burst that only jams electronics in a localized area. All I have to do is see if the chips are vulnerable to an EMP.

"I can produce miniscule nuclear explosions that would send out an EMP in a small radius of say fifty to a hundred yards. That's the answer—I think."

"It's that easy," JR quipped.

Roy was on his feet, he looked at Dekka and Tellek and said, "C'mon, we've got work to do."

Chapter Sixty-Three

Washington, D.C.

"That's one-hundred hospitals, nearly twice as many nursing homes, and fifteen of the leading mental health hospitals, hit this morning. The death toll stands well over five thousand already and is still rising," Cliff Willis concluded his report.

Grief and frustration washed through Daniel like a tidal wave. *So many people!*

Daniel said, "Pull in all the military resources you need, and reassign them to reinforce security at the possible targets Salome identified."

"Yes, Mister President. Is there anything else?"

"No, Cliff. Just get those troops reassigned before the end of the day," Daniel replied. What he didn't say was, *I just hope if we have a strong troop presence at all targets, those lunatics will not attack them.*

The end of the day! Good grief! Blinking in surprise, Cliff hesitated slightly before responding, "Yes sir!"

Pausing with the phone halfway to his ear, Daniel asked, "Is there a problem, Mister Willis?"

Hearing the edge in the President's voice, Cliff responded quickly, "That's a lot of troops to reassign in a very short period of time, but I'll see that it's done."

"You can only do your best, Cliff. Nothing more," Daniel said.

It was shortly before midnight when Salome stepped into the Oval Office for a hastily called conference.

"Hello Daniel," she greeted with a smile.

"Hi Salome. That smile tells me you must have good news."

"Got a text message from Roy."

"I can see why that'd put a smile on your face."

"It did, but not entirely for the reason you might be thinking."

Video conference

Before Daniel or Salome could continue their conversation, Daniel's mirror phone rang; it was JR asking him to join a video conference.

Beckoning to Salome to join him, he seated himself in front of the screen and activated the conference link.

Salome took a seat next to Daniel and greeted Sinclair and the rest of the Musketeers at the Rabbit Hole.

"How's everyone doing?" Daniel asked.

"We're all fine here, but very concerned about what's happening with the Re'an of course. These attacks are terrible."

"As are we all," Daniel said.

"What's this meeting all about?" Luke asked.

"I'm not sure. JR said something about a new idea of Roy's."

"It will probably be a humdinger, then," Luke said.

Daniel nodded with a grin, noticed Salome's smile, and realized why she hadn't stopped smiling since entering his office.

She knows. Roy's got a plan!

Thinking of his injured friend and former operative, Sam inquired, "Have you heard how Jack is doing?"

Shaking his head, Daniel said, "Last I heard, he was still in bad shape, but the Eighth Cycle medical techniques have been doing wonders for him. Rebecca said he'd make a full recovery."

"I'm here, Sam," Jack said, joining the call from the canyon site.

Still heavily bandaged, he looked pale and pained, but Sam was relieved to see him up and about.

"Good to see you, Jack!" Sam exclaimed. "We didn't think you'd be back on your feet for a while yet."

"And he shouldn't be," Rebecca said, stepping into the picture, glaring at Jack. "You told me you were going to the bathroom."

"I got lost," Jack replied sheepishly.

"Sure, you did. You're still lost, this is not the bathroom."

"Well, I'm here, I might as well stay for the meeting, don't you think, JR?"

Very diplomatically, JR replied, "Jack, it would be nice to have you here, but usually the doctor knows best," and he winced at the daggers in Rebecca's eyes for not siding strongly with her.

"Chicken," Jack said.

Termination

"Wouldn't you be?" JR asked nodding toward Rebecca.

"No, I wouldn't," Jack said, but when he caught sight of the look on Rebecca's face, he flinched slightly and added, "Well, maybe… but only a little."

Rebecca threw her hands in the air and said, "You can stay, but I'll be the sole judge and jury of how long." She sat down in the chair next to him to keep a close watch on him.

Jack nodded with a grin. "Yes, Doctor Rossler."

By now, everyone who had been called to the meeting was in their places and Sinclair started. "Apparently, our resident electronics genius has done it again."

"Roy, why don't you fill us in," JR said.

"This is Dekka and Tellek, two of the L'gundo scientists," Roy introduced them to those who hadn't met any of the scientists from the Tunguska site. "Robert and Linkola you already know.

"I've been working with them, and with Raj, to develop a way to knock these soldiers out, and we think we've got it."

Full of energy, Roy left his chair and paced as he spoke. "Daniel, do you remember that warehouse I destroyed a while back with that Nano nuclear weapon I tested?"

Daniel cringed, remembering the empty warehouse about a mile from the Foundation's former headquarters in Boulder, Colorado. Roy had tested his newly developed Nano nuclear "bomb" on it, utterly destroying it and creating a legal and social headache for Daniel. The invention was impressive; the local fallout was equally impressive.

"I remember," Daniel acknowledged.

"With the help of the team here, we've been able to re-engineer and miniaturize one of my nano nukes and test it. It's tiny and it produces an electromagnetic pulse that is effective up to about seventy-five yards. By 'effective', I mean powerful enough to disable the Re'an chips, instantaneously rendering them unconscious."

"There he goes with them nano nukes again," Sinclair jested. "But if that's the way to stop them, then go for it, Roy."

Roy grinned and continued. "Once they're unconscious, we move in and vaporize them with the laser weapons. The rest is simple – sweep up the ashes, collect all their weapons and technology, and get the hell outta Dodge."

There was silence.

Dennis broke it. "How long will it take to build these devices and deliver them to my teams?"

"Actually," Roy replied, "the devices are fairly simple to build from materials that can be found at local hardware and department stores. I'll provide a list of materials before this meeting is over.

"As soon as your teams have purchased everything they need, we'll meet via video conference, and I'll step them through the process of constructing the devices."

"I thought you said these were nano nuclear devices," Dennis objected.

"They are," Roy confirmed, then added, "sort of."

"Wait a minute," JR said. "What do you mean 'sort of'? How are you going to keep it quiet?"

Roy replied, "We've modified the nano nukes I built in the past. Dekka was able to combine Eighth Cycle knowledge and technology with Eleventh Cycle products and equipment and come up with something very similar that will mimic a nuclear explosion and the accompanying EMP effect we need.

"Don't think in terms of a big explosion, JR. These explosions will have a bit more destructive power than lighting a match and produce less than a quarter of the noise of a very small firecracker."

"So, the big thing here is not the explosion but the EMP," Raj added.

Dekka added, "Other than knocking the soldiers out and destroying the devices that deliver the explosion, there will be very little if any other damage."

"Are you absolutely positive about the power of those explosions, Roy?" Daniel asked.

"We've already tested one here, and other than a barely audible 'pop', we haven't destroyed anything!" Roy added happily. His expression became somber. "Other than the destruction of one of my spyflies and a spyder," he added.

"How…," JR started to ask.

"Just accept the fact, JR… it works," Raj said. "The explanation gave me a headache, and I still don't really understand it."

"Okay," JR shrugged.

"How do you plan to deliver it?" Luke asked.

"With the spyders. The spyflies will scout the room or area properly, then send the spyders in with their loads and detonate them at the opportune moment."

"Every chip and electronic device within range will be fried?" Eric asked.

"Exactly, and then you can send in your teams to finish them off with the lasers."

Dennis nodded, deep in thought. "This is going to make the teams smaller and more mobile, not to mention safer, I'd say this sounds like our new Plan A."

Everyone started nodding.

Roy noticed Daniel's frown. "Well, what do you think?"

Daniel's pen tapped quietly on his knee for a moment more, and then he leaned forward directing a steady gaze at

Roy. "What," he asked carefully, "could go wrong in this scenario?"

Roy cocked his head sideways and bit his lower lip as he thoughtfully considered the plan. He spoke softly and measuredly while he worked through the issue. "I suppose if a soldier happened to be outside the perimeter of the EMP's effectiveness, he would be unaffected by the pulse."

Dennis said, "Based on our observations of them so far, that's fairly unlikely to happen; they tend to stay together when they go out on their missions, and after that, they go back to their safehouses and stay there."

Roy added, "Other than that, I don't see any other issues, not from a technical perspective, unless of course, the EMP devices fail to explode."

"To mitigate that risk, we could build two devices per site and keep one as backup," Dekka said.

Roy nodded in agreement. "I'd say that's the way to go."

Nearly a minute passed in silence, while Daniel's pen once again tapped a slow pattern on his knee. "Very well," he said. "Let's do it." Then he turned his gaze to Dennis and said, "As you know, we're expecting another wave of attacks, maybe tonight. But let's hope that the fact that they'll find the targets heavily guarded will hold them off for one night. We have to assume by tomorrow night they will have regrouped and proceeded with their attack. We need to get Roy's EMP devices built and ready by no later than tomorrow evening."

"Understood," Dennis replied.

"I just sent you a message with the list of materials you need," Roy said. "Once you have all of it, it will take about three to four hours to construct the devices."

Dennis nodded. "Let's set a time for 1:00 p.m. Phoenix

time tomorrow for the video conference to help us build those EMP bombs."

"That works for me," Roy said.

Daniel closed his eyes and whispered loud enough for everyone to hear, "Thank you, God."

Everyone bowed their heads and spent a moment in silence.

Before they ended the meeting, Dennis said, "Give me an hour or so to inform the teams and get this list off to them. Then I'd like to return to the canyon to direct this operation with you from there. If that's okay with you?"

Roy replied, "I'm the gizmo guy, Dennis, you're the commander. It'd be good if you're here."

"See you in a few hours then!" Dennis replied and reached to close his connection.

"One moment," Deszik interrupted. "Since I know these soldiers and their capabilities better than anyone here, I think I should join one of the teams and take some of the Eighth Cycle weapons with me."

After a brief discussion, consensus was reached.

"That's great!" Dennis said. "You can catch a ride back with the helicopter that brings me out."

"I will be ready," Deszik assured him.

JR grinned at Daniel. "These numb-nuts are going down."

Daniel smiled back. "Yes, they are."

Chapter Sixty-Four

Eighth Cycle Site, Grand Canyon, USA

Daniel and everyone else was extremely grateful when the sun rose the next morning and Re'an hadn't launched another wave of attacks. It was what Daniel hoped and prayed for—just one day's grace. They got it.

Dennis reported that the Re'an were flustered when they turned up at their targets and found them heavily guarded. Their team leaders had called them back to the safehouses, and it was apparent that they were stressed about the fact that they had no contact with Viktor to get fresh instructions.

It was just as Deszik had predicted, once they were confronted with a situation that they weren't briefed on, they were in shambles. He also pointed out that it would not last. Their original instructions were to destroy those targets, and they'd soon come to the conclusion that they'd have to do it, even if it meant killing everyone that stood between them and their targets.

Termination

A few hours later, Dennis confirmed it. The Tectus surveillance teams had picked up conversations between the Re'an team leaders who agreed they'd return to their targets that night, decimate the guards, and then blow up the targets.

The control room was bustling with activity when Rebecca stepped in several hours later, her flashing eyes scouring the room for her errant patient.

Dennis had arrived back from Phoenix a short while ago, and with the others, was watching with fixed interest as Dekka and Roy instructed the Tectus teams in making the tiny weapons.

Robert, forehead creased in concentration, had his eyes glued to the monitor where data from the AVO was scrolling slowly down the screen.

"Has anyone seen Jack?" Rebecca asked.

Silence.

"Well?" she prompted.

"I thought you... uh... took him back to the medical unit," JR answered without looking up.

Rebecca's eyes narrowed suspiciously. "JR? Do you know something I don't?"

"No, I don't," he said. He was lying. He knew, as well as all the others in the room, that Jack had packed some stuff and hitched a lift with the helicopter that dropped Dennis off earlier. He would've been close to Phoenix by now. They'd given him their word not to let Rebecca know what he did.

Rebecca knew a conspiracy when she saw one, but she also knew there was much more at stake than just Jack's life, and it was not the time to cause a commotion. She did feel the need to say, "Need I remind you guys that Jack is recovering from near lethal injuries and should be in bed resting? His injuries could still kill him if not properly cared for.

"If I find out that any of you know anything about his disappearance, there's going to be hell to pay!" Giving them a final glare, she turned and left the room.

JR and Roy looked at each other in concern. Roy started to speak, but JR cut him off. "What's done is done; can't change it now."

JR returned his attention to the video conference. *If something happens to Jack, I'll never forgive myself, and neither will Becca.*

By the time the Tectus teams were all equipped with their EMP devices, and the video conference ended, Jack had arrived in Phoenix and reported to Eric.

Eighth Cycle Site, Grand Canyon, USA

"Deszik is assigned to team two, and all teams have reported in as on-site in surveillance mode," Eric reported. "It will be about an hour until nightfall on the eastern seaboard. We don't expect any action before then and probably not for another five or six hours, since they all seem to strike at the same time across the nation. The teams will continue to monitor the subjects and notify us at once if there appears to be a change in their MO."

"Good," Dennis replied. "You've all done a spectacular job in getting ready and deploying the teams with such a time crunch."

"Thanks," Eric replied. "Thanks again to Roy and Dekka for the training."

"Keep me posted, and I'll be talking to you again soon."

Dennis closed the conference call and turned from the communication console. "That's it, guys! It will be a few hours before the action starts. I'm going to grab some dinner."

"Hang on just a minute and I'll join you," JR said.

One of the few remaining team members left in the control room, Korda, rose to his feet. "Me too," he said.

Dennis glanced at Robert, still hovering over the station receiving the AVO information feed. "Coming, Robert?"

No answer.

"Robert?"

Still no answer.

Dennis stepped across the room to stand by Robert. He observed the data Robert was examining for a bit. *What's got him so intrigued?* "Robert."

"Huh?"

"Are you joining the rest of us for dinner?"

"In a minute, in a minute," Robert said distractedly.

"What is it that has you so engrossed?"

Robert pointed at the data scrolling down the screen in front of him. "That!"

"I assumed that much," Dennis replied. "What about it is so interesting?"

"It doesn't make any sense!" Robert replied. "None of this makes any sense! What the hell is going on up there?"

Dennis patted Robert on the shoulder and said, "It's okay buddy, everything will be okay."

Robert harrumphed and planted his elbows on the desk so the heels of his hands could support his chin while he stared at the screen in frustration.

Dennis shrugged and left to join JR and Korda.

When the three of them arrived in the dining area, they found Rebecca and some of the others there. By now,

Rebecca had received the news about Jack's arrival in Phoenix and was still steaming.

JR apologized and explained that other than putting Jack in restraints, there was nothing they could do to stop him.

Rebecca was quiet for a moment before she said, "I just hope that he doesn't sustain more injuries; another blow to the head or torso could kill him."

"I'll talk to Eric and ask him to make sure Jack is kept out of the thick of things," Dennis said.

"You do that," Rebecca said, got up, and started to walk away.

JR said, "Rebecca, if all goes according to plan, there's not going to be much action. Definitely not physical combat action."

She stopped and said, "In that case, why didn't he stay here? He could've followed the entire operation as it unfolded from right here."

"You're right," JR said. "I told him that, but he said he *had* to be there, that he couldn't sit around here while the Tectus members are out there risking life and limb."

Rebecca didn't reply. She just shook her head, turned, and walked away.

Chapter Sixty-Five

Jack's eyes were glued to the front of the house as he listened to the status updates from Eric's team.

For the past hour, they had remained motionless, listening through their connection to Roy's Spyflies as the six soldiers moved about inside the house.

When a short, stocky soldier mentioned the location of their target, another Tectus team had been dispatched to the site in case of need.

Following doctor's orders, Eric had ordered Jack to remain at the local headquarters to help track the Tectus teams moving through the city.

Jack had agreed to stay behind. *But I didn't say for how long.*

Five minutes after Eric's team left for their assigned position, he quietly picked up the gear, slipped out of the building, and drove his rental car to within three blocks of the team.

From there, he made his way to the site and stealthily

moved to a position in the tree line where he could see what was happening.

From his position on the west of the Re'an occupied house, Jack identified the location of the members of Eric's team.

For an operative trained in observation and detection, Jack was surprised that it took him nearly three minutes to locate the Tectus members. After some consideration, he decided that it wasn't because of any lapse on his part, but due to the considerable skill of the members. *Damn, but these guys are good!*

Although he couldn't identify the actual person, Jack knew that one person was further down the tree line from him, and the other three hidden in the foliage of neighboring yards on the other three sides of the house. *It really is a shame, though, that these guys are going to be taken out so quietly and while they're unconscious. I would really like to inflict some damage on one of them.*

Jack was pulled from his musings by Dennis' voice coming over the headset. "Stand by; one of the West Coast teams is preparing to move."

"Delta 1, Delta 3," Eric called. "Eyes."

"Delta 3, Delta 1. All six members are present in the house, sir. So far they are still spread out too far for the EMP to be effective."

"Keep your eyes on them, Delta 3," Eric commanded. "Delta 1, Delta 4. Eye assist."

"Delta 4, Delta 1. Acknowledged."

"Delta 1, Delta 2," Eric called to the young Tectus member who would be first through the door, "stand ready."

"Delta 2, Delta 1. Standing ready," the tall, trim young

man confirmed as he got quietly to his feet, assuming a crouched stance to stay hidden.

Fifty feet down the tree line from Delta 3, Jack watched the movement in the house with the intensity of a hungry lioness waiting to pounce on the prey.

Inside the house, Commander Ruslan finished cleaning his weapon, stood, and called the five members of his team to the living room for a final briefing.

As the men joined their commander, Eric's team watched in anticipation.

"Delta 3, Delta 1, they are all within range!"

"Delta 1, Delta 4, activate the pulse!"

"Delta 4, Delta 1, activating."

Commander Ruslan wasn't sure if he actually heard a faint click or if he was reacting on some inner, gut level knowledge, but at that moment he flung himself over the back of the couch landing hard on the floor and rolled into the kitchen; his second in command, Nickolai right behind him.

Scrambling to his feet, he saw the rest of his team scattered on the floor of the living room as if dead. From the corner of his eye, he glimpsed through the sliding glass door, a figure moving across the backyard at high speed.

He quickly turned to check the front window and saw another man quickly approaching. "It's a trap!" he shouted. "Get on your feet and get out!"

As he turned toward the back door, a shower of glass rained down on him accompanied by a body. Letting the force of the impact drive him to the floor, he rolled away from the body as he hit the ground.

San Francisco, California 10:00 pm PST

Tectus captain, Harold Rawlins watched the interior of the house with frustration. *Where are the other two?*

"Eagle 2, Eagle 1, they're just not in the house. Heat sensors show only four in there."

"Eagle 1, Eagle, understood."

Damn!

"Eagle 1, Base. Has our onsite team spotted them?"

A few moments that seemed like an eternity went by while Rawlins waited for a reply.

"Eagle 2, Eagle 1, it looks like they are getting ready to leave. We're out of time."

Rawlins' thumb hovered near the activation switch. "Eagle 1, Eagle 2, stand by."

"Base, Eagle 1, no sign of them at the site yet."

"Eagle 2, Eagle 1, they're heading for the front door."

Rawlins' thumb moved over the activation switch and pushed. He wasn't sure what he expected, but it seemed like nothing happened at all, except all four of the soldiers suddenly toppled to the floor.

"Eagle 1, team, they're down, let's go."

With quick but careful steps, his team entered the house and set about the business of eradication, retrieval, and clean-up. They were out in five minutes.

Across town, two Tectus sharp shooters kept a close eye on the hospital building. The soldiers would show up. *And when they do, they will die.*

Chicago, Illinois midnight CST

"Lieutenant Walker, Yankee 2 reports all the soldiers are gathered in one room," said a small woman dressed so that she was almost undisguisable from her dark surroundings.

"Activate the device," Walker ordered. He had started to rise and head toward the house when the woman's husky voice stopped him.

"Yankee 2 reports no effect; they are continuing to move to the outside; they're coming out the door now."

Walker could see the soldiers with his own eyes. "What the hell happened? Why aren't they dead?"

"The device must have malfunctioned, sir," she replied.

"Yankee 1, Yankee 2, is the backup device ready to go?"

"Yankee 2, Yankee 1, confirmed, but it won't do any good now."

Watching the soldiers as they approached their van, Walker asked, "Can you get it in the car with them?"

"Already on it, sir. Stand by."

Walker watched in dismay as each soldier entered the van and closed the door.

"Fly and Spyder are in," Yankee 2 reported just as the van's engine started.

Walker reached for the second activation device and flipped the switch. This time, he was rewarded by seeing the occupants of the vehicle slump and remain still.

"Gottem," he stated softly. "Let's get this mess cleaned up and get out of here."

Phoenix, Arizona 11:00 pm MST Team Two

Deszik braced himself and hung on to the grab handles in the SUV. His teammate, Alex, a no-nonsense woman retired from the Marines, sped through the streets of Phoenix, tires squealing as she slid the vehicle around corners, sparks flying against the pavement when the vehicle hit the ground after 'jumping' a dip in the road. He had been told she was an excellent sniper who 'never missed,' but he hadn't expected her to be such an accomplished driver.

Like the soldiers observed by team one, the soldiers they were assigned to eliminate were ready to go when team two reached the house. Unlike team one though, they had already held their final briefing hours before the EMP devices could be slipped into the house and were in the process of leaving when the team arrived.

Having parked five blocks away, it had taken them time to return to their vehicle, and now they raced for the site, hoping they could stop the Re'an before they could set off another explosion that would kill many.

Deszik felt his side of the car lift from the pavement as they flew around yet another corner, and his grip tightened on the bar to hold himself in place.

"Almost there," Alex informed him loudly over the racing engine and squealing tires.

She'd barely finished speaking when she brought the vehicle to a screeching stop and exited it in one fluid motion, rifle in hand.

Deszik quickly left the SUV and set off at a run to catch up with her. "Where are they," he asked, looking around the residential area.

"Two blocks ahead and one to the right," she replied without slowing her pace.

Within minutes, they were hidden in the foliage of a yard across the street from the Peaceful Healing drug and alcohol rehabilitation center.

"I don't see anything," she said.

"Me neither."

"Let's split up and move around to the back."

Deszik agreed, and they set off on their own.

"Keep your comm open," she threw back over her shoulder as she moved away.

Moving carefully but quickly, Deszik reached the side of the building and paused to look back over the front of the building he just left; still nothing.

Where are they?

Just then he heard a brief, high-pitched whine that signaled the firing of an Eighth Cycle weapon. Before he had time to wonder who fired it, Alex's voice came over the comm link.

"Be ready," I got one of them, and the other four scattered in your direction. Following."

He had only taken two steps when the first of the four soldiers rounded the corner, followed closely by a second.

They saw him, but before they could react, he lifted his weapon and fired twice in rapid succession. Both soldiers fell.

He saw a third soldier and fired again, but the soldier pulled back behind the building.

Running up to the edge of the building, Deszik peered quickly around the corner. The two remaining soldiers were caught between him and Alex, and he heard them exchanging fire.

Checking the location of the soldiers again, he noted that one was closer and had his back turned to him.

Ducking around the corner, Deszik barreled toward the soldier crouching behind a short brick wall.

Sensing the attack, the soldier spun and fired at Deszik hitting him square in the chest.

The shot knocked Deszik to the ground, forcing the air from his lungs and the weapon from his hand.

Momentarily stunned, he lay still trying to breathe. The soldier, thinking he had killed a man from the 21st Century, turned his attention back to Alex and fired a shot that missed but toppled the equipment she was using for cover on top of her.

Deszik quickly got to his feet and launched himself at the soldier. The force of impact took them both to the ground. Trained in hand-to-hand combat, Deszik grabbed the man's head and gave a sharp twist and upward pull, breaking his neck.

As he dropped the body, another shot glanced off his arm. He fired a shot and the fourth soldier was no more.

Climbing to his feet, Deszik took aim and vaporized the dead soldier, then turned to help Alex who was struggling out from under the equipment that had fallen on her.

Phoenix, Arizona 11:05 pm MST Team One

As soon as he saw the tall man jump, Jack knew something was wrong. His gut told him things had just gone to hell in a handbasket, and Jack trusted his gut above all other information.

Forgetting his pain, Jack burst through the brush along the tree line, just as he saw the man fly over the couch and out of the target zone.

Pushing himself to the limit, Jack sped across the back yard. *Looks like I'm going to get to inflict some damage after all*, he thought. Giving a primal yell as he reached the glass door, he used his last step to propel himself through the glass and into the Re'an soldier.

Jack rolled, coming up in a fighting stance, ready to take on the Re'an.

"You are either braver or stupider than I expected," Commander Ruslan said to Jack. "I think stupider."

"Think what you want," Jack retorted with a quick movement that ended with his weapon shattering on the Re'an body armor.

"Stupider," Ruslan yelled as he spun, his foot connecting with Jack's ribs knocking him to the floor.

Gasping for breath, Jack lunged, hitting his rival in the knees, throwing him off balance.

The tall man fell to the floor, and Jack threw himself on top, but the soldier rolled to his side and Jack slipped to the floor. Flipping over quickly, he whipped his arm around the soldiers' neck securing it in a chokehold.

He felt a vice-like grip on his arm, then the soldier leaned forward, pulling him forward with a twist guaranteed to break bones. His shoulder gave a strange pull followed by a numbing, burning sensation, and his arm came loose from the soldiers' neck with a stabbing feeling. Jack's head snapped backward with a punishing force, and he saw stars when his chin took the impact from an armor covered knee.

As he fell limply to the floor, he heard men's voices shouting around him. He tried to get up but felt the pressure of a hand on his back and a voice, Eric's voice saying, "Stay down, Jack. You're badly injured."

"I'm fine, I gotta get that guy," Jack said angrily, then hissed in pain as he drew a breath.

"You're a long way from fine, buddy," Eric said and held his bloody hand so Jack could see it. "That's not from your bloody nose, by the way, it's from your side; your ribs are sticking through your skin."

Jack groaned. "If I don't die, Rebecca's gonna kill me."

"Probably," agreed Eric. "Just stay still, we'll get you out of here."

"But what about the tall guy?"

"He's gone along with one of his soldiers. But don't worry, the rest of the team has gone after them."

Jack groaned and knew no more.

"All the reports are in, Mister President," Dennis said. "With a few exceptions, everything went as planned, and the Re'an soldiers have been eliminated."

Daniel frowned. "What exceptions?"

Dennis gave Daniel a brief synopsis of what had happened with the four teams that had had problems.

"Did any of the Re'an get away?"

It was the one question Dennis had hoped Daniel wouldn't ask. He sighed. "Four of the soldiers got away. Two in Phoenix, one in New York, and one in Chicago."

Dennis didn't apologize. His teams knew their jobs and were especially good at them; they were not to blame. Sometimes things went wrong.

"I was hoping we would avoid that scenario," Daniel said. "Did we lose any of our team members?"

"No, sir. There were some injuries to those at the sites where the four escaped, but no deaths." *Yet*, he thought. He wasn't sure if Jack would survive his injuries, and if he did, if he would survive Rebecca's wrath. Being on a conference call several hundred miles apart had done nothing to shield him from her reaction. *I've seen riled up mother grizzly bears that couldn't compare to her anger when she heard Jack was being brought in severely injured.*

"That's good to hear!" Daniel said. "Very good. What are your plans for dealing with the escapees?"

"Dekka, Roy, and Raj are working on ways to locate them. Depending on where they are, we will plan accordingly for dispatching them."

"I thought we could already track them?" Daniel asked, confused.

Dennis sighed heavily as Raj stepped up beside him. "Mister President, Daniel," Raj said. "We were able to trace them because they were in close proximity to the equipment. It appears that they have moved out of range. We're working on ways to locate them and will let you know as soon as we have an answer."

Daniel gave a slight shake of his head and sighed heavily. "Just do your best." Then he added with a slight smile and a wink, "and be quick about it too!"

Smiling back, Raj replied, "You got it!"

"Rebecca!" Daniel acknowledged when he saw her step into sight at the command center in Phoenix. "How is Jack?" he asked with concern.

"Alive, barely," she growled.

Roy stepped hesitantly toward the monitor and asked softly, "How bad is he?"

Crossing her arms and still glaring, Rebecca answered, "He has four broken ribs on his left side and six on the right, three from his original injury and the rest from today. One of the ribs on the left is close to the heart and will kill him if it shifts before we can repair the damage. Two ribs on the right have punctured his right lung. His arm and shoulder are broken, along with two vertebrae in his neck, and he has a severe concussion, not to mention his internal bleeding and having glass embedded in his skin."

Roy hung his head. "I am truly sorry," he apologized.

"Save it for Jack, he's the one you nearly killed."

"So, he will live?"

"The next 24 hours will determine that. He's a very strong individual, but he has recently been taken to the point of death twice. Every body has its limits, and his has been pushed too far – *way* too far. We are having trouble stabilizing him. He's in surgery as we speak. They're trying to stop the internal bleeding and then will work on getting the broken ribs away from his heart and lungs. Once he's out of surgery, if he remains stable for a 24-hour period, I'll take him back to the canyon; the Eighth Cycle technology can help him recover much faster, although now that I think about it, a long convalescence would serve him right."

At the back of the control room, JR heard every word of the exchange and deeply regretted letting Jack sneak off. Keeping his eyes focused on the monitor before him, he didn't look up to face Rebecca; he would deal with her later, and in person.

As the conference calls ended, Korda entered the room with evident enthusiasm. "Excuse me!" Korda's voice cut through the silent aftermath of Rebecca's report. "In anticipation of victory, I have prepared a feast to celebrate! If everyone will join me in the kitchen, we can continue the celebration with a real party!"

A brief lull followed. When the silence continued, Korda's excitement began to fade, and he began to frown wondering what he'd done wrong. Then whispers of surprised appreciation floated across the room. "Well, what are we waiting for? Let's party!" JR shouted.

His energy rekindled, Korda broke out into a grin. "This way folks!" he said heading for the door.

Enthusiastic voices responded as they all began to vacate the control room. Korda, happily, led the way.

"C'mon, buddy," said JR, attempting to haul Robert out of his chair. "You're not missing this!"

Robert said, "I'll be there in a few minutes."

"No, you won't; you've had your eyes and ass glued to that spot for the last 18 hours. If I don't make you leave, you'll still be there when doomsday comes." JR laughed.

"It may be closer than you think," Robert said softly.

JR frowned. "What's that?"

Realizing that JR wasn't going to relent this time, Robert got up, stiffly. *I have been sitting there too long!* He made a show of stretching and said, "Nothing, I'm coming."

JR paused briefly, looking at his friend with a peculiar expression.

"What?" Robert said. "I thought I heard someone say something about a party; let's go find it!" and headed for the door.

Glancing at the information still scrolling on Robert's monitor, JR gave a shrug. "Guess it isn't important," and he followed Robert.

In the cool of the desert night, two figures made their way carefully, silently toward the Superstition Mountains due east of Phoenix. The glow of sunrise was just beginning to reveal the high, jagged rocks where they would conceal themselves while they planned their next move.

The stench of dried urine, old rat turds, unclean bodies, and mold assaulted the man's nose as he entered the old, long abandoned tenement building. Covering his mouth, he stepped over a snoring body on the floor and began to climb the stairs, jumping the ones whose treads were missing. *I wonder if any of the others survived?* He would settle in at the top of the building and consider the possibilities of how he might contact them if there were any.

Scurrying from his hiding place, a man sprinted along the New York City train track to catch the moving train. Grabbing hold of a stair rail, he hauled himself up and into the empty boxcar. He didn't care where the train was going, he just needed time to regroup, to think, and to get out of the crowded city. *What the hell had happened?*

Epilogue

The feast was truly delicious, and they talked late into the night. Eleven hundred miles to the northwest, pressure began building beneath the mountains of Washington, and a small unnoticed earthquake rolled through northern California.

Late that night, as the celebration raged on, Robert slipped out to sit alone in the control room. His eyes focused on monitoring the AVO sites, he listened to the last of the incoming reports from Tectus teams returning to base.

He had been interested by some of the AVO readings and returned to satisfy his curiosity. He was now troubled.

The AVO equipment was recording major activity beneath the Kanga Stratovolcano at the northern corner of Kanga Island and steadily increasing seismic activity beneath Pavlof, another stratovolcano on the high northeast flank of the Emmons Lake Caldera.

The two volcanoes between Kanga and Pavlof, Bogoslof and Cleveland, were unmonitored seismically, but he suspected they were experiencing similar activity.

Alaska's mainland volcanoes, mounts Trident, Snowy, Katmai, Augustine, Redoubt, and Spurr were showing a minor increase in pressure. The readings also indicated an increase in minor earthquake activity along the Explorer Plate west of British Columbia.

Robert pulled a map from one of the file cabinets and began carefully marking the locations of the AVO equipment and the events they were recording.

When his task was complete, he stood back for an overall view of the map. He took a deep breath, let it out, then marked the location of the new volcano at the Tunguska site and the location the USS Montana, aka Trepang, had been lost.

After looking at all the information, Robert sat down heavily and rested his head in his hands, massaging his temples. *How is this possible? This is not good, not good at all.*

Urgent beeping from one of the monitoring stations brought his head up abruptly. Quickly accessing a satellite view of the area indicated, he stared in astonishment watching a bloom obscure the area.

Twenty-six hundred miles away, at AVO Fairbanks, Andrew Smyth and Bud Winthrop watched open-mouthed as monitoring cameras recorded the unexpectedly violent eruption of the Kanga volcano.

"Thank god that is an isolated area," Bud said.

"No kidding," Andrew agreed. "I didn't think Kanga was prone to events of that magnitude."

"She's not," Bud said and added slowly, "this is the first event of this magnitude in her known history."

For the next half-hour, they watched in fascinated silence the destructive capability of Mother Nature. Neither of them noticed the triangular monitoring signal at Bogoslof turn red, warning of an imminent eruption, or the orange triangle at Cleveland beginning to glow indicating escalating activity.

Finally, Andrew pulled his eyes away from the screen. "Bud! Look at this!" Andrew cried pointing to the red and orange triangles. "This looks as if a major event is brewing."

"Could be," Bud replied, not liking the readings he was seeing. "I just don't see how this is possible! That new Tunguska volcano can't be responsible. I don't know what caused it, probably some Russian weapons experiment gone wrong, but it isn't part of the Pacific Ring of Fire, so it shouldn't be affecting any of what we're seeing."

"Maybe we're missing something."

"I can't see what, but let's go over everything again."

The Itinerant hung in the ocean darkness, its internal instruments humming, clicking, and beeping as they worked. She and the Mystic Sea had remained in the Pacific, working in tandem to study the unusual amount of seismic activity along the Aleutian Chain and trench.

"Reading another earthquake, sir," Taka reported.

"Bill, is the equipment still working correctly?" Marcus asked.

"So far, it's collected and stored all the information we want on every activity without a hitch."

"That's great! No one has ever had the opportunity to observe and collect this much information at one time. This is going to put our geologists years ahead in research!" Taka exclaimed.

"This much information is going to take them years to sort through!"

"They'll be in seventh heaven. Trust me, I know those Rockhounds."

For a time, the bridge was silent, each of them lost in private thought. A sudden spurt of activity at Taka's station alerted Marcus, but the report he received was more than he expected – much more.

"Sir!" Taka exclaimed. "According to these readings, I believe Mount Kanga just erupted!"

More by JC Ryan

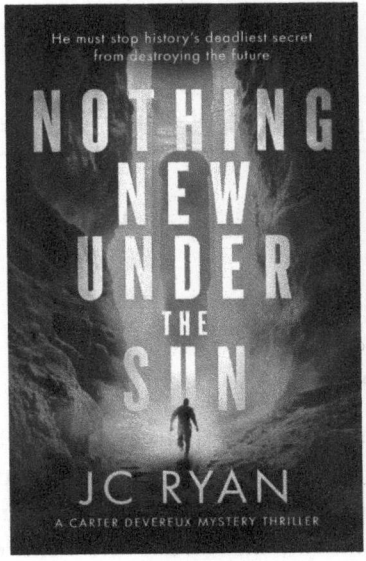

vinci-books.com/nothingnew

What if everything we know about history is wrong?

Archaeologist Carter Devereux's groundbreaking research suggests that ancient civilizations possessed technologies rivaling our own. As he follows clues across continents, he discovers texts describing prehistoric nuclear devastation. With powerful forces seeking to exploit these artifacts, Carter must unravel the secrets of humanity's past to safeguard its future.

Turn the page for a free preview…

Nothing New Under the Sun: Prologue

Ten miles off the Coast of Florida, USA

Carter Devereux leaned over the rail of the barge, dallying with one of the women who operated the crane while he looked down at the diver coming up to the surface.

A diver's masked face broke the surface a few yards away from him. It was Ahote – he couldn't get his mask off quick enough. "Carter!" he yelled. "What do you have for testing for gold?"

Carter's heart started racing. "I've got a few basic chemicals. What do you have?"

"Get them over here!" Ahote yelled again, unable to contain his excitement.

Carter spun around and ran down the stairs to get the testing kit from below deck. He arrived back just as Ahote climbed on board.

"Sabrina is bringing up something big!" Ahote shouted above the noise of the crane's engine.

Although Carter could speak several languages, and

understood several more, he couldn't make out any of the rest of Ahote's babbling – it could have been English or Hopi, or maybe even a few others. Carter could not comprehend anything else he was saying.

Just when Carter was about ready to grab Ahote by the shoulders and shake him to calm him down, Sabrina emerged from the water indicating to the crane operator to start the pull.

Sabrina climbed on board stripping off her mask and tanks, dropping them on the deck. Turning to look at Carter, she smiled.

Carter remembered the smile from the last time he'd been with Sabrina - on an unauthorized night dive – and grinned. Sabrina was part Greek with a fiery temper but had a sweet side that rarely surfaced unless they were alone.

Sabrina was an Olympic class swimmer, tanned, with long black hair and a bust line that could stop traffic. Somehow, Ahote always found the hottest women to work for him, much to the consternation of his wife, Bly.

"I've got it!" the winch operator cried out as the net broke the surface. It landed on the deck with a dull thud as seawater poured everywhere.

Ahote, a Hopi Indian, whose name translated as 'restless soul' ran to the object in the net and started scraping away the encrustation. He found something sparkling and gave it to Carter. "Here, test this!"

Carter was on summer break from a Boston University where he was working on his Master's degree in archeology. He'd found records of a sunken Spanish galleon off the coast of Florida and convinced his grandfather, Will Devereux, to fund the undersea expedition.

Will, intrigued at what they might find, employed Ahote's salvaging company to undertake the actual diving operation to locate the galleon with the aid of underwater radar. They failed to find the galleon, but instead found the remains of an unnamed Viking dragon-prowed longship two days ago.

Carter opened the lid of his chemical kit box and started the test. A few minutes later he shouted, "I don't believe this! ... It doesn't happen! Ever."

"We got gold?" Ahote shouted, dropping to his knees next to Carter.

"It's not possible" Carter shivered with glee as the rest of the crew surrounded them. He turned to Ahote. "Is your wife still on the mainland?"

"Yes, she is. Why do you want to know?"

"Have her bring the champagne," he said. "It's solid gold! All of it! You never find gold on a site! Unless... unless...." He never finished that sentence.

Sabrina grabbed his head and planted a passionate kiss on his mouth – holding him for a long time.

While he was trying to tell everybody they all were going to be rich beyond measure, Sabrina dragged him down below deck, peeling off the rest of her diving suit as she went.

When Ahote's wife Bly arrived with the alcoholic beverages as requested, Sabrina was coming up from the lower deck wearing only the bottom part of her bikini.

Bly was busy tying up the rope to the side of the barge when she spotted the topless Sabrina. "What in God's name is going on?" she yelled at Ahote. "I hope you have a damn good explanation for this!"

"Gold, my love. Pure gold is what's going on." Ahote grinned.

Bly's aggressive demeanor vaporized like mist before the

sun as she started breaking out the champagne - the party raged through the night.

Ahote and Bly finally disappeared into the wheelhouse and stayed there. Bly reappeared the next morning wearing a big smile.

There was more gold than anyone would ever have thought possible at the bottom of the Viking ship. Even after the taxman had taken his share, there was well over $100 million that the crew divided before going their separate ways.

The last Carter heard from Sabrina was a post card from her resort in Fiji. She had a special Christmas card made up of her standing next to the rough young men she kept on hand to do a variety of jobs at her resort.

How a Viking longship came to be off the coast of Florida was anyone's guess. The discovery of the ship caused a rumpus across the historical and archeological communities. Archeologists were still debating over how the ship ended up thousands of miles from the Viking lands in Europe and as many miles from the only known Viking settlements in Nova Scotia.

Viking longships were built for fast attack and not long sea voyages, making them unsuitable for hauling anything heavy for long distances.

Nothing New Under the Sun: Chapter One

A DOZEN WHITE ROSES

Ten years later.

Carter Devereux held the sword and worked on focus which was crucial in the Chen style of *T'ai Chi Ch'uan* and even more so in the use of weapons. His master had finally allowed him, after years of studying the non-weapon styles, to take up the art known as the way of the sword.

For 30 minutes, he practiced the *Jian* - thrusting sword - position. There were at least 49 positions to learn with this weapon and he intended to come to terms with them all. He visited his master's training hall, the Center of Harmonious Gratitude, located over a Chinese restaurant in downtown Boston, twice a week. It was small, just under a thousand feet, but Master Hong took very few students. Carter would spend hours holding the postures Master Hong imparted to him despite the nauseating odor of a variety of unfamiliar foods cooking below and whiffing up through the floor. He dared not disrespect his Master by showing his aversion to the smell, as it was Master Hong's primary income.

He put the sword down and went back to the stances of the weaponless style. Master Hong stressed the fact that no one ever completely mastered a martial art; they only became less cumbersome at it. Carter had progressed better than most - his dedication was legendary among Master Hong's students.

Carter made his first appearance at the center eight years ago, shortly after his twenty-seventh birthday. He had wanted to pursue an oriental martial art ever since watching an old Bruce Lee movie on late-night television when he was a kid. Someone told him about the old Chinese man who taught a very traditional form of *T'ai Chi Ch'uan*, or 'Tai Chi' as most westerners called it, which roughly translates into 'The Supreme Ultimate Fist.' The style was thought to have originated with Buddhist monks who needed a method of protection while they traveled across the ancient Chinese Empire. It was considered a 'soft' martial arts style since the practice reacted to violence as opposed to initiating it.

Master Hong had an extraordinary philosophy regarding whom he would teach. He felt non-Chinese should not be allowed to learn the secrets of the tai chi style he taught. Therefore, first, when prospective students turned up he would ignore them, and they tended not to come back. Second, should they come back; he would show them some pain. They would leave humiliated and not show up again. Finally, if they returned for the third time, he would teach them since it meant they must have been Chinese in an earlier life and deserved to be taught.

Carter's first day at the center, not knowing the old man's philosophy, was his most difficult. He found himself ignored - forced to sit on the sidelines and observe, not knowing what was going on. The second appearance Master Hong unleashed every student on him until he had engaged each one in combat. He'd barely managed to climb the stairs to his condominium afterward, but he had no intention of giving up. The third time he'd arrived at the center, Master Hong smiled and started to teach him the basics.

Carter concluded his morning practice with a set of deep breathing exercises. For him, tai chi was a daily ritual he had not neglected since the day he started eight years ago. He showered, had a light breakfast, packed his briefcase, and made his way to his office on the University campus.

When he arrived at his desk, it was almost eight. He prided himself on arriving before the clerical staff and working well past office hours. His dedication had served him well over the years and awarded him a tenured professorship of archeology at the young age of 25. Having an opulent grandfather whose money funded several of the tall buildings on the campus grounds didn't hurt either. Nonetheless, Carter achieved his academic and financial successes through sheer brilliance, hard work, and enthusiasm for his subject.

His grandfather's prosperity meant he never had to worry about funds while studying. While other students were stuck in pointless internship positions over the summer breaks, Carter could spend his on archeological digs in the Middle East, South America, and undersea exploration.

To those who called him a lucky man, he always imparted a bit of wisdom learned from his grandfather; "Luckily good fortune is often found in partnership with conscientiousness."

He turned his attention to the box on his desk, which had intrigued him since its arrival an hour earlier, taking his time to examine it. When the shipping department brought it to him, they saved the packaging so he could see where it had originated. The return address was in Spanish and listed Peru as its point of origin. The rest of the return address was smeared and hard to read, causing Carter to surmise the sender didn't want the location known. He wasn't concerned - any package coming to the University was examined by campus security and passed through an X-Ray machine. The anthrax scares ten years ago had mandated this additional level of safety.

The box was wood with a thin strand of string tied around it in a constrictor knot. *Who went to such trouble just to secure a box?* Thinking better about it, Carter took several pictures of the box with his smartphone. Instead of cutting the string from the box, he used an awl from his desk to untie it. He would keep it with the box in case he wanted to know more about the source.

The lid hinged on one side of the box. Security might have been able to tell him the contents before he opened it, as they surely would have seen the insides as it passed through the scanner, but it would have ruined the surprise for him. Inside, he found cotton packing. Again, he was intrigued. No one packed objects in cotton these days - too expensive. Most of the time they used vermiculite, Styrofoam peanuts, or bubble packing, but the sender considered the contents of this box special enough to use cotton wadding.

He peeled back the cotton to expose a golden hummingbird. With a cotton glove on his hand, he picked it up. Although the figurine was about an inch long and three-quarters of an inch wide, it felt heavy enough to be gold. He would test the metal composition later, but Carter was willing to bet this was 24 karat gold.

Who sends a gold artifact through the mail? The postal systems of the world were rife with underpaid workers who just might be tempted to list an uninsured package, as a 'loss' if they thought something inside was valuable. He looked at the packaging from Peru - there was no postal insurance stamp on it. *Someone was willing to take the risk of this artifact's loss in the mail just to get it to me.*

He pulled a loupe out of a drawer and looked closer. *Wait a minute; this isn't pure gold.* The gold on most of it was shaded red, which meant it was some kind of alloy. The gold used in the construction of the figurine was altered to give it the red hue before the hummingbird was made. The eyes were black. From the way they glimmered under the light, Carter decided the eyes of the bird were obsidian, plentiful in South America, but difficult to fashion.

He pulled his special digital camera from the desk and mounted it on a small tripod to photograph the bird. For the next hour, he took a series of photographs at different levels of magnification and uploaded them to his desktop computer for closer scrutiny.

As he enlarged the shots, Carter could see the marks of hand tools on the bird. Someone had spent a long time fashioning this creation. He would need to confer with other researchers in his department, but if this artifact was as old as he suspected, it was a major find. He couldn't tell the exact age, but he was sure it was not created in the last 500 years.

The level of detail was hard to believe. This hummingbird was far more realistic than anything he'd seen before. The feathers were created so that each one had a level of precision only visible with magnification. He toyed with the idea that this might be some kind of fake artifact meant to fool him, but a phony one would not have this level of skill in its creation. Three-dimensional printing had just appeared on the market, but to build this artifact up from a computer design would have cost more than any hoaxer's budget would tolerate. It would take an SLS machine to do this job, and he was unaware of anybody who had developed one that could print with gold. And, why reproduce the marks and errors of a skilled artisan? No, this hummingbird figure had to be real, and pre-Columbian.

He gently returned the hummingbird to its box and looked at the container. Nothing on the package showed where it had originated, other than the Peruvian postal stamp. Could this be one of those 'ooparts' - out-of-place artifacts? Most of those turned out to be misidentified or fakes, such as the famous crystal skull of the Incas. He had to put the box in a safe place. The gold in it alone would make the artifact a tempting object for anyone who wished to score a quick buck.

He got up and prepared a mug of coffee from the machine behind him. *Wonderful thing technology, it gave the human race nuclear weapons and coffee machines.* As he added the cream from his small office refrigerator, Carter looked again at the photographs. He had another thought and uploaded a copy of the images to his online secure cloud repository where he stored most of his valuable documents.

He sat back with his hands folded behind his head, contemplating lost advanced civilizations antedating written history. His grandfather, who raised him and instilled in him a sense of wonder for ancient civilizations, regularly suggested there was more to the past than anyone cared to admit.

Carter had a collection of documents about lost civilizations, ancient astronauts and the wisdom of the Great Old Ones. He remembered a movie he watched as a young child where an archeologist found the lost battle-ax of a conquistador revived after being struck by a lightning bolt. In Europe there were so many tales of sleeping kings and Holy Grails, it was a wonder one couldn't just stick a shovel into the ground and find one or more of them.

But then again, there were plenty of artifacts that just didn't fit the era or strata where they were discovered, or didn't make any sense to modern day scientists. There was the ancient battery discovered in Baghdad by Wilhelm Konig in 1938. It was anyone's guess what it was used for. *Was this an invention by the ancients, or were they working from an older design they couldn't understand?* The Byzantines had invented napalm, but no one today knew what its exact composition was. He also knew about a team of investigators who built a model aircraft based on pre-Columbian figurines in an attempt to prove the ancient Tolima civilization had jet aircraft technology. The model really did fly. Also, there was the ancient Indian flying machine or 'vimanas' to contend with . . . *those drawings were too technical; the information was much more than what would be relevant only to pilots for them to be fantasy.* Similar unexplained objects were also discovered in Costa Rica, Brazil, and Argentina.

Then there were the gold spirals found in the Ural Mountains of western Russia around 1991. Gold prospectors had brought them back from a trip to the Narada River. Some of them were as small as 1/10,000 of an inch. *The initial studies on the spirals inferred the micro-objects were shellfish, but this proved to be incorrect. It was indeed gold. No one was able to figure out where the objects had been made, or how.* Some researchers thought they might be over 20,000 years old.

The hummingbird figurine had come from Peru, where

the Lost Golden Garden of the Incas was supposed to be located. The Spanish conquistadors claimed to have discovered a city with an entire garden constructed out of gold, silver, and gemstones. They reported every aspect of the garden, which was sacred to the Inca royalty, was made from precious metal and precious stones. Even the roots of the plants were reproduced in gold or silver. The garden even displayed animals, hand tooled from gold which resembled the originals in every way, shape, and form.

"We did not know if they were living objects fashioned from gold or statues," the Spanish Knight Don Carlo Del Mache had written back to the King of Spain in the year 1565.

Most astonishing of all were reproductions of tigers and lions, animals not native to Peru or anywhere else in South America at any time in the past. The Spaniards were thunderstruck by what they saw as they entered the sacred city. *Present day archeologists wonder if the conquistadors were mistaken in their accounts. Others speculated that the Incas had traded with the Middle East using some sort of unknown technology.*

The Inca royalty had tried to hide what they could from the greedy invaders since the Spaniards tended to melt down the gold and send it back to Spain. The monks accompanying the conquistadors considered all the artwork produced by the Incas to be pagan idolatry. Some people felt the Spaniards account of the garden of gold was mistaken for the sacred Inca city of Coricancha. *I wonder if the hummingbird came from this golden garden of the Incas.*

Carter pulled out his smart phone and called his grandfather, Will Devereux. This little piece of archeological mystery was something that would definitely excite Grandfather Will. His grandfather traveled in less rigorous archeological circles and could often be found in the company of travelers and seekers of adventure. Just last year he'd financed a trip to the Greek Islands to locate the lost Minoan civilization of Atlantis. They hadn't found anything, but his grandfather vowed to return next year with a submersible.

"Carter!" the voice on the other end of the line greeted him. "How good of you to call! We're looking forward to your visit next week. Anything new and exciting in Beantown?"

He smiled at his grandfather's little slight at Boston. Will Devereux, although American born and bred regarded himself as a Quebecois these days and they looked down on the upstart nation to the South. They often said, "Vermont should never have joined that rebel alliance. Nothing good has come out of the state since they declared independence from Quebec in the 18th century."

"I've got something to send you, Grandfather. Look in your cloud account; I've uploaded some pictures of a hummingbird artifact that arrived in the mail earlier today. It appears to be pre-Columbian, and I'm sure you'll find it interesting."

"Why, thank you, Grandson. I'll look for it. See you up here next week."

At approximately 10:00 on that same morning, Carter was involved in a collision. Although it was not the kind normally reported in the local news, it would have a greater impact on the future of human civilization than any other collision reported in the news on that day.

Carter taught an undergraduate class, Introduction to Historical Methods, and needed to get to the lecture hall before his students arrived. Unlike most of his colleagues, he didn't mind teaching the introduction classes. He found them an excellent way to put the students on the path to scientific reasoning and it helped to identify the bright minds that would in due course make significant discoveries. One of his former students was a featured commentator on one of the educational channels and credited Professor Devereux as his inspiration to further his studies and obtain a doctorate degree.

Books and laptop computer in hand, Carter was doing his best to keep the golden hummingbird off his mind when he turned the corner and ran into another moving object. Books and flash drives flew through the air, but they both were able to grab their laptops before either of them hit the ground. Carter took three steps, righted himself, and turned to see whom he slammed into. It bothered him he'd been so careless. His pursuit of tai chi was supposed to keep this from happening. Master Hong would have laughed at his student's maladroitness had he been present.

Carter whirled around to help the person whom he struck, praying it wasn't a senior administrator. An incident like this would not be a good thing for a person of that position to have in mind during budget talks. The person he collided with was down on bended knee and slowly rising, having retrieved what had been lost. As Carter walked toward the figure, he could only see a green business suit. Then she turned around to face him.

He was speechless. Standing before him was one of the most beautiful women he had ever faced.

She was a vision in scarlet. She appeared to be in her late twenties and was nearly six feet in height. For a moment, Carter, who stood six-four, was enveloped by a vision of an ancient warrior princess emerging from a burning castle. The woman he faced had flaming red hair tied back with a dark green ribbon. She possessed a heart-shaped face, her eyes were emerald green, and the nails that gripped the books and laptop matched them. Her physical proportions conformed to the golden ratio.

Most of the college staff dressed down at this University, feeling the title of 'Assistant Professor' allowed them to look any way they wanted. Carter was one of the few who wore a suit and tie, as did this vision of beauty in front of him. Could she be an instructor of some type? Hardly, with her look of professionalism.

"Could you watch where you are going?" she snapped at him. "You damn near knocked me over. Do you have any idea how much that laptop cost me?"

"I'm really sorry," he apologized. "I was on my way to a class full of freshmen …"

"I've got a class to teach too," she retorted, "and I'm late already." She turned and walked away.

Carter stood watching her divine form and then noticed she had a bit of a limp.

"Did I cause that?" He ran to catch up. "My apologies again. Are you hurt? Can I help you carry your stuff?"

"Don't worry I'll survive. Try and not collide with any more people today." She turned again and continued on her way, high heels clicking on the concrete.

"I think I've just met a goddess, a Valkyrie," He mumbled as he watched her vanish into the trees. A smile played on his face at this thought of the fierce Norse warrior maiden of antiquity, a daughter of royalty, with flaming crimson hair who would choose those who die in battle to spend the night with her in heaven.

He made sure to take a more conservative turn around the next corner and continued to his lecture room.

Termination

Dr. Mackenzie Anderson was angry. It was her first lecture, and not only was she late, but her foot was now stinging, and that annoyed her intensely. "Wretched fellow - tall, dark and handsome - far too pretty - probably a bear of very little brain."

He returned from his class, dropped some forms off to the department's secretary, and checked to make sure the golden hummingbird remained locked in his desk – no reason to leave it lying about. Then, all thoughts of it vanished as he sat down at his computer and pulled up the staff profiles on the University Intranet. A few minutes later Carter located his goddess again.

There she was in all her glory: Dr. Mackenzie Anderson, the adjunct researcher in human molecular biology, Department of Genetics. He looked at her stunning picture and rubbed his eyes to make sure this was the same angry woman he'd encountered. She had been with the department since receiving her doctorate three years ago. Why wasn't this woman pulling down the big money working for a pharmaceutical company?

He picked up his phone and made a call. "Hello," he said when a voice answered on the other end. "I would like to have a dozen white roses delivered to someone at the University, and I would like the arrangement delivered today."

Grab your copy...
vinci-books.com/nothingnew

About the Author

JC Ryan is a bestselling author renowned for his intricate espionage, archaeological thrillers, and conspiracy mysteries. With over 30 acclaimed novels, including the popular Rex Dalton K9 Thrillers, Rossler Foundation Mysteries, and Carter Devereux Mystery Thrillers, Ryan has captivated readers around the globe.

Drawing from his diverse professional background—as a military officer, lawyer, and IT manager—Ryan creates compelling narratives that skillfully blend historical accuracy with thrilling adventure. He is celebrated as a master storyteller, known for crafting riveting plots, meticulous historical details, and engaging, multidimensional characters. Ryan's meticulous research lends authenticity and depth to each story, immersing readers in richly constructed worlds filled with intrigue, suspense, and adventure.

Fans of David Baldacci, Lee Child's Jack Reacher, Tom Clancy's Jack Ryan, Nelson DeMille's John Corey, Vince Flynn's Mitch Rapp, Mark Greaney's Gray Man, Gregg Hurwitz's Orphan X, Robert Ludlum's Jason Bourne, Daniel Silva's Gabriel Allon, Brad Taylor's Pike Logan, Brad Thor's Scot Harvath, James Rollins' Sigma Force, Steve Berry's Cotton Malone, and Dan Brown's Robert Langdon will find JC Ryan's novels equally compelling and unforgettable.

When not writing, Ryan enjoys spending time with his college sweetheart, whom he married in 1978. They are proud parents of two daughters, have two sons-in-law, and are grandparents to two grandchildren.

www.ingramcontent.com/pod-product-compliance
Ingram Content Group UK Ltd.
Pitfield, Milton Keynes, MK11 3LW, UK
UKHW020044211025
464173UK00003B/95